Praise for The ey

~ This has to be one of the best and most original crime thrillers that I have read.

~ Exquisite and totally believable.

~ Another stunning instalment in the fantastic Eddie Collins series.

~ The Death of Jessica Ripley will haunt you for a long time to come

~ A suspenseful revenge thriller.

~ Everything about this book is enthralling.

~ The Death of Jessica Ripley starts at 100 mph and then speeds up!

~ The action does not pause for a second and when you find yourself at the end of the book, it's quite a shock that you ended up there so quickly.

~ The story around Jessica Ripley is desperately sad, brilliantly executed and full of compassion.

~ It's a book you wish you hadn't read so you could read it afresh again.

~ Whilst the story, and the plot, are great, the real star of this book is Eddie and the way Andrew Barrett continues to develop his character.

~ I love books where I can tell that the author had great fun writing it.

~ As usual with Andy Barrett's books, once you get into this, you lose the use of your legs, sitting in one place until you have finished it.

~ Send the family out for the day, forget the chores, nothing should get in the way of this one.

The Death of Jessica Ripley

Sometimes you can't forgive and forget

by

Andrew Barrett

Chapter One

How it began

Freedom leaked unseen from her life as the smoke leaked out of the oven door. Thirty minutes, maybe less.

Jessica Ripley stood at the sink, washing up the plates from yesterday so they could eat off them today. Her mind was screwing about with the past; tormenting her like Sebastian used to, topping up her stress levels. To her right, Michael screamed from his bedroom doorway so loudly that he could have been pressing his mouth against her ear.

She clamped her jaw closed, and heat prickled her skin, but she was determined not to break down. What the hell had she done to deserve this? "Michael!" she yelled. "Shut up!" Her reflection in the cracked window above the sink showed her the veins standing proud in her neck and the tears dancing on her eyelashes, ready to fall.

The oven timer dinged but she didn't hear it. She didn't smell the burning food; and the stinging in her eyes was just the prelude to more tears. Her mind had latched onto the two-year-old's screaming until nothing else existed.

Her hands became still in the hot water. Soap bubbles popped against her skin.

Anger grew in her chest, and her breathing trembled. Inside, the clouds were gathering and the storm was about to break.

He screamed.

She closed her eyes and the tears fell.

When the smoke alarm shrieked, Jessica jumped, and her anger exploded. She pulled her hands free of the sink and smashed them furiously back into the water. Her reflection burst into a thousand droplets just as the pain hit.

Michael screamed louder. The alarm screeched, but the new pain claimed all her attention. Jessica pulled her hand out of the sink; watery blood flowed down her forearm from the knife wound and dripped from her elbow onto the wet floor. The soap bubbles were red, and—

"You should get that seen to."

Jessica squealed.

Sebastian stared at her. He hadn't shouted over the alarm, but she'd still heard him.

"Jess." He wore a shirt with no collar, buttoned up tightly under his chin. Sleek, fashionable.

Panic slapped her, eyes darting everywhere at once. "The fuck are you doing here?"

He nodded at the blood running from the gash in her palm. "Here." He passed her a tea towel.

She snatched it from him, stepped back, and shouted, "How did you—"

Holding the knob between fingertip and thumb, he turned off the oven, and fanned the smoke alarm but for now it continued to shriek. "Shouldn't leave your door open."

Michael's scream filled the background and stabbed at her.

Sebastian smiled like he was her saviour. "Not round here," he said. "Not safe around here."

There was a knife on the draining board. "Get the fuck out."

He took a step closer and tilted his head towards the bedroom. "Can I see him?"

"No."

"He's crying. He needs his father."

"Get out before I call the police."

Sebastian retracted his step and peeked into the lounge. He was scanning the place, sneering at the slowly dissolving sofa, the shiny, stained carpet. Demeaning her without even trying. "Do you have enough credit left on your phone to call the police? I could lend you a fiver if you like?" He returned his attention to the kitchen; the torn lino in front of the oven, the mould on the wall above the cracked window. "This is 2007, Jess. You're living like it's the Middle Ages. It's disgusting."

"It's home."

"Home?" The bewildered smile lingered. "Boyfriend coming over tonight?"

"None of your business. Now please—"

"You don't belong with a bus driver," he sneered, "and you don't belong here. Neither does my son. You belong with me." The smile was gone. It had been a façade, anyway.

'You belong to me', you mean.

She pulled the tea towel around her hand and winced. "And you belong in a psychiatric ward. I'm not going anywhere with you. And if you take one step towards Michael, I'll slit your throat."

"So that's how you feel?"

She snorted, "It's taken you a year to work that out? Go home."

"Not without you." He grabbed her arms. "Not without him. We're a family—"

"We're *not* a family. Why can't you understand that? It's finished. Now get off me, and get out of my house." She hated herself for trembling. She hated herself for staring into his black eyes and feeling the coldness spreading out from her heart, feeling the old pain, the old fear resurrected so long after she'd thought it was dead.

The noise was deafening.

"I mean it. This is your last chance to make all this right again." He let his hands fall away from her reddening arms and took the knife from the draining board.

"Sebastian. Wait."

"You can change all this," he waved the knife around the room. "You can be back home within half an hour. Michael can sleep in his old room, and we can start again. It's all in your hands, Jess. His future lies with you. *Our* future." He smiled again. "*My* future."

Jessica's heart tripped over itself. But despite her fear, she wouldn't beg – he wanted her to beg, like she'd done before; he wanted her to kneel, to plead for a life she daren't return to. Not this time. Pride with a sickening tinge of panic glowing at the edges stopped her. She snarled, "You're fucking mad, Sebastian. We're not—"

He turned the blade on himself and his shirt creased just beneath his sternum.

Did he mean to do it this time?

The façade melted away. There was no smugness; there was no emotion at all. His eyes were flat discs of black. "Last chance to make all this right again."

"Don't," she whispered, almost reaching out to him.

Michael screamed.

He raised his eyebrows again in a silent question; a prompt, an offer.

Blood seeped through the towel, and she clenched her fist. "No."

The tip of the blade pierced his skin. His white shirt spotted red and she gasped again.

"I'll do it. And my death will be on your conscience. You know it will. How will you ever forgive yourself? How will you explain it to him?"

"Sebastian." Her voice quivered, and for a minute even Michael's piercing scream seemed diminished as her entire focus lay on the blade at his chest. He'd threatened it before, to make her forgive the latest bruises when apologies and flowers had failed.

He'd threatened it – even sank a blade into his wrist once. But like all his promises, it had been hollow. Like this was surely hollow. Another of Sebastian's mind games.

Don't trust him. Don't let him manipulate you again. It's a trick!

Resolve straightened her face.

He twitched the blade but there was no fear in her.

He had lost, and as the blood bloomed on his shirt, confusion bloomed on his face. "A new start," he said. A desperate half-smile tried to break her reticence. "A clean slate. We begin again. Paris next weekend, Brazil next month."

She looked from the knife to his eyes and back again.

I could push it in. One quick jab and it would all be over.

He'd never threaten her again, he'd never induce this fear again. She bit her lip.

Michael stopped screaming.

Jess blinked herself back to reality. She took a step back. "Just fuck off, Seb."

She turned away and went to Michael. She could feel the tingle running up her back as he watched her leave.

"Jess!" He screamed, "I mean it! Jess!"

* * *

Less than an hour later, the police led her from the flat. Bewildered, she glanced over her shoulder at the body, and watched in absolute shock as Michael reached out to her from the arms of an officer. There were no sounds, just the sight of his frightened eyes, and his shaking hand.

How it ended

DAY 1

Chapter Two

"That is some serious fucking anger."

Eddie stood at the end of the driveway, cigarette hanging from his bottom lip, as he studied a picture he'd taken on his phone. He looked from it across to Troy. "Perhaps the murderer worked with *you* for a day."

"Very clever, old man." Troy grinned, chewing gum.

Eddie watched as Troy walked back towards the body with some kind of street swagger in his hips. He found it incredibly annoying. At the end of each stride there was something like a controlled collapse, a limp perhaps, but he made it look cool.

"Why don't you go sit behind your desk and scribble some report? Leave the proper work to me."

Eddie stared after him; his dislike of the new CSI seeped ever closer towards hatred. There was no joking in Troy's laughter, no humour in his insults. He meant every word.

"Come back, Duffy, you old bastard," Eddie muttered. "All is forgiven." He sighed, put away the phone, and clambered into a scene suit, almost tripping up over the stupid thing. He could feel his anger growing, keeping pace with his embarrassment as he hopped around, trying to get his foot in the hole. "Fucking thing!" He spat the cigarette away.

Troy looked back over his shoulder, then turned and laughed. "You need a hand? Arthritis getting too much for you?"

"I am going to fucking batter you in a minute."

"Ha. Like you could ever catch me."

Eddie gritted his teeth and pulled the suit hard enough that his hand tugged a hole straight through it. He heard a cough behind him, and saw Benson pretending to be dignified, as though he wasn't really laughing at all.

"They're a twat to put on," Eddie said. "How come people can't appreciate that?"

"No one else seems to have the problems you do."

"That's because I'm more creative; my mind is elsewhere while I'm getting suited up."

"Mind?"

"They need redesigning; they're shit. Now what the hell do you want?"

"I'm a Detective Inspector at a murder scene, Eddie. Take a wild guess." Benson stepped closer, aware that there were PCSOs and quite possibly press floating around nearby. "He still pissing you off?"

Eddie zipped up the suit, ignored the split running from chest to abdomen, and said, "Is it really that obvious?"

Benson grinned. "I think you hide it well."

"Why can't I pick my own staff? Stupid system."

"Because Personnel would be out of a job." Benson took a Mars bar from his coat pocket, cracked the seal, and said, "So what have we got here then?" through a mouthful of toffee.

"Get a suit on and come see for yourself."

"And have people laughing at me too? Forget it. I'll settle for the description."

"He's a brief, right?"

"Was."

"Defence?"

Benson nodded.

"I've never had a body where thousands have a motive for killing him."

Benson peered down the driveway. "Go and supervise your new bulldog and make sure he doesn't fuck anything up. Boss wants this one filed quickly."

"Has he ever said, 'Take your time with this one, Tom'?"

* * *

Eddie crouched by the body and felt the tear in his suit grow longer. And even though Troy had his mask on, Eddie knew he was laughing as he chewed his gum like a cow grinding cud. "If you don't wipe that grin off your face, I'll wipe it off for you."

"Get out of the wrong side of bed this morning, Eddie?"

"Both sides are the wrong side."

"You need vitamins. They won't bring back your youth, but they'll take away the aches and pains."

"You getting another job somewhere far away from me is the only thing that would make me feel better."

"You don't like me, do you?"

"Give me your assessment of this scene, and then I can leave it with you."

Troy slid his mask down so it nestled under his designer-stubbled chin like a G-string under a pussy. "I said you don't like me, do you?"

"I thought I hid it pretty well. Damn, Benson lied!"

"I'm good at picking up on people's feelings."

"Sharp lad, well done."

"Why don't you like me?"

"We haven't got that long." Eddie looked at the body. "Get on with this."

"Come on. I want to know."

"Job first, pissing competition later. Get on with it."

Troy sighed and stood up. "Look, I'm not one of your trainees. I'm not fresh out of college; I'm your equal and I know what I'm doing. So if you wanna go and leave me to it, that's fine."

Eddie stood, cringing at the pain in his knees but refusing to show it. "I don't care who you think you are. You're working a scene with my name at the top of the sheet, so I want to know that you're thinking about it logically."

"You always said logic was—"

"Never mind what I said. Run me through it."

Troy stood with his hands on his hips for what seemed like minutes, and Eddie grew steadily hotter and hotter with anger. And then Troy pulled up his mask, stepped closer, and said, "Male. White. Fully clothed, sitting in the driver's seat of his Mercedes. Pickaxe sticking out of his neck. Glass everywhere. Blood everywhere. Briefcase on the back seat."

"Succinct. And your plan of action?"

"Asphalt surface: no good for footwear, so we have a safe path around the body. I'd begin with photography."

"Back up a bit."

Troy sighed, folded his arms. "I've checked that there is a cordon across both entrances to the driveway; there is a scene guard on each entrance and another at the back of the house. So we're free to examine the scene. There is no threat of rain, and no one overlooking us, so there is no need for a scene tent."

"Carry on."

"Happy so far?"

"Carry on."

"Is this an exam? I mean – do you stand over all your CSIs like this? Why can't you just fuck off and let me get on with my job?"

"You're two degrees from a disciplinary. One degree from a punch in the nuts. Okay?"

Troy cocked his head and took a little step forward, chest out, just a few shades away from being threatening. "I've heard about you. I know you're cocky, I know you don't mind assaulting people, and I know you've got a shit attitude." He smiled at Eddie, chewed the gum. "I don't care. I don't find you in the least intimidating."

Eddie tapped his foot, blew hot air into the mask, and watched closely as the boy grew ever more animated.

"I was top in my class for all forensic studies and practical examinations. I've been a CSI in Bradford for two years, working my arse off to get a fucking job in Major Crime. I'm good at my job, and just because you've taken a dislike to me, doesn't mean I don't know what I'm doing."

Eddie reached out and grabbed Troy by the throat of his suit, and hauled him away from the body. And in a relaxed voice, with no pressure bubbling beneath the surface because he'd learned to disguise it, he said, "Get your suit off. Get in your van, and fuck off back to the office."

Troy knocked Eddie's hand aside, straightened his suit and fronted up to Eddie. He opened his mouth.

Eddie got there first. "Be very careful what you say to me next. You could end up back in Bradford."

Troy thought about it, then tempered his response. "I can do this shit in my sleep, Eddie. You know I can. You've seen my report, you've read my file—"

"No," Eddie said. "You're very wrong. I haven't read a word about you. I observe, I take note of what you do at scenes. I couldn't give a flying shit what your record says; I want to know how you perform today. Now."

"But—"

"Go back to the office. We'll talk when I get back."

Troy's mouth opened again and Eddie gave a warning look. That was enough for Troy to turn and walk back to the cordon, slap his way under the tape and slam his van door a minute later. The van screamed away from the scene, and Eddie was left staring at Benson. "He's a cock."

"He's you twenty years ago."

"I was never that arrogant."

Benson cocked an eyebrow.

"I wasn't!"

"How many new CSIs have you got?"

"They sent me two. But it was easier with just me and Kenny. Now I've got to babysit them."

"You mean you've got to… manage them?"

"Yeah, that. I didn't want this job in the first place, remember?"

"I remember. But you've got it. You're doing it, so you should do it properly."

"That's what I'm trying to do. But I've got that prick fighting me all the time."

"For a CSI you're as blind as a bat."

Eddie looked at Benson sideways on.

"He's trying to impress you."

"Ha! My arse. All he's doing is pissing me off. He's got twenty-four hours before I transfer him back to Bradford."

"I think you're being too harsh and too hasty."

"Firstly, no I'm not. Secondly, I don't give a shit what you think."

Benson bit into the Mars bar and a string of toffee clung to his chin. He nodded at the body. "What you got?"

"I haven't started the exam yet, so I've got nothing."

"No. You haven't. So now I have to wait till you get a CSI down here that you like and start from scratch. All because you had a tantrum."

"Up yours." Eddie walked to the body. "I'll do it myself."

"And what about your bulldog? Thought you were going to meet him back at the office."

Eddie stopped. His shoulders slumped. "I didn't say when."

"Come on, Eddie. Get a grip; I want this wrapping up *tout suite*."

"Course you do. You got a wanking class on tonight?"

"Oi!"

Chapter Three

How things had changed from her dream life with Sebastian – mixing with the other lawyers, the skiing-and-ponies set, living in a large detached house on the outskirts of Leeds, her Range Rover parked next to his Mercedes on the gravel drive… it had been nothing less than idyllic. Except for the fists. The fists put a dampener on things.

After the bravery of running away, she'd found herself trembling in her new home; a miserable two-bedroom flat on the third floor of a tower block. It was damp; the buzzer didn't work, the lift didn't work. But the mild paranoia and the depression were always reliable.

There was occasionally Tony. A bus driver. No more Range Rover – just a Day Rover, courtesy of First Bus. Using public transport had lanced the snobbery like popping a boil. He was a decent enough man, content rather than ambitious, meek rather than sharp, and at least he didn't beat her for a laugh.

Following the little visit from Sebastian, though, she was given a new place to stay.

For twelve years.

* * *

It became easier to lie.

At first there was a part of her mind that writhed in agony just at the *thought* of lying about it, and it went into meltdown when she actually had to do it. Taking the blame for something she had not done was unnatural, but actively admitting it was harder still.

But admit it she had. And no doubt those on the outside would be patting each other on the back, with her guilt now verified by admission. They had forced her to. It was part of her rehabilitation, they had said, that she admitted her guilt, dealt with it, and began to move on.

As soon as she had admitted killing him, life had got a whole lot easier – even if sleep still wouldn't come. She was given counselling, all the understanding pats on the back she could ever want, all the tissues she could dampen. But most important of all, she was given a parole date.

She'd had a picture taped to her cell wall, a six-by-four colour print of Michael. He was two years old, a toddler with a killer smile and a giggle that could melt ice. She would spend the hours after mealtimes lying on her bunk, staring at that picture, blinking away the tears, craving him again. She never stopped loving him.

And when the cell doors had closed and the lights dimmed, she'd peel away Michael's photograph and hold it to her chest, revealing a smaller one on the wall where Michael's had been. It showed a man in a smart grey suit; a receding ginger hairline caught the sun and made his head glow like it was on fire. He was looking directly at the camera, but there was no smile, no sparkle in his dark eyes; just contempt.

His name was Thomas Marchant.

As the man most responsible for putting her in prison in the first place, Jessica reserved a special hatred for him. He was her defence barrister. There were others, of course, but he was the worst offender. She'd never forget his face. And now she was out.

But first she had more important things to attend to. Michael was the only thing in life that mattered right now. The *only* thing. He was the tether that held her to her past, and now that she was out on parole, he was also her future.

She ascended the creaking wooden stairs to the first-floor office of the West Yorkshire Probation Service. Her probation officer – or, as they now termed themselves, Offender Manager – was John

Sidmouth. She'd met him twice before, and he always came across as a man who'd rather be doing something else, *anything* else, than taking care of the shambles of an ex-prisoner's life.

She remembered his fingers: fat stumpy things that punched keys ungraciously, stabbing at them as though playing a game of whack-a-mole. Mr Sidmouth was portly, and wore greasy black-rimmed glasses. He made her feel nauseous; perhaps it was the way his gaze lingered on her a little longer than it should. Perhaps it was the way he sighed often, the way his eyes screwed up as though scrutinising her.

Jessica knocked and Sidmouth called her in. He didn't stand as she entered, just gestured towards the wooden seat and barked, "Sit, sit."

She pulled her jacket across her chest and sat, watching as his tongue glided across his lips, quick as a lizard's scenting the air.

For twenty minutes he recited the terms of her parole, and the licence conditions she had to live by for the next eighteen months. She nodded constantly, and when asked if she was abiding by those conditions, the nod was vigorous. And it was true. Mostly.

"So when can I see Michael?" It came out quickly, like an urge that couldn't be restrained.

Sidmouth ran a finger under his collar and flushed slightly. "Soon." He licked his lips again. "I have to liaise with Social Care. But… maybe next week."

"Next week?"

"All the paperwork has gone through. Don't worry about that. Social Care are supportive of your visit, so everything's going in your favour. I am in consultation with Michael's foster carers through Social Care, and I'm confident we'll have a date very soon." He folded his arms and sweat spilled out onto his brow.

"I sense a 'but'."

"So long as you stick rigidly to your conditions in the meantime, there'll be no problem." His tongue flicked again.

She eyed him, and he looked away.

He cleared his throat. "All that remains is for me to visit your home address, just to check everything's in order."

"A visit?"

He punched the keyboard, and she could see it bouncing on his desk. "You're at 42 East Gate Walk. Flat Two. Yes?"

"Yes," she said. "Why do you need to visit?"

"Routine. I have to make sure that you actually live there. This is one of the conditions of your licence."

"But—"

"You *are* abiding by the conditions, Jessica, aren't you? Because if you're not—"

"Yes, of course—"

"…Because if you're not, we cannot allow you to see Michael. And you will go back to prison." Dead eyes looked at her.

"But—"

"I thought we'd made that perfectly clear. Wasn't it clear?"

Of course it was fucking clear! You don't need to fucking remind me!

"It was clear."

"Then there should be nothing to worry about."

When Jessica closed his office door, she let out a breath that seemed to last forever, and when she stepped out onto the street, she knew trouble was right behind her.

Chapter Four

Eddie took a photograph to show the illuminated dash lights and the key at position two in the ignition. It told him that it had been the beginning of a normal day: eat breakfast, ignore the wife, grab the briefcase, climb into the car, start it up; his mind had probably been an hour in front of where his body was. It was probably engrossed already by his first meeting, his first client, and how to get them off whatever charge they'd fallen foul of.

That's how this kind of lawyer worked. They took defence work, and they disregarded honour, revelling in getting clients off even if they were obviously guilty. And this guy looked like he was particularly successful at it. New Mercedes, large detached house in a select neighbourhood two miles from Harewood House, six hundred yards from Alwoodley Golf Club, in north Leeds.

He wondered who had found the body. He wondered how the ignored wife was taking this: with sadness, or relief? Her life was now changed forever – for better or worse. Once the shock had worn away, would she be happy?

Eddie reached through the smashed glass with a gloved hand and turned the motor off. He stood for a moment – the new silence deafening, a breeze tickling the hood of his scene suit – and listened to the hot exhaust clicking as it cooled.

He'd get the photography out of the way, and when Kenny arrived, Eddie would leave him to it. He could trust Kenny; he'd do a thorough job, without any babysitting needed.

Eddie took shots from all corners of the car, then closed in on the driver's side, paying attention to the shattered window, the pickaxe handle poking out of it like a Cadbury's Flake from a sundae. The business end of the pick, the chisel end, had gone through the lawyer's throat, more or less dead centre. Eddie opened the rear door and peered in at the back view. It had travelled right through and was lodged between the top of the seat and the underside of the headrest, pinning the head in place. He photographed it.

Back inside the front of the car, Eddie stared at him. His chin, bloodhound flab flanking it, rested on the rusty metal, specks of blood flecked over his cheeks. His eyes were still wide open, and he looked shocked – understandably, Eddie thought – as though he'd seen it coming but had no time to react. He was almost bald; just a fine stripe of ginger hair circled the back of his head from ear to ear, like his pet squirrel couldn't bear to leave home.

It must have been terrifying, for the ten seconds it took his mind to pack its belongings and leave the body behind.

There was a rustling alongside him, and Eddie pulled his head back out into the sunlight to see Kenny.

"Which coffee shop does he work at? Must pay well. That's a brand new—"

Eddie tutted. "He's a barrister, Kenny. Barrister, not barista – justice grinder, not coffee grinder."

"Sure it said barista on the log." He stared at the dead guy. "Looks like a big game of KerPlunk gone wrong."

"I think we can rule out suicide," Eddie said, and turned away from the car.

"You going now?"

"I have to meet Troy."

Kenny's demeanour changed; his mouth curled and his eyes became slits.

"Not your favourite?"

"He's a tosser. Just make sure you put him in his place. I wanted this afternoon off, but because he's a knobhead I'm stuck here doing his job."

"Sorry, mate."

Kenny took a breath, let it out slowly. "What do you want me to do?"

"Photography's done, but feel free to take your own. The pick is our main source of evidence: use DNA mini-tapes on the smooth parts of the handle, then wet and dry swabs for the rougher bits. See if you can find any fibres, too. Keep a look out for manufacturers' or owners' markings and photo as required. Take a swab of blood. Then pull the axe out and package it ready for chemical treatment."

"You sound like a fucking forensic manual."

Eddie closed his eyes. "Sorry. Sometimes I forget that at least *you* know what you're doing."

"Yeah, well. That lass is supposed to be starting today too, so you got your hands full."

"Yay," Eddie said. "Give me a shout when you're done here, and I'll arrange body snatchers and vehicle recovery."

"Go on, get yourself out of here; I'll drop you a report when I've done. Want me to go along to the PM when we're done here?"

"You don't mind?"

Kenny shrugged. "My afternoon is shagged now, might as well get some overtime in."

"I'll send the new girl down to help."

"Isn't she going to need an orientation day with you first?"

"It'll take ten minutes to show her where the toilets are, where the kettle is, and where we keep the Valium. And Sid can always do that shit with her another day."

Chapter Five

Jessica took a mouthful of coffee and stared at herself in the mirror on the wardrobe door, studying a single blurred blue dot where her eyes were meant to be. The doorbell rang out in the hall; the blurred blue dot blinked and both eyes came into focus.

She went out to the communal corridor with its high ceiling and dirty matt paint that had once been white, and trudged to the front door. The bell chimed again, and through the frosted glass she could see the silhouette of a man standing on the step. His arm was extended, ready to push the bell again.

The door of a bedsit on her right opened and a greasy-faced, long-haired man lurched out. He squinted at her and said, "What's up?"

"I'm sorry," she whispered, and her shoulders hunched up as though she were protecting herself.

He looked at the front door. "What's up?"

"I… I don't know." She looked at him; he was staring at her, so she looked away again. She heard the door close, and the greasy-faced man had gone back to whatever he was doing before.

She swung the front door open. At first she didn't recognise him, but when she did, the colour left her face like blood draining down a plughole. "Mr Sidmouth," she said, "what are you doing here?"

"Ms Ripley." And without invitation he was up the steps, and into the hallway, and Jessica found herself staring out at an empty street, wondering if she should step inside and close the door, or step outside and close the door. She felt cold, and now she felt vulnerable.

"Which is your flat?"

Jessica blinked, closed the door and turned to face him. She made herself smile, and said, "This way." She took him into her bedsit, glancing quickly around to make sure there was nothing out of place. No, not out of place. Incriminating. "I thought we agreed on a visit tomorrow?" She could feel him gazing at her. If his eyesight had strength it would be pushing her down onto the floor. She felt a prickle scoot up her neck, and turned to face him, plastic smile on a pale face. Why hadn't he replied to her? "Can I offer you some tea?"

Sidmouth put down the briefcase and took off his jacket. He wore a dark striped shirt with sweat patches under the arms, frayed black braces, and slacks that were too short. Orange socks peeked out. "No. Thank you. I'm here for two reasons. Firstly, to make sure that this is your registered dwelling and that you do actually live here."

"Yep. This is me." Her smile widened and then crashed. She got no response from him. It was as though he were deep in thought, concerned not with her or her feelings, not with social etiquette even, just with his thoughts. Deep thoughts. She handed him a rental document.

He barely glanced at it. "Good. That's fine."

It was awkward. They stood facing each other in a room crammed with a bed, a wardrobe, and a tiny kitchen. If you listened carefully you could hear the mould on the wall by the cracked window growing, spreading.

Jess shuddered. "And the second reason? Is it Michael? Can I go and see him?"

Sidmouth wiped a sleeve across his forehead, and stared at her. He licked his lips again and turned to his briefcase. "Michael, yes. It's Michael."

Jess clapped, held her laced fingers in a nervous fist under her chin. "When? Today? Can I see him today?"

"Patience, Ms Ripley." He withdrew a slim sheaf of papers, licked his finger, leafed through them and slid out a yellow sheet. "Social Care have agreed to an accompanied visit. I have here the details of your contact, who is expecting a phone call from you this afternoon to fix a convenient time. This," he said, "is a form 68 which you sign as a declaration that you shall not harm or molest the child in any way, and that you shall abide by the terms laid down in…" he reached back inside the briefcase, and pulled out a leaflet, "…here: 'Your First Supervised Visit'." He stared at her. "Once you've signed the 68, everything can proceed." He swallowed again.

This was the moment she'd dreamed of for the last decade; the moment she finally made arrangements to see Michael again. And in all the dreams of this moment, she'd been jumping up and down, tears of pure happiness spilling down her cheeks, a rush of anticipation churning her stomach.

But she felt cold.

Numb. Empty.

"All it needs is your signature," he said. "And my signature. And *then* you can see him."

Jess allowed herself a tentative smile. "Do you have a pen?"

He nodded, staring at her.

She took the 68, took the pen from his wet fingers, and placed the form on the counter next to the sink. She bent over, and signed.

"And again overleaf."

She flipped the page and signed again, handing him back the pen and folding her arms tightly, scared that she would start to shiver. What the hell was going on?

He stood in silence for a long time, pen still in his outstretched hand, trembling slightly. And then he cleared his throat, and said, "Before I sign… I want you to do something for me."

Chapter Six

Eddie flicked away the cigarette through the van's window. The Major Crime Unit's darkened glass exterior reflected sunlight that was diluted by thin cloud hanging in the air like it didn't know what to do. That air was still and felt oppressive, as though a storm was brewing – in more ways than one. That thought led directly to Troy Ainsley and his attitude – an attitude so big that it surely couldn't be contained inside just one head.

Bigger than my fucking ego.

Eddie climbed from the van and trudged towards the double door and the TAC access card reader. Some days he hated his job. Most days, actually. Only scene work held any degree of fascination for him now. The rest of it – the scene management, the personnel issues, running the office, coping with the paperwork and the irrepressible march of change – was a nightmare to deal with, and he longed for days when he was up to his elbows in blood and clues.

And he'd just given one of those days away to Kenny. All part of being a fucking boss, he assured himself. Magnanimous to a fault.

Idiot.

Eddie sighed as the door clicked open and sighed again as it closed behind him, trapping him in a cool silence that pressed in on all sides. How he hated being here. The relative darkness of the foyer greeted him. Moneypenny might have nodded as he walked past; he wasn't sure.

"Eddie?"

He stopped and turned to face her.

It had become something of a ritual between them and he didn't know why she kept doing it. She would stop him as he walked along, and keep him chatting for ages. Well, a minute or two, but it seemed like ages. Not for the first time did he wonder if there was another way in. "I have to go and bollock someone."

She cleared her throat and scratched the back of her neck. "I just wondered—"

The phone on her desk rang. Eddie seized the opportunity to glance at her cleavage as she bent forwards to answer it, and he waved, mouthing 'see you later'. She waved back, but it looked like a forlorn goodbye.

What the hell is up with her? Whatever happened to the good old days when I could stare at her chest without the risk of a conversation erupting?

At the top of the two flights of stairs, Eddie peered across the main office. Benson stared at the computer screen, head in his hands. "What's up?"

Benson didn't look up. "The barrister." He shrugged, slapped his hands on the desk. "I have no idea where to start. So far this year he's represented twenty-eight people in Leeds Crown Court alone. I haven't even started on his family yet."

"So narrow the clients down. Some of them will be inside—"

"I know that!" he shouted. The office quietened, hoping for a row, and he looked around. "What? Get on with your bloody work!"

Eddie took a step back and hid a creeping smile. "I love it when you get angry," he whispered.

"They can hire a hit from inside, Eddie," he said. "Honestly, this guy has so many fucking enemies it's a wonder he didn't die years ago."

"Why did they choose now to hit him?"

Benson shrugged again.

"I have no idea how you made Inspector. Sometimes you are truly shite at your job."

"I want to thank you for your opinion. Now piss off and leave me alone."

"Don't look for people he represented this year. Look for the ones who got out of prison this year."

Benson growled, "Get out of my…" He stopped, looked to the ceiling.

Eddie laughed. "I did it, didn't I? I hit the one thing you hadn't thought of."

Benson began typing. "Get lost, Eddie."

* * *

He signed the paperwork as Jess buttoned her blouse, her vision blurred with tears.

He only said, "Don't forget our next appointment. Three days." Then he slid his jacket back on, collected his briefcase and let himself out of the flat.

Jess heard the front door close and raced along the corridor to make sure he was gone. She dropped the latch, stood with her back to the door, and wailed.

Chapter Seven

Eddie walked into the CSI office, intending to grab a coffee at the kitchenette before heading straight into his own office and closing the door behind him. He knew the 'discussion' with Troy would turn into a confrontation, and he wanted to be ready. He had to prepare himself not to punch the crap out of the little shit, because he knew that wasn't a smart option even though it was the easiest one.

He could hear voices from the kitchenette. Most noticeable was Troy's, loud and brash; he was concentrating on being the centre of everyone's universe, and Eddie could feel the hackles rise on his neck. He decided against the coffee and marched straight into the CSI office.

Sid was the first to see him, and like a dog seeing its master return home, he smiled and hurried towards him. Black lipstick and red eyeliner made him look like a sick and twisted Coco. "Eddie! Eddie, she's here!"

"Is it Hallowe'en already, Sid?"

Sid cocked an eyebrow. "Not nice, Eddie."

"Who's here?" Eddie peered over Sid's studded shoulder pads and all he could see was Troy's million-dollar smile; he could smell the spearmint from here. His lip curled.

"Nicki, of course! Come on, come on, let me introduce you." He trotted down the office, and if he'd had a tail it would have been wagging.

Eddie worried that he might have a little accident on the carpet if he didn't curb his excitement.

"Nicki, he's here." Sid spun on his platforms, sweeping an arm in Eddie's direction. "This is Eddie Collins."

Nicki stared at Eddie, mouth open.

"Fuck me. It's love at first sight," Troy laughed.

Eddie glared at him. "Inside my head I've punched you in the face three times already." He put his hands in his pockets, hoping it might dissuade her from offering him her hand. It didn't work, and inside, Eddie screamed. He shook briefly, wondering what the hell to say to her. What do you say to a stranger? "Welcome to the madhouse."

"You didn't welcome *me* to the madhouse."

Eddie looked at Troy again. "Because you're a prick. And make that four times."

"Shall I fix everyone a drink?" Sid clapped, his effervescence not exactly captivating, but mildly endearing. "Tea? Coffee?"

Nicki smiled at Sid, "Tea. Thank you."

"And a coffee for me. I couldn't get in the kitchenette when I arrived, for the ego blocking the doorway. And bring out the garibaldis, Sid. This is a celebration."

Troy shook his head, and Eddie turned to him. "Have you shown Nicki where the drugs are?"

Troy's mouth froze mid-chew. "Drugs?"

"Valium? Diazepam?" He turned to Nicki. "You'll soon be on a repeat prescription for them, working here, love."

The smile slid right off Nicki's face.

"Troy. My office. Now."

Eddie stormed off to his office, and Troy followed.

"Close it. Sit down."

Troy sat, feet tapping on the floor, hands rubbing at his legs, fingers scraping the fabric of his trousers. "You fancy her, don't you?"

Eddie just stared at him, watching him grow ever more nervous. "You seem a little agitated. Everything alright?"

Troy nodded, "Yeah, yeah, I'm cool."

"How on earth do you not choke on all that bullshit coming out of your mouth?"

"What?"

Eddie looked away. "I said that out loud, didn't I?"

"Very funny."

"You have anything you'd like to share with me?"

"Like what?"

"I don't know. It was just a friendly enquiry."

"You can have a stick of Wrigley's if you fancy…"

Eddie wondered if this was how parents felt as they prepared to lecture their child on the correct way to behave. He hadn't exactly been looking forward to it, yet he relished thc chance to get the little bastard by the neck and squeeze – just enough to frighten him. "You are a disgrace. You will never walk into a scene like that again, with your funky swagger, your chewing gum, and your back-chat."

"I never—"

"Shut up. I don't care what bits of paper you have that prove what an excellent student and scene examiner you are. They don't impress me. All that will impress me is your scene work, and your ability to produce high-quality reports based on what you've seen and recorded and recovered. I expect you to provide me and the investigation with your conclusions based upon what you perceive, and in association with any witness account you may be privy to."

Troy crossed his legs, his airborne foot flicking around.

"At a scene, no one is above listening to suggestions – including me. Everything is on the table; all possibilities are taken into consideration. No one is trying to get one over on their colleagues, because that means the victim loses. Everything we do is focused entirely on the victim. So if you're busy battling me, we're both busy not doing our jobs. Is that clear?"

Troy nodded.

"Good. Because the next bit of news I have for you might come as a shock."

"Go on."

"I'm your boss."

Troy looked around the room. He shrugged. "Yeah. So?"

"So? So you don't fuck about with me; you treat me with respect; you ease off on the competition, because it's not a competition, it's a fact-finding mission. It's not a game, Troy."

"I see Kenny having a laugh with you. That's all I was doing."

"No, it isn't. You were winding me up; you were showing off. I have banter with Kenny. Get it? Banter. We have a laugh, and we take the piss out of each other because we've known each other a lot of years, and…"

"And?"

Eddie swallowed. "And I trust him."

Troy threw his head back. "Ah, I see. So…"

"And I like him."

Troy nodded to himself. "You've got it in for me—"

"You know what I like about you, Troy?"

"No. What?"

"Fuck all."

"I get how it is. You can have banter with the other geriatrics, but new blood comes in and you get scared, and you see it as a threat." Troy leaned forwards in his chair, his voice growing louder, more venomous. "You make me sick, you old fag, that you can have it in for me before I've even fucking started. I'm the best CSI you're ever likely to get in this shithole of an office. So you should think yourself lucky I even volunteered to come here and fish your crap-show out of the stagnant—"

Eddie reached forward and took a handful of Troy's jet-black hair. And he pulled. He yanked him down off the chair and onto his knees, and Troy yelped and then shouted. "Get the fuck off me!"

Eddie pressed his face into the carpet. "Now listen to me, you arrogant little fuck. You start treating me and this department with some respect—"

"Or what? You'll beat me to a pulp?"

Eddie considered this. "Yes," he said, "something like that."

And then the office door opened. Nicki stood there; she gasped. "What's going on?"

"We're having a meeting. Close the door."

Sid appeared in the doorway, carrying a tray.

"Get Nicki a coffee, Sid, and bring me a digestive with that, would you?"

Sid reached in and pulled the door closed.

"Get off me before I have you arrested for assault."

Eddie let him go, and when he stood, Troy's face was red, his hair ruffled and his eyes wide.

"I'm so gonna fuck you over for this."

"Well, that induces in me a level of fear I've never felt before."

"I mean it!"

"Empty your pockets."

"What?"

"I thought only old people were deaf."

"You can't make me."

Eddie folded his arms. "Based on our recent physical relationship, I'd say I can make you do pretty much anything I want, wouldn't you? Now empty them before I do it for you." Eddie sighed as the door opened again. "What?"

Jeffery now stood in the doorway. "Eddie," he said, "everything okay?"

Eddie shrugged. "Fine."

"Troy?"

Troy looked at Eddie. Eddie had no expression on his face; just a knowing look in his eyes.

"Everything's fine, Mr Walker. Thank you."

Jeffery hovered for a while, knowing there was hostility but seeing only harmony, until, with no way to prove otherwise, he tutted and left, barging past Nicki on his way. Now she stood in the doorway again.

"I saw what you did," she said to Eddie. "I didn't like it."

Eddie shook his head. "I don't care."

"Well, you should!"

"What's the best way to stop a cat playing with a mouse until it's dead?"

"I have no idea—"

"Shoot the mouse."

"What are you talking about?"

"I have no idea, but it shut you up for a minute. Like I said before, Troy and I are in the middle of a meeting. A private meeting. Close the door. And this time leave it closed." He watched her shut the door, then walked over and flung it open again. She shuffled away quickly, and Eddie grunted and retook his seat.

"You're lucky I've mellowed in my old age. A year ago you'd have been through that window, minus your warrant card." He motioned at Troy to sit. "Look," he said, "I'm sorry I did that to you."

Troy looked up quickly.

"Before you get the wrong idea: I'm not sorry I did that because *she* saw me, and I'm not sorry because Mr Walker came in. I couldn't give a shit about either of them. I'm sorry because I embarrassed you."

"Whatever. I'm fine. I'm not embarrassed."

Eddie thought about it, and nodded. "Okay – that's what you want me to believe, so I will. But I know different. Us old folk have a sixth sense about this kind of shit. And we also have a sixth sense about other kinds of shit. Know what I mean, Troy?"

Troy fidgeted again.

"Don't throw it all away. You could be really good at this."

Troy bit his lip, looked at the carpet, and nodded minutely.

"Someday soon, you'll be subject to a random drug test. I hope you pass it."

"How can it be random if you know about it?"

"Because I have friends who'll say it is."

Chapter Eight

It struck Kenny that when the time came to remove the pickaxe, there was every chance he would destroy any potential evidence along the bottom edge of the shattered window. And so he got out his torch and used oblique light across the panel to see if there was anything that needed attention right now; something like stray fibres that had clung to the paintwork, perhaps.

There were none, but he thought it prudent to carry out a fingerprint examination too. The car was silver, almost the same colour as the aluminium fingerprint powder, so he opted for a black granular powder that would give much better contrast.

He treated himself to a brand-new squirrel hair brush, and liberally coated it in powder. He worked in smooth straight lines along the door, keeping a keen eye for any fingerprint ridge detail.

With aluminium powder, you used a circular motion, and when ridge detail began to appear, you'd concentrate the powdering in that area, developing the mark, enhancing it until it was sharp and clear. And then you might even use a clean brush along the ridge detail to clean it, to remove any excess powder.

You couldn't do that with a globular powder. If the brush showed any marks, they were very fragile. Over-brushing simply broke them up and erased them, and no amount of swearing would bring them back again.

In any case, all he got in return were weather marks, dried-on water droplets. Not a single fingerprint. Sad, but to be expected. The important thing was that he could now work against the side of the door without compromising any potential evidence.

He stood back and observed his scene, thinking through the things Eddie had requested, before satisfying himself there was nothing further he could do with things as they were. Now it really was time to withdraw the axe from the guy's throat while preserving it as best as he could for chemical enhancement of any latent fingermarks.

He laid out a sheet of brown paper and stacked up the packaging materials he'd need. And then he put on fresh gloves, two pairs, and leaned into the car. He knew the killer had held the axe at the lower half of the handle – certainly during the fatal blow – because the risk of his hands colliding with the car's window or frame would be minimised.

So that meant he had to extract the pickaxe using points of contact along the upper half only, preferably the upper third. Of course, the killer might have held the pickaxe anywhere along its handle, and indeed anywhere along its head, but Kenny had to take hold of it somewhere. But that didn't mean he didn't take care, and so he thought hard about how best to remove the stupid thing.

He hoped that if he applied gentle pressure, like pulling lightly on an oar, the axe would slide out of the throat easily. He took hold and pulled gently, and it was easy to imagine the movement of an oar in the rowlock of a boat on Lake Coniston… but this was nothing like pulling on an oar.

"Fuck."

He pulled again, and the dead man's head rocked as though it were listening to some private funky tune. But that was all. The pickaxe didn't move.

Kenny reasserted his grip, ignored the sweat collecting on his brow, and yanked harder on the handle. The head nodded again, this time as though it had awoken with a start, but the axe was stubbornly anchored in place.

The dead man's throat opened slightly and a clot of blood fell out onto his shirt like a slug taking a dive. Kenny closed his eyes. And then it struck him: he needed to open the car door so he wouldn't need to lean in at such an awkward angle. He'd be able to get more purchase too. But the door would only open eight inches before the frame collided with the axe handle.

By now the sweat was running down his face, and he'd started looking over his shoulder to see if anyone was watching this comedy.

He slammed the door, and stood with his hands on his hips, staring at it. There had to be a simple solution; after all, the fucking thing went in, didn't it? Surely it should come back out again!

He needed more pulling power. He needed to be able to brace himself somehow so he could exert more force; as it was, he was just pulling himself along the edge of the door. The smudges of black powder across the abdomen of his white scene suit were evidence of that.

Kenny took one last look around, raised his left leg, jammed his knee into the window opening, took hold of the axe, and pulled.

* * *

Eddie had told Troy to take the afternoon off, with good reason. The kid was high on speed or something.

After Troy had left, he wondered why he'd been so lenient. He sighed; was it a sign of weakness? The kid deserved a second chance. Everyone deserved a second chance.

Getting soft in my old age.

He stepped out into the office.

Nicki looked up from a desk that had been transformed from a simple wooden slab with two monitors and a keyboard into a Walt Disney shop display.

"What the fuck is that?"

Sid coughed. "I helped her. Good, eh?"

"Good? No. Not good."

"You always said we should be free to express ourselves." Sid marched over from his own desk, and Eddie inspected the furry critters surrounding the monitors, and the Seven Dwarves lurking behind the keyboard. "You always said we weren't just a number to you, that we were people. Come on, Eddie, be reasonable. What's wrong with Sneezy and Doc?"

"Reasonable? Me?"

Nicki folded her arms. "Bit much to ask, isn't it, when you're more of a headlock kind of man?"

Eddie winked at her. "I didn't have him in a headlock; I just had my knee on the back of his neck."

"You did not!" Sid's hand was over his mouth.

"But I was tempted."

Nicki said, "That was disgraceful behaviour."

"I know, but I think he's learned his lesson. He won't do it again."

"Not him – you! I so should have reported you."

Eddie leaned in and whispered, "You do what you think is right, love, and leave me to run my office how I see fit. Okay?"

Sid smiled at him. "You're Grumpy."

"And you're an arsehole."

"No," Sid pointed at the figures, "you *look* like Grumpy."

"Flattery will get you nowhere." He was staring at Nicki. "I suppose you're Happy, Sid?"

"I like to think so." Sid was beaming. "And which one is Nicki?"

"I'm Bashful," she said, "because I'm actually quite a shy person."

Eddie raised his eyebrows. "Well, I sent Dopey home, so that leaves Kenny as Sleepy, I suppose."

"So can I keep them?" Nicki looked up at him.

Eddie strolled off down the office. "Get your stuff together, Nicki, you're going to a PM."

Nicki gasped. "Shouldn't I have an orientation day first?" She licked her lips. "I mean, there's so much to know." She turned to Sid, hoping for some backup.

"Told you he was a nice fella really. Once you get to know him. And if you're good at your job. And if he's in a good mood."

Chapter Nine

Eddie and Nicki parked behind Kenny's van.

"So why did you send Troy home?"

He shut off the motor and looked across at her, hiding his eyes behind his shades. "It takes a long time to build a team in an office like ours. It's not like CID out there in the big office; they're all back-stabbing bastards who'd climb over their mother's corpse to get promotion or a gold star. We're different; we look after each other. Implicitly. We are a closed shop. And once we've been together for a while and I feel we can all trust each other, I'll answer a question like that from you. But until then I have a duty to keep my mouth shut."

"I wouldn't have reported you."

He stared at her.

"I mean – I should have, you know, all things being equal."

"But?"

"But they're not equal. I think you actually had a good reason to do what you did."

Eddie opened the van door, took off the shades and threw them onto the dashboard. "Don't do me any favours. And don't say things just to butter me up. I'm really not the buttering-up kind."

"But—"

"Listen. I'll let you into a little secret."

Nicki moved across the seat, leaned in a bit. Her blouse gaped.

Eddie shook his head and got out of the van. "Get a scene suit on."

She met him at the back of the van. "So what's the secret?" She unzipped the suit he'd thrown her, then bent over and pushed her feet into it.

Eddie turned his back on her. "This is my secret: I hate my job. Every day I wake up knowing I've got to come to work, I could cry. There's so much else I could be doing if I didn't have to come to this shithole and look after people like you."

"I beg your pardon?"

"Don't take that the wrong way. It's not an insult. The truth can never be an insult."

She stood up, pulled her arms into the sleeves so that her chest was about three yards in front of her, and Eddie looked away again. Once she'd zipped up, he turned back. "I hate the office and I hate the people in it. That includes you. I only come to work to get to places like this. This is what I do best." He pointed to the cordon and the lonely copper checking messages on his phone. "Scene work gives me a buzz. The rest is payment for that buzz. It's the gristle you get in your steak. It's the hangover in the bottom of a bottle. See what I mean?"

"So I'm an inconvenience? I'm a lump of gristle?" She was smiling, but it was shallow, masking concern.

"I didn't apply to be a supervisor. It was given to me; I didn't really have a choice. But if I'd had a choice, I'd be Kenny. I wouldn't be me. Kenny gets to play out all day doing this stuff; I get to sort out pricks like Troy Ainsley, and I get to wonder if pretty novices are going to stab me in the back because they don't like the way I manage my office. And I *have* managed it, through some fucking hard times over the last few years."

She stared at him, but there was no regret on her face.

He stepped closer. "My aim is to be fair. Nothing else. You break my rules, you too will get walled up by the throat. Abide by them and you'll be fine."

"So what are they?" Her voice had an edge to it, unlike her fucking Disney toys.

"Honesty. In everything. Oh, and everyone deserves a second chance."

"If you preach honesty in everything, how come you actually lied in front of Mr Walker?"

"Jeffery is an exception to my rule. He makes allowances for my management style because he knows I'm being fair. If he has to get involved it usually entails a lot of shouting and swearing, and he doesn't like that. So he has the world's largest blind eye. You very nearly got him involved in something much bigger than you knew."

"Which was?"

"Which was none of your business. Don't try to second guess me, and don't flash your tits at me hoping I'll be extra lenient on you. It doesn't work. Got it?"

Nicki looked away.

"I'll take that as a yes. You do your job well, you ask for advice when you need to, and you do what I say, and we'll never have a cross word. And when I can trust you, I will."

"Okay," she whispered.

"Now let's go and take the piss out of Kenny. This really is the strawberries and cream part of the job."

* * *

Eddie gave his details to the copper with the clipboard and stopped at the scene tape. He nudged Nicki. "Look!"

Kenny had his knee in the window of the car, heaving for all he was worth on the pickaxe handle, and issuing a stream of profanities. Eddie began to laugh, and then he began to howl. Pretty soon, Kenny stopped what he was doing and turned to see Eddie and Nicki walking up the drive towards him, laughing hysterically.

"It's not funny!" I've been trying to get that bastard out for twenty-five minutes!"

"Correction: it *is* funny. And I've got the photos to prove it."

"You twat!"

"Pleased to be of service. Anyway, Kenny – this is Nicki. Nicki, this is Sleepy."

They nodded at each other in lieu of shaking hands. Shaking hands wasn't the done thing at a crime scene.

"Any ideas?"

Eddie peered into the back of the car and looked at the headrest. He pushed in a plastic clip on each side and gently eased the headrest up. Then he went around to the driver's door, leaned in and withdrew the axe from the dead guy's throat as easily as pulling an oar through water. He laid it on the brown paper sheet, ready for photography.

"I hate you, Collins."

The dead man slumped, his head resting easily onto his left shoulder, exposing the hole and displaced vertebrae in the back of his neck. A stringy tendon hung out of the wound and draped over the otherwise pristine collar of his shirt.

"I fucking hate you."

"Pleased to be of service." Eddie bowed. "Nicki is with you for the rest of this scene, and take her to the PM too, alright?"

Kenny nodded, his attention now on the axe. "Yeah, no problem."

Kenny pulled Nicki to one side and explained in minute detail his thought process for the rest of the scene exam. Once the axe had been packaged, he would place clear plastic bags over the dead man's hands, feet, and head. Then he'd open out a body bag and get him out of the car. There would be some leakage, he said, but it was unavoidable.

He would call in the undertakers, or body snatchers as Eddie liked to call them, and have the vehicle recovered for a more thorough examination later.

As Kenny talked, Eddie stepped away. He'd been thinking about this scene, and it was entirely Troy's fault that he hadn't had the time to give it more intense thought earlier. He wondered where the attacker had secreted himself, for secreted he surely must have been. It had happened in full daylight.

Hiding in the conifers would have provided the perfect cover while still allowing a view of Marchant preparing to leave for work.

Eddie looked at them. For a full minute, he stood there doing nothing else but looking. And during that time, his mind didn't wander, it was focused on the job, it was paying explicit attention to those trees and the ground around them.

There was a small gap between the low branches of two neighbouring trees. Eddie slid his torch from the pouch on his belt and knelt on the asphalt.

He crept forward. He imagined the attacker would have been kneeling in the gap as far away from the driveway as possible, with an eight- or ten-pound pickaxe at his side, ready to pounce. And he'd have been there for what, half an hour? An hour? Several hours?

Deep in the scrub of small sticks near the base of the conifers, there were several freshly broken twigs, their sandy-coloured flesh standing out against the surrounding darkness. On the ground, amid the thousands of fallen brown needles, was a clump of flattened nettles. This was the killer's nest. There were four feet of thick scrub between the conifers and the wall.

Eddie stood and walked around to the entrance, looking at the gaps between the other conifers as he went. There were no similar signs of disturbance in any of them. He ducked under the blue and white police tape and walked along the footpath. The gap, only slightly visible from this side, presented itself on his left. He stood, hands on hips looking at the top of the wall. It was rough stone, like a dry-stone wall, but fixed with mortar. Running along the crown stone on the highest part of the wall was a fresh scrape, a shallow gouge that, like the broken twigs, showed up light against the mossy and blackened surroundings.

He peered over the wall and into the darkness below. The torch lit the trees and the carpet of brown needles, it showed him more broken twigs, but it didn't show him anything else.

There were no clumps of fibres clinging to the branches, there was no blood soaking into the broken twigs, no hairs floating in the breeze. There were no fresh cigarette ends or drinks containers. There was nothing. Lots of nothing.

Eddie could see this murder ending up in the 'unsolved' box.

Chapter Ten

Charles wore his pinny, and even though Eddie had stopped laughing at it ages ago, he still found it funny. But what made it even funnier was the shirt and tie he wore beneath it.

"You practising for a waiter's job? It's good to see you getting back into society. Being one step up from a tramp is so last year."

Charles came over to him with a tray. On it was a plate of pork chop, chips and salad. "What?" He handed Eddie a napkin.

Eddie gawped at it. "You after a Michelin Star?" He studied the napkin. "We normally use our sleeves."

"Not any more. We're going to behave like normal people from now on."

"Normal? You?" Eddie snorted. "Hey, have you been sniffing glue, because I told you it's bad—"

"Why can't you just enjoy it? Why must you turn everything into a major event?"

Eddie caught a scent, and then squinted. "You smell like a Lynx advert. Have you been stealing my aftershave?"

"I might have borrowed a splash. You can have it back when I get home. Anyway," he smiled, "what's an advert smell like?"

"Very clever. Had a brave pill today, have we?"

"Nope. A happy pill."

Eddie paused. "Where are you going?"

"I met someone. Wendy. Wonderful woman."

"You're going on a date?"

"You are so sharp, son. I'm proud of you."

Eddie's mouth fell open. The food wasn't burnt. It looked good and it smelled good. He'd even dressed the salad. "This is freaking me out. What the hell's going on?"

"You like it?" Charles smiled, rubbing his hands together. "Wendy gave me a few pointers."

"What, like getting someone else to make it?"

"All made with my own fair hands, boy." He tossed the pinny into the kitchen, stood before the tall mirror behind the front door where he adjusted his already immaculate tie, and said, "You'll have to wash up tonight, I'm afraid. Don't know what time I'll be back." He winked, opened the door, and checked his watch. "Come on, come on."

"Who you waiting for?"

"Taxi."

Eddie got up and walked towards Charles. "I have to say, Dad, that I'm impressed with how you've turned things around."

Charles looked at him sideways.

"No, really. I mean it."

He puffed out his chest. "Thank you, son. It means a lot."

"Are you… er, are you… packing?"

"Packing? Eddie, we hardly know each other. I ain't moving in with her."

"No, no, you missed my point. I mean are you – packing?" Eddie nodded, winked, and slapped his arm. And Charles stared at him blankly. Eddie sighed. "I'm too old to have a new younger brother."

The penny dropped. "You're disgusting! This is a purely tectonic relationship."

Eddie bit the smile to death. "Well, I hope the earth moves for you." He gave Charles a look that a father would give his son on his first date: Be careful, but have fun. It said, I'm worried for you, but you're growing up now; but mostly it said, don't be a prick, and leave while you're still sober. "How did you meet?" He took a mouthful of coffee.

"Facebook."

Eddie spat coffee across the floor, and coughed until he doubled up. "Facebook!" he screeched. "How old are you? I was joking, the other week, about it being the modern way to find true love. And you *believed* me?"

"Just because you're a cynical dinosaur doesn't mean I am too. Look at you, stuck in here night after night wishing you had a woman."

"No chance. Been there, got the carpet burns."

Charles patted Eddie on the arm, "I can see the jealousy in your eyes, son."

"That's not jealousy, it's fucking amazement! And I'll tell you something else too, Patrick Swayze, she's going to be mighty pissed off when she finds out that you accidentally posted a picture of Brad Pitt on your profile."

Charles shook his head. "You can say what you like, you little toerag, but I know when the green-eyed monster's come out to play."

Eddie returned to his seat and used the napkin to wipe coffee from his chin like a normal person. "It's your one-eyed monster that worries me! Christ, Dad, I thought you'd have grown out of puberty by now." He watched Charles standing in the doorway, nervously – or excitedly – checking his watch, and he supposed there *was* an element of jealousy there. Maybe it *wasn't* natural to spend every night in here, looking at the same four walls and listening to his dad farting the national anthem before bed.

He thought back to Nicki, and how she'd made a not-so-subtle move on him. There was an age gap of about ten years, an intellectual gap too – one that put her at a significant advantage – but such a match wasn't unheard of. She probably just wanted to get inside his boxers to advance her career, though. It was obvious, and he'd seen it when she was in the van with him: how she draped her top open like that, using her femininity and assuming he'd fall for it. As though all he ever thought about was a pair of tits; as though Eddie Collins was really that shallow. It was puzzling, wonderful, and frightening. But it was the frightening part that had finally made him blink and walk away.

He found himself frowning. "What the hell's got into you?" he whispered. "Cut it out."

"Taxi's here," Charles shouted. "I'm off. Enjoy your pork and your solitude."

Eddie grinned. "Damned right I will."

And then his father was gone.

"Don't be late home!" Eddie called. "I ain't waiting up for you!"

He looked at the meal. His appetite had gone. He wondered if anyone actually found him attractive – besides those who wanted to further their career, of course. He lit a cigarette, folded his arms and found a wall to look at.

"Fucking Facebook."

DAY 2

Chapter Eleven

"My, you've grown." Jessica looked away from the mirror, embarrassed, as she rehearsed the first words she would speak to her son in twelve years. "'My, how you've grown'. Is that the best you can come up with?"

She sat on the toilet, pulled off a yard of paper and wiped the tears away. She was trembling. She knew she'd be nervous, had expected it, but this was beyond nerves; this was well on the way to terror.

It wasn't supposed to be like this. It was supposed to be the happiest day in the last decade; it was a reunion with someone she loved. "Love. With someone I *love*. With the only person I love, actually."

She stood again, gripped the damp toilet paper in her clammy hands and stared with new determination into the mirror. She looked hard, and she smiled, she made herself smile even though she hadn't done it for so long that it felt unnatural. The muscles soon ached. "Hi, Michael—"

Someone banged on the front door and Jessica almost had a heart attack. "Fuck, fuck, fuck." She ditched the toilet paper and flushed, plumped up her hair again, pulled her blouse straight and darted out of the bathroom, out of the flat, and along the hall where a figure presented itself through the frosted glass just like Sidmouth had done. It caused her to pause for a moment, but it wasn't him; this figure was much shorter, much rounder.

This was her.

She opened the door, pre-ordered smile already in place, and a large rain-drenched woman beamed up at her.

"Jess? Hello, dear. I'm Marilyn from Social Care." She stuck out a wet hand and Jessica noticed the chewed nails. Jessica shook hands, and then stood aside. Marilyn-from-Social-Care stumbled up the final step and into the hall. As she walked by, Jessica noticed the smell; like the dampness you might find in a cellar. Fusty, mouldy.

Back in the bedsit, Jessica grew more nervous. All the officials who came to see her knew where she lived – obviously – and they knew how she lived, just a rung or two up from the alkies next door, living in squalor. But it was the way things had to be for now; it was her version of a halfway house. They wanted her to get a job and return to society's all-embracing arms as soon as possible. They wanted her to be normal again, and to let the past live in the past.

"It's good to finally meet you," Marilyn said, looking around, beige folder held tightly to her chest.

Jessica noticed that her wedding ring was almost totally encased by the skin on her finger, hidden away inside sore-looking folds. "And you. I can't begin to tell you how much I've been looking forward to today."

"Nervous?"

Jessica nodded. "I haven't seen him since he was two. He won't know me, I know that, but I hope—"

"Small steps, Jess. Hope is good" —she reached out that chubby hand and placed it on Jessica's own— "but don't keep it round your neck like a weight. Don't expect too much from today. I hate to say it, but you're a stranger to him."

I know I'm a stranger. You think I don't fucking know that? You could drag any woman in off the street and present her to him – it wouldn't matter, he doesn't know me any more.

"He probably doesn't even care," she whispered.

"Oh, I'm sure he does, dear." Marilyn's friendly smile plumped up her cheeks. "Shall we go?"

"Yes, yes, of course. Don't you need me to fill out any forms first? There must be a lot of paperwork—"

"Hey. Try not to be too nervous. It'll be fine, you'll see."

* * *

From beneath a pink umbrella, Marilyn knocked, Jess behind her, eyes closed, rain soaking into her hair, hands laced before her as though she were in prayer.

The door opened, and a woman with copper-coloured hair exchanged whispered pleasantries with Marilyn, who then stepped aside. Jessica looked up at the woman who'd brought her son up.

"Hello, Jess. I'm Valentine." She held out a hand adorned with jazzy acrylic nails. "Don't be afraid. He's turned into a wonderful young man. You'll be so proud."

Jessica smiled, but even after all the pep talks she'd given herself on the way here, she found herself in tears again. This Valentine woman had ruined it already. *A fine young man. You'll be so proud.* These were things she wanted to discover for herself, not have some stranger hand her a resumé. On trembling legs, she stepped inside, aware that Marilyn was right behind her. Valentine gestured through into the living room. "Go on," she whispered.

Jess almost threw up, but she pushed the door open.

Chapter Twelve

It was raining heavily as Benson stood in reception at the Major Crime Unit, staring into his reflection in the silvered glass windows by the door. To his right, Maggie Darlington mumbled into the phone, and he saw her sneak a quick glance at her watch. Benson did the same. Four o'clock, and counting. He'd been in since seven this morning, but had no desire to leave work and head home to his lovely, adoring wife.

Because he didn't have a lovely, adoring wife.

Look up the word battleaxe in the encyclopaedia, and there's a good chance her photo would be alongside it. "Cow," he said, trying to peer into the carpark. The clouds had brought a premature darkness to the day, causing the automatic lamps out there to blink on and cast their unforgiving white LED light, and its sharp black shadows.

The wind hurled rain at the door, and Benson considered how wet he would be before he made it to the car – wherever it might be. He held in his hands the keys to a Corsa – one of sixty or seventy out there. He could cope with a moderate drenching, but wasn't prepared to go further than that. He dug around his pocket on a Mars bar hunt, but all his hand pulled out were half a dozen chocolate-smeared wrappers. "Bastard," he whispered.

And then he wondered if this enquiry would keep until morning.

He was on his way to a building site – just the place to visit when it was pissing it down like this. "Be up to my arse in fucking mud."

"Sorry?"

He turned. Maggie was off the phone and was now smiling at him.

"Nothing. Just plucking up the courage to head out." He indicated the rain.

"You need a brolly—" And then she was gone, eyes downcast as she took another call in her headset.

Benson's polite smile drifted away and he looked back out into the rain.

Maybe I should delegate. Send out one of the cocky young bastards. No point being a DI and doing all the donkey work myself.

But he couldn't.

His shoulders slumped. That was the old-fashioned way of policing: get the sprogs to do all the shitty work, while you and your gaffers went down the pub. It didn't work like that any more; these days everything was much fairer, much more above board. Transparent, they called it.

And anyway, it had never really been Benson's style. He'd always preferred to be out there doing the legwork and pulling in the answers, rather than sitting at some desk, getting eye strain and headaches. Computers could only tell you so much. If you relied on the young ones to get your answers for you, you could guarantee you were getting their mistakes too, getting their omissions. Wasn't worth it; better get soaked and get what he needed.

He pulled up his collar, hit the big green button on the wall, and punched his way out into the deluge. By the time he'd found the car, he was wet through. As he climbed in, he could see them all standing up there in the main office, looking out through the windows – and he could see a good portion of the bastards looking down here and laughing at him. No matter – he was out of there now. Cold, shivering, but away from them.

It was at times like this that he could really understand where Eddie Collins was coming from. There was nothing quite like being alone to really focus the mind. Give it something to think about and keep it away from the pollution of others, and it's amazing how much better you could feel coming out the other side. People say physical exercise makes you feel good – something to do with endorphins being released. Surely it was the same when you had a spell alone?

Eddie Collins was a strange creature, though. They disliked each other, but there was a good amount of respect there too. Since Eddie came to Major Crime a few years ago, they'd worked all kinds of jobs together and got into some truly life-or-death situations. The kind of situations that can really make two people bond – whether they want to or not.

* * *

By the time Benson reached the housing estate, he had his headlamps on full, and the wipers struggled to clear his screen. He brushed a hand across the misted-up side window, and stared out at the bunting that was flapping so violently that it risked taking flight. He could see the sales office, and beyond it a blue perimeter fence with Portakabins stacked two high, forming the site offices of a new-build construction site a couple of miles from Alwoodley Golf Club. He turned off the engine and cringed at the rain hitting the roof, at the rain hitting the earth and bouncing mud up the side of the car.

He took a deep breath, opened the door, and made a mad dash for the entrance.

* * *

He stood before a three-bar electric heater with steam coming off his hands and his head like he'd just stepped out of a Turkish bath. From a stand by the door, his coat dripped water into a layer of mud that formed a trail right into the cabin. One of the guys placed a mug of tea on the desk to his side. "Should've left it till tomorrow," he smiled.

The mug was cracked and looked as though it had never been washed out. "By which time, the tape would have overwritten itself again. It's just my luck." He reached for the tea, sipped gratefully, and curled his hands around it like it was his best friend.

Five minutes later, he was parked in a chair next to some security man who wore body armour and a dark blue knitted jersey with elbow patches. Benson wondered if he'd once been a copper and couldn't quite shake off the habit. But he didn't ask – you're likely to end up in a year-long conversation if you start talking about the job with an ex-employee.

"Here he is." The officer pulled his chair in closer to the monitor. "Over the fence, casual as you like."

"Why are there tools left out overnight?"

The security man shrugged. "I think they're supposed to put them in the storage containers. You know what people are like, chief."

Benson stared at the monitor, watching the man walking straight through the floodlit area to a small trench next to a stack of breezeblocks. There, leaning against the stack, were the pickaxe, several spades, and a cement mixer with a tarp thrown over the top. The man was white, tall, maybe six-one, six-two, very well built, and bulked out further by the padded coat he wore. He turned, grabbed the pick and a small hand axe, and immediately started walking back the way he'd come. "Beard. Yellow cap. Blue coat and jeans."

"Cat Diesel Power cap," the officer said. "I'd recognise them anywhere."

"What's that mean? Cat Diesel Power?"

"Caterpillar? The earthmovers? They have diesel engines. It's just a trademark kind of thing. 'Cat, diesel power'."

Benson nodded, still confused, and looked back at the screen as the intruder leapt the fence again.

"There you go, chief. Twenty-eight seconds. In. Out."

"What time?"

"Oh-five-twenty-two."

"Twenty-eight seconds. Wasn't worth me getting wet for."

"I could've had it dropped off for you."

"No matter. It's good to get out in the fresh air."

The security man raised his eyebrows and laughed.

"Can you copy that for me?"

The man handed him a disk and smiled. "Already done, chief."

* * *

Benson arrived back at the Major Crime Unit after all the nine-to-fives had clocked off, and the place was quieter. Ironically, it seemed to him, he also arrived back just as the rain stopped. Dead. It didn't peter out; it just stopped as though the director had shouted 'cut'.

The reception area was eerily quiet. If he listened closely, he could hear the water dripping onto the tiled floor from his coat. The silence didn't last long enough before the double doors opened and Collins appeared, dragging a cigarette from a packet.

Chapter Thirteen

She tried to gauge his reaction, but failed somehow.

He was tall, dark-haired, and gangly. Not an ounce of fat anywhere. His eyes looked at her, but they had no love in them; he was just waiting for this to be over so he could get back to his computer game.

What had she expected? That he'd come running and fling his arms around her?

"Michael," she whispered, and took a step towards him.

He stared. "Hello."

"I've… I've missed you."

Silence.

Jess took a glance behind her, needing some reassurance, but they too just stared at her; Marilyn with concern, Valentine with raised eyebrows and folded arms. They were all looking at her, waiting for the drama to start – she was the star attraction, this murderer who'd laughingly come to reclaim her long-lost son. "I wrote to you. A thousand times." She smiled, not wanting to aggravate him, but needing to ask, "Why didn't you reply?"

He was cold. A stranger who preferred it to stay that way.

"Have I made a big mistake? Coming here? Should I have stayed away?"

"I was in a play at school," he said, his voice still high-pitched, but filled with such self-assurance that she felt intimidated. "Couple of months ago. They gave me a lead part."

"Oh, that's fantastic. Perhaps I can come to—"

"I was a soldier. In the Second World War. And I'd been injured and sent home. It was a really good play."

"Sounds wonder—"

"And my mum and dad came to see me in hospital. That only lasted for a scene, or maybe it was two scenes. I can't remember now."

She nodded with enthusiasm. He was warming to her.

"And then I was at home. Healing. And my friends visited me, and my mother would make squash for us, and we'd remember our comrades who were still fighting in the war."

Jess turned for another look around. Everyone looked as confused as she was. When she turned back to him, his face was made of stone. There was nothing there for her, there were no feelings. He was talking to a wall. It was rehearsed, just bullshit to make her shut up and go home. Alone.

His voice was sharp enough to cut through any ambiguity. "She was a better mother to me than you ever were."

Valentine shouted, "Michael, what did we agree?"

His eyes didn't even flicker. They remained on Jess. He blinked once, and then said, "You can't just walk back into my life from stage left and start acting like my mother, pretending you sent me letters. It doesn't fucking work like that, yeah? You are messing with my head, now fuck off and leave me alone."

"Michael!"

"The show's over," he said. "No repeat performance." He turned to his right and walked out of the lounge, closing the door behind him.

Jess turned, and the rest was black.

Chapter Fourteen

Eddie kicked open the double door, pulling a cigarette out of a packet with his lips. As he looked up, he saw Benson standing there looking like either he'd just shit his pants or he was halfway through a favourite tree impression.

"Has it been raining?" He laughed as Benson pulled his best 'very funny' face. "You in a rush to get home?"

"I was trying to think of an excuse to avoid it, actually."

"Consider me your excuse. Starbucks?"

Benson stared.

"They do a good breakfast in a bun. And fantastic blueberry muffins."

* * *

"Starbucks is my new McDonald's," Eddie said. "Much classier. And we struck it lucky," he said, cocking his head. "Sometimes they play jazz. I have to shout at them when they play jazz."

"I like jazz."

Eddie looked at Benson and shook his head. "Explains a lot." He put the drinks down and then brought over the food. "I'm in no rush to get home either."

Benson sipped.

"My dad's turned into a younger man than I am. He's fallen for this old tart called Wendy. Keeps fawning over her on Facebook. I can't go near him without gagging."

"Young love, eh?"

"It'll pass." Eddie set to work on the muffin, keeping his eyes on Benson whenever Benson wasn't looking. Something was wrong. "You okay?"

He nodded. "Yep."

"Lying bastard. Home getting you down?" Eddie could see that was the very question that put a hole in Benson's hull, and now he was filling with water and sinking.

Benson went quiet – not that he'd been saying much to begin with. But this was a different kind of quiet – contemplative, remorseful even. He just nodded and took a bite of the breakfast bun.

And Eddie did what most men would do in this situation. Ignored it. "Why are you so wet?"

Benson chewed and swallowed. "Hmm, got the CCTV of the murderer stealing the pickaxe."

"How do you know he's the murderer?"

Benson rolled his eyes. "Don't be so fucking pedantic. For once, just shut up, nod, and say 'well done, Benson'. Okay?"

"Hey, well done, Benson. What's he look like?"

"Like a tramp. Big, tall, has a beard and a yellowish baseball cap with Cat Diesel Power on it."

Eddie looked confused. "What's a tramp doing mixing with the likes of Marchant?"

Bensons shrugged. "I can't think of a connection."

"How's the list coming along? I mean, it could be someone straight off your list, or it could be someone paid by someone on your list."

"I know. Why are you always trying to tell me my fucking job?"

Benson raised his voice, and several of the other guests – polite people, much better than the riff-raff who patronised McDonald's, thought Eddie – looked his way. Eddie cocked an eyebrow and stared back at them. "I'm always telling you how to do your job because you're shit at your job, you fucking Mars bar muncher."

"Shit? Me?"

Eddie smiled, tipped his mug at Benson.

Benson sighed. "Over the last twelve months, Marchant has defended twenty-four people—"

"What about those released—"

"Shut up." He pointed a finger. "Don't interrupt me ag—"

"Why are you always so touchy?"

"Now you're sounding like my wife, and I have to tell you that I find it disturbing, okay?"

"Sorry."

Benson carried on. "He defended twenty-four people. Eight of those made a formal complaint, against either the sentence or Marchant's handling of their case."

Eddie raised his eyebrows again.

"No" —Benson shook his head— "it's normal, those stats are about average. Of course, we don't know how many of the remaining sixteen are also pissed off at him but just aren't inclined to make a formal complaint."

"I think we can discount any that would want to draw attention to themselves by making a formal complaint."

"Really? You don't think it'd be a good bluff? 'Why would I complain about him if I was going to kill him?'"

"So you still have a list of twenty-four?"

"Two of them died. And we have the families, of course. And the families of those he successfully defended against – victims can be nasty when it comes to losing."

"So there are lots of people who wouldn't mind seeing him wearing a pickaxe for a tie?"

"He's not short of enemies." Benson sipped, dug a nail into a chunk of food caught in his teeth, and sucked it off.

"It's like eating with my dad." Eddie turned away. "Have you finished playing with your food?"

"I've got Khan and a team of seven working on that little lot."

"Should have it wrapped up by tomorrow, then." Eddie smirked.

"How long before we get results back from the DNA mini-tapes from the axe handle?"

"Don't pin your hopes on them."

"I'm not. But how long?"

"Five days."

Benson nodded.

Eddie continued with his own line of thought. "So how about the list of people he's defended who've been released over the last few months? That must be a lot shorter."

Benson smiled a little. "Four."

Eddie nodded. "If you did your job properly, I could take the rest of the week off."

"And who's going to oversee your office?"

"Don't remind me."

"Of the four, one is a woman currently out on license for murdering her ex-husband. She doesn't look physically capable of swinging an axe.

"There's a man who had admitted to killing a rapist. He didn't blame Marchant for his sentence, but he has no alibi for the date of Marchant's death."

"How do you know?"

"I had someone speak to him already. He lives in North Yorkshire."

"Oh."

"Can I continue?"

"Be my guest."

Benson sighed. "One is a rapist who had been sent down, got released, and is now back inside for sexual assault.

"And the last one is an arsonist with mental health issues. He has an alibi – he's in Juniper Hill."

"So that means it's the rapist killer. We should let him go; he's doing a valuable public service."

"By killing the rapist or killing the defence lawyer?"

"Either. Both. He's medal material, really."

Benson made a start on the blueberry muffin.

"So where does that leave your investigation?"

Benson spat crumbs across the table as he said, "With Khan's enquiry, more or less. Unless your DNA mini-tapes give us a name."

Eddie stared at him over the rim of his mug, and felt his hackles rising. Benson shrugged; content, it seemed, to wait for the murderer to fall into his lap, clutching a signed confession. Eddie couldn't believe that Benson wasn't pushing forward with an active enquiry. "How about we go and see the rapist killer?"

Benson worked the muffin like there was a toad in his mouth trying to get out. "It's on my list."

"Short, is it? This list?"

Benson's eyes narrowed tight. "I'll do it tomorrow. Satisfied?"

"Want me to come with you?"

Benson dropped the plate on the table. "Why the fuck would I want you to come with me?"

Eddie stood up, threw the napkin on the table and dabbed his lips with his sleeve. "Suit yourself, you miserable twat."

Chapter Fifteen

The wind blew leaves and litter around what was loosely termed the front garden. It took Jess a few seconds to work out who the woman was, standing on the top step, clutching a small handbag in immaculate hands. Over the woman's shoulder and beyond the leaves and litter, she could see a dark blue BMW – one of those big ones – parked at the kerb.

And then Jessica's eyes were drawn to the woman herself; to the deep copper-coloured hair waving at her from beneath a fur-lined hood, and the tight lips that tried and failed to raise a warm smile.

"Valentine," she said.

The woman pulled her coat even tighter against the wind. "Can I come in?"

Once inside the flat, Jessica found herself standing before Valentine with her hands planted across her groin, arms pulled in tightly over her breasts. She was fully clothed, but she felt naked, as though her lifestyle was under scrutiny. She began to bite her lips again, but she tried to maintain an illusion of decorum. "Can I offer you some tea?" She nodded towards the plastic kettle.

"I'd love a green tea, if you have any?"

Jessica screwed up her face. "Sorry."

"It's okay, I'll pass then. Thank you though."

"I can do coffee. Instant."

"I'll get to the point, Jessica. We – that is, my husband and me – we've been taking care of Michael for twelve years." And now it was Valentine's turn to screw her face up. Embarrassment – fake or real – forced her to take a deep breath and spit the words as though they were bullets. "We want to adopt him. There," she said, and let out the breath.

Jessica's legs became hollow and for a moment she thought she might just fall over sideways, but she turned and grabbed the worktop.

"We love him," she continued. "We're a close family."

Jessica turned to face her, eyes squinting with something approaching hatred. She kept one hand resting on the worktop to steady herself. "I've lost all those years," she said, keeping her voice quiet but strong; no hesitation, no cracking. "But despite that, I will get to know my boy again, and he'll grow to love me—"

"That's not going to happen. You saw him—"

"At least give me a chance. I'll change him!"

Valentine's lips tightened, her eyes focused on Jessica's, and she took another breath before saying, "This is a one-time offer. I'll bring the papers tomorrow, you sign them, and I hand you a cheque for fifty thousand pounds."

Jessica's mouth fell open.

"We're a family now, Jessica. It would be cruel to pull him away after all this time. He has school… exams…" She blinked, looked around the room. "You'll never be more than a stranger to him. I mean, look at—"

Jessica took her hand off the worktop and slapped Valentine's smug face so hard that she fell against the door. Valentine drew fingertips across her lips; they came away smeared red. She turned to open the door, but before leaving she said over her shoulder, "When it all goes awfully wrong for you, Jessica – remember today. This was the beginning of it all." She slammed the door. From the other side of it she said, "And we burned all of your letters. He didn't get a single one of them."

Jessica buried her hot face in her cold hands.

DAY 3

Chapter Sixteen

Charles had come home at a fairly respectable eleven-fifteen.

Eddie had been in his darkened room listening to Floyd through his headphones, filling his ears with sound and his mind with images. The only light came from his glowing cigarette end, and the hated alarm clock on his bedside table. He was sinking into 'Wish You Were Here' when a slice of light from the hallway glided under his door. He pulled the headphones off and sure enough, there was Charles, singing something shit by Englebert Humperdinck.

He'd been tempted to go and take the piss out of him, but decided it was better to leave the old fella alone with his new-found happiness. He'd put the cans back on again, closed his eyes and turned the volume up.

And now, at ten to eight the next morning, he stared at the Major Crime Unit building from the comfort of the Discovery with something approaching hatred, cigarette dangling between his lips, arm out of the window and Floyd playing gently on the stereo. His mind was a million miles away, in a much better place.

Even the timid rain dampening his shirt failed to draw him from his reverie. It was almost blissful – like spending the last few minutes in bed under a warm duvet replaying the disappearing tendrils of a fantastic dream before letting reality intrude.

It seemed to sum up his life, that building. Ugly, bland, hiding everything behind a façade of clinical uniformity where there was no danger of any character being allowed even to exist, let alone flourish. He sighed, took a drag on the cigarette, and tried to sink into his thoughts again – they weren't particularly pleasant, but they were his, and they were comfortable.

But they weren't allowed to return. Eddie heard the gate rattle across the car park entrance on its bent rail, and then a mobile boom box destroyed any chance of sinking back into casual thought as it parked right next to him. Eddie took a long slow blink and let out a mammoth sigh in preparation for the first ignorant prick of the day.

The boom box was a black Vauxhall Astra with a spoiler bolted above the rear window, some kind of home-made splitter under the front valance, blacked-out windows and a *No Fear* decal across the door. This thing was dripping cool, thought Eddie, shaking his head. "Why me?" he whispered.

The engine stopped, but the music did not, and Eddie resigned himself to having his morning prematurely shot to death by some ignorant twat with poor taste in music and a misdirected understanding of what constituted 'cool'. But then the music – the noise – did stop and the car rocked as the driver climbed out. He smacked his door into Eddie's car.

"Hey, old man! I see you even drive a granddad's car!" Troy howled to himself and slammed the door. The spoiler wobbled. "I bet you listen to Fleetwood Mac, eh? Or Simon and Garfunkel?"

"How fucking dare you." Eddie wound up his window and climbed out of the Discovery. He was in no mood for a confrontation, but sometimes other people just couldn't resist goading him. "I've never listened to a Simon and Garfunkel song in my life." He stepped up to Troy, slapped a hand on his shoulder. "Don't ever insult me again. And while we're having a friendly chat like this, let me remind you that dinking someone's car on purpose is criminal damage, okay? Do it again and I'll pull your face off." Eddie began to walk away.

"Really?"

Eddie stopped and turned. He flicked his half-smoked cigarette at Troy's car, pointed a stabbing finger, and said, "And playing noise like that is a pollution offence, you ignorant bastard. Other people exist, you know. Selfish prick."

"Like you'd know about other people." Troy held out his hand, palm up. "Pay me."

"'Scuse me?"

"Your cigarette blistered my paintwork. Pay me twenty quid and we'll call it quits."

Eddie surprised himself by laughing. "You're taking the piss, right? If I gave you twenty quid, I'd own the fucking car! *And* I'd want change."

"Twenty quid or I take this further."

The smile simply rolled off Eddie's face and his eyes grew dark. He stepped forward, but Troy remained planted to the spot, hand outstretched. Eddie slapped it aside and stepped right up to his face. "This can end in one of two ways."

"Oh goody, here comes the threat."

* * *

In reception, Maggie checked her watch, straightened her suit again and cleared her throat. She tapped fingers on her desk, waiting. A voice came from beyond the double wooden doors that led up to the MCU first floor. The doors opened and Jeffery Walker entered the reception foyer, chatting to a besuited man who'd entered the building almost an hour ago without even looking at her.

Jeffery was laughing, hands never still, nervous, as though he were trying to impress him. The stranger offered no smiles in return, even polite ones. He stared at Jeffery, and eventually Jeffery ran out of steam and stood there like a dog offering its throat to the alpha.

"And who leads the forensic effort at the coalface?" His voice was quiet, but all Maggie could concentrate on was the reflection of the overhead lights on his bald head – surely he must polish it.

"The coalface?"

"Who's below you, Mr Walker?" He began walking until he was level with Maggie.

She hoped the phone wouldn't ring – she didn't want him analysing her like he was analysing Jeffery.

"Feel free to call me Jeffery." He smiled, fidgeted.

"Who's below you, Mr Walker?"

Jeffery looked around, either to see who was watching this embarrassing spectacle, or to ask for help. Maggie smiled at him.

"Mr Collins is our man at the coalface."

"I'd like to meet him."

Maggie saw Jeffery's eycs widen slightly – and she wasn't surprised. But she *was* surprised when his mouth fell open as though he was about to throw up. He stared at Maggie, and then over her shoulder. She stared back, wondering what the problem was.

Jeffery flicked his eyes again, and she turned.

Eddie was in the car park. He had Troy six inches off the ground by his jacket collar, snarling into his face. She squealed, and hurried around the reception desk towards the stranger, holding out her hand. "Good morning, I'm Maggie Darlington, receptionist. Pleased to meet you."

The stranger stared at her until her smile shrivelled and her hand fell back to her side. She felt herself glowing red.

"Maggie, this is Mr Crawford, our new Superintendent."

She shuffled around to block his view.

Jeffery stared on in disbelief as Eddie dropped Troy onto the bonnet of his car and lit a cigarette.

"Very pleased to meet you, Mr Crawford. Can I get you some coffee?"

"Had I wanted coffee, I would have asked." Crawford turned back to Jeffery. "I want to meet Collins."

Jeffery turned green. "Are you sure?"

* * *

"No threat, Troy." Eddie curled his fist into Troy's jacket and lifted him clean off the ground. "I'm sick of pricks like you spoiling life for people like me. You're like those scum who ride around on scooters. I hate them as well. You pollute my life and think it's funny. Well it's not funny. You're not funny."

"Put me down. This is assault."

Eddie got nose to nose and growled. "If I had my way I'd terminate people like you. And I'd do it for free. I wouldn't even take a meal break."

"Very funny. You've had your giggle, now put me—"

Eddie dropped him on the bonnet of his Astra, dusted his hands off, and lit a cigarette. He pulled out his wallet, stroked a twenty from inside, and stuffed it into Troy's jacket pocket. "I want a receipt. And don't play that shite near me again. It makes me angry. Got it?"

"You're a psycho, Collins!"

"Wanker," he said, and walked to the ugly glass doors. "Touch my car," he shouted, "and I'll have yours crushed into a paperweight for my desk." He reached the glass doors, impressed that at last someone had washed all the dirt off them enough for him to see the despair in his own face. He took a last drag on the cigarette, flicked it away and opened the door.

The foyer was brightly lit, but always seemed dark and depressing. The only entertainment he found in this dreary part of his journey into hell was Moneypenny and her rather splendid cleavage. But when he looked up to find it, neither it nor she was behind the reception desk; they were standing in the middle of the foyer with Jeffery and a man who looked like Telly Savalas. They were all looking at him. Eddie glanced over his shoulder but when he turned back, they were all still staring at him. "Is my fly down?"

"Eddie" —Jeffery beckoned him— "this is our new Superintendent, Mr Crawford."

"Hi." Eddie walked past the group and barged through the double doors, heading for the stairs.

Jeffery coughed. "Eddie!"

All three heard him tut as the doors squeaked open again, and Eddie dragged his feet to Mr Crawford's side.

Crawford nodded and held out his hand. "Mr Collins."

"Can I offer you a lollipop?"

"I'm sorry?"

Moneypenny stifled a squeal and hurried around to her desk again, hand cupping her mouth. Jeffery looked blank.

"Ah, yes. I see now. You're the very first person ever to liken me to Kojak. Can't tell you how funny that is."

"I have a thing for originality," Eddie said. "But this is good; first time we meet, and you're already apologising. I like that in a boss."

"I have no idea what you're talking about." Crawford looked up at Eddie and closed the gap down just as his green eyes closed to slits. "But I find you most disagreeable."

Eddie shrugged. "Good. It wouldn't do to have too many yes-men, would it? I mean, look what happened to your predecessor. Nearly drove this old boat into the fucking rocks because no one would dare question him."

"And you are that man?"

"Well, it's definitely not Jeffery." He looked at Jeffery. "No offence." Eddie smiled and turned away, heading not for the double doors, but for the reception desk.

Moneypenny's smile faltered, then left her face completely. And in that one moment, Eddie found her blank face very attractive; there was nothing concealed, it was all on show, no nasty surprises about to leap out and grab him. He leaned on the chest-high counter and stared at her, resisting the urge to let his eyes travel south.

"Eddie," she whispered.

"I'm waiting."

Moneypenny blinked, shrugged. "What for?"

He tapped his fingers… and decided to go ahead and do it. "Italian?"

Her eyebrows dropped from hopeful to confused, and she said, "I'm from Doncaster. But I used to drive a Fiat."

"Eddie!" Jeffery snapped. Eddie looked over his shoulder to see one of the double doors closing behind Crawford. "That was very rude."

"He's new here; I forgive him."

"You asking me on a date?" Moneypenny's face gathered all the happiness it could muster; her eyes were on fire.

The glass door opened and Troy skulked in, eyeing Eddie as he passed the desk.

"Troy," Eddie said, "my office in five minutes. Bring coffee. And don't spit in it."

"Eddie," Jeffery said, "my office in fifteen minutes."

"I'm going to need longer than ten minutes with him," Eddie pointed at Troy, ignored Jeffery's tut. He turned to Moneypenny. "I'll meet you at The Italian Job in Garforth. Seven o'clock."

"Okay," was all she could say.

Chapter Seventeen

Blackness.

There was no place in hell darker than where Jess found herself now. She lay motionless under the duvet. The tears had long gone, leaving a void of despair so intense that she feared even death might not pull her free of it. She'd disappeared into a stupor, where voices came and went, and thoughts filled the pocket of stale air under here, disappearing into a vortex the moment she tried to concentrate on them.

On the worktop, well out of arm's reach, sat a full bottle of Bell's whisky and three boxes of paracetamol. They'd been there since yesterday, and Jess had been considering their potential.

Options.

Though much of the journey back home with Marilyn was already forgotten, she remembered her saying, "You can try again. He'll be more receptive next time, you'll see. It was a shock to him. Next time will be better."

Those words rattled around her empty head like a bullet ricocheting off the walls. Next time. "Next time."

They shouldn't have needed a next time. It had been drilled into her in prison that you suck the pill and you do your time. Dwelling on it caused the time to slow down, and caused distress. But there was simply no stopping the gnawing anger she lived with each day, that injustice was to blame.

That the system had failed her massively. Had she been guilty of murder, or manslaughter, then doing the time for it would have been a lot easier; she'd have sucked the pill and done the time. But the knowledge that she was in prison simply because people had fucked up had been like a slow torture.

How frustrating it had been, trying to convince people in authority that they'd made an error. They don't make errors. They *never* make errors. Not collectively. Not the whole fucking system!

And now she was semi-free, but her life was in shreds.

No job.

No son.

No house.

No future.

The only possible cure – and it wasn't certain – was death. The ultimate freedom.

"The death of Jessica Ripley," she whispered. It sounded good. It sounded inviting; it sounded like the only option for her to finally break free. She lifted the quilt and felt comforted that the bedsit was in darkness, that there was no harsh daylight to make her challenge her decision. It was just a case of opening the bottle and drinking. Simple. And then you sleep. Forever. And the pain is gone.

When it all goes awfully wrong for you, Jessica. Remember today. This was the beginning of it all.

Valentine spat those words at her yesterday. As if yesterday hadn't been bad enough.

Always room for something worse. "Fifty grand." Like that could ever replace my boy. Bitch.

Jess swung her legs off the bed, and when her feet touched the cold floor it felt good, like a contrast to the warm blackness she'd lived in, a stimulus. The curtains were open, and through the fogged window she could see the house opposite, silhouetted against a lighter sky. But in here the shadows clung like poisoned thoughts. On shaky legs, Jessica padded across the floor to the bottle. Her head ached, and her stomach cramped. Her body creaked. She could already smell the whisky; it was as though her brain knew what was coming and tried to simulate it.

She could make out the bottle on the worktop, and reached for it. But even before she picked it up, she could see something was not right.

And now that she'd come round a little, she noticed another smell: the rank odour of sweat. A shiver trickled down her back, and she broke out in goose pimples. She was gripped by an irrational fear that made her freeze; eyes wide, heart hammering, limbs cold, fear hot. Her wide eyes saw nothing. She moved her hand back and forth, searching, and when her fingertips found the worktop, she scooted around for the cutlery drawer.

Knife in hand, Jess found the light switch and turned it on.

He sat on the chair, glaring at her. "'Ello, Jessica."

Chapter Eighteen

It took a moment for Jess to recognise the stinking man in the chair. He wore a grubby, battered, yellow baseball cap with CAT Diesel Power across the front. He'd grown a beard that he clearly used as a bib, and which seemed to sparkle each time he moved his face. He wore a padded jacket, shiny with dirt, and jeans with holes in the knees, through which poked a second pair. And boots that looked like army issue from World War Two.

He smiled. The stench that came from his mouth was like the ethylene from overripe bananas.

"No welcoming hug, then?"

Jess took a step back.

"I'll take that as a no, shall I? Suppose that means a shag's out of the question too?" He laughed and winked at her.

"What the hell are you doing here?" Jess held the knife out, but he made no attempt to move from the chair.

The smile and wrinkles never left his face. His eyes sparkled as though they were damp. "You didn't seek me out."

"I wouldn't have recognised you even if I had. You look like a disease."

"You old flatterer. I'm a tramp. I'm a wanderer. Hey, they even turned me down as a *Big Issue* seller." He tried to laugh, but it ended in a coughing fit. He pulled a small tin from one of his many pockets, and took out a premade roll-up.

"Not in here, Tony."

"Bah." He lit it and breathed out a grey cloud. "I saved your life." He pointed at the empty whisky bottle. "That went down the sink. Tablets went down the toilet; pretty much like my life when you left."

Jess threw the knife back in the drawer and slammed it shut. "Left?"

"Got arrested, then. Same difference to me. You weren't there. They wouldn't let me see Michael – not a blood relative. It works against you. Got to drinking a bit, and I lost my job, as you're likely to do if you're knocking back a bottle of gin while you're in charge of a double-decker. My flat went next, the council wouldn't even consider letting me have yours, and before long I found myself stealing clothes off people's washing lines.

"It's why I never visited you." He smiled, but it was tinged with regret and embarrassment. "I should have, I know. But you wouldn't have wanted me to." He took another drag on the roll-up, holding it with shaking, brown-stained fingers. "Still a bit gutted you didn't try to find me when you got out."

When it all goes awfully wrong for you, Jessica. Remember today. This was the beginning of it all.

"My first thought was Michael." And then the blackness hit her again, and the disaster of hearing your own child telling you to fuck off and never come back. "I'm a failure." The room blurred and she let the tears fall.

"Go on, lass. Get it out of your system. They dry up eventually, trust me."

And as though she'd been waiting for permission, she did. The sobbing came, the blocked nose, the tears so hot that they stung. She eventually collapsed onto the floor, howling, shrieking. Tony sat there smoking, watching her. "It's not fair," she said, over and over again. "It's not fair what they did to us. To us all."

"I'm working on it," he said.

She propped herself up on her elbows, dragged a sleeve across her eyes, and said, "Working on what?"

"Making it fair. Well, making it fairer, I should say. Because there ain't nothing that'll give back Michael, or these missing years.

Or my dignity. Nothing. No can do. No time travel," he grinned, "not even in a bottle of Bells and a packet of painkillers.

"But you can get some recompense for your loss," he whispered.

"Victim support?"

He laughed again, a full-on belly laugh with a sizeable coughing fit at its tail end. "Yeah," he said, "if that's what you want to call it. No forms to fill out, though, and you ain't getting a single penny in compensation. This is a different kind of recompense, and it feels better than any amount of money."

Chapter Nineteen

Eddie banged on the bathroom door.

"What?"

"Hurry up, you old reprobate, some of us have appointments."

"Bugger off. Some of us have dates!"

Eddie growled. "My appointment… *is* a date."

Charles pulled the bolt and opened the door a crack.

Steam billowed out and Eddie almost choked on the smell of aftershave. He stepped back. "Jesus! I hope you're taking her a gas mask. You smell like a tart's handbag."

"A date? You?" Charles grinned from the cover of the doorway, his eyes suspicious. "Does it have four legs?"

"I don't have time to wisecrack with you. Come out."

"Does it involve a cruise up the red-light district?"

"You are so gross. I should disown you."

"I *knew* you were jealous. I knew it!"

"You'd better not have used all my aftershave—"

"Here," Charles passed him a bottle through the gap. "Now leave me alone."

"What's up? Polyfilla not set yet?" Eddie shook the bottle as Charles locked the door. "This is empty, you old git. Buy your own!"

"Don't come back too early."

Chapter Twenty

"They changed me."

Tony rolled a cigarette. "How?"

"I was normal—"

He laughed and coughed.

"I was! I was as normal as anyone can be. And they got it wrong."

"Have you spoken about this to anyone else? Inside, outside, wherever?"

Still on the floor, Jess was shaking her head. "Nobody. If you don't admit to your crimes" —she curled her fingers into quote marks— "you have a hard time. They encourage you to confess. It also goes better for you with parole. So the system spat me out here, into the loving, caring hands of people like John Sidmouth."

Tony stood, slipped both of his overcoats off, dropped them in a heap on the floor, and took his seat again, lighter at the ready. "John Sidmouth? Probation Officer?"

She nodded.

"Little fat fuck with a briefcase?"

She squinted at him. "How do you know?"

"Since I found out where you lived, I've kept an eye on you."

"That's creepy."

He laughed. "Yeah, I suppose it is. But I wanted you to be safe. Things have changed in twelve years; safe places ain't safe no more. Someone has to watch your back."

"I want him dead."

Tony's mouth fell open. He looked around, as though there could be eavesdroppers, and at last said, "No, Jess. You're a smart girl. You don't want to go around talking about killing people."

"You saying I can't trust you?"

He leaned forward, elbows on knees, and pointed at her. "Girl, I'm the only one you can trust. And I know they all got it wrong. I never asked you if what they were saying was true, because I know you didn't stab that prick."

She looked at the floor. "It was just one careless mistake after another. And I kept on thinking it would be caught at the next stage, and the nightmare would be over. But then the next stage messed up, and the one after that, and before I knew it I was counting bricks in a cell. For twelve years."

He nodded, "It's a bastard."

"But the bigger bastard is what it did to my family."

"You'll get him back. Stop punishing yourself; he's a kid. Give him time."

"They put me away for twelve years, Tony! And they took away my baby. He's a teenager now! He hates me; he thinks I want to ruin his life again by taking him back."

"Sounds like every parent-teenager relationship."

She looked away, closed her eyes for a moment, and said, "He's better where he is."

She thought about Michael's christening present from Sebastian's parents, a small golden box. She'd always told him it was a box of truths. She opened that box now, inside her mind, and she saw that he was immeasurably better off where he was.

Maybe Valentine was right.

And learning this new truth was as fearsome as being buried alive – it was inescapable. And though the words had just tripped off her tongue – because that's what all shit parents say when they have their kids taken away from them – she hadn't really meant them. They were taken straight from the pages of *Good Parenting*: thou shalt not be selfish.

But she *wanted* to be selfish; she wanted Michael back again even if he *was* better where he was because then it really would be like having a second chance at life, it would be like none of the bad things had ever happened and she'd just been in a coma for twelve years. Of course it was a lie – she wasn't stupid, but it was the best she could hope for. And it was way better than any fifty grand.

That selfishness was something she daren't admit to anyone – even Tony, the man she could trust more than any other. That was a secret for the box of truths only.

"How can I stop it? I can't bear it eating at me like this, day in and day out. I can't bear it!"

He took a breath. "I could come over there and console you, which I'm pretty sure ain't high on your wish list. Or you can get a fucking grip. Take charge of your life, Jessy." He smiled, and winked at her.

Her anger dissipated. "And how do I do that when I'm already in their sights?"

"Stay in their sights. But be covert," he said, "like Jason Bourne. Take your revenge, and you'll sleep better, trust me. I just proved it."

She watched his face, the way the dirt in the wrinkles turned almost black as he smiled. "What have you done?"

"Not read the news today?"

"I'm depressed enough as it is." His smug grin intrigued her. "Why, what's happened?"

Tony leaned forward, elbows on knees, and he whispered, "Who do you hate most for killing you? For killing us?"

"Sebastian."

"No, no, no. Apart from him. Who do you blame?"

"Marchant."

Tony sat back, crossed his legs, smugness personified. "He ain't no more."

Jess closed her eyes, then said, "Why can't you just speak plainly—"

"I killed the fucker."

Her eyes sprang wide.

Tony nodded, laughing. "I did him proper, Jessy. You'd've been proud of me."

"You killed Marchant?"

He nodded again.

She leaned back against one of the cupboards and felt the wind being kicked out of her until she couldn't breathe any more. Collapsing like a dying balloon.

How long before they come for me? "You fucking idiot."

"What?" His proud smile faded.

"I'm on licence. They'll come straight round here and put me in cuffs."

Tony slapped his leg. "No they won't, lass. Ain't no way you could've killed him the way I did. I swung a pickaxe right through his car window and through his throat." His smile returned, loaded with more pride, and then turned to laughter. Only when he risked choking on his own euphoria did he quieten down and look across to her, sitting on the floor, her face wet with fresh tears. "Oh, come on, Jessy! I did it for you, woman! Why can't you be happy?"

"Because I wanted to kill him."

Chapter Twenty-One

It was Tony's turn to be dumbfounded.

"I dreamed about it all the time I was inside. I longed for Michael, but I dreamed of killing that bastard. He bent over so easily in court; he just accepted everything, challenged nothing, and all I needed was for him to fight for me. To do his job. He was on the take. Had to be."

"You ain't no killer, Jess." He sat forward again, a challenge on his face. "You might've dreamed about doing it, sure. You might've imagined shooting him or drowning him, setting him on fire, maybe." His tormenting smile drifted away and he became serious. "But it's a lot different than you might imagine. Knowing you've taken someone else's life is..." he searched for the word. "Breath-taking. No. No, it's not; it's nauseating."

He cleared his throat, and used his hands to try and get the feeling across to her. Jess was mesmerised. "It's their eyes. You see their eyes change. I ain't talking about the dead fish-eye thing, y'know, the milkiness, cos I wasn't around long enough to see that. I mean the fear.

"If they see it coming, their fear is contagious. It grabs you, and your heart kicks against it. You see their fifty years of existence coming to an abrupt end like... like..." He clicked his fingers. "You ever seen one of them tower blocks being demolished, or a chimney stack? It's like that. They've spent a whole lifetime building their tower, growing, getting families and networks and whatever else it is that people fucking do, and" —he clapped his hands together— "bam! It's gone. All of it. In an instant. Their whole history." He stared at her. "And *you* did it. You."

"I still—"

"I thought it would be a lot easier than it turned out to be. I wasn't sick, but I nearly was. And not because of how gruesome it was; *that* didn't bother me. But I was the one who demolished his tower. It's a big deal, Jess. It's the biggest there is."

Tony began to slide from the chair, and Jess gave him a sharp look. He sat back. "I'm sorry," he said. "I didn't know. I thought I was doing you a favour. Honest I did."

She sobbed, hands over her face, crying like she'd lost a parent. And she was like that for ten minutes before she peered through her sticky fingers and said, "Why now?"

"Huh?"

"You had twelve years to kill him. Why wait till I get out?"

Tony sniffled. He rolled a fresh cigarette, looking at her all the while. He lit up and took a long drag. "You have no idea, do you?"

She stared, waiting.

"While you was away, I found out where they all lived. All of them what put you behind bars when they should have released you without charge. I followed them, each of them, Jessy. And I made notes in a little book; got their addresses. Even learned their routines. Some of them, anyway." He patted his jeans pocket. "Still got them, right here."

"Why, Tony?"

He held out a hand. "Shh. Give me a chance, will you?" The smugness was dead. "I didn't kill him while you were away because our lives was on pause. In my head, anyway. I thought when you came out, we… Well, I thought we'd pick up right where we'd left off, you know." He stared at her but she gave away nothing, simply watched from between her fingers. He continued, "And when you *did* come out… Well, I could see that you was different. Of course you was; how could I be so stupid! I could see, Jessy" —his voice shrank to a whisper filled with cracks and pauses— "that they'd broke you, done some real damage. The bastards. There was no chance we could just pick up where we'd left off.

"It was dead. We was dead." He dropped his head, and the cigarette shook between his fingers.

"Is that why you didn't come to my door wearing a three-piece suit to impress me?"

He shuffled a snort out of his nose. "Honestly, if I thought I had a chance, I would've." He shrugged. "Anyway, this is my street gear, keeps me warm on cold nights."

"You might be a scruffy git, Tony, but I appreciate you being a gentleman."

"Me! Ha!"

"It's true. I like that you didn't come here to get me back." She noted the hurt in his eyes. "I mean, that wasn't your priority. You tried to look after me first before thinking about anything like that."

He nodded. "That is true. But they'd taken you away from me, and I cherished you so much; I'd have done anything to keep you with me. Anything at all." He settled a wistful gaze on her and held it there. "That's why it hurt me," he said. "I waited every day of those twelve years, holding on to us being together again. Eventually I needed help, you know… getting through." He looked up, smiling, but it was a failed attempt at bravery. His tears said so. "They'd taken you away from me, see. And I knew I couldn't let them get away with it; I knew you'd not forgiven them and decided to move on. They killed you, Jess. They killed us.

"So as well as locking you away and crushing you; as well as splitting you up from your son, and breaking us two apart, they'd imprisoned me too, killed me. They turned me into this." He blinked and a tear rolled into the creases of his false smile. "I killed him, selfishly, for me, not for you. He ruined my life too."

Jess dropped her hands away, pulled a sleeve across her damp face and stared at him. Those last few words… They sent a shiver up her back.

Hope sparkled in his eyes. "And I did it because I wanted to get rid of all the shit in your life, Jess. I wanted to be your knight in shining armour. Do you understand me? It's complicated, I…" His voice cracked.

She nodded. "I think so."

"And there's something else, too. I found out he was up for retirement in a few weeks. He was moving abroad. Florida, I think. And once that bird took off, there would be no chance of nailing him. It had to be done quick. So can you forgive me for stealing your thunder?"

The sobbing came again. "It can't end here, though," she whispered.

Chapter Twenty-Two

"Why, Miss Moneypenny… you do scrub up well." Eddie smiled at her. It wasn't the smile he reserved for meeting new people he wasn't allowed to be honest with – that was a fairly flimsy affair and easily dislodged. This smile, the one he pointed at Moneypenny now, was genuine, and it shone in his eyes.

"Thank you, Eddie." She reached her arm out awkwardly.

Eddie tried to shake, missed her hand and masked the awkwardness by leaning in for an air kiss and bumping heads.

She smelled good. Better than his dad did.

She sat down opposite him, and Eddie soaked up the view. Between them was a small vase with some plastic flowers drooping over its edge, and next to it a wooden contraption with a stack of menus, the dog-eared laminated kind covered in greasy fingerprints, tomato ketchup, and old sneeze-matter. They were so large that she was hidden from him. He peered around them, and then just picked one up and dropped it on the floor

How come he'd never seen past the cleavage while at work? How come he'd walked past her every single day?

"How did your meeting with Mr Crawford go?"

"Who? Oh, the new boss man." He shrugged. "Same suit, different arsehole."

She nodded as though she knew what he meant.

"Anyway, we didn't come out to talk about work…" He rubbed his hands together and realised his palms were sweating. He felt like a youth again: clumsy, uncertain, and full of doubt.

She obviously felt a little uncomfortable at being scrutinised so closely. "How come you call me Moneypenny? Are you suggesting you're James Bond?"

Eddie's smile gave birth to a small laugh. "Me? James Bond? Nah. I'm more like Mr Bean." He stared again.

"So…?"

"Oh. Well… I know your surname is Darling, or something. I've seen it on your lanyard."

"Darlington."

"Yeah, that's it. But I don't know your forename. Moneypenny suited you. I mean – it suits you." He didn't know it, but he was smiling again, and it made her look away. "So, what *is* your name, Miss Moneypenny?"

"It's—"

Eddie's mobile phone rang. It was 'Who Are You' by The Who.

Her smile died, and Eddie's heart sank. "I thought I'd left this bastard thing at home." He read the screen, and closed his eyes.

"Everything alright?"

"Sorry," he said. "Work. I have to answer."

She nodded.

"This is like every cop show since 1978, isn't it?" He pressed 'ok' and said, "Collins." He listened for a moment, eyes wandering around the restaurant as it grew busier. He made an effort not to look at her but his gaze was still drawn, so in the end he just stared.

"You're fucking kidding." It came out louder than he'd intended.

Moneypenny's head disappeared into her shoulders with embarrassment, and she mouthed, "Sorry," at those who glared and tutted at them.

"Right. Give me twenty minutes." Eddie put away the phone and sighed across the table at her.

"You're leaving?"

"Sorry. I feel really bad."

"It's okay." She stood and gathered her handbag and phone. "Perhaps we can do it again sometime? Only for a bit longer?"

Eddie was at her side, pulling her chair out so she could stand, and he felt almost heartbroken. Five minutes. That's all the gods could spare him for – five fucking minutes? Really? He gritted his teeth and although there was genuine anger there, he felt such remorse, such sorrow. "I would love to. And I promise not to bring my phone with me." He found it hard to smile, but he didn't want his anger to be the last thing she saw of him. The screaming tantrum could wait.

"Must be serious?"

He nodded. "Murder."

"I don't know how you do your job; I couldn't face all those bodies, all that blood."

"I'm not a real human. Anyway, when you've seen people skinned and disembowelled, you're kind of immune to the ordinary stuff."

Someone nearby retched.

He realised, too late, that there were certain things one didn't discuss in polite company.

He walked her back to her car and watched her drive away. "What's your name, Miss Moneypenny?"

Chapter Twenty-Three

It took her twenty minutes to walk around the block.

The orange street lamps cast cones of putrid light, turning the raindrops to flashes of gold as they fell through it, allowing them a brief moment of beauty before they became annoying again. Just another lie.

Cold. Jessica pulled up the collar of her coat, squinted into the rain and stared at his house.

She saw him in the lounge, reflections from a cinema-sized television shooting flashes of coloured light around the walls.

Tony had given her this address.

She walked up the driveway, around some big flash car, a Jaguar maybe, confident there was no CCTV anywhere near this place. The closer she got to his front door, the more shredded her nerves became.

To distract herself, she played images of Michael on the private screen inside her head: the show where the coppers led her from the house, cuffs out front digging into the knobbly bone on her wrists, people looking on, staring at her as some copper mumbled something about missing his meal break because of her, the selfish bitch. She thought of Michael, and strangely, she thought of the washing-up – how it needed drying and putting away. A job unfinished.

The nerves fled; the old anger returned and settled in for the show. This, too, was a job unfinished. But this was something she could put right.

Jessica walked up a single step and into a porch with a gentle overhead lamp that glowed through a tangle of dusty webs. She stared at the door: ornate black studs against white paint. They reminded her of the old entrance to Armley jail.

Anger got comfy and nodded its head at her.

She knocked and through the bay window she saw a shadow grow tall on the wall, and then fade. She saw the hall light go on, and the top of a bald head bobbed along the hallway towards her. The latch clicked and then the door opened.

An old man peered out. The lines on his face were fissures. His watery blue eyes seemed to squint even though his lower lids drooped. He looked her up and down, then those eyes settled on hers, and eventually he smiled. "Hello."

His ears were longer, his hair thinner, whiter, and his nose redder, tiny veins creeping near the surface. The last time she'd seen him, he'd looked considerably larger around the waist, considerably younger. But that's what happens to a person after twelve years of feasting on the deaths of others.

"Hello," she said in her friendliest voice, "I'm really sorry to bother you, but I wonder if I might use your telephone to ring the AA?" She held up her phone, and smiled an ironic smile. "Battery's dead."

The old man studied her, paying no attention to her prop. "Come on in out of the rain, dear. You must be wet through." He opened the door wide, and the opulence smacked her right in the face like a wad of cash. She marvelled at the velvet wallpaper, the oak panelling, the walls adorned with proper paintings, and a grandmother clock ticking seconds in the corner behind her like death's metronome. She shivered.

The door closed behind her, and she could feel him staring. "Telephone's through here. Come on through, won't you?"

She followed him along the hall, watching his unstable gait, shuffling twisted feet in old man's slippers, his back bent from leaning over stainless-steel tables all day, and he led her into a kitchen that was larger than her entire bedsit. Dazzling white lights from above, mellow LEDs set into the marble floor, central breakfast island with leather stools placed geometrically around it. "Wow," she said. "I bet your wife loves spending time in here. I'd live in here if I could."

"She did. Not now though; been dead eight years."

"Oh, I'm sorry, I didn't mean—"

"No, no, that's okay. Death comes to all life," he smiled, and his long yellow teeth peered out at her, framed by wire-thin lips. "I have a very philosophical view. And anyway, despite all this," he whispered, as though his wife might still be listening, "she couldn't cook to save her life." He laughed, "We spent more time unpacking takeaways in here than cooking."

Jessica laughed too. Anger tapped its fingers, and she felt admonished.

"Let me take your coat; it's wet through. You'll catch your death."

She stared at him, at his unfortunate choice of words, but she allowed him to remove her coat, feeling the need to get him onside and lower his defences. Anger shook its head and shouted, "Get on with it!"

He'd already hung it on a coat hook by the back door by the time she remembered her knife was in the inside pocket. The one she'd brought here to stab him with. He turned and stared at her again, and she wondered if her nervousness shone out.

He wasn't exactly subtle; his old eyes clung to her curves like a drowning man clutching a buoy.

He didn't recognise her, though. Why would he, after all this time? She wondered how many people he'd cut open in the last twelve years, and how many times he'd fucked up and given the wrong information to the police. How many times had he made the wrong call because he was incompetent or lazy, or both?

Still he stared at her. Unashamedly. Eyes roaming, feasting. Anger looked on with new concern.

"Forgive me," he said.

And that made her heart trip. Did he recognise her, after all?

"I really don't mean to be rude; I know it's jolly bad manners to stare. But I am unable to avert my eyes from beauty. I love art, you see, and you are a goddess among angels." He smiled warmly. "I hope I don't come across as a dirty old man, I really don't mean to. But I don't get many goddesses in my house these days." He laughed, a high-pitched chortle that made her smile. "I have a cleaner who calls twice a week, Mrs Watkins. She's more of a gargoyle than a goddess."

Jess caught herself smiling. Anger tapped on the floor, and asked her what the fuck she was doing. Had she forgotten why she was here, had she forgotten the missing years, the pain, the tears? *You don't give an animal a name when you know you have to kill it.*

"It's a beautiful house. What do you do for a living?" she asked, eyes on the knife block by the sink.

Anger smacked its forehead with a sweating palm.

"Oh, I don't, any more. These days I enjoy getting up late, and doing as little as possible. I intend to enjoy my remaining time. You never know when you'll take your final breath."

You are fucking kidding! Is he doing this on purpose?

"I used to be a Home Office pathologist. Did it all my life, right from university. I suppose that's made me quite pragmatic." He shuffled to the kettle, groaning, "Tea? Or coffee, perhaps? I make a splendid Americano."

I can't do this. I can't. "No, thanks. I'm okay."

He checked his watch. "I have pizza coming soon." He smiled at her. "You're more than welcome to share it with me; I like to indulge in a meal with a film. I'd be grateful of the company."

Was it a ruse?

Pizza will be here soon? Jesus, he knows! "I already ate, but thanks. You must have seen some horrific sights in your time."

"Came with the territory."

"Shootings? Stabbings?"

"Oh, yes; with a certain inevitability. Several a month. Fascinating, though." He grinned. "If you like that kind of thing. It's not for everyone."

"So can you tell, say, what angle a knife goes into a body?"

He paused for a second before answering. "Indeed you can. When I had a homicide, I'd work quite closely with the Crime Investigator people, and the police. We used…" he clicked his fingers, trying to remember the term "…trajectory rods to determine angles of penetration. And then they'd photograph them in the three axis. It's quite interesting, really." He shut the tap off and put the kettle on its base.

"Fascinating. So I guess that means you could determine if a stabbing was murder, or if it was self-inflicted?"

He turned the kettle on. "Well, yes, if…" He stopped, seemed to reappraise her, to see her anew. Eventually, he smiled at her, cocked his head slightly to the left, and then rested a shrivelled hand on the granite worktop to steady himself.

Jessica's heart kicked, and Anger slapped her in the face. She smiled back, eyes sharp, ready.

"Is this to be my last evening?"

Chapter Twenty-Four

She bit her bottom lip and pulled a pair of clear plastic gloves from her jeans pocket.

"I mean, I don't want it to be." He winked, hoping to provoke a smile. None came. "Is there anything I can do to… I really would do anything. Just to die a natural death," he said. "Not keen on the thought of a forensic post mortem. If you see what I mean."

Jess looked at him. She shook her head.

He held onto the worktop tighter. "Ah well," he whispered, watching her thread her hands inside the gloves. "The phone thing… it was just a ruse?"

She nodded.

He nodded in reply. "You certainly got me. I thought my luck had changed," he said. "At least I'll get to see my wife again. She'll be nagging me again in no time." His eyes watered. "I thought I recognised you. You stood just like that in the box at Leeds Crown if I remember correctly. Proud. Straight. How long has it been?"

"Twelve years."

"Twelve years," he echoed, lost in thought.

She walked to the back counter by the sink and pulled out a knife. "It's time."

"Yes, of course." His voice cracked slightly, but he held his composure. "Don't suppose I have a last request?"

Jessica took a long breath in. She'd named the fucking puppy, and now it was looking at her with those eyes, whimpering. "What is it?" Her mouth was dry, but her hands were clammy inside the gloves.

"I'd rather like a glass of whisky. And if I might, just a few puffs on a Cuban? Mildred would never let me smoke in the house, and I more or less let go of the habit. But I still have a box of them; beautiful aroma. If I might?"

Jessica nodded, stood aside to let him through, and then said, "Why did you lie?"

He paused and rested against the worktop again. "I didn't lie. I was sure. The trajectory rods were in a position where the wound might have been self-inflicted, but he could also have been stabbed if the offender was at his right side, the arc of the… Well, we considered the options, and on the basis of what we knew, we decided it was more likely that he had been stabbed."

"You were sure?"

He nodded, paused. "Yes. Fairly."

"Fairly? You jailed me because you were 'fairly sure'?"

"My dear—"

"You've got a good memory."

He nodded again. "Your case stood out. We believed the account you gave the police – but at the same time… I thought you'd stabbed him. Conundrum. You don't forget those easily."

"We?"

"The SIO and myself."

"SIO?"

"Senior Investigating Officer."

"Who?"

"I don't think—"

"Who?"

Bolton sighed. "It hardly matters now, does it, dear?"

She took a step forward. "Quick or slow?" She blinked. "It matters to me, so I'll make it matter to you."

He licked his lips, eyes fixed on the blade, hands trembling. "Detective Superintendent Masters."

"Your decision cost me twelve years. Cost me my son. Ruined my life."

He looked away, nodding slowly. "I understand that. Though it won't help now, you have my sincere apologies. Despite your intentions, and if you can find it within yourself, I would ask that you forgive me."

Sweat ran down her back, and her chest felt tight, as though the air had become considerably thinner, but she kept her focus, remembered Michael screaming, remembered Michael telling her to fuck off. "Go get your cigar," she whispered.

His face was full of regret as he stepped forward.

The blade sank into his chest with almost no resistance, stopped only when her fist collided with the fabric of his shirt. Face to face with him, much too close, she saw the shock in his old blue eyes, saw the pain in his twisted face, felt his body stiffen against her, and smelled the hot blood rushing across her gloved hand to drip onto the floor, pattering like the seconds from the grandmother clock.

He watched her; and then he slowly took his hand from the worktop and sank to the floor on his knees. He fell backwards, his head hitting the marble with a crack.

Jessica breathed hard as bile rose in her throat, set her chest on fire, and turned her legs so weak that she staggered backwards and fell on her backside. She almost threw up, but turned away from the body, taking long slow breaths until the room settled down.

The colours were bright and the lights blinding, and her heart beat loud in her ears. She concentrated on one of the pleasant LED lights in the floor, marvelling as its light picked out an old dribble of coffee or tea down the immaculate drawers beneath the steaming kettle.

Nothing is as perfect as it first appears. Another lie.

A hot belch came out and Jessica almost passed out, but she watched the light, watched the dribble, and she came back at last. And when she did, her fury was vile.

Chapter Twenty-Five

The old man had been complicit in ruining her life and the lives of the people she loved. Him and the other arseholes. They were supposed to be professional; they were supposed to be above cockups of this magnitude. Their public image was golden, their ability unquestionable, and their honour beyond reproach.

But it was all a fucking lie.

Everything about the establishment and the people who made it up was a falsehood. They weren't infallible at all. There was no overlord of unimpeachable sense – it was all so flawed and imperfect. It was too human, too easily corruptible; subjective, ad hoc. There was no safety net.

She stared at him.

Inside, her anger – not only at what he and his colleagues had done to her all those years ago, but at what they'd turned her into now – grew so hot and so fast that it blinded her. But not so much that she couldn't see what else they and the grievous error had caused, what it had created.

Their apathy had turned her into a murderer.

And it wasn't as though killing them one by one would incrementally return her old life in pristine condition, to be lived again a second time as it should have been lived the first.

Ironically, his death made no difference. At all.

And yet it did.

If this was it – if this was the way things actually were now, and she couldn't reclaim her old life – then this was how it had to be. She had to make sure that *they* weren't a part of it. She had to be free of *them* if she were to live from this day on without forever pulling her hair out over the past she'd been denied. She swallowed, content that she was making progress at last.

She had worn gloves, but already blood was running up the cuff, beneath the latex, working its way deeper along the fissures in her skin, spreading. She held out her hand, the one still holding the knife, and it shook badly. The blade quivered in the overhead lights and she could see the smear of red caught in its teeth. Across her right hand, up her wrist and coating her dark blue sweater was a gauntlet of deep red. Beneath her arm hung a quivering curtain of it that dripped onto her jeans and onto the floor. She could feel it cooling quickly until it became uncomfortable, until she could no longer bear it on her skin.

And although her head wasn't swimming any more, her breathing was fast, almost hyperventilating, and her vision was still colour-saturated with a grey vignette around the edges. Jess felt far from normal.

She dropped the knife, reached up and swiped a tea towel from an orderly stack on a shelf. She scraped the blood from her arm and her gloved hand, scrubbed it from her jeans, and watched it smear into the fabric. For a moment or two, she concentrated not on the blood, not on the body lying a couple of yards away, but on her breathing. She closed her eyes and tried to make a grab for calm, tried to pull it towards her and bring herself and her tripping heart back to safety.

And it worked; her eyes slid open again, and Jessica Ripley began the long walk back to a normality that had been torn from her more than a decade ago.

She stood on legs that still trembled, bent again to retrieve the knife and tea towel and looked around to make sure—

The doorbell chimed and Jess nearly fainted.

Instead she dropped down just in case whoever was at the front door could see along the hallway and into the kitchen. She'd only been able to see the top of the old man's head as he approached the door, but a taller person might see more.

Standing at the end of the breakfast island, she scanned the kitchen, saw a doorway to her left and scooted towards it. She found herself in a large dining room with an eight-seater oval table in rosewood, complete with candelabra centrepiece. A pair of sideboards adorned with figurines along the right-hand wall, and in between them a heated food trolley. All this, she thought, and he orders a fucking pizza?

The mantelpiece over the dark fireplace to her left bulged with more figurines and a silver clock the size of a head stood silently at its centre. Paintings covered ninety percent of the walls. It was like stepping back into Victorian England.

Beyond the dining room, an open door led into the dimly lit lounge; an enormous wall-mounted TV was paused on a woman's face halfway through a blink. Jess crept through the lounge and peered through the slightly open door to her right, out into the hallway. She couldn't see the front door from here, so she crept past Bolton's wingback chair, with its array of remote controls, tiny side table with teacup and saucer, footstool in front, and walking sticks to the rear.

She crept closer to the doorway and flattened herself against the wall, listening. The doorbell rang again, and her heart pinged in her hollow chest.

Someone knocked on the door.

Only a few moments passed before they knocked again.

She breathed out. It must be the pizza.

All this for a stuffed crust.

She held her breath again as the front door opened and someone called.

"Mr Bolton?"

Oh, fuck off. Put it down to a no-show, and eat it yourself!

"Mr Bolton? It's Rasine from Mikka's Pizza and Kebab." It was a thick, heavy accent loaded with back-of-the-throat consonants; Polish or Slovakian. Jess closed her eyes, dug her nails into the wallpaper, as the woman entered the hallway.

In her mind's eye, Jess saw the woman treading carefully; afraid of being labelled an intruder yet genuinely worried, perhaps, for one of her regular customers who seemed to be behaving oddly. She imagined her placing the pizza on the hallway table, imagined her taking more steps towards the lounge door – the one Jess cringed by. She held the knife aloft. Ready.

"Mr Bolton?"

Jess stiffened as a hand floated into the room and fingertips landed on the door, ready to push it all the way open. But the hand stopped, and Jess heard Rasine gasp. The hand fell away and there were hurried footsteps along the hallway towards the kitchen.

Jess pulled the door open and quickly tiptoed into the hall and through the open front door without looking back.

As she ran down the driveway, she heard a scream from behind her.

* * *

Fifteen minutes later, she walked along Stonegate Road as casually as she could. She'd expected that by now her heart rate would have returned to normal, but it was still hammering away inside a chest that felt too constricted for it; her hands and feet tingled with a fearful anticipation, her eyes were wide and she trembled.

Up on her right was a pathway from Stonegate Road that led into a wooded parkland. She left the relative safety of the streetlights behind and tumbled into the obscurity of a soothing darkness. Moments later, the trees flickered with a vibrant blue light that died as quickly as it had arrived. Several other police vehicles sped past before she could get deep enough into the trees to hear no more.

Even though there were no streetlights in here, it wasn't completely dark; there was enough light to see by. Jess took herself off the track and stalked deeper into the woodland. Stopping by a large tree with a mass of black bushes beneath it, she buried the knife in the thicket, and then sank against the tree, sweating and shivering.

Silently, she cried. And it wasn't until she began to feel cold that she remembered that her jacket was hanging in Bolton's kitchen. In its pocket was a knife from her own.

Chapter Twenty-Six

The further Eddie drove, the angrier he became.

He wanted to have just one evening to see whether his inner self was correct: that he was dating Moneypenny because he was jealous of his old man, and not because he'd suddenly matured enough to participate in a grown-up relationship again. But the chance to see which of his options – which of his personalities – was correct was snatched away from him, like so much in his life, by his bastard job.

And what angered him still further, the icing on the shit cake, was that Nicki Murphy was in the office when the call came through, and so she'd be working the scene with him. "Deep joy," he mumbled. He was too angry to wonder for very long why she was there at that hour; probably sucking someone's dick to make her promotion run smoother.

As usual, it was fairly easy to identify the scene of the crime because there was no room to park. The house was on a junction: busy road to the front, and quiet lane to the side. The quiet lane looked like the police station car park, and so did the footpath.

He dumped the Discovery half on the footpath at the front of the house, cut the lights and engine, and sat in silence for a minute, feeling the car sway as vehicles sped by. His eyes quickly grew accustomed to the semi-darkness; the streetlamp beneath which he'd parked puked bile-coloured light in a tight circle that wasn't so much a pool as a puddle.

Eddie took a moment, lit a cigarette and pondered on what was to come. He pondered lots more besides, but the scene sat on top of the slush pile in his mind and shouted the loudest. Sitting at the bottom, growing stale now, growing mouldy too, was the old question: what the hell am I doing this job for? There must be something better for me, something that doesn't involve evening work, weekend work… work.

And then Benson slapped a hand on the window and Eddie jumped hard enough to bang his knees on the dashboard. "Bastard!" he screamed as Benson walked off, laughing.

* * *

Eddie sought out Nicki's van and was surprised to see her still sitting inside it, in total darkness, the same way he'd been sitting moments ago. He wondered if she was also in deep contemplation of her future too, and the temptation to smack her window, as Benson had smacked his, was almost too much to resist.

But he didn't want to pull himself out of his bad mood by inflicting sore knees on someone else and laughing about it; he wanted the bad mood to continue. You knew where you were with a bad mood, but a good mood… well, that could cause no end of unforeseen things to happen – dating a woman you barely knew, for example.

He shook his head, dismissing thoughts of Moneypenny, and tried to shove aside all that human stuff and just concentrate on the job before him.

He opened the van door and Nicki jumped anyway. "What have we got?"

She looked nervous. "Erm, dead guy in the kitchen."

Eddie waited.

"I haven't been inside, actually. I was waiting for you."

"So who *has* been inside? Who found him?"

"I don't know; I've only just arrived."

Eddie looked at all the police vehicles blocking her van in and doubted that very much. "What the fuck have you been doing? Why haven't you supervised the cordon, or started on the exterior photography?"

"It's your job, and I didn't want to stand on your toes."

"Stand on my toes? Christ, you were all for stealing my office yesterday." He stepped back, out of the way. "Come on, we need to get suited up. Get your camera gear sorted. Chop chop."

He sighed, walked away from her and peered over the hedge into the driveway. He could just make out Benson and headed in his direction, hoping for a modicum of sense.

Benson looked Eddie over as he approached. "How come you don't look like a tramp?"

"I was out," he said. "Restaurant."

Benson raised his eyebrows. "Restaurant, eh? Been on a date?"

"And they said you'd never make a detective."

"Who with?"

"Can we just get on with this shit, please? I'm in a bad enough mood as it is."

Benson shrugged. "Fair enough. I'm just pleased to get out of the house."

Eddie sighed, and folded his arms.

"Having an argument with the wife."

Eddie stared.

"And I was losing. As usual. I often wonder why—"

"So who is the dead guy?"

Benson gawped. "You amaze me. You ram your fancy date down my neck, but as soon as I mention… You don't give a flying shit, do you? I'm going through hell every time I have to set foot inside that house, knowing that nagging bitch is waiting for me, and you do not give a toss! Here I am spilling my heart out…" He closed in on Eddie. "You're not even listening, are you?"

"Sorry." Eddie looked at his watch. "Twenty past eight."

* * *

Eddie lifted a finger towards Benson. "I know what I meant to ask you," he said.

"I sent Khan."

"What? To interview the rapist killer? Why would you do that?"

"Because I'm a manager, and I'm allowed to delegate if I so choose."

By twenty to nine Eddie, Benson, and Nicki were standing in the ample reception of the house, wearing full scene suits, overshoes, masks, and hair nets. Anywhere else and it would have been a hallway; here, it was a reception. Anywhere else and they would have looked like painters and decorators; here, they looked like CSI. A chaise along one wood-panelled wall, a grandmother clock in the corner. Nice.

Nicki looked puzzled. "We haven't enough stepping plates for this place, Eddie."

"I know, right! You'd think they could've murdered him a bit closer to the door, eh?"

"So what are we going to do?"

"We could just drag him this way a bit. No one would know. It'd make our lives—"

"Seriously."

Eddie cocked an eyebrow. "Seriously, you say?" He straightened his back. "Well, okay. Put three down here," he said, "leading us to the lounge. We'll walk through the lounge and through the dining room, and we can use the rest of them in the kitchen, okay?"

"How do you know the murderer didn't go in there?"

"I don't. But it's carpeted, and so we won't be destroying any footwear marks even if he did."

"How do you know it's carpeted?"

"Fuck's sake." Eddie sighed and performed a good long blink, raising his eyes to the elaborate plasterwork on the ceiling. "I looked through the front window." He smiled at her. "Okay?"

Nicki nodded, and set to, clanging the noisy aluminium plates on the hardwood floor.

"You gonna tell me who's bought it, then?" Eddie asked Benson. "Or are we playing twenty questions?"

Benson had his arms folded, bottom lip out, sulking.

"Look," Eddie whispered, placing a hand on Benson's shoulder, "about you and your wife. I know things are tough…"

Benson unfolded his arms and turned to Eddie, nodding, ready to open up the conversation again.

"…but no one gives a fuck. So can you please tell me who's dead, who found him, blah blah, and then you can go home and sulk some more. Okay?"

"I hate you, Collins."

"I don't care. Now fucking tell me!"

Chapter Twenty-Seven

Eddie and Benson stood on a pair of plates by the head. Nicki was on the plate behind them, trying not to look.

"His name's Dr Stanford Bolton."

Eddie turned sharply. "Doc Bolton? *The* Doc Bolton?"

Benson nodded.

Nicki tried to peer over their shoulders. "Who's Doc Bolton?"

"I thought he looked familiar. See what death buys you," Eddie waved an arm at his opulent surroundings. "Wonder if I'm in his will."

"See what hard work buys you," countered Benson. "I couldn't do what he did."

Nicki tried again. "Who's Doc Bolton?"

"Our old Home Office pathologist from years ago," Eddie said. "I've spent many a happy hour watching him slice and dice. Must've retired ten or twelve years ago."

"I wonder if Prof Steele will enjoy this one?"

"I bet he squirms a bit," Eddie chuckled.

"Who's Prof—"

"Our current Home Office pathologist. You and Kenny did the barrister's body with him, remember?"

"Ah, yeah, I didn't really pay too much attention to his name, actually. I was trying to stop myself from barfing across the mortuary floor."

Benson and Eddie shared a look.

Eddie nodded towards the body. "Who did it, and why?"

"I'll just pop out and ask. Back in a minute." Benson lurched past Nicki and was out of the room in seconds, taking the rustling noise of his suit with him.

"Was it something I said?"

Eddie looked at her. "Probably. But then again, he's a strange bugger; I wouldn't worry about it."

"I'm glad he's gone, actually," Nicki said.

"Cut him some slack. You get used to the smell."

"I mean, it gives me a chance to apologise again about sticking my nose in with the Troy business."

"Okay, I'm happy for you. Now shall we concentrate on him before he rots away?" He turned back to the body.

"I'm just trying to be friendly, actually. Trying to start over, because I've noticed a touch of frostiness towards me, and I don't know why."

Eddie sighed and turned around to face her. "Look," he said, "I don't know what your game is—"

"Game? I'm not—"

"And you wouldn't believe how not fucking interested I am. In the meantime, I'm frosty towards you because you're a stranger. I don't like people, but I'm forced to live among them and work among them. And I *really* don't like strangers. I have no idea if you've got my back or if you'll stab me in it, but if I had to guess, I'd go with the knife every time. But we're not here to discuss that." He pointed at Bolton's body. "We're here to make sure this man gets a top-notch service from CSI. I think he's earned it, don't you?"

"Well—"

"How about you leave your broken personality and your fake platitudes at the door?" He smiled at her. "And let's make a start." He clapped. "What do you say?"

She stood perfectly still, eyes wide, and Eddie could see her jaw grinding away angrily.

"Are you going to storm out in a temper, or are you going to tell me what you'd do in a murder scene like this one?"

She continued to stare at Eddie for some time, all stiff shoulders and stiff upper lip. Then, as though deflating, she rounded, went limp, and began to look at the room. A full minute later she said, "Well, we know who he is, so we're in no rush to get a formal ID. We can leave him alone for the time being until we've done our preliminary work."

"Which is?"

"Recording the scene."

"Excellent. Do it."

Nicki prepared the camera, made adjustments to the flash, and proceeded to quarter the room, making the body the subject of her images as she gradually closed down the gap to it.

Eddie watched her work, and he couldn't get his first impression of her out of his mind – how she'd tried to roll him over so she could get him into bother with the gaffer. He didn't like it, didn't like how she worked, didn't like how underhanded she was. And it set him on edge whenever he was around her.

Had he been here with Kenny, they would have split the jobs between them and just got on with it, stopping every now and then for a chat or a farting competition. But with her he was tense, didn't even know if she could do the job.

Time to find out. "Do we think it's a robbery, or a burglary? Do we think it's motiveless? Targeted? What are you thinking?"

She looked up at Eddie, let the camera swing on its strap, and took a breath. "I… I don't know."

"Well of course you don't *know*. But think it through, give us some starting points."

"How could I possibly know if it was burglary? I don't know if anything's missing."

"Who would?"

She shrugged, deflated further. "Actually, I don't know."

"He has a housekeeper. So his housekeeper would know if anything's been taken. I mean, the TV's still in the lounge, but we don't know if anything else has gone: cash, jewellery. We haven't even been upstairs yet. It might be turned over up there." He stared at her. "Mightn't it?"

"Could be."

Eddie nodded to himself.

Light dawned on her face. "So we should go and check."

"We will. Soon," Eddie said.

"Anyway, how do you know he's got a housekeeper?"

"Because his wife is dead."

Nicki laughed. "How could you possibly know that? She might be out at bingo, or a WI meeting, or—"

"She's in an urn in the lounge. We walked right past her. No more bingo for Mildred Bolton."

"But someone else might live here with him. He might have family here; there are lots of photos on the hall walls."

"He lives alone. He has a housekeeper. She calls around once or twice a week, and her name is Mrs Watkins."

Nicki stared wide-eyed at Eddie. Eventually she broke into a grin, and then a small laugh fell into her mask as she pointed a gloved finger at him. "I get it, I get it. So you're taking the piss out of me." She held up her hands, "I admit, you got me then. Hook, line and sinker."

Eddie looked confused.

Chapter Twenty-Eight

Benson appeared in the kitchen doorway. "Nothing seems out of place upstairs."

"We thought you'd gone home for a shower." Eddie looked up. "In and out pretty quick, then?"

"Seems so."

"So someone walked past a houseful of high-value items, and didn't even search upstairs. They wanted him dead."

"They might have been scared off by someone."

Both turned to Nicki. "You forgot the pizza," Benson said.

"Oh. Yeah." She looked down and got back on with her work. "It was only a suggestion."

"Judging by the TV on pause, he wasn't expecting a lengthy visit. She came to kill him and then left again. She came for one thing only, and when she'd done it, she walked. Nice and calm."

"Except for the pizza delivery," Nicki said.

"Except for the pizza delivery, yes."

Nicki dropped her roller, sat back on her haunches, and said, "So now you're starting to freak me out, Eddie."

"He has that effect on most people, love," Benson said. "Why?"

"Were you here when it happened? You seem to know—"

"He knows shit-all, love. He's doing what he always does: pissing in the wind and hoping some of it sticks."

Eddie twitched his head like a pigeon. "You been eating mixed metaphors again?"

"No way can you deduce the attacker was female," Benson folded his arms and leaned against the doorframe.

"Well, based on the size of the footwear marks, it's either a female or a very small male."

"You got footwear marks?" Benson lurched forward and peered across the breakfast island. Nicki rollered a black gelatine footwear mark-lifter into position and then gently peeled it off again. She flipped it over so the gel faced upwards. Eddie passed her the torch and she shone its beam at ground level across the gel.

"Nike Cortez," she said proudly.

Eddie nodded. "Yep."

"How do you know it's the murderer's?" Benson said.

"Because there's another one over there in blood. We're going to swab it. I'll bet you next month's pittance it comes back as Doc Bolton's blood."

"Can I come in?"

"Be my guest."

Benson walked around the breakfast island, his suit crackling.

"Just don't stand between here and the hallway door."

"Any sign of the knife?"

"Nope."

"I'll have OSU search the drains in daylight," Benson said.

"Good."

"Okay, well, I might as well get out of here."

"You might as well arrange the body snatchers; we're almost done with him."

Benson's phone rang, but before he could unzip the suit and reach inside his pocket, the caller rang off. "I hate these bastard—"

Someone swung the front door open and called, "Tom?"

Benson's eyes widened, and Eddie watched him dash back across the kitchen floor, through the dining room and lounge, and into the hallway. He reached for the front door handle.

"Stop!" Eddie shouted. "Don't touch that door, Benson!"

Benson almost skidded to a halt, his hand an inch from the handle. He turned and shouted, "Nearly gave me a bleedin' heart attack then!"

"Better luck next time."

Someone coughed. "Is there a problem?"

Both turned and looked at the bald head peering at them around the edge of the door.

"Boss." Benson said.

"Fuck," Eddie whispered.

"Don't you like him?" Nicki asked.

"He's a gaffer. I'll have to spend half an hour telling him what we've done and what we've found and he'll still want a briefing in the morning. Then he'll come up with some stupid suggestion or he'll mess my scene up. So – no, not really."

"I tried to ring you, Tom," Crawford said.

"Sorry, yeah, couldn't get—"

"It's okay. Can I come in?"

Eddie blinked. Benson shouted, "Can the boss come—"

"I heard. Yes. Just don't touch the interior door handle. In fact, wait, wait, hold it there. I'll come to you. Fucking Kojak."

"We can wait till tomorrow's briefing Eddie, if you'd prefer?"

Eddie almost fell over. He looked back at Nicki; she was laughing.

"I don't want to make a nuisance of myself."

Too fucking late for that.

"No," Eddie said, astonished, "it's fine." He arrived in the hallway and pulled the door open by the top edge; Crawford, dressed in a full scene suit, stepped inside.

"I brought coffee and some chocolate bars."

Eddie opened his mouth but nothing came out. He grunted a 'thanks'. "Did you get yourself a lolly while you were there?"

Crawford looked at Eddie, his mouth turned down.

"Well, *I* thought it was funny."

Crawford ignored him. "You okay, Nicki?"

"I'm fine, thanks."

"Good." He looked at Eddie and Benson. "I don't want to hold you up; I know you're very busy. But is there anything that I can help with, anything I need to action?"

Eddie pulled down his mask. "Erm, we were just saying you can call the body snatchers; we're almost done with him."

"Tom, can you sort that?"

Benson nodded, "Sure, I'll get right on it." He sneered at Eddie.

"And I think he has a housekeeper," Eddie said. "You might want to trace her."

"You never told me that," Benson said.

Eddie winked. "You were busy searching upstairs. Tom."

"Did you find any records of her, Tom? Name? Address?"

"No, I… Er, no. I didn't come across—"

"Her name's Mrs Watkins."

Benson stared at Eddie, and Nicki looked up.

"There's an envelope in the kitchen with her name written on it. Fifty quid inside."

"I never saw—" Benson stopped talking. He squeezed past Crawford and out into the cold night air. "I'll run a check for all Watkins in a mile radius."

"Splendid," Crawford smiled as Benson sank away into the darkness. He turned to Eddie. "Why didn't you want him touching the door handle?"

"I haven't mini-taped it yet. The killer might have opened it. Got to be worth a shot."

Crawford nodded. "Indeed."

DAY 4

Chapter Twenty-Nine

Eddie woke up with a stiff neck and a mouth as furry as a beaver's belly. He clacked his tongue, adjusted his boxer shorts and walked from his bedroom, aiming roughly towards the kitchen for today's first coffee infusion.

He was vaguely aware of the radio playing somewhere nearby, some female disc-jockey spouting bollocks; he tried to blot it out and refocus his mind on the thinning fog of sleep – which in turn was preoccupied with last night's scene. The footwear would prove pivotal in that case, he could tell – all he could hope for was that the offender wasn't bright enough to throw them—

The woman screamed and Eddie jumped back so far that he hit the sideboard and knocked over his favourite vase of plastic flowers.

"Eddie," Charles rushed over, "what the hell are you doing—"

"Stop fussing, Dad, I'm fine."

"I wasn't fussing."

"I know!" Eddie pulled at his ever-stiffening neck and looked up from the smashed vase. He found himself staring across the lounge at a pale woman who held a hand to her chest, eyes and mouth wide open. "Who's this?" He looked down at Charles, who busied himself with the breakage, and only then did he remember that they didn't even own a radio.

"This…" Charles stood, put the biggest bits of glass on the sideboard, and kicked aside the plastic flowers.

"You know those hydrangeas were antique, don't you?" Eddie said.

"Eddie, I'd like you to meet Wendy." Charles swallowed, looked across at the woman and smiled. "Wendy," he said, voice croaking, "this is Eddie. My son."

They always said that first impressions were the most important, so Eddie held in the fart for once. "Morning." He eyed her – she was grandmotherly, but by no means cuddly. Her wavy lilac hair was clamped in place by a black net and two silver clips, and she wore a white dressing gown blown to bits by prints of massive red roses. Her hands were claws and her nails were red talons. Her puckered mouth was defined by sharp red lipstick, and her eyes peered suspiciously at him through a thousand folds of loose skin.

Eddie couldn't see the appeal. "You must be an excellent cook," he said, and made an effort by smiling in her general direction as he shuffled towards the kitchen. "Brew?"

He reached the sanctity of the kitchen, having not heard a word from her. Indeed, the silence seemed to grow heavier; he suspected there was a whispered conversation going on without him. "Would you like a brew or not, Wendy?"

Behind him, a throat cleared. "Earl Grey, if you have it. Please."

"Earl Grey?" Eddie laughed, filling the kettle. "We have Morrisons' own—"

"No, Eddie. Eddie," Charles was in the kitchen quicker than a ferret down a hole, barging Eddie aside, grabbing the tea caddy and laughing as though Eddie's sudden amnesia was funny. "I told you, remember: the Earl Grey is in here."

"But that's where—"

"Come on, son, step aside. I'll sort it out."

"All that's missing is a nudge and wink, Dad." He looked between Charles and Wendy, and enjoyed his first sigh of the day. "You okay, Dad?"

Charles laughed again as he continued to move at sixty miles an hour in a twenty zone. "Course I am. Let me make you a coffee, and then you can go get your shower, and get off to work. Did you work late last night?"

"Yeah, I was on—"

"You're one of those CSI chaps, aren't you?"

Charles stopped moving and grew instantly fragile. Only his wide eyes moved.

Eddie turned to her. "A CSI chap. Yes. That's me."

"Sounds frightful."

Charles closed his eyes.

"Having to work with all those dead bodies."

"I can think of worse people to work with." Eddie stared at her. "And what do you do, Cruella?"

She stared at him. "It's Wendy."

"It is, and I think we're due some rain, too."

"I said Wendy, not windy… Ah, I see. You were having a joke at my expense."

"Nonsense. It was free of charge."

The kettle clicked off, and Charles threw a spoonful of coffee into a mug. "Just get the milk," he said almost musically, pulling open the fridge door as Wendy and Eddie stared at each other, unsmiling, prickles growing through each other's skin. "This is nice," he said, looking from one to the other, and stirring the coffee so briskly that it sloshed over the side.

Wendy saw the mess and shook her head.

Eddie smiled and picked up the coffee, slurped his first mouthful, and watched the growing distaste on her face at his absence of manners. As he walked out of the kitchen and back though the lounge, he heard her ask, "And he stays here how often?"

Eddie pushed the fart out.

Chapter Thirty

Eddie turned off the engine and turned off Floyd too. He hadn't been listening anyway; the journey from home had been completely on autopilot and he was sure he'd slept through most of it. He stared at the glass monstrosity and lit his second cigarette of the day, elbow out in the breeze.

Today was going to be more difficult than usual, because today, as well as only having four hours' sleep, there was a woman in there – probably watching him right now, in fact – who he had let down last night. Okay, the job had come in and shattered their evening, but it was hardly a good start to the relationship.

"Relationship?" Christ, he was one step away from wedding bells.

Okay, not a relationship then; more an acquaintanceship.

Eddie shrugged; giving it a different title didn't make things any easier. He was about to sink just a level or so deeper and begin analysing his reasons for wanting this acquaintanceship when the gates rolled across the track again, and a black Astra, minus a spoiler, drove into the car park. Eddie noticed something else was missing, too: the terrible music. Perhaps he was making progress with Troy.

The Astra parked at the far end of the car park, and Eddie watched Troy slobbing his way towards the glass doors, head down, rucksack dragging on the ground.

Maybe he only got four hours' kip as well.

Eddie wound up the window, climbed out and locked the car. He fell in beside Troy. "How you doing today?"

Troy grunted.

"I see you lost your spoiler. From your car."

"Yup."

"No need to go on about it so much." Eddie smiled but Troy's fascination with the tarmac under his feet was obviously much greater than his interest in small talk. They stopped at the doors, and Eddie peered up at the glass turd and took a last drag before flicking away the cigarette and opening the door. "And Troy, if you'll let me get a word in edgeways…" Still no reply. "You're staying in the office today. Okay?"

"Whatever." Troy wandered through the reception as aimlessly as a disease, finally making it through the double doors and, presumably, up the stairs. The doors closed and Eddie lost sight of him. To his left, peering over the top of the reception desk, the one with the visitor's book with the chained pen perched on top, were a pair of green eyes.

Eddie smiled and walked towards them. "Miss Moneypenny."

She stood, smiling, but still too shy even to speak; which, for a receptionist, was an odd characteristic.

"I'm so sorry about last night. Of all the times to be murdered."

She laughed. "It's okay."

"Some people are so inconsiderate."

Moneypenny giggled, but her eyes never left his. Which was a shame, because he wasn't afforded the freedom to cop a quick glance down her top.

Never mind. It'll keep.

"Fancy trying again?" she said.

"Sure. When?"

"I took the liberty of booking the same table again for tonight."

"Really?"

"Hope you don't mind? It's a bit forward of me, I know, but..."

"See you there. Seven o'clock."

Moneypenny's smile widened right across her face. "Deal."

"Provided no one else gets murdered, of course." The chances of it happening again were minuscule; he was on safe ground. And, although he'd spent less than a minute with her, he thought it all went pretty well, and he needn't have worried.

Eddie walked towards the double doors. He didn't see Troy moving quickly out of his way as he barged through them and bounded up the stairs like a man who'd had a full and gratifying eight hours' sleep.

Troy smiled to himself and took the stairs rather more slowly.

* * *

Eddie opened the CSI doors and wasn't surprised to hear Sid singing some undistinguishable tune at his desk while flicking through a magazine.

"Sid!" he bellowed.

Sid looked up, clutching his chest. "Don't do that, Eddie!"

"It's the only bit of fun I get."

"Imagine if it gave me a heart attack and you had to do CPR and mouth-to-mouth on me."

Eddie stopped in his tracks and thought about it as he stared at Sid's black lipstick. "Fair enough. I won't do it again." He walked further in, his nose twitching. "Coffee?"

"No thanks, I have Darjeeling. It's monumentally awesome. Really, you should try some; it's very good for the complexion."

"How would you know? You wear more makeup than Lady Gaga. Coffee?"

"It's on your desk. Two garibaldis as well, because I bet you've had no breakfast again." He stared. "Have you?"

"No. I had an argument instead."

"Why am I not surprised?"

Eddie sniffed the air again. "Where's Troy and Kenny?"

"Not here yet. And you have to be in Mr Crawford's office in" —he lifted his arm and stared at a huge wrist watch— "eight minutes."

"The fuck is that?"

"Do you like it?"

"No. It's gross. It looks like Big Ben."

"Cheek. It's a birthday present from my mum."

"In that case, it's lovely. What is that damned smell?"

"Airwick. Scents of the Forest. Like it?"

"Smells like sheep shit." Eddie turned around and headed to his office.

"Oi, that cost me six quid!"

"You were robbed. Tell Kenny he's doing a PM at ten o'clock. He can take Nicki with him."

"Righto."

Eddie retrieved the coffee from his desk, stuffed a biscuit in his mouth and went back into the main office, almost bumping into Troy. "Where did you get to?" He spat crumbs.

"Toilet."

Eddie nodded towards his office, and Troy followed him inside. He closed the door. "Today is your random drugs test."

Troy's eyes closed and his chin hit his chest.

"You're going to fucking pass. Aren't you?"

He looked up. "Eddie…"

"Don't 'Eddie' me. Just make sure you pass." Eddie snatched the other biscuit from the desk and headed out with his coffee. "And don't leave this office before I get back."

Chapter Thirty-One

Jess woke up, staring at the blood under her fingernails and caught in the creases of her knuckles. At first she thought she'd somehow cut herself overnight, but then reality hit her like a hammer blow to the chest, and she shrieked.

And then she surprised herself by laughing.

Last night, she had come home to an empty flat. She'd expected Tony to be there, sitting in the chair, smelling. But judging by the air quality, he hadn't been around all day. His absence had been disappointing; she'd wanted to share Bolton's killing with him. She'd realised he was the only person in her life she could trust. And she'd wondered if sharing her burden would bring them closer again.

When she'd closed her eyes last night, she'd been fearful of every noise in the building, of the junkies shouting at each other from the next room, the toilet on the first floor flushing, expecting the coppers to put the front door in at any second. But she'd slept, and she'd slept well, and she couldn't remember having dreamed of anything at all, let alone anything about taking someone else's life. The only thing that had kept tugging at her mind was the thought of the jacket and knife she'd left behind. But what the hell could the police do with a sodding jacket anyway? Nothing. She was home free. And the same went for the knife: she'd put it in the pocket straight after washing it up – it was clean.

She'd run a long warm bath and scrubbed her nails and her arms, used a piece of broken mirror to inspect her neck and face, and even though she couldn't see any of Bolton's blood there, scrubbed them anyway. She'd washed and rinsed her hair half a dozen times before climbing, wrinkled and reddened from the tub, and then poured a bottle of bleach down the plughole.

Now she dressed in a t-shirt and sweater, and one of her last pairs of jeans. She bundled yesterday's bloodied clothes and gloves into a shopping bag, ready to go into someone's bin as far away from here as she could get.

She crossed Bolton off her list and got used to the idea of being a killer. And any time she doubted that she'd done the right thing, all she had to do was replay his evidence against her in court, and replay Michael telling her to leave him alone. Vindicated. Job done.

Sticking the blade in had been the hardest part. The build-up to it hadn't exactly been a picnic, mind. But she'd realised that once you're committed to it, and you feel the blade thrusting towards someone, it becomes a feedback loop where you wonder how hard to push and how deep to go. As it turned out, she'd set both dials to 'full', and it had worked out just fine. But it had still been the hardest part.

Watching someone's life end because of you was like flicking a switch. You shifted from wondering what it would be like to kill someone to remembering what it was like before you had.

Once you're over this side, there's no going back.

Twelve years later than the justice system had given her the name, she became a murderer.

She tried on the new title for size and decided that it was easy to live with, and even gave her confidence. She stood before the little cabinet mirror in the bathroom and smiled at herself full-on. Suddenly, life didn't seem so terrifying any more; suddenly there was an option for when things didn't go your way.

"Maybe it would have been better all along if I *had* killed Sebastian."

Jess picked up her keys and the bag of bloodstained clothing, and slammed the door.

* * *

She had dumped the bag of clothes in a nearby bin.

The door banged shut behind her, and traffic noise dimmed to a hum. Jess suddenly came awake from the daydreams she'd had on her journey here. The plaque on the wall said West Yorkshire Probation Service, and suddenly felt not quite as brave as she had been in the bathroom earlier.

As she climbed the stairs, the old fear of meeting Sidmouth leached back into her mind, and she could feel the new wall of strength crumbling. It was sad, that her new superpower was made of fucking meringue. The higher she climbed the drier her mouth became and the wetter her hands grew. But *this* was the hardest part, wasn't it? The anticipation? Set all your controls to full, and it'll be fine.

Except Jess didn't quite believe that.

She stood before his office door and knocked.

"Come."

She took one last deep breath and entered John Sidmouth's office. There he sat, a sickly little smile on his thin pink lips, like he had a secret about her that only he knew of, like he was playing with himself under the desk.

"Sit." The grease on his nose and his forehead glistened, and she could see long hairs sticking out of his ears.

She almost retched. She pulled the chair away from his desk, sat and crossed her legs, and folded her arms tight across her ribs.

"It didn't go well with Michael, I hear."

She shook her head. "I need to see him again."

His eyes and his smile grew a little bit wider. "I can arrange it. But I should warn you

Don't make me, don't make me, don't make me

that Michael has been suffering recently."

"Suffering?"

Sidmouth pushed his own chair back, rubbed his eyes beneath the thick black-rimmed glasses. "He's been in bother with the police. Twice in the last few months."

"What kind of bother?"

"Petty stuff, mostly. The worst thing was stealing his foster mother's car. He didn't damage it, and she didn't want to proceed with any action, but…" He nodded. "Well, it's not good. I think he's mixing with the wrong kind." He paused. "Unless of course, *he* is the wrong kind."

"How can I help?"

Sidmouth smiled at her. "I don't see how your intervention could help him at all. He began going off the rails shortly before your release from custody." He raised his eyebrows. "What does that suggest to you?"

"He needs to get to know me again, Mr Sidmouth. He's worried, that's all. Once we're back to normal, he'll calm down."

"I don't see a 'back to normal' anywhere on his horizon, Ms Ripley."

Jess felt numb. "She offered me money."

"Who offered you money?"

"Michael's foster mother." Jessy leaned forward. "She wanted to buy him!"

"Really?"

"Is that all you can—"

"Ms Ripley. Think of your position. Think of your *future*. That kind of thing is illegal, and—"

"Fifty grand."

Sidmouth stopped talking, mouth still open. When it closed, he licked his lips and said. "If you look, however, at *Michael's* future, one might conclude…"

Jess's eyes widened. "Are you—"

"I'm merely speculating… I would be willing to act as broker if—"

"I'm not selling my own son! He's not a," she tried to find the right term. "He's not a—"

"Liability?" He let out a breath. "Could be a new start for both parties. And a healthy one for you."

"You were telling me it was illegal a minute ago."

"Just thinking of your wellbeing, Ms Ripley."

"Well *I'm* not giving up on him!" She sat back, deflated. "And I'm not selling him, either."

Sidmouth appraised her, his eyes straying from her face and settling on her chest. "Glad to hear it," he whispered. "I need to make recommendations first, of course. But I'm sure there won't be a problem in arranging another visit." He stared at her. "Will there?"

"Are we going to do this dance every time I want to see him?"

Sidmouth smiled at her.

"You are sick."

"I am also in charge of whether you see your drop-out son or not."

She made to get out of the chair, but Sidmouth didn't flinch.

"I am the man who decides whether you stay free or go back to prison; you're on licence, Jessica, remember. Life can be pretty tough for someone in your position. Better get used to it."

"But—"

"I would suggest that makes me your best friend, wouldn't you? Someone you'd like to keep on the right side of?"

She was about to argue, but his voice had grown stronger and louder, and hers meeker, quieter. She was shrivelling up again, she was losing again.

Where's your superpower now, Jess? Where are those options now?

He leaned forward, elbows on his desk, fat fingers playing with each other. "I shall conduct another home visit the day after tomorrow."

Her eyes closed, and she felt her bottom lip quiver.

"And I'll be leaving the paperwork here. I'll sign it once I'm satisfied, and once I've returned from your bedsit. Is that okay?" He smiled at her again, greasy pink lips shining. "Jessica?"

* * *

Jess cried most of the way home.

She tried not to, of course, but she couldn't help it. This was what the phrase 'over a barrel' was designed for. This was what hell felt like. She wanted to be thinking of Michael now, coming up with a way to help him, maybe with Marilyn's input, not to be worrying about having to blow off some fat bastard who could turn nasty at any time. He was the kind of man who saw a little power over someone and exploited it to the max. There really was no telling where the end might be, but she couldn't imagine him ever saying, 'You done good, Jessy. Everything's back to normal now, and we'll never see each other again'. He would make sure she went back inside, if for no other reason than to exercise his power.

She was on licence for another eighteen months; it would be a long time to suffer.

She resolved not to.

Chapter Thirty-Two

Eddie entered the main CID office, glancing at Melanie, who sat alone at a semicircular desk in a sea of other desks. Detectives and other researchers like her engaged in a low hum, speaking on phones, sharing a joke. It could be any medium-sized office anywhere in the country. They could be a sales team; it could be an architects' office, a solicitors' office.

But these people were all engaged in catching evil.

He stared at them and realised the truth of that last thought. They were engaged in catching evil. These people were the last stop in determining whether murderers and rapists, current or historic, got to go free, or got to live in a cell for the next fifteen years.

These were the people on whom the victims' families depended to make sure their dead ones or their damaged ones were given the justice they deserved, and they were the ones charged with keeping those villains away from the law-abiding citizen. They were charged with keeping people's faith in the police and the justice system.

Didn't it all sound like a cliché? Didn't it all sound like a game? Didn't it all sound like bullshit?

But it was true, and it didn't hurt to be reminded of that every now and then; how important their work was. Eddie felt a little guilty at taking the piss out of them – out of the victims. But it was how he coped. Without it he'd split in two and some little nut-job would jump out, start killing people, and end up in a straitjacket in Juniper Hill with the arsonist.

Melanie was smiling at him.

He hadn't noticed at first, was too busy staring at the office while lost in thought. But then he became aware. He squinted at her, looked behind him, but it was him she was grinning at. And then she winked. Eddie was confused. He began walking towards her, meaning to ask why she smiled at him. "Is my fly down?"

"Eddie?"

Eddie stopped and turned. Crawford.

"Are you lost?"

Eddie looked to Melanie, but she was staring at her monitor as though he'd dreamed the smile and the wink. "No," he said, unsure what was going on. "I'm coming."

He closed the door of Crawford's office, and chose to stand in the corner. This used to be Cooper's office, and it had always looked too big for him, like an ill-fitting suit, like a personality smaller than the laugh that carried it. He had been a fake, but Crawford suited this place, he filled it well, and those sitting in the chairs and standing by the window thought so too – they were calm, respectful. Crawford was the kind of leader this place had needed for years.

That calming effect even seemed to work on Eddie. At first he tried to resist it, but then he gave in as though tired of the constant battles.

Crawford was smiling at him. "Okay?"

Eddie nodded. *See*, he thought, *this is so unnatural.* He felt his hackles rise, the ones that warned him of things like this – unnatural things, things not in the right place, not in the right order – and he tried to pat them down again as though he were stroking a dog. It looked at him, shook its head, and bit his hand off. Eddie snapped awake, blinking eyes that settled on Benson.

Benson screwed up an empty Mars bar wrapper and stuffed it in his pocket, his jaw working the chocolate so noisily that Eddie had to either look away or throw up on the carpet right there and then. Nicki was here too, and her presence confused Eddie. He mouthed, 'What are you here for?' She shrugged, pretending not to understand him. So he said, "Why are you here?"

Crawford took up his seat, and said, "I invited her. She worked the scene with you last night; she might have valid points to raise."

"Yep." Eddie considered it, eyebrows arched. "She might, but I want her at a PM at ten." Crawford looked like a model from a glossy men's magazine, red braces over a cream shirt latching onto tailor-made tan slacks that probably cost more than Eddie's house. Eddie's nausea at seeing Benson macerating a Mars bar intensified a little at the sight of how good Crawford looked. Was that a little intimidation, Eddie? he asked himself. He almost laughed aloud.

There were a couple of new faces, and one old face missing. Jeffery usually attended these briefings; he was the one responsible for formulating forensic strategies, for liaising with the SIO, for developing a coherent way forward through an investigation, and for scheduling evidence for laboratory analysis in a specific and cost-efficient way. He was needed here.

In a way totally unlike that of his predecessor, Crawford opened the meeting by welcoming them all to his office and saying, "For those who don't know me, I'm Lloyd Crawford, and I've come from Nottinghamshire Constabulary to fill the void in MCU left by Mr Cooper. I've been in policing for thirty-two years, but I'm not an old-school copper. I believe in leading by example, and I believe in treating people fairly and with respect. We move forward as a team, and we all bring something valid to the table. It's why you're all here. I look forward to getting to know each of you a little more over the coming days, but for now we have some pressing business to attend to."

Eddie was impressed. At last, a gaffer who was decent, and wasn't a coffin-dodger.

Crawford cleared his throat. "His name was Doctor Stanford Bolton. He was a Home Office pathologist working the Yorkshire and Humber region for almost twenty-five years before retirement eleven years ago." Crawford didn't even look at the notes on his desk. "He dealt with roughly thirteen hundred suspicious and sudden deaths over that time; about ninety in his last two years before retirement.

"He was seventy-six. He lived alone; his wife, Mildred, died eight years ago. He has a housekeeper, Mrs Watkins, who comes in twice a week for a few hours." Crawford nodded at Eddie. "Mrs Watkins confirms that to the best of her knowledge nothing has been removed from the house, or appears out of place, except for a knife missing from the block by the microwave. Suppose it could be in the dishwasher, we should check—"

"Dishwasher's empty," Eddie said.

"So the murderer took it with him." Crawford gave this some thought before resuming. "He banked with Barclays, who report no suspicious activity on his accounts." He stared at the room. "It's a stranger murder."

Eddie's brow folded up over his face and he snorted. "Bollocks."

Everyone turned to stare at Eddie, and Crawford said, "Remember my opening speech where I outlined that we all work with respect, Eddie?"

Eddie bowed his head slightly, "Bollocks, Boss."

Crawford let it go. "What makes you think it's not a stranger murder?"

Eddie sipped his coffee. "Just because *you* don't know who killed him, doesn't make it a stranger murder. A stranger murder is random—"

"I know what a stranger murder is. And since we have no motive for the killing—"

"We only don't have a motive because we don't know who killed him yet. When we find her, we'll see that there *is* a motive and that they knew each other. Therefore, it's not a stranger murder."

Crawford turned a slight shade of crimson. "In Nottingham, three years ago, a man was stabbed in his own bedroom by a stranger. Nothing was taken, nothing was disturbed. In. Stab. Out. Left the door open and walked away whistling some happy tune. We found the killer twenty minutes later, covered in blood, on a bus heading out of town. It was a stranger murder. Same kind of murder this is."

Eddie shook his head. "This victim of yours, was he a prominent pathologist as well?"

"He worked in a Post Office, actually. What's your point?"

"Your murderer was suffering mental health problems. Our murderer, *Doc's* murderer, is perfectly sane. And they knew each other. Yours was a stranger murder, this… isn't."

Crawford smiled. He laced his perfect fingers with their perfect nails together across his flat stomach and took a deep breath. But it was easy to see that he'd love to smash the desk with a frustrated fist. He did well to keep calm. "Okay, I'll humour you: how do you know Bolton's murderer was sane? How do you know they knew each other?"

"Don't humour me. You don't owe me any favours."

"Eddie," Benson warned.

Eddie looked back to Crawford. "Sorry. I didn't mean to be rude."

Graciously, Crawford waved a hand.

"Your murderer was seen by people on the bus, and was heard whistling as he walked away. He didn't think he'd done anything wrong. It was just another day to him, just another event. He did it in the daytime and made no effort to conceal either himself or what he'd left behind.

"Doc's murder was at night; she talked her way in, and she took away the murder weapon and nothing else, so it shows premeditation, it shows purpose. It took some effort to conceal. It was done by a female – statistically less inclined to kill a disabled old man than a male is – and she kept it quiet. I bet she didn't walk away whistling."

"I'm not getting into a pissing competition with you, Eddie—"

"Good; I have a really short willy."

"So how did you know he lived alone?" Everyone looked across at Nicki. "You told me last night that he lived alone. How did you know?"

Eddie sighed and wished there was somewhere he could sit down – this was getting tedious. "There was moss on the windows and in the gutters of his Jaguar on the driveway. Seeing as he was so fastidiously tidy in his house, that pride didn't extend to his car, which I suppose means he didn't care for it very much, he didn't use it much; no one used it much. And his tarmac drive, wide enough for at least two cars, had more moss on it. If there'd been another car parked there regularly, no moss would have grown. So it stands to reason that no one else lived there."

"And how did you know he was disabled?"

Eddie shrugged. "Blue badge in his car window. Pair of walking sticks by his chair in the lounge. Another walking stick propped against the pantry door in the kitchen. It's not fucking rocket science, Nicki. You mostly just need to use your eyes and look."

"Proper Sherlock Holmes, aren't you, Eddie?" Crawford's grip on the high ground was slackening, and it was easy to see that he'd been rattled.

"Just bringing my little bit to the table, Boss." He winked. "Moving us forward as a team."

One of the new faces morphed into life as if Eddie had seen him for the first time – in the same way as he'd suddenly become aware of Melanie smiling at him out in the main CID office. This guy wasn't smiling at him, though. He was just staring. He stood to the right of Crawford, arms folded, still as a statue, and stared. At Eddie.

He reminded Eddie of Agent Smith from *The Matrix*. All he needed was a pair of shades and he could be his double.

Crawford straightened his already straight tie and tried to regain some of his composure. "Tom," he said, "anything?"

"Bolton was found by a pizza delivery woman, Rasine Wozniacki. She checks out, I've crossed her off the list."

Crawford nodded, tapping a pen against his chin.

"Leeds Watch have CCTV of a woman walking alone about eight o'clock last night up Stonegate Road. She disappears into that stretch of woodland between Stonegate Road and Carr Manor Road. Not seen her since. They're sending me the recording but have already said she appears relaxed, not in a hurry."

"Are you sure about the pizza delivery woman?" Nicki looked around the room, and then aimed her comments at Benson. "I mean, she's female, we found possibly female footwear marks at the scene. She wouldn't have brought her own knife, so would have had to use one from his kitchen. I'm just thinking aloud…" She looked at Crawford.

"Go on," he said.

"Maybe he invited her in, or she asked to use the toilet or whatever, and they argued, or she tried to extort more money from him… she sees the knife and kills him."

"Keep it in mind," Crawford said.

"If *my* life depended on it, I'd have handed her the envelope with the fifty quid inside," said Eddie.

Nicki looked away.

"But it's possible they argued," he said.

Detective Sergeant Khan spoke up. "I find it hard to believe that someone would go into someone's house with the intention of killing them, but without a weapon. So it's not pre-meditated."

Nicki smiled back at Eddie. Eddie drank more coffee.

"Pizza woman checks out," Benson said again. "Khan did that last night; her route checks out, and when you check her previous customers along a timeline against the time she called it in, it fits. She's off the list. We have her clothing and her footwear if you need them." Benson looked at Agent Smith.

"I'll bear it in mind."

"Won't Jeffery need to bear it in mind?" Eddie asked. "Where is he, anyway?"

"Tom, will you organise background into Bolton's past, please? I want to know who he worked with at the labs, who he came into contact with at the mortuaries, who had any contact with him since he retired. And get all the information you can on his remaining family, and any children. Okay?"

Benson nodded. "Boss."

Eddie coughed. "Where's Jeffery?"

"We'll come to that, Eddie, don't worry."

"When someone says 'don't worry', I tend to worry."

"Anyone have any final words before we close?" Crawford stood, ran his thumbs around his waistband and looked at the shaking heads. "Okay, great. Let's meet back here at sixteen-hundred for an update."

Everyone began to stand.

"Has anyone thought to check if it could be linked to Thomas Marchant's death?"

Crawford's face was that of a father proud of his son's theory, even though it was ill-conceived. "I think we're on safe ground there, Eddie."

Eddie shrugged. "Thought I'd just throw it out there. It's not often we get two professionals murdered within days of each other."

"Thanks, Eddie," Crawford smiled. "Have a catch-up with Tom. He'll fill you in about Marchant."

Eddie's embryonic fondness for Crawford keeled over and died. All that bullshit in his maiden speech was just designed to make everyone here, himself included, think he was the new and invaluable saviour of MCU. But like everything else in this life that seems too good to be true – like dating a woman and it going according to fucking plan! – it was a plastic façade covering a mass of lies and uncertainty. It was the smile on the lips of a liar. Eddie wanted to punch him for smiling at him like that. Patronising fucker.

People shuffled past him, and Eddie was vaguely aware of a strange, almost apologetic, sorrow in Benson's eyes as he walked out.

Eddie looked at Agent Smith. He didn't move. He really was cast out of bronze.

The room was empty now; just Crawford, Agent Smith, and Eddie were left, staring at each other.

"It's unfortunate timing, Eddie," Crawford began. "I'd wanted the changes brought in when we all had the chance to absorb them, rather than when we're busy trying to solve two murders." He smiled again, apologising with his mouth while his eyes said, 'I don't give a shit, let's just get this one last lie out of the way'.

Eddie sipped the dregs of his coffee. Waited.

"I had to let Jeffery go, I'm afraid."

Eddie gasped. He let the thought sink in for a moment before saying, "Had to let him go. Why? Did he steal the petty cash?"

"No, he—"

"He stole your lollipops, didn't he? The bastard!"

Agent Smith moved a tiny amount, and Eddie wondered if he was still plugged into the wall.

"He's back at Division. Went last night."

"Why? He was very good at his job."

"I'm sure he was—"

"Then why—"

"If you'll let Mr Crawford speak, maybe you'll find out." Agent Smith had changed colour slightly, and his eyes had narrowed.

"And you are? Wait, let me guess. You are his replacement?"

"This is Detective Sergeant Victor Weismann. I brought him with me from Nottingham. He's an excellent forensic manager with many years under his belt, and will be a big asset to MCU."

"Really. How did the Personnel department feel about it?"

"They were very accommodating," Crawford said. "Everything's gone through. It's all above board."

Eddie glared at Agent Smith. "Got friends in Personnel, have we?"

"I didn't feel that Mr Walker was quite… up to the task. Mr Weismann is your new boss, Eddie. I'm sure you two will get along like a—"

"House on fire?" Eddie closed the door after him.

Chapter Thirty-Three

Jess sat in the bus shelter on Heath Road. It was one of the new ones that had a seat inside and an LCD screen telling you how late the next bus was. And, strangely, it hadn't been smashed yet; it was all pristine.

She sat in the centre of the bench where she had a good view of the house; she'd been there forty-five minutes. Her bottom was numb, her feet tingled, and her back ached because she was slouching, but she didn't move. It was as though she were dead. And if it wasn't for her shallow breathing and her occasional blinks, other people who came into the shelter might have thought she was.

Buses came and went. A few people asked if she was okay, but she didn't reply. If they blocked her view of the house, she would either look up at them until they moved again, or she would look around them. She didn't speak.

It began to rain, and pretty soon the silence of the bus shelter gave way to the comforting noise of rain beating on the metal roof. It was all the same to Jess. She was in the kitchen where Sebastian died amid a melee of noise, she was in Michael's bedroom as he screamed his tits off, she was in the dock where she suffered through the silence of that hollow-chested moment as the jury found her guilty.

Her life had begun attacking itself; it was like a virus, it consumed anything of goodness and from it the badness grew. They do say that the more you think negative thoughts, the more negative your life becomes, like a self-perpetuating circle of shit. Conversely, thinking happy thoughts created happiness. Simple!

Jess smiled.

It still rained, both outside on the shelter roof, and inside, where the darkness bled out like a wound.

She smiled wider.

He walked along Heath Road, the rain seemingly not bothering him at all. He was with a school friend, and they laughed about something as the sky grew darker. He was thinking happy thoughts.

Jess stopped smiling and got up. Her fingers tingled and her throat was dry. She cricked her back, and watched the two youths part company, Michael unlatching the small wooden gate that led to his front door.

She stepped out of the shelter and walked away, mulling something over in her mind.

Chapter Thirty-Four

"Why's Eddie keeping you in today?" Sid pushed a cup of tea across the desk towards Troy.

Troy didn't look up, just shrugged.

"You know that if anything's bothering you, I'll always listen." Sid smiled, tongue-stud glinting. "And I'll always try to help."

"Go away."

Sid stiffened. "And I have to say, despite his brash exterior, Eddie is always—"

"Fuck off, Sid."

"Oi!" Kenny threw a pen across the office at Troy. It missed by a yard, but the accompanying sentiment struck home, bang on target. "Watch your lip, boy."

Sid's nostrils flared and he stood back, ready to open fire for Troy's bad manners, but the phone on his desk rang. He breathed out the tension, grew a smile and answered. "Good morning. West Yorkshire Police Major Crime Unit, CSI Department, Sid speaking, how may I help you?" Sid nodded a few times, looked back at Troy – who had his head on his desk – thanked the caller, and put down the phone. "There's a gentleman to see you, Troy. He's on his way up; a Mr Gibbon." No reaction from Troy. "I'll go and show him in."

"No." Troy stood, grabbed his jacket from the back of the chair, and marched down the office. "I'll sort it."

"And Troy," shouted Kenny, "don't monkey about." He laughed as the door slammed.

Sid turned to Kenny. "That was a bit cruel."

"Funny, though."

"You know Eddie wants you to do Bolton's PM at ten o'clock with Nicki?"

Kenny gritted his teeth. "Fuck off, Sid."

They both laughed.

* * *

Nicki came out of Crawford's office amid a group of detectives, and split away from them, heading towards CSI. But no sooner had she broken free than she saw Troy marching from the CSI office towards the stairs, his limp barely noticeable. She was about to call out to him, but his face was angry and afraid; his eyes were wide yet they stared into the distance. He met a man at the top of the stairs. Nicki paused, watching them shake hands. She couldn't hear, but Troy was doing a lot of nodding and spending time looking at his feet. She felt inclined to follow as they descended the stairs.

It was all very strange, especially since Troy had his jacket with him. Were they planning on leaving the building together? Who was that man, and what did he want with Troy? All information was good information… and so Nicki swept down the stairs in time to see them heading into an open office just off the hallway, near the stores.

It was quiet here. She rounded the corner and pressed her back to the wall and was rewarded almost instantly. She heard the man proclaim that he was from a private company specialising in employment drugs testing. She noted that Troy didn't speak. The man did, though; he went on to say that it was a voluntary test, and that Troy must sign the consent forms if he wished to proceed.

"I don't have any choice, do I, Mr Gibbon?" Troy said. Not a question; a statement.

Gibbon provided an answer anyway. "No, you don't have to cooperate. But if your employer has asked you to participate, then you'd be wise to take the test. If it ends up at tribunal, refusal to have this test would look very bad for you."

There was a pause, Nicki's eyes were wide, and she could feel her heart chugging. She knew there had been something wrong with Troy, the way he was always at sixty thousand feet, always full of himself, and ready to argue with anyone, but she never suspected drugs; she always thought he just had a very big opinion of himself and an even bigger ego.

"Thank you," Gibbon said. "Here's a sample bottle. Where are the nearest toilets?"

Nicki turned, hurried back along to the stairs and climbed them with a hearty smile on her face.

* * *

Eddie closed Crawford's door and was thinking about stealing some of Kenny's coffee when he spotted Melanie. Perhaps it was time to find out what was going on.

He perched on her desk and made her jump, which was an added bonus.

"Eddie."

"Melanie." He watched her.

Her straight face cracked, and she began to smile again.

"There it is. What's so funny? Or are you on the love beads again?"

"Funny? No, you misunderstand. I'm pleased. For you."

"Me? No one's ever been pleased for me."

"And for Maggie too."

"Maggie?"

"Jesus, Eddie. When are you going to stop giving people imaginary names and start learning their proper ones?"

"I don't know what you mean. Doing something like that would be very childish, Cher."

"But you *are* dating the receptionist?"

"Moneypenny?"

Melanie sat back and folded her arms.

"Yeah, well, keep it to yourself. We haven't even had a proper go at it yet."

Melanie raised her eyebrows.

"Dating, I mean. Filthy woman." Eddie looked up and saw Nicki cresting the stairs into the main office, then turning right towards CSI. That in itself wasn't strange; what *was* strange was the smile on her face, like she'd found twenty quid. He continued to watch her but asked Melanie, "What do you think of him?" He nodded towards Crawford's door.

She whispered, "I thought he was lovely."

"But?"

"He practically threw Jeffery out last night. Him and his sidekick walked him out of the office. Apparently Jeff was almost in tears."

"The bastard."

"Yeah. So – watch your back."

Eddie patted Melanie on the shoulder and walked across the office to Benson.

"Cher?" she called after him.

"High cheekbones." He smiled at her. "And Botox," he whispered, "Lots of Botox."

Eddie approached Benson, and said, "How come you never use your own office?"

"And miss out on all this happy banter? Anyway, I'm a DI, I'll leave all that ivory tower shite to people like him."

"He's a knobhead. You know that, don't you?"

"I am a fucking detective, Eddie. I'd worked it out, thank you."

"I don't understand how they'd let him bring his own man in and turf Jeffery out?"

Benson shrugged. "I have no answer. I suppose he must have a good record, and maybe they were so desperate to fill Cooper's chair, they bent over for him. He'll have negotiated his own terms."

Eddie put down his empty cup, sat on Benson's desk and folded his arms.

Benson sighed. "Not going to be a quick visit, then? I have a lot of work to do."

"I know. How far have you got with the list from Thomas Marchant's murder?"

"Look, we'll have a sit down sometime, you and me, okay? I'll go through what I've got and we'll take it from there. But right now…"

"Why would you do that?"

Benson smiled. "He's kicked Jeffery out; how long have *I* got left, I wonder?"

"Seriously?"

Benson shrugged again. "I don't know. I might be talking bollocks, but he's too nice a man to work here. There are no nice people working here, which means he's a slimy bastard. And it means he's good at hiding stuff. So my advice is to keep your nose clean and stay out of his way. Don't pick fights with him, Eddie."

Eddie laughed. "Yeah, okay, whatever you say." He stood, collected his mug. "I ain't changing for no prick like him, and I ain't scared of Agent Smith, either."

"Who?"

"His sidekick. UnWeismann."

"Well, on your head be it."

Eddie walked towards the CSI corridor and met the drug-testing man at the top of the stairs. "Okay, Gibbo? How did it go?"

Gibbon held out his hand, remembered that Eddie didn't do contact, and casually dropped it again. "He was—"

"Wait," Eddie looked around. "Come into my office, eh?"

* * *

Eddie closed his office door with a foot and handed Gibbon a coffee. "Don't tell anyone I gave you a drink. I had to steal the coffee again."

"Why don't you buy some?"

Offended, Eddie stared at him, then sat down. "How did it go?"

"He was bricking it. His hand was shaking as he signed the consent forms."

"Good. I hope it teaches him a lesson."

"He's a clever lad, though."

"I know, that's what's so infuriating. He could be good at this job if he'd climb down off his ego. What do you think he's on?"

"What's his behaviour been like?"

"Apart from today where I couldn't get a word out of him, he's got masses of confidence, very chatty…"

"Good stamina?"

"Oh, yeah; he never stops."

"Could be any number of stimulants, but I wouldn't be surprised if he was on amphet."

"He's on fucking speed?" Eddie thought for a moment. "Is it worth getting it tested after all, just to see what he's on?"

"I said he was a clever lad. I figured he was too willing to cooperate, you know what I mean? He was too willing to oblige. I let him go into one cubicle and then I stood on the toilet in the next one and peeped over the top."

"You old pervert."

"He took a vial from his jacket pocket, poured it into the container I'd given him, and then had a pee."

Eddie was grinning. "Sneaky little bastard. I wonder where he got it from."

"Blocked urinal somewhere, I should think." Gibbon shrugged and sipped his coffee. "Didn't you put sugar in this?"

"I'm not stealing Kenny's sugar as well. What do you take me for?"

Gibbon stood. "Well, I'm off to Costa, then. You okay with me binning his sample and the paperwork?"

"Yep; I've learned all I need to know, cheers."

Eddie opened his office door just as Nicki walked away. "Hey," he called after her. "What were you doing?"

"When?"

"Just then. I opened the door and you almost fell inside!"

She appeared suitably confused. "I'd just called back for my radio, that's all. Happened to be walking past your door, actually."

Eddie eyed her as she waved and left the office. He looked at Gibbon, decided he ought to shake his hand. "You okay seeing yourself out?"

Chapter Thirty-Five

Eddie stared after Nicki. There was something about her that he didn't like. He couldn't put a finger on it, but it was there nonetheless, like a smell that he couldn't identify. He went back into his office, grabbed his coffee and took it to sit on Sid's desk. "What do you think of her?"

"Nicki?"

Eddie nodded.

Sid swallowed, and cracked his knuckles. "Well…"

"I know it's not a fair question, but I value your opinion."

Sid sat a little straighter, puffed out his pigeon chest a little further. "I haven't made up my mind yet."

Eddie nodded and began to heave himself off the desk, but Sid hadn't finished.

"And that's not good. I know people. I know instantly whether I'm going to get along with them or whether I'm going to stab them with a teaspoon, y'know. "

Eddie sat again.

"The fact that I haven't formed an opinion about her yet spells trouble. To me, it means she's hiding something. Whether or not that's a bad thing" —he shrugged— "I don't know."

"Thanks," Eddie said, shuffling towards the desk edge again.

"And I'll tell you something else, too. The way they got rid of Jeffery Walker was very underhand. He wasn't an outstanding piece of work by any means, but he was honest and reliable, and I trusted him. He made good decisions."

Eddie stared at him, and the smile that tried to rupture his straight face barely made a show before he throttled it. He loved how Sid ranted, appreciated his unbiased appraisals, but found his delivery

– a constant barrage of words with no pause for breath or consideration – very funny.

"He'd done nothing to deserve such treatment. I mean, imagine how he feels, having given his best to MCU for eight years only to be shunted back off to division with his tail between his legs to do some made-up job collating stats. He must find it bewildering and embarrassing. Not to mention how angry he must feel at being ousted by a DS from Nottingham! I mean, no selection process, no interview? What's all that about?"

The doors banged. Both men looked around to see Troy standing there in his own little cloud of bad mood; his eyebrows turned his eyes into slits, and Eddie was sure there was a little sneer as his top lip quivered.

Sid resumed his typing and at last Eddie stood. He faced Troy. "You okay?"

Troy nodded. "If you've nothing for me to do, can I go home? Please?"

Eddie glanced at the clock on the wall, and decided he wasn't going to give someone half a day off because he felt a bit low. "No. You can come with me."

Troy's shoulders slumped further. "Where?"

"Grab your coat and your van keys, and you'll find out. It'll be a surprise. Oh look, you've already got your coat." Eddie clapped his hands. "Think of the fun we'll have!"

* * *

"Wow, you're a little ray of pitch black, aren't you?" Eddie was deafened by the silence on the way, but he felt comfortable with it; if the kid was too depressed or too angry to create conversation, then fine, fuck him. "Park here. Then get suited up."

"I thought you'd sorted this last night."

"Still work to do. I want some fingerprinting doing."

"They'll have worn gloves. What's the point?"

Eddie thought about it for a moment. "You're right. Let's go to Starbucks."

Troy looked at him. "Really?"

"No. Not fucking really. Get a suit on." Eddie slammed the van door and walked up to the tape.

The Police Community Support Officer on the cordon met Eddie. "You going in?"

Eddie pinched the bridge of his nose, and then smiled. "No," he said, "we can do the fingerprinting from out here."

"Sarky bastard. What's your numbers?"

"I'm B72, and if you just write 'Knobhead' for him." Eddie nodded over his shoulder as Troy's arms bulged with suits and overshoes. "Everyone will know who you mean."

The PCSO blinked, unimpressed.

"I'm B16," Troy muttered.

"Well it would be, wouldn't it," Eddie growled. "BIG. Did you choose it yourself?"

Troy shook his head and the PCSO lifted the tape for them to duck beneath.

Eddie walked up the driveway, following Troy. "Is it open?" he shouted back at the PCSO.

"No," said the PCSO. "But if you turn the handle and push, that usually works."

"Touché!" Eddie half-smiled and resumed his walk up the driveway. "Smart bastard."

Outside the porch was a scene tent, like a small marquee, held in place by weights dropped onto its feet to stop the wind pulling it down the driveway. It was a place to get changed in, it was a place to handle the exhibits, and it's where they had reversed the private ambulance last night so they could load the body without the indignity of being spied on by press or public.

Troy dropped the suits and overshoes onto a small trestle table, and Eddie unshouldered the kit and the camera. In silence they suited up, and Eddie was relieved that the kid didn't make fun of him getting into the suit. In fact, he was silent.

For a moment Eddie was undecided whether he liked this new, quiet, Troy better than the old loud one. He was also unsure whether *he* was responsible for the kid's bad mood. He thought about it for a second or two and then dismissed it with a shake of the head.

"How long we going to be doing this shit for?" Troy asked.

Eddie considered this. "Well, let's see. They've just increased the retirement age to sixty-fucking-seven. But by the time we reach our sixties, they'll have moved the goalposts to the seventies. Pretty soon we'll have commodes for office chairs so we won't need to get up to take a piss, and they'll have to expand the disabled parking outside the front door—"

"I meant," Troy shouted, "how long are we doing *this* shit for?" He pointed at the house, jabbing with an irritated finger. "This shit, this scene?"

That was the last time Eddie would try and share a joke with the miserable little bastard. Yes, he definitely preferred the quiet Troy, but he cut him some slack this time on account of his own possible responsibility for the sulky mood. He also resisted the temptation to slap him round the back of the head.

Little shit.

"This 'shit' is your fucking job! It's what you're paid to do, Troy."

Troy glared at him, and almost imperceptibly shook his head.

Eddie closed his eyes and breathed deeply. Once calm, he said, "Get inside before I pull your petulant face off and feed it to you."

Chapter Thirty-Six

Once in the hallway, Eddie closed the door behind them, and near-silence pushed aside the noise. Eddie said, "Nicki did a good job yesterday. She recovered footwear marks from here" —he pointed to the hallway floor— "and the kitchen floor. We're free to stand wherever we please, but take care; you never know what else we might find."

Troy shrugged. "Like what? What else is gonna be on the floor?"

"Would you like me to punch you on the nose? How the hell should I know? It's just a general warning to keep your boogie fever under control until we've finished."

Troy tutted, and walked off.

Eddie growled and swung a frustrated fist at the spot he'd vacated.

The sitting room curtains were still closed from their examination last night – trying to shield themselves from interested bystanders. Now it was fine to pull them open again, and when he did, everything that had been so subdued last night came to life and grew a fresh and vibrant layer of colour. Eddie saw blood on the doorframe – something everyone had missed last night as they worked by torchlight and the dull uplighters scattered on each wall.

He came in close, hoping for fingerprint ridge detail in the blood, but it was just a contact smear. But that in itself was interesting. It meant the killer had left via the dining room and the sitting room, then out into the hallway and finally out of the front door. She didn't leave the kitchen directly into the hallway and out.

Why was that? Eddie asked himself.

Perhaps she wanted to do a quick search for any valuables before she left? Eddie took his time looking at the room, and knew that nothing had been disturbed, and as far as valuables were concerned, he knew Bolton didn't have any of the laptops or tablets, or expensive phones, or gaming equipment that an intruder would like to take. Bolton had a wall full of books, that was his entertainment; that, and whatever shit he was watching on the TV.

Eddie turned off the TV, sick of seeing the woman's face paused halfway through a blink.

Doc's valuables were of a different type than the youth of today craved: intellectual. He doubted very much that the attacker had a penchant for first edition Brontës or the complete works of Shakespeare and Wordsworth, or lots of books by some Italian guy whose name he couldn't pronounce.

And that was another reason why Eddie thought it was a targeted attack and not some burglar hoping for spoils.

He smiled. "She left this way because there was a girl out front delivering pizza."

"What?" Troy shouted from the kitchen.

"Nothing." He could see it. The panic in the killer's eyes as someone knocked on the front door. He could picture her holding her breath in here by the doorframe as the pizza girl plucked up the courage to enter the house and wander up the hallway where she could see into the kitchen. "That's when the killer left," he said.

Eddie walked through the antique-filled dining room and stood at the entrance to the kitchen, watching Troy work. He had his LED torch out and he was going over the worktop with a squirrel brush and some aluminium powder. A cloud of it hung around him like his bad mood had. Particles of dust sparkled in the torchlight, and Eddie watched the concentration in Troy's eyes. He liked to see people concentrate on a job.

He flicked on his own torch and then edged into the kitchen, keeping the unfocused beam pointing straight down onto the floor, and now that the stepping plates were gone, he saw more very faint red stains on the tiles as he approached the breakfast island. Again, they weren't drops; they were contact smears, and when he took out his magnifying glass and closed right up on them, he expected to see more Nike Cortez. But these had a stippled pattern, like leather glove marks, or like—

"Latex glove marks up here," said Troy. "Or nitrile."

"Latex," Eddie said, thinking. "Latex or nitrile here too."

"Why was she on the floor?"

A good question, Eddie thought. And not only that, it suggested that Troy was engaged with the scene. It wasn't about ticking a row of boxes on a sheet of paper any more; it wasn't about just finishing this 'shit' and moving on. Sure, there were boxes that needed ticking, but no one knew what the questions were yet – this kind of scene work was a blank sheet where the CSI not only ticked the boxes, but created the questions leading to those boxes.

And that was when the other box presented itself. He almost remarked on it there and then, but no; Eddie wanted to stand off and let Troy sink deeper into the scene to see if the little shit was as good as he thought he was.

"Unless they'd been involved in a fight? It would explain why the killer was on the floor." Troy raised his eyebrows. "The stabbing might even have been accidental."

Eddie nodded. "What else?"

"Is there anything else?"

"I have no idea."

Troy thought. "We have glove marks. You and Nicki got the footwear marks last night. You took a DNA mini-tape of the front door handle, too—"

"Oh, you read the report, then?"

"How about we powder the glove marks on the floor, and try swabbing them for DNA?"

Eddie folded his arms and thought about it. "Good call. Do it."

Troy pulled a yellow marker from the camera bag and stood it with a grey scale beside a stain, just beyond the breakfast island, the furthest of the bloody marks on the floor. "Is there much chance?" He photographed it from a distance – a location shot – followed by several detailed shots.

"One in five hundred."

"How the hell do you know that?" Troy took a new squirrel brush and began powdering the dried stain. He kept the marker and scale in place, and rephotographed it.

"We used to do it years ago with burglary scenes. You'd powder up the offender's glove marks and try to get DNA from it. If the offender had rubbed their face or their forehead while they wore the gloves, we hoped to get the DNA from transferred skin cells. Good idea – but lousy in practice. And it cost a fortune."

Troy found the glove mark surrounding the red contact stain on the floor, and moistened a plain sterile swab. He worked it into the powdered mark, staying clear of Doc's blood, hoping to swab only the offender's cells. "When will you get the results?"

Eddie stood and arched his back. He wanted a cigarette, and his mouth was dry, but they were on a roll, and he didn't want to stop the kid now things were going so well. "I can get that swab turned around in five days." He knew he could get it turned around in two if he paid the premium.

"I didn't mean the results from this. I meant the—"

"Oh, the drugs test. I thought you didn't want to talk about it?"

"When?"

Eddie pulled back the sleeve of the white scene suit and looked at his watch. "Another two or three hours." He leaned against the island. "Not worried, are you?"

"Nope. Not in the slightest."

"Good." Beneath the mask, Eddie grinned.

Once Troy had written out the evidence bag and dropped the swab into it, he asked, "Can we take off the masks now?"

Eddie shook his head. "Better not. I don't know if there'll be any further DNA work here." He was amazed; this was a different person, as though Troy had rented out his skin for someone decent to live in for the day. Gone were the endless boring snipes about him being younger than anyone else outside of junior school; gone was the gum-chewing swaggering arsehole, and in had stepped someone who did the job with a little more diligence, and someone who didn't seem interested in challenging Eddie at every chance.

Troy nodded, and closed the kit box. "There is one other thing I noticed."

"Oh?"

Chapter Thirty-Seven

Back in the office, Nicki glanced at her watch at the same time as Eddie had glanced at his. Sid looked at her from his desk and smiled. She smiled back, gave a polite nod to go with it, and put her head back down. She clenched her cheeks, wondering whether it was the right thing to do. And then she remembered words her father spoke several years ago, that there was no room for sentiment when it came to career advancement. She could see him now, his hands gently on her shoulders, thumbs circling.

She hoped it had worked to ease his nerves, because it sure as hell did nothing for hers. In fact it irritated her. "When you get ammunition, use it. That's what it's there for." And when she'd tried to challenge his statement with reason, the thumbs had pressed in just a little bit harder than was really necessary.

She stood, ready to leave the office, but Sid looked up at her, pinning her to the spot with his stare. His face was like a silent challenge, and Nicki swallowed.

"Everything alright, Nicki?"

"Tea?" she asked.

Sid sat back and folded his arms. "I'm okay, thanks. You go ahead, though."

She smiled. "I will, I think, actually." She felt his eyes all over her as she walked down the full length of the office. How the hell could he know what she was doing?

"Nicki?"

She stopped, and turned to him, trying to build a reassuring smile in the time it took her to rotate. But it grew twisted, malformed.

"You sure you're okay? You look a bit green."

She laughed, one of those polite laughs from the same box as the polite nod. "I'm fine." She made herself walk slowly out of the office, forgetting all about making tea, trying to keep her walk slow and casual when she really wanted to run.

She rounded the corridor into the CID office and noticed her hands were sweating. All the people; all looking at her, all judging her. To the right was a row of small individual offices with floor-to-ceiling windows, like a terrace of greenhouses.

The blinds in one of them moved, and then the door opened.

She walked towards him.

* * *

Eddie stood with his arms folded, willing Troy on.

Troy faced the patio doors that looked out onto the expansive garden. Next to them was a row of coat hooks on the wall. Here in this *Ideal Homes* exhibition of a modern kitchen, all glass and chrome, these black cast-iron Victorian things with their elaborate swirls and cascades looked out of place. On the hooks were three or four coats; one a bodywarmer with a million pockets, and next to it, on top of the others, a blue raincoat with orange slashes down the sleeves. Below the hooks were a pair of Wellington boots and an iron bootjack.

"Over there. It might belong to the housekeeper, that Mrs Watkins. There's a coat. Small."

Beneath the mask, Eddie beamed. "Hey, so there is!"

Before going to the coat, Eddie cast a focused beam low across the floor and could see nothing of interest; impressions of feet inside socks, something that looked like it could be a pair of slippers, but no Nike Cortez. That was good news because it meant walking over there wouldn't destroy any evidence, but it was also a conundrum: it meant that Bolton must have hung up the coat himself.

Did he know his killer?

Troy stood before it, clamped gloved fingers on the cuffs and the bottom of the coat. His gloves came away damp. "It rained that night, didn't it?" he said, looking at Eddie. The top of the coat, across the back and the shoulders, was dry; the rainwater had made its way south, and the high ambient temperature inside the house had dried the rest of it, leaving only the lower extremities still damp. "It could be the murderer's."

"Could be. It's definitely not Bolton's; far too small. And I doubt Mrs Watkins would have left it. Good spot, Troy. Let's open it up on some brown paper and see if there's anything in the pockets, eh?"

Troy nodded. "I'll just photograph it first."

Inside, Eddie cheered. Now that the bad Troy had gone, Eddie could see that beneath the façade there was actually a diligent examiner. His hopes for him grew, and he stepped back out of the way as Troy took aim and fired off a few shots.

Once on brown paper, they photographed the coat again – even checked out whether there was a name tag anywhere inside – but they came up with nothing. "Still good for wearer DNA though," Troy said.

It came out as a cross between a statement and question, so it showed he was still unsure despite his claims that he was the best examiner in the office – he had certificates! But Eddie gave him the benefit – perhaps it meant that he was stepping aside to let Eddie take that decision? He didn't know for sure, but Eddie chalked up another plus in the kid's favour.

"Okay. Let's see if there's anything in the pockets, then."

Chapter Thirty-Eight

Sid was leaning back against his desk, feet crossed on the floor, one of them tapping to an angry tune only he heard. His arms were folded and his face looked sour, like he'd bitten into a chocolate bar and discovered it wasn't chocolate at all.

The doors opened; when Nicki rounded the bend and saw him, she stopped short.

"What have you done, Nicki?"

No polite smile this time. In fact, she bypassed denial and went straight for justification and defence. "Someone needs to bring this office into the current century, Sid."

"And that's your job, is it?"

The beginnings of a sneer spoiled her prearranged fury. "My job is none of your fucking business. Understand?"

"I understand that perfectly. But I hope you know what you're doing."

"Is that a threat?"

Sid's own effort at a smile failed. "I don't do threats, dear," he said.

The office door barged open and Eddie and Troy bounded in, sharing a joke as though they were best drinking buddies. Troy clutched an evidence bag and a knife tube. He strode to his desk, oblivious to the atmosphere hanging like a fog in the midst of the office. The temperature was verging on frosty, but he was glowing. "You did great—" Eddie stopped. He looked between Sid and Nicki. "Everything okay?"

Still looking at Nicki, Sid said, "*He* does the threats round here." Sid's arms dropped; he looked relieved that Eddie was back, but there was still tension in his face. "I need a paracetamol."

"What's up?" Eddie dropped the camera bag on a desk. "Been stealing each other's nail polish again?"

"Ask her."

Eddie looked at Nicki. She swallowed and took a pace back.

"Someone going to tell me what the fuck is going on?"

Nicki stuck her chest out, nose in the air, eyes half closed. "So I know you made Troy have a drugs test today."

"Is that right?" Eddie's face grew serious. "And did you know you've now spread confidential information around the fucking office?"

"What was that?" Troy said, dumping the evidence sacks on his desk.

"And furthermore," she continued, "I know that the drugs test was false. It was bogus."

Troy joined the loose circle. He looked at Nicki, who stood defiant. "How the hell do you know— how the hell did you know I had a drugs test at all?"

"I just do."

Troy grabbed her arm. "You spied on me?"

"I was trying… I found out that it was a ploy, actually. To frighten you into quitting drugs, Troy."

Eddie slapped a hand over his face. "You just keep digging that hole deeper, don't you? Shut up, Nicki. You can't broadcast private information—"

"Is it true?" Troy asked Eddie.

"Is what true?"

"That it was bogus," he said, voice only just above a whisper.

"Well, since you used someone else's pee it doesn't really matter, does it?"

Troy's eyes widened further, "*You* were spying on me too?"

"No, but—"

Troy took a pace forward and punched him in the stomach. Eddie's legs buckled and he hit the floor on his knees, clutching his guts.

Nicki screamed.

Sid hid his face behind shaking hands.

Troy shouted, "I was just getting to like you, you bastard!"

Eddie looked up and coughed. "Good punch, mate." He struggled to rise, holding on to a desk for support.

"It was bogus?" Troy looked distraught.

"So what? It worked, didn't it? Look how well you performed today. We haven't had a cross word and you've been—"

"I can't believe you'd trick me like that."

"It was no trick; it was—"

"It was so bogus, Eddie," Nicki said.

"Shut up, you!"

"There's more to come," said Sid, peering around one of his hands.

Everyone turned to face Nicki.

She cleared her throat. "I felt compelled to report the matter—"

"To Weismann," growled Eddie.

"To Mr Crawford," Nicki said. "You left me no choice. Really. The way you run this office is disgraceful, actually."

"You slimy back-stabbing bitch!" Sid yelled.

"Sid," Eddie said. "She's not slimy."

Eddie took a stride towards her, his eyes screwed into slits. "We may work in a slightly unorthodox way in this office. It makes sure everyone is treated well and fairly; it makes sure that everyone is given the help they need to succeed. Of course," he said, "there are short cuts. But you'll find they never fucking work." He raised his eyebrows. "Never. You've broken that delicate mechanism, and now we have what?" He slowly turned, looking at the hurt and betrayed faces of his crew, "Anarchy."

Eddie got into her face so closely that he could smell her sweat. Without taking his eyes off her, he pointed to Troy. "I respect him. He punched me in the guts, and he got his point across to me, face to face. He didn't run and tell poison tales. Yes, he's got problems, but we were working through them, and making sure they didn't affect his performance at work…" He shrugged. "But now what? What's going to happen to Troy now you've declared him a junkie to Crawford?

He stepped back. "Have you any idea how to handle people? Have you any idea what you've donc?"

"I'll tell you what she's done."

Everyone turned around, and Kenny strode up the office. He pointed an angry finger at her. "Don't ever expect me to work with you again, love."

Nicki sighed, frustration making her growl.

"Fuck's sake," shouted Eddie. "Now what?"

"She came with me to the post mortem, and in the middle of the examination I turned around and she wasn't fucking there!"

"So I don't like dead bodies," Nicki said. "I'm okay with them at scenes, but I'd prefer not to engage with them at a PM."

Eddie laughed. "'Prefer not to engage with them?' This is the Major Crime Unit, love – we deal in death every bastard day!"

"I will not back down, Eddie, so stop trying to intimidate me. I had other things to attend to today, Kenny. Better things. I'm sorry, I should have—"

"Piss off," Kenny shouted. "You've been set on getting your feet under the table ever since you came here, and all you've done is make waves. You have no idea how to blend in; you have no idea how to treat people! Now leave me the fuck alone. I mean it." He turned to Eddie. "Don't shackle me with her again."

Nicki flushed red, and sweat popped out onto her forehead. "There will be consequences to this—"

"Oh, I can't stand this." Sid shrivelled into a ball of angst and rolled out of the office.

"Sid?" Eddie stared at Nicki. "See what you've done? There will be consequences, alright; if you've upset him—"

"The consequences will affect you, Eddie." Crawford stood in the doorway. "And they will affect you too, Troy."

Eddie closed his eyes, shook his head.

"Nicki, are you alright?"

Nicki breathed out and the relief on her face turned it red. There was a tear in the corner of one of her eyes. "Dad, I just can't—" Nicki planted a hand over her mouth, but it was too late; the horse had not only just bolted, it had set fire to the stables too, and then hurled grenades up and down the paddock. Her eyes flicked around the room, and everyone stared back at her, disbelief on their faces.

Chapter Thirty-Nine

"Dad?" Eddie said. He looked at Crawford, incredulous. "Fucking *Dad*?"

Crawford glared at Nicki, lips pursed.

"I'm sorry," Nicki whimpered.

"I thought necrophilia was illegal." Kenny barged Eddie out of the way. "So you've been greasing the wheels for your daughter to—" He gasped, pointed at Crawford. "You were prepping her to take over this office. Weren't you?"

Eddie nudged him. "I think you mean nepotism, Kenny."

"Who gives a flying shit? She's here to steal your job, for Christ's sake!"

Eddie stared between Crawford and Nicki. "It would explain why you run to Daddy every time I try to discipline my office."

"I was merely protecting Troy's—"

"Leave me out of this, you fucking cow. You used me to get one over on him!" Troy shoved her out of his way and walked down the office to the door, where Crawford grabbed him.

"You dare touch my daughter like that—"

"Whoa, whoa," Eddie shouted. "You" —he pointed at Crawford— "take your fucking hands off him before I put you in a coma, and you" —he turned to Nicki— "you want this job so much that you're prepared to hang Troy out to dry? You despicable piece of shit."

"Collins," shouted Crawford.

"Shut the fuck up, you." He looked at Nicki again. "You want the keys to this sinking ship? Is that what you want? Is that why you've fawned over me, is that why you've reported me? You are sick. Take them, they're yours."

"What?"

"You heard. If you want control, fucking take it." He looked from her to Crawford. "I'll be fucked if you two clowns think I'm going to constantly bow down to you. Forget it. I'll send you a thimble." He smiled. "My way of helping to bail you out. But on one condition: you leave him alone."

Nicki looked from Troy to her father, her eyes sparkling, and she was filled with nervous energy that would have seen her dancing up and down the office had she been alone. Crawford breathed deeply, relief giving him the higher ground that dignity commands. "I think you're making the right decision. It would have ended bitterly if we'd taken this through disciplinary."

"Disciplinary?" asked Eddie. "If anyone should be disciplined, it's you two."

"Falsifying a drugs test… Could look very bad for you, Eddie."

"I'm used to looking bad. I have my own naughty chair in PSD. Them upstairs have been looking for someone like you to come along and force me out for years."

"You forced yourself out the moment you engineered an illegal drugs test—"

"Listen. Think about it; you'll ruin that kid's career for no reason. He was getting back on track, no big brother breathing down his neck, clean record, able to move on. And he has the makings of a bloody good CSI. Is all this worth it? I'll go, but leave the kid out of it."

Nicki – lips tight, arms folded – stared at him, shaking her head.

He snorted. "Why would you want to ruin him? Vindictive, perhaps? Selfish? Jealous?" Eddie's eyebrows rose at that one, and Nicki turned away. "You could have done well for yourself without Daddy's help. You could have *earned* your status instead of being handed it – that's a fucking insult, by the way. And you know what; you know how much trust people have in you now? None. Not a fucking droplet; no one from CID will trust you, and none of your staff will either. That sinking ship I mentioned? You're just an empty figurehead."

"Actually, I think I know how to handle staff a damned sight better than—"

"It's not over yet," Kenny barked at her. "If he goes, I go."

"Kenny," Nicki cooed.

"I mean it. I ain't working for you, love. And I ain't having your dad tugging my strings through you, either." He grabbed his coat off the back of his chair. "So fuck you very much. You'll find the PM disk in my tray. Upload it yourselves, if you can bear to look at the images."

Nicki stood resolutely at the end of the office. Her tongue flicked at dry lips, her knuckles were white, shoulders tense. "Kenny, I mean it; this is your last chance."

"Shove it up your arse." Kenny barged past Crawford without so much as a look. Troy followed him out of the office.

"Troy! You get back here now. You hear me?"

The door closed behind him.

No one could have blamed Eddie for grinning triumphantly right then. But he felt too hollow. "Look what you've done. Your new kingdom consists of… you. Congratulations."

"Eddie, don't be hasty."

Eddie pointed to Troy's desk, to the evidence bag on it. "There's a coat in there," he said. "It belongs to a female, and I don't think it's Mrs Watkins, on account of the steak knife Troy found in the inside pocket. You should submit it to the lab; have them check it for wearer DNA. You'll need to fill out an MG21, okay? DI Benson or DS Khan will be able to help you with possible suspects and where to go from here. Listen to him," he said to Nicki, "he'll help you with the paperwork if you need it. And the swabs from the knife—"

"What's going on?"

Eddie looked up at Weismann, who now stood next to Crawford. He ignored him. "The swabs from the knife go on a 21 too. There'll be scene work if we… there'll be scene work if he identifies a suspect. There'll be lots of work, okay, so you'll need help from division—"

"I said what's going on?"

Eddie strode down the office, eyes never leaving Weismann's. "Really?" He said, coming to a halt well inside Weismann's space. "You have no idea? All this" —he swept an arm at the empty office— "is a complete surprise to you?"

"Yes. It is." He looked over Eddie's shoulder to Nicki – who clearly didn't know whether to preen herself or shit herself, and had settled on something in between – and then across to his boss, Mr Crawford – the man to whom he owed his current position. "Sir?"

Crawford gritted his teeth. "There's been a development. We need a meeting."

The office felt cold to Eddie now; strange, foreign, the way it might if he were just a visitor. Behind him was his successor; in front of him, two men in suits who probably had no idea what a crime scene looked like, let alone how to process one. But the scary thing was that these men were in control of the quality of forensic examinations across the region under the umbrella of the Major Crime Unit. It was embarrassing. It was dangerous.

But the worst thing? These people were responsible for bringing justice to victims like Doc Bolton. He pitied Doc; the odds were suddenly in favour of the criminal.

Eddie shook his head, and closed the door on a disaster waiting to happen.

Chapter Forty

Eddie walked down the stairs, the commotion in his old office a thousand light years behind him, unheard. He watched the stairs trickling backwards underneath him, his jacket slung casually over his shoulder, the cigarette lighter in its pocket thumping into his back. And then he was on the ground floor, eyes open but seeing nothing. He was thinking about Doc Bolton, about the scene and about the processing yet to be done. And he was wondering how it would all get done with a monkey and two arseholes in charge.

As he punched through the doors, Troy smashed him in the face.

Eddie fell square on his backside, sunglasses crushed in his back pocket. He looked up at Troy. "If you've broken my shades, I'm going to tie you to the gates and then open them."

Troy panted as though the adrenaline pumping through him was genuine five-star leaded petrol, circling his fists as though ready for another bout. Miss Moneypenny shouted, and there were footfalls on the marble floor as Eddie checked his jaw still worked.

Eddie looked up. Kenny held out his hand.

"Kenny," Eddie smiled, and gained his feet.

"You fucking sold me out!" Troy shouted, assuming the stance of a nineteenth-century boxer, fists curling through the air.

Eddie was about to offer the case for the defence when Moneypenny barged Troy out of the way. Eddie watched, stunned that she felt the need to do that for him, and stunned that she actually *could* do that for him.

He was mesmerised, even as Kenny slapped him on the shoulder.

"Why the hell did you let them have it?"

Eddie swivelled to Kenny. He could see his crooked bottom teeth, the grey whiskers on his flabby cheeks, and he could see the hurt in his eyes. And Eddie went cold – he hadn't considered anyone else when he'd given the mad bitch the keys. He'd made his point, and he'd walked.

The consequences were in front of him now.

"I ain't working for her, Eddie."

Eddie looked at Kenny, felt Moneypenny and Troy nearby, and heard footsteps behind him on the stairs; big clodhopping boots, the kind that Sid might wear. And he suddenly felt very hot, and very guilty. He began walking across the foyer.

"Where the fuck are you going?" Troy yelled.

"Eddie, you're letting everyone down," Kenny shouted. "Eddie!"

"Eddie," Moneypenny whispered.

Eddie stopped. Stared at the glass door which was now less than a yard away from his outstretched hand. He held his breath and turned around to see them all staring at him. To their right the security guard – the one with the bent nose that looked as though it had been broken a year or two ago – stared on, arms folded, unmoving. And then the double doors opened and Sid joined them. "What?" Eddie asked them. "You want a fucking miracle?"

"We want answers."

"Answers? Go and ask them upstairs, Kenny. They have your answers."

"That it, then? You just gonna shrug and waltz off into the sunset?"

Eddie looked at the floor. He tried to put on his sunglasses but the lenses had fallen out. He threw the frames into the rubber plant and looked at them all. "I'm sorry," he said. "I'll call you, Moneypenny."

DAY 5

Chapter Forty-One

Eddie poured coffee as Charles skulked around the corner. "Cruella leave you high and dry last night, then?"

"Stop being so petty. Her name's Wendy, and you know it. No, she stayed at her own house last night. Has to be up early this morning," Charles said. "Doctor's appointment."

"Venom top-up?"

"Eddie."

Eddie laughed, "Sorry, but you're just so easy." Eddie stirred his coffee. "Would you like tea?"

"Please."

"Earl Grey?"

"Eddie!"

"Sorry." Eddie took the smile away, folded it up and slid it into a drawer for future use, and said, "Toast?"

Charles squinted.

"What? I'm having some – thought you'd like some too."

"Two slices. Please."

"Would you be kind enough to get the butter?"

Charles opened the fridge door and bent to reach the butter.

"You know there's a thumb imprint on the top of your head, don't you?"

"Get your own bleedin' butter!" Charles stomped out of the kitchen and Eddie howled with laughter.

"I'm sorry," he squeaked. And then he laughed again.

* * *

There was always an uncomfortable silence in the lounge whenever Eddie and Charles ate together. Eddie hated sharing mealtimes with anyone – even himself. He couldn't bear the sound of someone munching or mulching food. It sent him from his usual calm persona into a rage almost instantly. There was probably a medical term for it, but he wasn't interested enough to find out.

He contemplated turning on the TV just so he could get some relief from the sound of eating, but the shit on TV was even worse, and so he sat with anger stomping across his face in time with his chewing until the toast was gone.

He looked over at his father, watching the jaw working the toast as though it were losing an arm-wrestling match with it.

The giggles in the kitchen forgotten, he said, "What's the crack with you two?"

"Me and Wendy?"

"No, you and Saddam Hussein."

Charles sighed and put down his plate. "Why do you have to be so rude all the time?"

"Because there's nothing more entertaining on the telly."

"I wish you'd get along with her. She means the world to me."

Eddie studied Charles's face for traces of humour, absolutely sure there was a punch line on its way. But no; he was serious. "Really?"

"Yes, really."

Wow. Eddie blinked. *Takes all sorts.* "She seems… She seems to be a little on the manipulative side to me, that's all. Don't you feel that? Don't you notice how domineering she is?"

"She's a lovely, warm, and caring woman, Eddie. You've forgotten what it's like to be loved."

"Loved? You and her… you're in love?"

"Well, I think we're getting there, yes."

Eddie bit his lower lip until his eyes watered. "If that's love, I'd rather shove wasps up my arse."

"Well, I'm happy. And I'd like you to be happy for me too. I'd like you to be happy *with* me." His eyes shone at Eddie. "Why can't you do that?"

Eddie looked at the carpet, shame creeping like a red tide up his neck.

"Can you do that, Eddie? For me?"

Eddie thought about saying *if ignorance is bliss, you must be very fucking happy*. "Course I can. I'm happy for you, Dad."

Charles didn't let his eyes roam; they stayed locked on Eddie. "Are you ashamed of me? Or are you worried for me? With Wendy, I mean? Or perhaps you're jealous, maybe you don't want to see me with another woman?"

"Come on, Dad."

"I mean it! What's wrong with you?"

"I'm not keen. Okay? On her, I mean; I'm not keen on her. There's something—"

"Like you'd know!"

Eddie looked away.

"What success have you ever had with women? Eh?"

"Dad—"

"None! No success at all. You had one woman kill herself, and another run away from you!"

Eddie stood. "Dad—"

"Proper Casanova, aren't you? And you sit there lecturing me!" Charles stood to face him; the eyes were still shiny, but so too were his wrinkled cheeks as the tears tumbled through the white whiskers. "You selfish bastard."

They stood facing each other perhaps six or eight feet apart. Not since Charles had moved in had they stared at each other with such vehemence, such animosity. Charles's old fingers crunched into a fist and then someone knocked at the door. Both ignored it; it was like a gunfight without any guns.

"Is it because you think I'm being disrespectful to your mum's memory? Is that it?"

"What? No, it's not that."

"Then what is it?"

The door banged again.

"Like I'd fucking know, right? I drive all my women away; not shy of reminding me, are you?"

"Answer the door. And then go to work, I don't want to look at you."

Eddie went to the door, calling back over his shoulder, "Better get used to me being around. I walked out yesterday." He opened the door just as Weismann was about to knock again. Eddie growled, "What the fuck do you want?"

"I want—"

Charles pulled Eddie back into the lounge. "What do you mean, you walked out? Are you crazy?"

"I was being pushed out."

"No one pushed you out, Eddie," Weismann said.

"Why do you do it, eh? Soon as life gets a bit tough, you just walk away without a care in the world."

"What the hell would you know? You abandoned ship when I was sixteen!"

"Shall I come back at another time?"

Eddie looked back to Weismann. "How about you don't come back at all?" He slammed the door.

Charles rushed to open it. "Come in. Ignore him."

"Don't let him in; he's one of them who wanted me out!"

"I didn't want you out, Eddie. I was one—"

"See," said Charles, tears still spilling down his face, "how you take everything so personally, Eddie. You've got to curb your sensibilities, boy. Toughen up a bit."

Eddie turned to Weismann. "What do you want? You can see we're in the middle of a discussion here."

"I want—"

"If you've come to ask me back, then you've wasted your time; I've had enough of that daft cow and her father."

Something approaching disgust settled on Weismann's face. He held out his hand. "Van keys."

"What?"

"You walked out with the van keys in your pocket. Or were they tucked inside your bottom lip, the one you were about trip over?"

"That's you all over," said Charles, pointing.

"Shut up." Eddie walked past Charles and headed for his bedroom. He was back moments later and tossed the keys to Weismann. "That it? That all you came round for?"

Weismann nodded. "What else?" He nodded at Charles, "I'll let myself out. Good luck."

"What do you think happened in the office yesterday?" Eddie glared at Weismann. "That we all collectively got fed up and left, and Nicki volunteered to pick up the pieces and create a new team? Wow, she really is a martyr. And you're a fool."

Weismann gently closed the door behind him, leaving Eddie looking at Charles. For a moment, neither moved and neither spoke. And then Charles said, "I'm sorry. For what I said. Your women."

Eddie looked away and sighed. "I'm sorry, too. I was just trying to look out for you. I stepped over the mark, Dad." He reached out and embraced his father.

"It's okay, son. I know you're a bit concerned; new woman on the scene, and all that. You're worried for me, I get that. But don't be. I can look after myself."

"You sure?"

Charles nodded. "You know she'll never replace your mum, don't you?"

Eddie nodded, and they pulled apart. Charles went to the kitchen. "Do you want a fresh coffee?"

"Please."

"And then you'd better go and try and get your job back."

"Nope. They barged in, Dad. That Nicki lass I told you about – her dad landed a couple of days ago. He's the new head of Major Crime, a Detective Chief Super, no less. Don't stand a chance against him and all his fucking stripes and all her snooping, undermining me at every—"

"You don't know till you try. You just going to stand back and watch them ruin what you've built up? You going to let them walk all over you and your staff? What about Sid? He won't take it well, Eddie. You have to think of your staff."

Eddie wandered off. "I'm going for a shower."

"Good lad."

Eddie whispered, "But Wendy still has a face like a warthog's ballbag."

"I heard that, you bastard!"

Chapter Forty-Two

Benson swung through the double doors into CSI, clutching a slim wad of papers. He stopped short and squinted to the far end of the office, but it was empty. The lights were on, but no one was home. He nudged open Eddie's office door, and the squeaking hinges roused Nicki, who was sitting at his desk.

"Hi," Benson said. "You seen Eddie?"

"He doesn't work here any more. I'm in charge now." She stood, swivelled towards him, and smiled. "So how can I help you, Tom?"

Benson looked at the office, how neat the filing system had become. Each of the files had a place in the ceiling-high cabinet, and there was room to spare. The nicotine stains on the window were gone, the carpet had been cleaned too. The desk… it was tidy! "Just 'Benson' will do."

She nodded.

"Where is he?"

"He resigned, actually. But I want you to know that you'll hardly notice a ripple in the quality of the forensic support this office provides."

"I need someone to accompany me on a house visit. I'm chasing a suspect and I want a forensic input on footwear."

She smacked her lips. "Would tomorrow be okay? I'm trying to arrange cover while we recruit new staff…"

Benson nearly fell over. "You mean everyone resigned? *Everyone*?"

"Like I said, you'll barely notice a ripple."

"Then I want you to come with me now. If Eddie were still in charge, he'd—"

"But he's not."

Benson turned and almost bumped into Crawford standing in the doorway.

Crawford smiled. "We'll certainly do our best to maintain our excellent customer service record. But we do ask that you bear with us during this transitional phase. Nothing to worry about."

"She said I wouldn't notice a ripple. I'm noticing."

"Barely a ripple."

Benson continued, "Nothing to worry about? Boss, this is the police, not Marks & Spencer's. I don't want platitudes; I want someone to verify a suspect's footwear. And I want it now."

"Careful, Tom."

Benson nodded his understanding. "Or I'll be next, right?" He took a small step closer to Crawford's ever-present smile. "First Jeffery Walker went, and Weismann filled his boots. Now Eddie Collins has gone – *and* his entire team." He pointed a thumb over his shoulder at Nicki. "And this young lady is suddenly in charge of a whole – and very empty – forensic department? A forensic department with no staff."

"We're working—"

"Not good enough. We're live on air right now! This isn't a fucking rehearsal. Boss." Benson brushed past Crawford as though he wasn't there. "Never mind. I'll sort out my own forensic support." He stopped on the other side of the door, and turned to face Crawford and Nicki again. "You've got until this afternoon to fill those chairs with competent CSIs, or I take this upstairs."

Crawford bent slightly until he was eye to eye with Benson. The smile never left his face as he whispered, "This young lady is my daughter. Her name is Nicki. She has a degree in management, and has been a CSI for almost three years. She's top drawer, Tom." His smile widened as Benson's mouth fell open.

"Your daughter?"

"And we have the blessing of 'them upstairs'. Tom."

"Seriously?"

Crawford nodded. "Amazing what you can achieve if you promise to save money along the way."

Nicki spoke up. "Collins broke so many rules in his efforts to run this office, Mr Benson. They're all documented. I want to run things correctly. And with the support of my co-workers in CID, I can run it well. Actually, this place could be a beacon of excellence."

"Nice words, love." Benson paused, then turned back to Crawford. "As the head of the Major Crime Unit, how could you allow this to happen? CSI is crucial – *crucial* – to our operation. And you've let them all walk so your daughter gets to wear a tiara that she isn't entitled to wear, and gets to sit in Eddie's seat? You'd sacrifice the department and Major Crime's ability to investigate homicides just so your little girl gets to live out her fantasy?"

Crawford's face darkened. He looked at Benson with contempt, and said, "Consider yourself on a written warning. Do not tell me how to run my department."

Benson looked past him to Nicki. "Your degree in management," he said, "is laudable. But it'll only take you so far. You need a team who will work with you when they really want to go home, and when they really can't stand the sight of another dead body at three in the morning. Collins might have a wonky outlook on life, but everyone in here trusted him implicitly." Benson looked up at Crawford and nodded his respect. "I'll leave you with that thought. Sir."

Chapter Forty-Three

Her mind wasn't here. It was screwing itself up into a ball as Sidmouth made another move on her. It shuddered, and it closed its eyes against him and what he was about to do to her.

In reality, she was closing the external door and walking towards her bedsit. Her mind agonising over what would happen to her tomorrow when Sidmouth called around.

She dug in her pocket for the key to her bedsit, opened the door and screamed.

"Sorry," Tony said, hands out. "Didn't mean to scare you."

"Just who the fuck do you think you are, showing up whenever you please? This is my home, Tony!"

He climbed out of the chair, picked up his overcoats and made for the door. "I am sorry. You're right." As he went to pass her in the doorway, he stopped; concern cloaked his face. "Why the tears?"

She shook her head.

"Michael?"

"No…"

Tony thought for a moment. "Sidmouth."

Jess collapsed on the bed, burying her face in the mouldy quilt until she could barely breathe. She became aware of Tony stroking her hair.

"It's okay," he whispered.

A shiver pinged up her back, and she opened her eyes. What the hell was he doing? "I'm okay," she said, pulling away. "Go make a drink, eh?"

As he got up, Tony said, "He's holding you to ransom."

She sat on the edge of the bed, her shoulders rounded, her feet twitching against the floor.

He had his back to her, seemingly watching the kettle. "He's holding something you value more than your own body. More than your pride." Tony turned around, steam rising over his shoulder, and he said, "He's going to win every time, Jess."

She sighed.

"Don't ever lose your pride, lass. It's all you've got. Once it's gone…"

She looked up; there was a distant smile on his face, his eyes focused on nothing.

"…Once it's gone, there really is nothing left to fight for."

"You sound like you're speaking from experience."

He turned back to the kettle and made the tea. As he brought hers over, he said, "Look at me. Do I look like someone who's got any fucking pride left?"

"Why don't you clean yourself up, then?"

He pointed a finger. "Ah. No. You see, this is my camouflage. It's my invisibility suit. While ever I wear this, no one takes any notice of me. They might get nervous with the homeless guy watching them, but they don't do anything, see?" He nodded his mug at her and then took up his seat, slurped tea and reached for his tobacco. "I'll always remember seeing you in that courtroom."

Jessica's feet became still.

"You had pride then. You were a proud English lady in your suit. Your hair. I always remember your hair, all fastened up, all neat. Head held high."

She watched him as he drifted back in time to recall her trial. For her, they'd been horrible weeks; each day the dread becoming heavier and darker, the smell of it more and more rank, until the very end when the judge passed his sentence. All that weight, all that darkness, all that smell of desolation, how it all crushed her until she was nothing but a shell, a husk, a dead body with a heartbeat. Breathing death.

"I was proud of you." He smiled at her, almost shyly.

The mug in her hand shook. She remembered that day as though she were reliving it; the horror of it all having gone so wrong, and the long walk back into the bridewell, and then into the back of an SSS van. Next stop, HMP Whealston.

"That day in court was bad enough," he said. "But I still think of the day that put you there."

Her vision cleared, and she stared at him, *through* him; she was back in the kitchen among the chaos, fighting it, swimming through it as it dragged her under, drowning. She hitched a breath and pictured the blood running down her arm, felt the pain in her hand. The slash wound right across the palm, down to the tendons – *a defence wound*, they'd said. *We understand,* they'd said. *Just tell us, Jess. What happened next?*

Did you wrestle the knife from him? Did you pick another from the block? What was happening, Jess, tell us. Self-defence, they'd said, nodding to each other. Manslaughter instead of murder. You'd be out in three years, maybe less.

"It was horrible," she whispered, unblinking. "Michael was screaming his lungs out. And the smoke from the oven was making my eyes sting, and my hand was throbbing, and there was blood splashing on the floor. And he was standing there with a fucking knife against his chest, and that wicked smirk on his face. As though all he had to do was threaten me and I'd melt into his arms."

Jess's teeth were bared, her lips drawn back in a snarl. "I've never hated anyone so much. I watched him twist the blade, and I saw blood on his white shirt, and I thought, *my God, he's going to do it, he's really going to do it*, and I shivered, and I remember holding my breath, wondering what would happen next. And I didn't know what to do. Should I call his bluff and tell him to fuck off, see what he did? Or should I relent, should I say 'okay, let's go, just take the fucking knife away, Sebastian, you're scaring me'?

"But I didn't say anything. I watched his black eyes, I saw the smirk on his face, and I wanted to push that blade all the way home, and then push another one in for good measure. I wanted to kill the bastard; I wanted him fucking dead so he could never come back and threaten me, or try to steal my child. I wanted him dead so that I could sleep well for the first time since we split.

"The room was spinning, the pain throbbing, the smell was vile, burning food and fear. I was being crushed like they crushed me in the courtroom later. And all I could see was him sneering, and all I could hear was Michael screaming—"

"And the smoke alarm—"

The cup slipped from her hand and she screamed.

Chapter Forty-Four

She was desperate not to let him see her face. She was desperate not to look at him.

Tony almost fell out of his chair. "What?"

She stood, swiping her hands across her wet jeans. "Fucking hot. Get me a cloth."

Tony patted her legs with a wrung-out tea towel while she held an arm below her nose and wept hot tears, waving her hand to cool the scald.

"It's okay," he whispered again.

"I'm okay, I'm okay." She pushed him away.

Panic over, he tossed the cloth into the sink and refilled the kettle. "Frightened the shit out of me then."

Jessica's eyes were wide, unseeing, full of the past and full of tears.

He turned, arms folded again. "And then?"

She didn't see him; she was still seeing the past. He coughed, and she blinked awake. "What?"

"And what happened then?"

"I left him. I just turned around and went into the bedroom. I went because I didn't want him to corner me again; I couldn't stand the thought of being responsible for my own future – back with him and his fists, or alone with Michael and the ghosts of him and his sneer. So I left it in the lap of the gods. In the end it turned out I *was* responsible for my own future. For all our futures."

Tony made fresh drinks, but he could have been walking around naked for all Jess knew. She stared blindly at nothing, her mind bringing her back out of the bedroom, holding Michael in her arms, one injured hand dripping blood down her jeans.

Stopping right in front of Sebastian.

He was three-quarters of the way onto his back, the blade that he'd held at his chest lying on the floor next to his right hand, and a growing red wave of blood ruining his beautiful white shirt. It turned the stitching around the breast pocket red as it crept across his chest and dripped onto the floor, soaking into the torn lino, unstoppable. It was completely unstoppable. Like time.

His eyes were half closed, but still they laughed at her, still his sneer tormented her.

Michael screamed in her face and the smoke alarm shredded her thoughts, and there was her ex-husband on the floor. "Good riddance," she whispered as the smoke alarm stopped. Her ears buzzed.

She became aware of Michael struggling in her arms, and she had no choice but to put him down back in his room. He went stratospheric. But Jess peered through the noise and somehow managed to dial three-nines.

"Police," she'd said. The last free word she'd ever utter. *Where's the knife?* the operator asked. *Keep your son away from the knife, keep him safe.*

"Worst advice I was ever given," she said.

Tony was enraptured; he hadn't moved in ten minutes as he lived it all with her.

"My fingerprints in blood on the murder weapon."

"You'd think they'd take that into consideration."

She smiled, free of the past for the time being, back here in the shitty little bedsit with a tramp for company. "You'd think so. They played the tape back. The operator never told me to move the knife." She shrugged. "She didn't. I brought that upon myself. She told me to put distance between it and my son, to keep him safe, and I did that by putting the knife out of his reach. I grabbed it and moved it."

Tears ran into the creases of her dry lips. "I never was any good at following instructions.

Tony threw her mug into the bin; the handle had broken off when it hit the floor. He mopped up the rest of her cold tea using the cloth he'd dabbed on her leg. He had probably been talking to her, she realised later, but she'd not heard anything other than that smoke alarm from twelve years ago. It had been a shrill, piercing sound that drove away all reason. Just how was anyone supposed to think straight with that thing going off?

"It's funny," she said as Tony put on his CAT hat, "I never realised it before."

"What?"

"The smoke alarm."

"What about it?"

"It stopped. All by itself."

Tony dragged his coat on, shrugging into it. "It's what they do. They only ring for—"

"It was like I'd gone deaf. I could hear myself breathing again; I could hear myself moaning at the pain in my hand. I could hear Michael talking as well as screaming."

He stared at her, absorbed.

"The oven was turned off. I didn't do that."

Tony continued to stare at her, beard twitching slightly. And then his eyes moved away and he licked his lips. "I guess he did it before he stabbed himself, eh?"

I'm sure it was high on his to-do list. Kill myself. Oh wait, turn off the fucking oven first. She nodded to herself, shrugged, and said, "I suppose he must have."

"Make sure you've got all the bits of broken cup up before you start walking round here in bare feet." He opened the door. "And remember what I said about Sidmouth. Time to get your pride back, Jess."

Chapter Forty-Five

Eddie climbed into the Discovery, cigarette hanging from slack lips, and mind chasing its tail about the future.

He thought the visit from Weismann was very interesting indeed. Strange that the head of CSI at Major Crime would come all the way out here for the keys to a van that no one would need to use in the near future. "It was a recce," he told himself as he started the engine. He wondered what excuse Weismann would use for his next visit.

He wondered two more things to such a degree that he forgot to put the car in gear, and just sat there chewing over them. How were the others doing, and when would things get back to normal?

They need to, soon – for everyone's sake.

Perhaps he ought to go and see the top dog and explain what happened. Surely someone must have a brain cell they could borrow just for today? No way could MCU operate without a dedicated CSI department, and everyone knew it. They'd be shocked. Surely.

Eddie wasn't sure at all, actually. Crawford obviously thought that Major Crime needed CSI, but his predecessor, Francis Cooper, had tried to obliterate the department. Eddie smiled, reminiscing about how Cooper had tried to obliterate him, but the department had just happened to be in the way.

All this thinking was for another time, because right now the purpose of Eddie starting the car finally made itself known, and he selected reverse gear just as a plain blue Corsa parked right behind him.

Eddie put the car back into park and opened the door, expecting to see Weismann again, but it was Benson who climbed out.

"Thought I could smell shit," Eddie said, straight-faced.

"What the hell happened to your department?"

"Turned out that it wasn't my department at all. I was only borrowing it. Now it belongs to your boss's daughter. Probably a birthday gift. Easier to look after than a pony or a puppy."

Benson shook his head, hands on hips. "You really are so full of shit. In fact, I never realised just how full of shit one man could be."

"You want a mirror?"

"Very funny. Get in; you're coming to a scene with me."

"But I'm off the books."

"No, you're not. You might be out of MCU CSI, but you're still in West Yorkshire Police. So start earning your money. Get in."

* * *

Eddie flicked the cigarette end out of Benson's side window. "Do you know anything about Facebook?"

"What? What do you want to play with that shit for?"

"My dad got himself a woman by playing out on Facebook."

"You want a woman?"

Eddie sighed. This was much harder than he'd expected. "Forget women. Do you know about Facebook?"

"Not really. I was never much of a conversationalist. I prefer keeping myself to myself. You know me: shrinking violet."

Eddie looked across at him, unsure if he was just taking the micky.

"I never saw the need to advertise what I had for dinner, and I hate kittens and puppy videos. I suppose you need to ask a youth."

"Thank you for your wisdom, Glasshopper."

"So tell me why Nicki has cleaned your office and put her name on the door."

"You're joking – me and those stains go back a long way." He sighed. "I'm fed up of thinking about it. Daft bitch wants the hassle of my job, she can have it. I'm not going to talk about it." For the next ten minutes, Eddie filled Benson in about the drugs test, and how it became public knowledge thanks to Nicki's big mouth, and how Troy now felt the need to punch him every time he laid eyes on him. His jaw still ached.

Benson finally got a word in. "I asked *her* to do this, you know. She told me to come back tomorrow."

"What *are* we doing, exactly?"

Benson entered Beeston, cruised into the McDonald's drive-thru, and got them a couple of coffees. In the car park, as he added three sugars, he said, "Khan and his team are still working the twenty-odd people Marchant represented. He's less than halfway through." He tutted. "And he has seven staff working it with him." He looked at Eddie. "Seven. Back in the day, we'd have rattled that lot off and been in the boozer since Tuesday."

"How I miss the good old days."

"Why do you always have to be so sarcastic?"

"Because I find talking straight very boring. No fun at all."

"You just did it – talked straight."

"And I was right; it was no fun at all. Anyway, enough of this bollocks, how far have you got with your end of the shitty stick?"

Benson put the lid on his coffee and took a slurp. "I had four to look at, remember?"

Eddie lit another cigarette and opened the window.

"Why don't you take up vaping instead of smoking that stuff?"

"Because it annoys you. Now tell me, before I beat you to death."

Benson wound down his own window. "Of the four, one was a woman out on licence; one was a rapist-killer who didn't have an alibi – but it turned out he was in London the day Marchant had open throat surgery. So he *does* have an alibi now. Erm, one was inside, and the last one was a certified fruitloop."

"So that leaves the woman."

"Correct."

"You could have just said that we were going to see a woman. It would have been quicker."

"Are you in a rush?"

"No, but—"

"Well, shut up then."

"You said the woman didn't look fit enough to swing an axe."

"I know. And the axe-thief was a man. But she has to know something, doesn't she?"

Eddie shrugged. "I don't know. I just keep thinking about Doc Bolton and the woman's shoes we found at his scene."

"Small feet, you said. Not necessarily—"

"No, not necessarily a female's, granted."

"Well, let's go shake a tree, eh?"

Chapter Forty-Six

Eddie was thinking about Doc Bolton's scene again, and about the Nike Cortez trainer marks they'd found in blood on the kitchen floor. How small they were. And it struck him what a strange crime it was: women rarely stab someone to death unless they're being threatened. It was a classic domestic killing scenario. But it wasn't often you'd find that kind of death outside of a marital ding-dong.

He wondered about the robbery – or rather, about the fact that there *was* no robbery so far as they could tell.

It's personal. Has to be.

Having avoided the potholes along Elland Road, they were now waiting to turn right onto Cemetery Road. A lorry passed them, then another. Benson tapped his steering wheel as a bus drove past and indicated to stop.

A woman wearing a beanie hat and a red t-shirt ran across the road in front of them, also aiming for the bus stop. Eddie watched as the bus set off again, and the woman came to a halt seconds later, bent over in defeat, hands on her knees.

Benson looked left and then right, and made a dash for it, heading up the hill towards Beeston. But without warning he slammed on the brakes, and Eddie's seatbelt locked. Tyres squealed behind them, and angry drivers sounded their horns. Eddie looked across. "What's up?"

Benson indicated right and tried to spin the car around in the middle of the road.

"The fuck are you doing? This isn't Miami Vice!"

"I saw him." Benson revved the motor, both hands pulling the wheel as hard right as they could, edging out into oncoming traffic, oblivious to the cars behind him still sounding their horns.

"Who?"

A van coming towards them stopped and waved Benson round.

"Anytime you're ready is good with me," Eddie said.

"The cat man." Benson screwed the little car's engine through each gear. "On the bus that went past." He indicated left and sped down Top Moor Side. "The man with the CAT hat. Top deck."

"He was on the bus?"

Benson ignored Eddie, bounced over a mini roundabout and down Domestic Street where the bus was already indicating to pull away from another bus stop. He pulled the car in front and got out, slamming the door.

People going about their business stopped, watching with mouths open. Some got out their phones and began recording. It was the done thing these days – trying to catch out the coppers and ridicule them on social media.

"Bell end," Eddie said, following. "You're too old to play Starsky and Hutch!" he yelled, but Benson was already climbing aboard the bus. When Eddie caught up, the driver had his arms folded, and Benson was walking towards the rear. Eddie hopped up the step and asked the driver to close the doors behind him and to keep them closed.

The driver shrugged, flicked a switch and the doors closed as Eddie climbed the steps to the top deck. He looked at them all. No one was wearing a yellow baseball cap. Those who didn't have their eyes down concentrating on a book, or had earphones in listening to some cool tunes, studied him, wondering what the hell was happening. "Has anyone seen a man wearing a yellow baseball cap?" he asked, and heard Benson echoing his question on the lower deck.

A kid put his hand up.

Eddie nodded.

The kid pointed out of the window. Eddie followed his finger and saw a man running along an alleyway, saw the tiniest glimpse of a yellow cap just before he was swallowed by a spinney of trees. "Was he on this bus?"

The kid nodded. "I got on with him up Beeston Hill."

Eddie raced back down the stairs, yelling, "Open the doors, open the doors!"

He had to wait a second or two and then he was out, vaguely aware that Benson was behind him. By the time he reached the pavement at the back of the bus, he was already out of breath. And then he rushed across the road, ignoring the shouts and gestures from angry drivers, and sprinted towards the alleyway, running through bushes and trees. As he ran, he saw broken bottles, needles, and junk lining the path. At the far end, the bushes and trees stopped. And so did Eddie, next to a series of concrete bollards put there to prevent kids on stolen motorbikes using the path as a short cut.

To his left was another path running through a viaduct arch; straight in front, a path running into a housing estate; and to his right, a third path that ran into a light industrial estate.

He panted, scanning each one.

He heard slow, heavy footfalls behind him, and a few seconds later Benson came to a halt at his side, breathing hard, sounding like he was blowing bubbles into a glass of milk with a straw. "You sound like shit," Eddie said, throat and legs on fire, lungs having come straight out of ten minutes in the microwave.

Benson grunted, and eventually said, "Fuck." Thirty seconds later, he finished the sentence with, "You."

* * *

Benson pulled up outside a long, dreary terrace of Victorian houses, mostly converted into bedsits and used as cash cows by absent landlords.

They climbed out, and Eddie found himself staring over the road at a pub car park. He'd dealt with a murder there a few years ago. A shiver ran up his back, and he turned to watch Benson slowly climbing the concrete steps to the front door. He rang the panel of half a dozen buzzers, but even from here Eddie could see the wires hanging out like a frizzed-up hair style. Benson banged on the door but got no reply. And when he tried the door, it was locked. He turned and shrugged at Eddie before returning to the car. "We'll try again tomorrow."

"Literally cannot wait."

Chapter Forty-Seven

She sat still in the near-silence for a whole minute, contemplating Tony's words – especially the last few: *get your pride back, Jess.*

Easier said than done. But not impossible.

Jess was sure of two things right now: first, the police would soon come knocking on her door; there were murders now that she was the perfect suspect for, and so why wouldn't they come? Of course they would, and it wouldn't be long; today or tomorrow, perhaps.

And second: they'd convince themselves that she was guilty of those murders because she had the perfect motive: payback. It didn't matter what you called it, they'd find a way to make it fit her, like they had before.

But Jess was about to reclaim her pride. She'd be fucked by all the demons in hell before she'd go to prison again. The plan grew in her mind from the seeds Tony planted: *get your pride back, Jess.*

She grabbed her beanie hat, slammed the door behind her, and caught sight of him catching a bus that was heading into a traffic jam. She ran down the hill, hoping to get to the next stop before the bus did. But she didn't make it. She was almost alongside when it just seemed to float away from the bus stop and left her flapping and gasping for breath.

The bus trundled down Top Moor Side, crushed by a glacier of traffic that was slow, but not quite slow enough for her to catch up. A small dark car squealed past. Someone was in a hurry.

She jogged to a mini-roundabout at the top of Domestic Street just as the car swerved in front of the bus, and she saw Tony get off it and dodge his way through the traffic behind. He disappeared from view up the alleyway towards Balm Walk. There was a choice of footpaths there, but she knew he'd slither under the viaduct and away towards the city centre. And that was where she placed her bet, and began jogging.

She arrived at the junction of paths at about the same time as a tall man and a fat man – coppers, obviously, and both out of breath – and kept to the shadows, knowing that Tony was long gone. Eventually, the two men turned and left. She looked at the viaduct, annoyed that she'd missed him. Still, it would keep. She'd find out where he lived sooner or later.

Chapter Forty-Eight

Eddie chose not to drive home.

He had some thinking to do first, but strangely he found himself in the car park of Killingbeck Police Station – a place he'd vowed never to visit again. He looked up at the roofline, at the weeds growing out of the gutter, and the fat pigeons gossiping on the apex.

Everyone assumed that being on the top floor of any police station meant you'd made it, that you were the top dog and on top dollar. But there was a room on the top floor of Killingbeck police station that wasn't like that at all.

It was spacious – providing there was only one of you working in it. Not quite so spacious if there were three of you in there. And the view through the only window into the courtyard below wasn't exactly resplendent: you got an AC motor above and a water pipe just below it. Either way, the window wouldn't open because of the pipe and even if it did, you'd get bombarded by pigeon shit. And it was such an awkward window to get to that it hadn't been cleaned since the station was built in the late eighties.

The room number was GD13; someone had modified it slightly to read GOD. Eddie knocked and entered, figuring this would be a nest of deaf people and the chances of anyone inside hearing him were pretty slim.

He was right. There were three of them in there – one wearing a green cardigan and typing into an old keyboard using his two index fingers, his back to the rest of the office, bald head glaring under the fluorescent lights. Then there was the self-appointed boss, the one wearing a tank top and shirt sleeve garters, who was parked against the far wall where he would be able to observe his minions if he wasn't asleep.

Eddie blew out a sigh and walked in towards Jeffery.

He dropped into a seat opposite him and took a deep breath of the old man smell, in which Old Spice played a minor role. Jeffery put down his pen and looked up. "If you've come to gloat, you can piss off."

"I expected to see your Zimmer frame in the car park."

"Humour hasn't improved, then?"

"I tried to ring…"

Jeffery frowned. "He doesn't allow us… He prefers our phones on silent."

Eddie nodded, checked his laughter so as not to wake the bossman. He changed the subject. "Who did that to your door plate?"

"The God thing?" Jeffery nodded towards the 'boss'. "It's more a reflection on how close we are to dying up here than how close we are to Him. This is the Operation Research Facility." Jeffery ran a finger around his collar. "Otherwise known as the Obscure Research Fuckup. It's where they send the people like me who they want out but don't really want to fire. I think the altitude kills us off fairly quickly; oxygen's in short supply up here."

It was good to see Jeffery's smile, and Eddie tried not to let his sorrow at his old boss's position colour his face as he asked, "Why did you just walk?"

"When Weismann came?"

Eddie nodded.

"If there's a bull coming at you, I think it's better to stand aside than try to reason with it."

"We were all sorry to—"

Jeffery waved a hand. "Don't," he said. "Don't feel sorry for me. I'm okay with being here; it's like a preamble to retirement. No one bats an eyelid if you drift off for ten minutes or take half an hour on the loo. There's no deadline here, Eddie, except the one everyone finally crosses."

Eddie sighed. "The department has just sunk in the space of ten minutes."

"Well it's very kind of you to say so, but I don't think I was *that* integral to its survival."

That made Eddie stop for a moment.

How important are we, really?

They say any big organisation is measured by the quality of the people in it. But each individual is tiny, insignificant; the organisation wouldn't so much as twitch if any one of them died or left. Eddie had always secretly thought of himself as indispensable – not in an arrogant way, just in a 'there's only one of me' kind of way. But hearing how his ex-boss thought the place would collapse without *him*, when in fact barely anyone had noticed his departure, made Eddie's jaw drop a little. He felt saddened.

"We miss you, you fuckwit," he said.

"Tough," Jeffery smiled. "I like it here. No way I'm coming back, so if that's why you've come, you've wasted your time."

Déjà vu.

"That type of visit is above my paygrade," Eddie said. "I just wanted to see how you were doing." The sleeping boss let out a squeak of wind, and Eddie bit his tongue to kill the imminent laughter. "If there was a way back in for you, would you take it?"

"Not on your nelly."

You lying bastard. "Yep," he looked at the source of the smell. "I can see how you'd like it here."

And then Jeffery went quiet, stared at the computer screen. Together they watched the little timer spinning round and round.

Eddie smiled. "I see you've got the same high-quality equipment."

"A card would have been nice, though."

Eddie looked at him – but turned away swiftly as Jeffery's lower lids tipped a tear onto the desk. "Your departure… well, it was a bit swift. A bit sudden."

"You're here now. It's been a few days," Jeffery raised his eyebrows. "Forget it, did you?"

Eddie nodded. "Sorry."

"Eight years I was there. Eight years. I like to think I was a pretty decent boss; that I made a good contribution to the team. And here I am, listening to pigeons all day, doing work that no one needs, and enduring Laurel and Hardy's uncontrollable flatulence without being able to open a fucking window. If you want fresh air you have to walk along the corridor where you can open a window. People passing by wonder what you're up to. They think you're going to jump."

Eddie nipped the side of his leg and kept the laughter inside. "What do you actually do here?"

Jeffery blew into a tissue and composed himself. "We do research for people who don't need things in a rush." He looked at the revolving cursor on the screen. "We do research for people who can't be bothered doing it themselves."

"You could transfer to something else. Something a bit more dynamic. You don't have to settle for this, Jeffery."

"You've seen the state of the internal job market recently?"

"Just saying: keep looking, don't give up."

"I only have ten years until I retire," he snorted. "Think of the crossword puzzles I could get through in that time."

"I just think—"

"So how's he doing, this Weismann fellow?"

Eddie shrugged. "Not really had much to do with him yet."

"He's an office dweller – a copper too. It's a bad combination for forensics at Major Crime."

"I told them that."

"I thought you might." And then he looked directly at Eddie. "But be careful, or you'll be next. They won't stop at me, so take my advice and pull your neck in for a bit. Make yourself invaluable, Eddie. You're bloody good at what you do, so make yourself so important that no one else could do it."

"And how would I go about doing that?"

"I've no idea. I was thinking of doing the same thing when they kicked me out of my office." There was a shine in his eye. Eddie didn't know if it was the embryo of another tear or the glow of humour.

Eddie stood to leave, and then said, Columbo-style, "Oh, Jeffery, there *is* something you could help with. If you've nothing better to do."

Jeffery raised an eyebrow. "As it happens, I'm stuck on twenty-three across."

"Doc Bolton's case."

"I had very little to do with it before I was ejected."

"It's linked to Marchant's death, I'm sure of it. The common denominator is a woman called Jessica Ripley."

Jeffery squinted at the mention of her name.

"Can you find out about her? About her case, and who was working it?"

* * *

As Eddie trotted back down the staircase into the belly of Killingbeck nick, he felt saddened to see what they'd done to Jeffery, and realised that irrespective of all that stuff about a company being made by individuals, them upstairs didn't give a flying shit about people.

Eddie had watched *One Flew Over the Cuckoo's Nest* for the first time about twenty years ago. And it had saddened him almost to the point of tears. He looked at Jeffery now with the same sadness he'd reserved for Randle McMurphy and his lobotomised personality. Maybe a pillow over Jeffery's mouth would be a good idea.

He stood thirty yards along the corridor from the divisional CSI office.

Thirty yards.

He gritted his teeth, and he planted one foot towards that door, prepared to ask for his old job back; prepared to bend his knee to Peter McCain so he wouldn't be out of work. But all by themselves, his feet turned around; he watched them carrying him towards the exit. "I hope you know what you're doing," he said to them, as the door to CSI disappeared from sight.

Chapter Forty-Nine

Eddie lit a cigarette and opened a window, letting the smoke crawl up his arm and out into the fresh air. There were two reasons why his feet wouldn't allow him to walk up the corridor to the Divisional CSI office and ask McCain for his old job back. The first reason was this: McCain would grin at Eddie, rub his hands together and gloat – oh, how the mighty fall! This would cause Eddie to jump on him and snap his neck. So, within an hour of asking for his old job back, Eddie would be looking at life for murder.

And the second reason he couldn't ask for his old job back was that he hadn't finished with the current one yet.

He knew his walk-out looked final and, at the time, it *was* final, he'd meant it – he wouldn't work for either Nicki or her old man. It would never work – in fact it would possibly also end in a life sentence. No job was worth that. But there was no way Nicki could manage major scenes by herself. Even if Kenny and Troy stayed behind, she would mess up, and Crawford would have to take action – he'd have to!

He'd try to cover up her shortfall, of course he would, and he'd probably succeed some of the time, but Eddie knew that even Weismann wouldn't tolerate it for long. Yes, they had infiltrated MCU's ranks at the same time, turfing out one incumbent after another, but Eddie had the feeling that Weismann was no dummy.

Weismann needed the job doing right – he was head of forensic operations, after all. If Nicki fucked up once too often, Weismann's head would roll.

Eddie smiled just a little bit. He flicked the cigarette out of the window and started the engine. If he hurried, he might arrive on time. He might not be as sparkly as he was the last time, but nothing could be worse than getting into another aftershave war with his dad.

Chapter Fifty

Eddie ordered steak, medium rare, and watched her over the top of his menu.

"Eddie?"

"Sorry," he said and handed the menu over to the waiter.

"What were you looking at?" She was smiling at him again.

"I was just enjoying the view." Inside, he was still enjoying the view, but he was listening to himself too. And what he heard made him want to vomit.

What the hell did you just say?

Sometimes, you didn't want your conscience along for the ride. Sometimes, you wanted to be able to be romantic without your harsher self judging you.

Piss off. Leave me alone.

She smiled, but there was concern behind it. "Do you think this is right? Us, I mean?"

Eddie made a real effort to smile back, but the question made him close one eye. "You'd prefer it if I brought my dad along?"

"No, no, I mean with everyone walking out… leaving their jobs. It seems a bit, I don't know, wrong to celebrate."

"At least we're guaranteed not to get disturbed this time." He laughed across the table, but she only smiled politely. "I even remembered to leave my phone in the car."

She almost returned his smile.

"Look," he said, "the forensic department at Major Crime is tiny, but it pulls ten times its weight; it has massive power there. And despite having me in charge, it has a good reputation. Mostly. And I actually quite like my job these days."

"I know, but—"

"It's a difficult boat to steer, Moneypenny. And right now, it has a hole in it so large that it'll be at the bottom of the ocean within a week; less, if we have any more bodies."

She stared at him.

He stared back, really looking into her eyes, wondering what it was she didn't understand about what he'd just said. He cleared his throat. "Pressure will mount pretty quickly, and… They'll ask us all to come back again."

"You think so?"

"I'd bet your wage on it." He winked.

She didn't look so impressed.

Eddie sighed. "Do we have to talk about work? It's depressing enough being there without it ruining an evening away."

"Okay. Was that our first argument?" She was smiling at him.

"If you want it to be. I call it conversation, though."

Her eyes sparkled. "When is your birthday?"

"June. Why?"

Moneypenny nodded, and said, "That explains it."

"Explains what?" What the hell was wrong with him? She was trying to have a pleasant evening out with him, and so far his only contribution had been aggression.

His conscience rolled up its sleeves and shook its head at him. You haven't been aggressive, it said. Or confrontational. What you've been is distracted by the worst day at work, and you're finding all this small talk a drag – especially now you know she's one of them astrologists. It shook its head even more. Really, get a grip. We've had enough female hocus pocus to last us a fucking lifetime, man.

"You're a Gemini. Twins."

Eddie stared, aghast. He wondered how rude it would be to ask for the bill before the meal had even arrived. And the wonderful image he'd formed in his mind on the drive over here this evening began to crumble, along with his hope that he'd finally met someone with whom he could…

Wait. She was smiling at him.

Her hand went to her mouth, and then she began laughing at him. And when she took away her hand to free a full-blown belly laugh, Eddie started to chuckle too. People stopped eating to look at them and eventually they too began to laugh.

The wonderful atmosphere didn't last long. The laughter gave way to the sound of glass smashing, and shouting. Moneypenny shrieked, Eddie looked around and Troy's fist was on its way into his face again. Luckily, this time, the blow was aimed under the influence of something and its accuracy suffered substantially.

Eddie popped his head to one side and the fist missed by a yard but continued to travel until it was somewhere around the centre of the table, by which time Troy was fully off balance. Eddie caught him around the chest before he collapsed onto the table. And, amid the screams, amid the sounds of crockery smashing and cutlery chiming as it hit the floor, Eddie, with Troy in his arms, rolled off his chair and into his neighbour's table. More crashing, more shrieks, men screaming angrily.

Through it all, Eddie caught sight of Moneypenny. Everything had quietened, like an audio version of a vignette – the silence began at the edges and worked its way inward. And then so too did the vision. The outside world bled away from the scene until only she was there, standing alone, her petite hand to her petite mouth, large eyes staring at him with concern. He couldn't remember anyone being concerned for him before.

Ah, yes. Jilly had. Briefly. And then Ros. But it turned out hers was short-lived, like a candle giving its everything to light up your life, but dying as dawn came along, leaving you abandoned for another long day, leaving you facing the terror of another night alone.

But here, look. Concern anew. She cares.

Eddie was about to experience gratitude when life bled back into the scene, and Troy screamed, "I'm gonna fucking kill you!" It dampened the mood a little.

Eddie snapped to as a man in a black waistcoat dragged Troy to his feet. Eddie was standing a second later, and he saw the venom in Troy's eyes, saw how the little man in the waistcoat was just another obstruction to him, as he tried to shove him aside while keeping his eyes on Eddie.

Troy won and lunged at Eddie's throat, a vicious snarl pulling his lips back.

Moneypenny screamed again.

Eddie stepped sideways into the attack and casually rammed an elbow into Troy's face.

Troy hit the floor and rolled around on his back, hands cupped over his face. There was a curious mix of screams from the women present, and relief from the men there. Waistcoat Man tugged at Eddie's arm, and Eddie turned to face him. "Help me into the back room with him. I'm calling the police."

"There's no need," Eddie said. "Leave him to me."

"I don't want any trouble, sir, I just want—"

"No trouble. I know him; it was a personal attack."

"Eddie," Moneypenny looked across at him.

Eddie looked between her and Troy, the kid who was hell-bent upon ruining everything, right from day one, all the way up to tonight, and forward into Eddie's future with her. "I'll get him out. Leave the police out of it, okay?"

"Okay, you get him out now."

Eddie nodded. He looked up at Moneypenny. Her concern had gone – and he didn't know if that was a good thing or a bad thing. And then he thought about it, and knew it was a bad thing. She reached down for her purse. "I'll see you tomorrow."

"I'm sorry," he said, as she walked away. Again.

Everyone was looking at him. Some were retaking their seats, straightening out tablecloths, picking up chairs or cutlery or whatever, but they all looked at him like it was his fault, this disruption to their evening. He looked down at Troy, grabbed him by the sweater and dragged him to the entrance, where Waistcoat Man held the door open.

"I'll come back," Eddie said, "settle up for the damage."

Waistcoat Man only nodded, eager for them to be out of his restaurant.

There was no sign of Moneypenny.

Chapter Fifty-One

Eddie had gone back out to the Discovery and taken his phone off charge. There were absolutely no text messages from Miss Moneypenny. No missed calls either.

He went back inside. He nudged Troy's foot – slightly harder than necessary – but the little bastard still didn't stir.

He sighed and slid the phone away. He looked down at Troy as he lay like a broken doll on the sofa, huddled into his blue and white hoodie as though it were a blanket. All at once, Eddie felt like stabbing the little twat, or at least beating him to a pulp; something that would take Troy a few months to recover from, anyway. Troy Ainsley had been a pain in the arse since day one, and Eddie had had just about enough of him.

He sank into the leather chair with the chrome armrests by the cold, dead fireside and lit a cigarette, watching the smoke meander up to the ceiling. He looked around at the lounge. It was naked of clutter these days. In the days of old there had been figurines and ornaments everywhere, walls crumbling under the stress of all the paintings and photos on them, shelves sagging under the weight of the porcelain and the silver.

All gone now.

The ceiling had all but been replaced, the walls needed new paper, and the carpet was long gone, leaving bare floorboards and warped gripper rods. The smell in here was curious: a mixture of dampness and the wet musty smell of new plaster. Even the veneer on the lounge door was warped. It was, of course, in two pieces because his dad, hitting a DIY spell without gathering the necessary knowledge first, had thought the door was five foot six high. When he discovered it was six foot six, he'd tacked another twelve inches on the bottom and called it good.

Eddie found himself smiling. The memories this place held for him came whether he wanted them or not; Sunday afternoons with Jim Reeves on the turntable and the smell of roasting beef in the air. Where had it all gone? Time slithers away like a coward when you start looking for it. But while this was a place of sweet memories for him, it was also a place of vile memories. He grew cold.

Eddie stood and kicked Troy.

He moved and then rolled off the sofa, groaning. "Did you just kick me?"

"I'll do it again if you give me any of your lip."

Troy sat up and rubbed the back of his neck, squinting at Eddie, who stood over him looking for an excuse to land a wrecking ball in his face.

"Go sit down," Troy said. "I'm not getting up while you're hovering over me."

Eddie drew on the cigarette again, and then creaked into the chair, feeling the familiar stitching of the arm rest give way to the chrome tubing beneath. "What is your problem? Let's get it all out in the open, shall we?"

"I'd rather just keep surprising you every now and then." Troy stood and headed for the door.

"Sit down."

"You can't make me; I'm free to go."

"No you're not. I'll tie you to the fucking sofa if I have to. Now sit down."

Troy kept walking.

Eddie threw the cigarette down and reached him just as he reached the front door handle. He grabbed Troy around the neck and dragged him back into the lounge, kicking the door so hard that the bottom strip of veneer fell off. Troy was kicking and yelling all the while but Eddie paid no attention, just tightening his grip. Eventually he threw him back onto the sofa.

"I'm gonna fucking have you for false imprisonment! You bastard!"

Eddie pointed at him. "Can't do that from in here, can you? Now shut up whining."

Troy laughed. "You are in so much shit, Collins. You're going down for this."

Eddie took out another cigarette and lit it. He offered the packet to Troy, "Want one?"

"Shove it up your arse."

"Fair enough. Now listen, if you make another dash for the door, I'll turn your face into red mush, okay?"

Troy glared at him. "What the hell are you doing?"

"Talking. For now."

"Where am I?"

"What's up with you?"

"Nothing. I'm fine and dandy." His face was dark, eyes untrusting slits, nostrils flaring. He sat with his legs apart, elbows on knees, fingers wrapped around each other in something like a death grip, rocking back and forth. Anger leaked from everywhere.

"So how come you attacked me three times today?"

"Oh I don't really know." Troy faked a smile. "Perhaps it's got something to do with my employment status. What d'you think?"

"Two things: firstly, you're not out of a job—"

"Yet."

"Yet. But rewind a bit and you'll find that it was your drug habit that caused you – and me – all this grief. So don't blame anyone else, even Nicki, for that."

"Yeah. Whatever." Troy folded his arms and sat back.

Eddie mimicked, "Yeah, whatever. You fucking spoilt brat. Truth knocked you off your high horse?"

Troy looked over and snarled.

Eddie laughed, took a drag on the cigarette. "So go on, why are you so pissed off at me?"

He leaned forward and pointed a shaking finger at Eddie. "The drugs test—"

"The drugs test I warned you about?"

"—was fake."

"Just a minute. You're annoyed that I knew you were on drugs, gave you ample opportunity to get off them, and then, just in case there were still traces in your system, I cut you some slack and arranged a *fake* one for you? That's why you're pissed off?"

"You did it to scare me. You did it just to make me come off them."

Eddie stared at him, trying to process his incredulity into understanding.

"I needn't have stopped."

"You are fucking kidding, right? If you'd known it was a fake test, you'd have carried on using?"

Troy shrugged. "Suppose."

"Then you're a bigger prick than I gave you credit for."

"I'm pissed off because I lost my job for a pointless drugs test, Eddie. Pointless!"

Eddie hissed as the cigarette end burned his fingers. He threw it to the floor, dragged a boot over it and watched the sparks turn black. "Just let me add this: if you'd carried on taking whatever it was you were taking – I'd have fired you myself. Clear?"

"Got any water?"

"No. No water."

"Kind of house is this? No water?"

"Under renovation. No water so far as I know."

"Well, can you go check?"

"Of course. Would you like my car keys as well?"

"I only asked. Forgot I was being held prisoner for a moment."

"Yeah, well. Don't let it happen again." Eddie tapped his fingers on the armrest. "So how could it have been a pointless drugs test if it got you to stop?"

"And I'm pissed off because she found out! How the hell did she find out?"

Eddie shrugged. "Not a clue." He looked at Troy, who just stared. "Why would *I* tell her, dummy? And Sid wouldn't tell her, either."

"So how—"

Eddie put a hand to his forehead. "She overheard me and Gibbon talking in my office afterwards, I bet. I caught her loitering."

Troy gave a single nod, closed his eyes. "That'd do it." He smiled bitterly. "And then she trotted off and told Daddy. And everyone had a good old laugh about it afterwards."

Eddie nodded. "No one laughed at you."

"The pisser is… you just gave in. Just like that," he clicked his fingers. "Like you didn't give a toss about the office. Like you couldn't care less about any of us." He shook his head, consternation crushing his eyebrows into his eyes. "I just don't get it. You were supposed to be the boss, the one people looked up to. And you bailed. Just like that."

"I had the head of Major Crime and his daughter bearing down on me. If I didn't walk then, they'd have found another way. Every week they'd dredge up some shit until some of it stuck. Don't you get it? They wanted me out, and they wanted her in irrespective of how I run my office."

"*Ran* your office."

Eddie nodded. "Ran my office. But they wanted her in because of the status." He thought about that for a moment, and snorted. "My job doesn't *have* any bleedin' status! Anyway, they wanted her in for some reason, probably as a stepping stone to something better."

"To what? Weismann is new too."

"Well, maybe something better in another force. My job would look great on her resumé."

"Whatever."

"But as things stand, they have one member of staff, and no idea how to run a crime scene. That's got to be cause for a bit of hope, wouldn't you say? Let her see the grass isn't so fucking green."

Troy said nothing. He looked at the floor with shining eyes.

"Right now you think there's no way to get back in. You're a junkie and Crawford won't have you within fifty yards of the place, huh?"

Troy just nodded.

"See why I did a fake test now?"

Troy looked up.

"It was supposed to get you off the fucking drugs, mate, without causing any fuss, and without them even knowing you were on them."

"Why would you do that for me?"

Eddie looked away. He could see where this conversation was heading, and he didn't like it. "Everyone deserves a second chance. I got a second chance; Jeffery took me on. He didn't really want to on account of he hates me, but I was clean. He gave me a second chance. And I thought you deserved one too, and because you're bloody good at what you do – when you stop being a penis, and when you stop trying to make yourself look good at my expense, and when you stop trying to fight me every inch of the way."

Troy snorted.

"I'm not an ogre. And long before you were good at the job, I was better. Remember that. And know this – I always will be."

"In your dreams."

Eddie smiled. "Come into the kitchen. Let's see if there's any running water."

Chapter Fifty-Two

There *was* water.

Each man leaned against the worktop, staring at the other, coffee in hand. Eddie lit another cigarette and this time Troy accepted one.

"So what is this place?"

"My folks' house. Well – my dad's. Mum's dead."

"So where is he, your dad?"

"He's living with me."

"Just till he has this redecorated?"

"Something like that. He was burgled. They took his boiler and flooded the place. Ruined it. So he's staying with me. He's forgotten about this place now, I think. He never mentions it any more."

Troy winked. "Securing your inheritance, eh?"

Eddie dragged on the cigarette and glared across at him.

"Have I hit a nerve?"

"It's here for him when, or if, he wants to move back in. I'm doing it up a bit at a time when I can afford to pay the builder. He's welcome to stay with me for as long as he likes. I'll keep this place for him, so he has an option. But I couldn't give a shit about any inheritance. You should know I'm not bothered about stuff like that. Possessions." He shrugged. "Can't take 'em with you."

Troy looked away, and Eddie wondered if just the tiniest bit of him was embarrassed by what he'd said.

"I come here every now and then. Check up on progress. And I like to come here and think sometimes."

"So he doesn't know about the building work, your dad?"

Eddie shook his head. "Never mentions the place. I think he'd be scared to come back."

"So you're doing all this work for someone who'll never come back here?"

"It doesn't matter. It's my old family home. Fond memories, you know? And he's my dad."

"Proper Samaritan, aren't you? A do-gooder." Troy was grinning, hackles raised, hostile all over again. "You ever thought life would be easier if you just kept your fucking nose out of other people's business?"

"If you're referring to you—"

"Fucking perceptive of you!"

"No. You couldn't do this job when your head's all mashed up. Don't you get it? You were a menace at the pickaxe scene, but at Doc's scene you were almost brilliant."

Troy licked his lips, and his eyes flicked away from Eddie, knocked off guard by a simple compliment.

"You really are good at this. When you're not using."

"So how did *you* know the drugs man? I mean, you can't look up 'Fake Drugs Tester' in the Yellow Pages, can you?"

"Gibbon? He's become a friend of mine. Someone I trust with delicate issues." He sipped his coffee, grimacing at how awful it was. "He was my…" Eddie searched the ceiling for the word, or for a replacement. "He was *my* drugs tester. A real drugs tester."

There, he'd said it. Another dirty secret added into the air of this place. "I was an alcoholic."

Troy stood still and stared at him, perhaps enjoying watching him squirm. "So… you were where I am?"

Eddie nodded.

"And you managed to do the job with your head all mashed up?"

"Look, I know what you're thinking, that a fellow sufferer should have handled it differently."

"Yep, that's pretty much what I'm thinking. Like 'left me the hell alone' different!"

"Not while my name's at the top of every fucking sheet you fill out, from putting diesel in your van to submitting DNA swabs for a murder victim. Then it's *my* business, and I say whether you can get by being high or not. And I say not. Clear?"

"Two-faced bastard."

"They're stimulants, Troy. And they do two things to people like us: they create a façade that no one can see in through; and they create a façade that you can't see out through either. They are falsehoods, and while that might be fun for an evening or a weekend, they can't remove you from reality permanently – unless that's your intention – and while you allow them to build your façade, they're at work rotting your body and polluting your mind. It's their way – and eventually they win. They always win."

"Did you memorise that from an AA cheat sheet? It was very good. Loved the bit about polluting the mind."

"What I don't understand is why you started back on them again. You'd come off them, and you were doing well."

"I'd lost my chance, Mr Collins. Nothing to keep me off them any more."

Eddie nodded.

"God. You're even trying to be sympathetic towards me, like you know—"

Eddie slapped him around the face. "Don't fucking mock me. Don't act like you're the only person ever to have given something up. You should use me as an example."

"Oh yeah, the Great and Powerful Eddie Collins. A lesson in life to us all."

"Come with me."

Troy followed Eddie through into the rear lounge – the parlour, as his mother used to call it. On the mantelpiece was a full bottle of

Courvoisier VS, a layer of dust around its neck. "That is one litre of the finest brandy Tesco sells."

"Is it the builder's?"

"The builder's? No, Jesus, it's mine."

"What? Why would you have that here if you've quit the booze?"

"Because I test myself. I know it's there if I ever weaken. So each time I come here and I don't crack the seal and guzzle it, I leave knowing that I'm still the boss. And if I can do it, Troy, so can you."

Troy backed up and looked at Eddie. "You really are Mr Perfect, aren't you?"

"Well, I mean—"

"You make me fucking sick. I used to look up to you. But the more I've learned about you tonight, the more I fucking hate you."

Eddie stared on, confused. At first he thought Troy was just messing about, but there was steel in his eyes and hatred on his face.

"You really think you're something special, don't you?"

"That's just my point, you thick twat. *I'm you.* I'm an average arsehole who was caught up in something I couldn't handle. Why must you reinvent the wheel? Why can't you look around you and learn from those who've been through it? And why must you turn all your anger in my direction? Try looking at yourself for once, and maybe you'll realise where you've gone wrong."

"Who says I've gone wrong?"

"Ah, now who's Mr Perfect? It's the world's fault, is it?"

They said nothing for ten minutes or so. Eddie lit up another cigarette, tossed the packet and the lighter to Troy.

Eventually Troy broke the silence. "You going to open it, then? The brandy?"

"No. I'm in control."

"Can I open it?"

"No."

"Why?"

"It's my challenge. You need to get your own."

Chapter Fifty-Three

Ten o'clock. Nicely dark, quietening down. Not many people about.

Jess watched from the seclusion of a dark alley between two terraces, across the road from his house. Her arms were folded as she leaned against the wall, foot nudging the rucksack just to make sure it was still there. Behind her, further into the shadows, near a chain-link fence, was a canvas shopping bag.

Her mind drifted for a moment, and thought of what Tony had said when she'd told him how Sidmouth demanded blow jobs in return for allowing her to see her son. Tony had become solemn at that point, and Jess could see the anger pulsing in him, and when he finally looked up at her, his eyes scared her. "Are you sure you wouldn't like me to deal with him for you?"

She'd given it some thought, but no matter which way she spun the options inside her head, they always came back to a 'no, but thank you'. She had earned the right to finish Sidmouth off; she'd earned the right to pull herself up by one more increment on the road back to normality.

Tony had already robbed her of killing Marchant; she wouldn't allow anyone to rob her of anything ever again. She'd go and see Michael with or without a Home Office blessing; she'd get Marilyn on side, she'd work with her new probation officer, she'd do whatever it took to see Michael. Whatever it took – except blowing someone off.

"That should be his last orgasm," Tony had said, and any other time a remark like that would have been funny, something he could have built a thousand innuendos onto, but not now; Tony's hunched demeanour said that he was as angry towards Sidmouth as she. Almost.

Another car passed by and brought her from her reverie. Her eyes settled on his house again: just a standard mid-terraced stone-built house, one of thousands like it in Morley, south Leeds. She swallowed a lump of hope and a lump of fear; one was sweet and the other tasted like shit. She was sick of eating shit.

Fully prepared now, Jess picked up her rucksack, unzipping it halfway before shouldering it, and emerging from the darkness into the jaundiced light of the street lamps. She thought that the strength she had could be easily destroyed – a strong word or two and she'd be cowering on the floor begging for mercy. But Tony had shaken his head.

"The power you have is real," he'd said. "I've got it too, from Marchant. It's like you're invincible, like you're unstoppable. And you are, but only if you believe it, Jess. Nothing is real unless you believe in it. Peter Pan was right." He'd smiled, holding out his arms. She'd fallen into them, and let the tears come again with crushing pain. "You *must* believe in yourself. Don't you see, everyone is trying to put you down, everyone wants their piece of you, and it's easy for them because they believe in themselves or they see a weakness in you, a weakness that's caused by your own self-doubt. Confidence is king.

"Don't forget, this is not a level playing field, Jessy. He's holding the cards, he's holding you to ransom. He's holding the thing you value most, and he's going to win every single time until you tip the playing field in your favour. Know what I mean?"

She'd looked at him, studied his eyes, and he'd offered to do this for her. And she'd refused instantly, and that had made him smile. "Good," he'd said. "I'm glad."

Jessica stood on the doorstep and knocked.

* * *

The hall light came on and her heart bucked so violently that she thought she was going to throw up. But she didn't have the time to reconsider as the key turned and Sidmouth opened the door. Jess planted a smile on her face. She lifted her head slightly so that the shadow cast by the peaked cap she wore crept up her face and allowed the light from the hall to shine on her. She heard him gasp. "Mr Sidmouth. Or can I call you John?"

He stood there in a pair of over-large sweat pants tied by a cord that dangled around his groin. He wore a white t-shirt with added tomato stains, and half of his belly hung out beneath it. He wore his shock well, and it only took him a moment to recognise her and say, "Ms Ripley, office hours—"

"Please," she said. "I just want a moment of your time."

"For what?"

"I, erm…" She pushed the smile. "I wondered if we could conduct our business here and now, instead of at mine tomorrow." She was tempted to wink.

He swallowed, and because he was thinking with his dick, it didn't even occur to him to ask how she'd got his address. "I… er…" He glanced over his shoulder as if seeking authorisation from someone who wasn't there.

He rubbed his face, and almost instantly it changed from one of consideration to one of incomprehension as though he was thinking: *what the hell is she doing at my house at this hour?*

It was as though the penny had dropped. The incomprehension fled from his face, and fear took up residence.

Sidmouth tried to slam the door but Jess got her foot in there first. The door hit it and bounced back against the wall. He turned and ran up the hallway, his open-backed slippers slapping against the floor and against his bare feet. He shouted something incomprehensible, like the scream of a child being chased across the playground. She launched herself up the final step and into the hallway, her gloved hand already searching inside the rucksack.

"Everyone feels brave in their own office, Jessy," Tony had said, "but get him at home, see how vulnerable he feels then."

Sidmouth was halfway up the steep, dark stairs when Jess wrestled the axe from the rucksack. She sprinted up the first four stairs and then swung the blade like she was chopping wood. The back of Sidmouth's right heel split wide open; the axe cleaved the slipper and the stair carpet and became lodged in the wood beneath. Sidmouth howled like a wounded dog, and his ascent slowed but grew more frenzied as Jess got to work yanking the axe free.

Blood had splashed across the wall.

He took a quick look back and screamed again, a long string of saliva whipping from his lower lip.

Jess freed the axe as Sidmouth rounded the top step onto the landing, screaming still in a high-pitched boy's voice. It sounded like, "Mam! Mam!" He dragged his dead foot behind him, leaving a shining trail of blood on the filthy carpet.

Jess, teeth bared, clambered up the stairs, yelling a battle cry, and rounded the corner to see him cowering by the open bathroom door. His arms were already raised, palms facing her, tears mixing with the snot on his face, more saliva dancing in the wind from his mouth as he pleaded with her, "Leave me alone! Please, please, I won't touch you again, please!"

He saw her determination, and squealed, dragging himself across the floor and into a poorly lit bedroom with cobwebs in each corner of the ceiling. "I'll sign you off, Jessica, please. I'll get you full access to your boy. You'll never have to meet me again!"

Chapter Fifty-Four

She grinned. The logical part of her mind had stopped working altogether; only the animal was left, and it wanted blood, not false promises. She walked along the landing, turned, and saw him trying to squeeze under the metal frame of his single bed.

The bedding was orange, the pillows pink, blue, and white stripes. The carpet threadbare, the walls dark brown fleur-de-lys, the curtains faux velvet. Ancient stuff from the eighties – the room of a boy who had remained a boy into his forties; who only appeared to become a man in his tweed suit, carrying his briefcase. But it was feigned. His only pleasure lay in destroying the lives of damaged women, getting hard on the power they gave him.

She swung the axe at his other ankle but missed.

He screamed, his eyes so wide that she could see the tiny red veins in the corners. She tugged the blade out of the floor. He pulled his legs up but she struck bone with her next blow, and Sidmouth's screams became inaudible, petering into a series of hearty sobs, the kind where the bottom lip hangs out and catches the tears.

Fear propped his eyes wide still. She grabbed the bed frame and lifted it up, getting her strength from the same place he got his erections – the suffering of others. She pushed it away, and as it hit the floor, it knocked into a flimsy wooden cabinet whose doors opened as it fell forward. Sidmouth's toys fell out across the floor.

He was isolated in the centre of the room, an island surrounded by his own blood, confronted by his own sickness.

Jessica stared. The light was dire, but these were not the kind of toys you would find in a nursery school. They whispered 'apprentice dungeon master'. They said 'wannabe paedophile'; they shouted 'practising sicko'.

"I can explain!"

"Don't bother." She raised the axe.

John Sidmouth cowered, scrabbling on the bare wooden floor with his one good heel pushing like crazy; his damaged heel working too, but just slipping on blood. His eyes were hollow black holes of terror as she swung the blade at his hands like a fly-swatter, taking one off completely and slicing the other across the wrist until it hung by a strip of glistening tendon, a useless appendage. She wasted no time celebrating, but swung the blade again, this time aiming for his crotch. It struck home and suddenly Sidmouth went silent.

Blood sprayed into her face, misted on the cap.

His eyes and mouth were open wide; blood pumped from his arms in comical arcs, and more leaked into the floor. He gasped once or twice and then stopped breathing. The arcs stopped.

"You fucker," she yelled, and brought the axe down across his face.

Blood sprayed across the wall, trickled down the remains of his left ear, flowed across his shoulder and turned his almost white t-shirt red. But her anger hadn't diminished – it had increased. The fucker had made her do this! This wasn't in the master plan; this was a dangerous detour that might attract the attention of the police – again. But, if it was possible, she hated this man even more than the others; operating under a government umbrella for countless years, tormenting people while waving forms and privileges and freedom under their noses.

Jess stamped on his face and he slid to the floor like a slug. She almost spat on him – almost, but caught herself just in time.

She stood there panting, wanting to carry on until the bastard was nothing more than strips of meat and fat, and lumps of mushy red hatred, but she was exhausted. She stood, hands on her knees, head hanging limp, sweat-dampened hair twitching with each hammered heartbeat, air rasping down her constricted throat.

Jess heard whimpering and held her breath. It was coming from the bathroom to her left, and she *knew* the sick fuck had a kid in there. A prickle ran up her back – *that's* why he was so hesitant at the front door: he already had company.

She stood straight, took a fresh grip on the blood-smeared axe, and walked out of Sidmouth's bedroom, across the landing. She peered around the doorframe into the bathroom.

It wasn't a kid at all. A fat old woman in a knee-length nightdress was sitting on the toilet with her pants around her ankles. Her breasts fell outside of her legs. Her neck fat removed all evidence of a chin, just blended it perfectly into her chest. Her chalk-white hair sat in rows of curlers under a piece of black netting. Shaking old hands outstretched, pleading.

"My John," she whispered.

Jess entered the bathroom, breathing through clenched teeth. "You raised a monster."

"Please!"

She swung the axe.

* * *

Once back inside that cosseted place in the darkness of the alleyway, shaking and breathless, Jess propped the axe up against the wall. She pulled off her outer layer of clothes: baggy man's jeans, a grey sweater three sizes too big for her, and a CAT Diesel Power cap. It was too dark to see properly in here, but they all looked to have been spattered nicely with fresh blood. Last thing to come off was the swimming cap she'd worn as a barrier between herself and the CAT cap. Her hair was wet through with sweat.

She took the axe, the clothes and the cap, and dumped them all into the stout shopping bag that she'd secreted by the hedge. Once the latex gloves were off, she waved her hands about until the sweat on them had evaporated.

And then she walked casually back out into the comparative brightness of the streetlights, not even looking across the road at that open door. Strange, she thought, what goes on in people's houses. Who knew what Sidmouth got up to in his bedroom – or in the cellar, even? How many more Sidmouths were there in this street, in this town, this city?

The thought sent a shudder skittering up her back. She shivered at the coolness of the evening, and began the long walk home, dumping the gloves in a wheelie bin at the top of the street, confident it had been the best meeting she'd ever had with Sidmouth. "Very productive."

DAY 6

Chapter Fifty-Five

Eddie's eyes flickered open, and he wondered where he was. For an awful moment he thought he was in some shitty bedsit above a carpet shop in Wakefield city centre. He woke up quickly then, hands in the tangles of a sweaty duvet, and a racing panic in his skipping heart.

When he saw his room, the present-day normality leaked back in. He breathed out a quivering sigh and dropped his head back on the pillow, finding some kind of solace in the familiar cracks in the ceiling.

Was it last night's heart-to-heart with Troy that had brought the past back to piss on his bonfire like this? He thought all of that was behind him – all that he'd *hoped* was behind him. Whenever his thoughts were dragged back to Jilly or Sam, he felt weak and vulnerable all over again. And he'd worked hard to shift that burden to a disused section of his brain that was like a quagmire, holding onto past terrors and refusing to let them go. The quagmire had a steel shutter door and a padlock the size of a dinner plate; it wasn't easy for him to inspect those memories, and it wasn't easy for them to escape. But escape they had.

Sam had been killed by a hit and run driver just before his twelfth birthday. Jilly had decided that she couldn't live without him – and, furthermore, couldn't live *with* Eddie – so she bailed on him with a bottle of pills. Eddie had never been the same since.

He'd tried.

Ros had been the next in line to ride the Eddie Collins rollercoaster. And she'd done a great job of holding on… until her own ghosts had frightened her off, and Eddie was left holding the spare set of keys that he'd had cut for her. He was also left holding a heart that was in a dozen pieces.

So Eddie had grown a skin so thick that no one could break in ever again. He'd also developed a cunning master plan for keeping people out – acidity. This gruff exterior wasn't something nature had bestowed upon him; it was something he'd grown, something he'd worked at, and it had kept him safe until now.

Moneypenny was knocking at that gruff exterior, tickling his extra-thick skin.

He found himself shaking his head as he remembered Troy, and how he'd opened up a little about his own addiction. What the hell was going on? It wasn't long ago that Eddie would have kicked Troy's arse out of the door and never let him back inside, let alone actually helping the kid to get off the drugs.

It was all getting too personal. He didn't want anyone getting close to him ever again. And he didn't want to raise that shutter door and start inspecting memories of lives past. He wanted his old wounds to stay in the quagmire. He felt sure that a shrink would tell him otherwise – that to free your demons was to exorcise them.

Bollocks to that. He buried them, the deeper the better.

"The fuck was I thinking?"

Just inviting trouble. Inviting pain.

Eddie shook his head, and made a mental note to stop this stupidity before it became serious. Look at Dad, he thought, living under a cloud all the time just because someone on Facebook took an interest in him and taught him to cook stroganoff without getting poisoned. Flattery… that's how they do it. Every time.

Eddie just had to hope that the mental note wouldn't get lost in the wash.

He picked up his phone, unplugged it and noted the time was a very pleasing four minutes past nine. He felt quite pleased with himself, being able to laze for a change instead of getting up early and being sore-headed all day.

But being up late didn't wipe away his memories of the way Troy had blitzed his romantic evening with Moneypenny – and just her name caused him to gasp; not because she was utterly beautiful, not because she was good company, ranking a good two levels above tolerable, but because he had to think of a way to extricate himself without causing her any pain. He had no choice.

And then his mind wandered to the next topic, as it was apt to do when it wasn't constrained by time or by getting to work early. It wandered to Troy. And there it stopped until his finger pressed the green button on his phone's screen. Next to it was a generic grey cut-out of a person, and TROY was beneath it. He heard it ringing, and then he heard a tinny voice tell him no one was available to take the call, and would he like to—

Eddie pressed the red button, threw the phone on the bed, and got up. He opened the door and heard the same old female voice he'd heard only yesterday, the one he'd mistaken for a DJ on the radio. What the fuck was she doing here again? Eddie walked along the corridor until he reached the lounge, where he propped himself against the archway and watched Superbitch and his father chatting. Eddie's ears were about to get warm. And then they were about to catch fire and fall off.

* * *

"Fetch me some more tea, Charles. There's a dear."

Eddie heard the chair creak, and heard footsteps in the kitchen. He moved forwards and peered around the corner, watched her as she flicked through the channels on the TV, pausing at food channels but stopping mostly at the pay-per-view ones.

The kettle clicked off. "Would you like more biscuits, Wendy?"

"Digestives. Milk chocolate, not plain this time. You know I don't like plain."

Charles shuffled to her side with a tray of tea-making equipment that he didn't even know they owned. The only tea-making equipment Eddie was aware of was a mug and teaspoon, but here was a porcelain pot, another for the water, a milk jug, a silver sugar bowl and spoon, all sitting on an ornate tray with a plate of biscuits. Eddie nearly coughed, but he was too engrossed by the whole freak show to avert his eyes.

"Have you arranged a meeting with the estate agent yet?"

"Ah," said Charles, "it slipped my mind! I'll get onto it this afternoon."

"Nonsense. You'll get on with it this morning. We need to know where we stand, Charles." There was a pause as she snapped a biscuit and nibbled on it. "These *are* McVities, aren't they? I won't have own-brand biscuits, Charles."

"Yes, yes, McVities."

"You do understand, don't you, about the estate agent?"

"Of course I do." Charles wasn't smiling under her torment. His face was a delicate shade of scarlet. "I'll get on with it soon." He looked as fragile as the porcelain teapot.

"Well, we simply can't progress this whole thing until we have a value. So the ball, as they say, is in your court, dear."

"I know."

"And when are you telling Eddie?"

Eddie's heart kicked, and he almost fell over.

"Soon. I'll tell him soon."

"Hurry up about it. He can't stay, you know. You do know that, don't you?"

"Yes, dear. I've said I'll tell him. I will, just give me some time; it's delicate."

"Delicate? How? Would you like me to tell him?"

"No. No, it's fine; please just leave it to me. He can get a bit touchy."

Eddie pulled his chin back off the floor.

"I mean, I can't even decorate, Charles. Have you seen the state of his room?"

"He's a free spirit."

"No, I'm afraid he's not. He's just a slob. It smells in there, you know. Did you know that? It smells awful."

Eddie staggered back to his bedroom, feeling numb. Once at his door, he took a deep breath, he opened it, closed it, and broke wind. He could hear her 'tut' from out here. And although that caused him to smile a little, he was still dumbfounded by all her talk of decorating and kicking him out. He emerged into the lounge, trying to keep the smile away as he saw the satisfying disgust on Wendy's face. "Morning."

"Hi, Eddie," Charles stood. "I'll, er, I'll go have a shower."

"Whoa, big boy," Eddie said. "I'll go first. Just need coffee."

Charles sat down again, looking at his watch.

Eddie saw Wendy raise her eyebrows and nod her head in Eddie's direction. 'Go on', she mouthed.

"Eddie," Charles began.

"Want some tea, Dad?"

"Er, no, thank you."

Eddie peered over at Wendy. "Want your cauldron topping up?"

She squinted at him. "We want you out, Eddie. As soon as possible, but certainly by the end of the week."

"What?"

Charles slapped a hand over his face.

"We've discussed it, and it's the right thing for all of us. You shouldn't be living with your father at your age. You should start wearing long trousers, boy." She stuck her nose in the air, and peered down it at Eddie. "Make your own way in the world. Do I make myself clear?"

"How come you're not at work?" asked Charles, smiling as though none of this unpleasantness were real. "It's almost half nine."

"Never mind the work thing, let's rewind and listen to Cruella again."

"Don't be facetious! That's very rude, boy."

Eddie bowed slightly. "Yeah, well, diplomacy is for people who aren't fluent in sarcasm." He poured water, stirred his coffee, and turned around. She still looked confused. "Anyway, I'm going now because I don't have the energy to pretend to like you today."

"Seriously," said Wendy, "why aren't you in work today?"

"They gave me the day off on account of I work too hard."

"Answer me, Eddie."

Eddie sighed. "How come no one ever believes that fucking line?"

"Language!"

Eddie blinked. "British English. With a soupçon of slang, while leaning heavily towards I-don't-give-a-sideways-shit."

"What's happened?"

Eddie looked at his dad. "Surely you told her? Even Ursula isn't that good at fishing."

Charles didn't know where to look.

"You walked out. That's what happened." Her pearly yellow teeth caught the morning sunshine like a jagged row of hearing aids.

Eddie shrugged. "So?"

"You can't handle responsibility, boy." She took a couple of steps towards him and lowered her voice, "Your father's days of bailing you out when the world gets too tough for you are gone now. It's time you dealt with the consequences of your own actions. You will learn that you are totally dispensable and that the world will not collapse should you decide it's all getting too much for you."

"Ouch."

"We want you out by the weekend, Eddie," she said.

Charles looked at the floor like it was going to perform a trick. And then he looked up, a plea on his face as though Eddie had the power to crush his dreams with just a handful of careless words. Wendy sat down in the chair next to him, crunching a biscuit, and reached up to hold Charles's hand – united against Eddie.

Through gritted teeth, Eddie said, "Can I speak to you alone, Dad?"

"Whatever you need to say," said Wendy, "you can say in front of us both."

"I don't mind," Charles said to her. "If he needs—"

"Both of us."

Eddie took a breath, and then someone knocked at the door. He sighed it all out again. "I guess it'll keep," he said, opening the door.

Benson stood there. "Get dressed, you prick, we're going to knock on Jess Ripley's door again."

Eddie's shoulders slumped. And then he stood up straight, and turned to face them both. "What was that about being totally dispensable?"

"If you're having an argument, I'll wait in the car," Benson said. "Don't be long."

Eddie closed the door. Wendy stared at him defiantly, and Charles looked like a lost puppy. "Okay, Dad. It's time you came clean. I was going to just let things hang for a while and hope that it just sorted itself out. But I think we should tell Wendy. What do you say?"

Wendy's smile dropped off her face and her head swivelled around to Charles.

"Ah, yes." Charles scratched his ear. "I'd been meaning to have a quick word with you—"

"Charles."

"Erm…"

"Charles!"

He mumbled, "You see, the thing is… this is Eddie's place."

There was a moment where it was obvious that she expected the punchline any second. It didn't come. "You're kidding me, aren't you?" She patted Charles on the backside – Eddie cringed – and she said, "One of the things I love about you most, Charles, is your sense of humour—"

"He's not kidding," Eddie said, heading for the shower. "He's been trying to impress you. But since I don't like you, and I'm *not* trying to impress you, I can tell you how it is. And it is like this: I want you out by the weekend. Okay, love?"

"But—"

"And he doesn't have a sense of humour." Eddie stopped and stared at her, appraising the curlers in her fake blonde hair, the blood-red lipstick, the hoop earrings, and the rouge circles on her cheeks. "At least, he never used to."

Charles shouted, "Eddie!"

"And as for you. Grow up, or I'm disowning you!"

Chapter Fifty-Six

It was supposed to be a treat. She'd worked hard all night, right from killing that bastard Sidmouth. In fact, she'd been working hard since before then, gathering the things she'd need. And she'd had about twenty-five minutes' sleep.

But the piece of cold chicken that hung inches from her lips looked like the most wondrous banquet anyone could have prepared. Her stomach growled and her mouth watered.

The doorbell rang again. She dropped the chicken back into the box and wiped her greasy hands on the duvet. The bell rang a third time as she approached the front door, and one of the junkies opened his bedsit door.

"Sup?" he mumbled.

Jess stopped walking. She turned to him. "What's up? What's up?"

"I only—"

"Why don't *you* answer the fucking door for a change and find out!"

The junkie curled his lip at her and slammed his door.

Jess, eyes drooping, opened the front door. If she'd had a full stomach, she would have emptied it right then and there all over the two coppers who stood panting on the top step. How the fuck did they know? So quickly!

"Jessica Ripley?"

Her heart tripped, and for the briefest of moments she thought about barging past them and running away. She looked at the fat one, the one who was breathing the hardest, and then across at the tall one, who seemed to be staring at her feet. It was like a Laurel and Hardy sketch. "Yes," she said. "Can I help you?"

"I'm DI Benson, and this is Eddie—"

"What do you want?" Her mouth had turned very dry.

"Can we come in?"

Suddenly her appetite had vanished. She stepped aside. "Sure." There was no point in trying to smile; the motors working the smile muscles had seized up, couldn't even get a twitch going. She nodded into the darkness at the end of the corridor, and when the tall one – who was actually quite pleasing to the eye – stopped and said, "It's okay. I've got the door," she knew that her moment to flee had just vanished too.

Had she been prepared for their visit, she would have been out – obviously. But if she'd thought they would turn up on her doorstep the very next fucking day, well, she would have cleaned herself a bit more thoroughly to begin with; her hands, her nails especially, still had blood—

"Chicken," the fat one said, sniffing into the air.

And as well as her personal appearance, she might have put up a bit more of a fight on the doorstep. She was not friends with the law; not one bit.

The smell of fried chicken was still strong as the tall one closed the bedsit door behind them. Her hands shook, and she wondered if it was hunger or fear. "Would you like some? It might be a bit cold now, but…" *Oh yeah,* a small voice in her head said, *very unfriendly! Positively scathing!*

They both shook their heads, but she could tell DI Benson was tempted; a little flick of the tongue over wet lips. Dead giveaway. Also a dead giveaway was his yellow shirt and red tie combo – he'd been wearing something equally outrageous yesterday when he'd tried to collar Tony on the bus. So the first question, when it finally came, was no surprise to her – and she never even considered giving a dodgy answer.

If this was it, if this was the big one, then she needed them to think she was a good girl who was telling the truth and trying to cooperate.

"Where were you yesterday" —he looked at his watch—"about this time?"

Inside, she let out a sigh of relief; they were starting with the easy ones. She sat on the bed as they remained standing, cramped by the door. The fat one, Benson, put his hand on his colleague's arm, said, "Eddie," and gently moved him aside, so he could sit in the chair by the door, the chair Tony used to sit in. He'd never sit there again.

She folded her arms. "Am I under arrest?"

Benson snorted, "What for?"

"I don't know. What crimes do you have that need clearing up this time? You could always frame me for them."

Benson clapped. "Very good, Jessy. If we were framing you for anything, you'd be in cuffs right now, and I'd be stealing your KFC, okay?"

"Wow," she said, "déjà vu." She almost smiled, but smothered it. "Do I need a lawyer?"

"Look, love," said the tall one. "You don't need a lawyer, okay. He just wants to ask you some questions, I just want to look at your footwear, and then we'll be out of your way. Okay?"

"You want to look at my shoes? Do you have a fetish?"

She saw Eddie look down at Benson, and shrug; he said, "I thought I did the fucking jokes."

"Leave it to me, Eddie. Please?" He turned back to Jessica. "So. This time yesterday?"

"I was trying to catch a bus, actually." She offered them both a smile.

"Why?"

"There was someone on it that I needed to speak to."

Benson stared at her. "Look, if I'm going to have to nudge you every step of the way, then perhaps we could do it in more comfortable surroundings down the nick. Get my meaning?"

She did, and she'd always promised she was never going back inside one. Ever. "There was a man on the bus who'd broken into my flat last week. I wanted my stuff back."

That made Benson sit up. "You know him, this man?"

"Tony."

Benson raised his eyebrows.

She sighed again, and said, "Tony Longbottom. He's an old boyfriend of my mine from way back. I've known him since before Sebastian…"

"What did he steal?"

"A jacket. A knife from the drawer; I only had two! And you're going to ask why he stole the jacket, and I'm going to say it had my purse in the pocket." She shrugged. "Sorry."

"How much in the purse?"

"Fiver. Some change."

Eddie looked up and asked, "How did he get in?"

"Through the door. It's an old Yale lock. It'll open if you so much as breathe on it. Try it. The junkies next door told me about it. Been like that years apparently."

"Why hasn't it been fixed?"

"Because the landlord is more of a taker than a giver, I guess. You'll need to ask him."

"Did you report it?"

"To the police?"

Benson nodded.

"No. I mean, what are you going to do about it, send CSI round?" She tried to laugh but it was a crow's croak.

"That's exactly what we'd have done, yes."

"But Tony's been in here. Finding his prints would prove nothing."

"You actually saw him take your jacket? You know for sure it was him?"

"I saw him! I was coming home, walking up the road, and he was coming out of the front door with it. He was off like a whippet. And the next time I saw him was yesterday. He was on a bus, so I tried—"

"How did you know it was him?"

"His cap. He always wears a bright yellow baseball cap. Well, it *was* bright yellow. Mucky now."

Benson leaned forward, elbows on knees, and the chair creaked beneath him. He shared a 'told you' look with Eddie before returning his attention to Jess. "Have anything on it? An insignia, a logo?"

"CAT Diesel Power."

Benson slapped his leg and then sat back in the chair, satisfied. "Know where he lives?"

"If I did, I wouldn't be chasing after him on a bus."

"Does he have other friends around here, someone he might have been visiting?"

Until now Jessica had been holding her hands in check, squeezing them tight to stop them shaking, and she'd kept her feet crossed for the same reason, but now, ten minutes into this informal chat, she had to relax them both; her arms and legs were aching like mad from last night's exertion.

"I need a drink. Anyone like one?"

Both shook their heads, but Jess filled up the kettle and switched it on.

And that was when she almost keeled over again. On the crease of her left little finger was a red line, the remnants of a cut that she didn't even know about. And now that she'd noticed it, it began to sting, and a low groan tumbled out of her mouth and into the sink.

How the hell had she cut herself? And more importantly, *where* had she cut herself? It became huge, like a gash; unmissable, throbbing.

She wondered if they could see it too.

She swallowed, dropped some coffee into a mug, and turned to face them, folding her arms. "Anything else I can help you with?"

Eddie stepped forward. "What shoes have you got, love?"

Jess clenched her fist over the cut and looked down. "These flip-flops," she said, "and a pair of trainers in the wardrobe."

"Mind if take a look?"

"Help yourself." The kettle began humming, and Jess looked over to Benson. "What's with all the questions?"

"Do you remember a man called Marchant?"

And there it was: bombshell number one! Had she been able to watch her own reaction to that name, she would have been proud. Her eyes screwed into slits and there was a tremor in her top lip as though she was ready to rip pieces out of Benson's face. She snapped, "Prick. Of course I know him. I'll never forget his face."

"He's the man who defended you for Sebastian's murder."

"No, he's the man who handed my arse to the prosecution. He's more of a villain than most fucking villains. 'Scuse my French."

"Someone murdered him."

Chapter Fifty-Seven

Jessica closed her eyes, took a quivering breath in and felt the heat of impending tears behind her eyelids.

"So there *is* such a thing as Karma." She couldn't hide the relief. Nor did she want to. "How?"

The performance that followed was perfect; Kate Winslet couldn't have done it any better. Jess made her eyes open wide, sniffled, and dried her eyes on her sleeve. She took a step back, palms still out, but shaking this time too. "Don't look at *me*," she said, "I had nothing to do with it." She paused. "But you have to tell me how he died. I've dreamed of stabbing him, poisoning him." She looked to the ceiling as though daydreaming. "My favourite was always hanging, though. Closely followed by fire."

"Not exactly distraught, are you?"

She smiled, pleased that the muscle motors were working again. "I'm not going to lie. I couldn't be any happier. That waste of space stole twelve years of my life." She pointed a teaspoon at Eddie. "I'm not sorry the bastard's dead." She shrugged at Benson. "I'm not sorry at all. If I had some bunting, I'd hang it outside the front door. In fact, tell me where they bury him and I'll go and piss on his grave. He'll get no tears from me. Wanker."

The kettle clicked off and she jumped. She poured water. There was nowhere to store milk, so all hot drinks were taken black these days. She carried the mug to her bed, found a clear space on the bedside table and put it down. She sat on the bed, knowing that under the mattress was a Stanley knife with its blade fully extended. Just waiting. Just in case. It was but one small movement away.

A fleeting scene sped before her daydreaming eyes: she took out the knife and she slashed the fat bastard's neck with it, and then, as he turned around from her wardrobe, she slashed Eddie's neck too. She'd take great delight in watching sixteen pints of blood spew over the bedsit floor, and watching as two shrivelling men writhed in pain, spraying blood like a pair of Catherine wheels spraying sparks.

If it seemed to be heading towards an arrest, things would get messy in here very quickly. And then she'd walk and never come back. No way was she ever going back inside again.

"Tony was around, you say, when Sebastian was killed?"

Jess blinked awake again. "Not as such. We saw each other, but it was casual; he never moved in or anything. Nothing official."

Benson leaned forward again. "I don't recall his name on any statement or report at the time."

"You've looked at them all?"

"Of course."

"Why? Is this all to do with Marchant?"

"Yes. Just routine. We have to be thorough, Jessica."

"Ha! Don't make me fucking laugh. Do you mean thorough as in thorough, or do you mean the kind of thorough you were twelve years ago? Bastard!"

"Oi," Eddie said, "if anyone insults him, it's me."

"Shut up," Jess said, and turned back to Benson. "You bastard. How can you sit there lecturing me on thoroughness? It didn't matter when it was my neck on the fucking line and your lot left every stone unturned, did it? Different story when it's some twat in a suit, eh? What, is there more scrutiny when the victim is an actual lawyer?"

Benson looked away.

"Well? You gone deaf now?"

Benson seethed. "I'm doing this investigation the way I run any investigation, Jess. Okay? I'm not here to discuss whether your conviction was safe or not—"

"No, you wouldn't criticise one of your own, would you?" She shook a mocking head. "Oh no, couldn't do that!"

Benson shuffled in his seat. "Tell me about Tony."

She took a long blink, and the muscles in her cheeks throbbed as she ground her teeth. "There was no mention of Tony because he wasn't even there that day. I hadn't seen him for maybe three or four days, and I wasn't expecting him."

"You claimed throughout your trial that you didn't kill Sebastian. Did you ask Tony to kill Marchant for you?"

"Christ, you *are* trying to frame me!"

"Jessica—"

"If you can't pin it on me, you'll pin a conspiracy charge on me." She shook her head again. "Priceless, you lot are. Priceless." She reached for her coffee and felt the knife under the mattress as she moved. Five seconds, she reckoned, maybe eight, and they'd be out of her way. "It was always a straight fight between me killing Sebastian, and him doing the job himself. And I did *not* kill him."

"Therefore you blame the establishment. Your lawyer, the police…"

"Of course I do. Wouldn't you? But I'm not going to kill someone because of it!" She puffed out a breath. "I'm not keen on spending the rest of my life behind bars, Inspector Benson. Trust me, I'd rather accept the unfair punishment I've already had, and lick my wounds until my own dying day. I've no desire to go back to prison. And I'm not in the habit of getting people to do favours for me. I do everything myself. Trust no one." She smiled. "It's my new motto. Like it?"

"Then who *did* kill Marchant?"

"I don't know; you're the detective."

A snort from over by the wardrobe.

"Did Tony kill him?" Benson asked.

"Why would he?"

"You said you knew him back then; he was your boyfriend."

"Yes."

"You didn't mention Tony at the time."

"Why am I answering the same questions again? I already told you: I was never asked. Like I said, it was always a fight between me having killed Sebastian, or suicide; no mention of a third party."

Benson persisted. "But do you now think he might have killed Sebastian?"

Silence. Jess sighed across the steam curling from the coffee mug. Calmly she said, "I was out of the room. Sebastian was alone with a knife at his chest. I hadn't seen Tony for a few days, and I wasn't expecting him." She watched Benson from the corner of her eye. He seemed to be thinking hard about what she was saying, or rather what she was omitting.

"Why?"

"He drove buses. Shifts. They didn't always add up to a lot of time together. He lived in his own flat, by himself."

"Was he working that day?"

"I never knew what shifts he was working. He'd just show up."

"So he could have shown up that night?"

"Could've." She shrugged, leaving a pause just long enough for Benson to really consider his own question. "If he did, why run away after he killed him, why not stay?"

"Because he'd be a murder suspect."

"But he wouldn't leave *me* as the suspect, surely?"

"You know him, Jessica, not us."

"Doesn't look much like a bus driver now." Eddie closed the wardrobe doors and stood up. "What's he do for a living these days? Where's he staying?"

"He's a merchant banker. Got a penthouse overlooking the River Aire."

Eddie was trying hard not to smile, she could tell. He turned away, and she worked her hand under the duvet, slid it down the side of the thin mattress, and took hold of the knife, all the time shielded from view by her crossed legs and the bedside table. No way would she ever hear the sound of metal doors closing again; the sound of sobbing as the lights dimmed.

Jess watched Eddie's reflection in the mirror on the wardrobe door, and decided that she didn't much like him – he was a black or white kind of man, no grey, no doubt, no wiggle room. She put the mug down again; the blade was inches away under the duvet now. "Sebastian's death ruined more than just my life. Even Tony said that." Her eyes glossed up as tears formed across them. "Me going away. Michael being taken into care."

"Could Tony have killed Marchant for ruining his life too?"

"He would have told me."

"And he didn't?"

She clicked her fingers. "Shit, now you come to mention it, I knew there was something I had to tell you." She glared at Benson. Eddie looked amused by her sarcasm. She shrugged.

Eddie moved into the small kitchen and opened the cutlery drawer.

"Got a warrant for that?"

Eddie closed the drawer again.

"But he could have killed him and said nothing to you?" Benson didn't take his eyes from hers.

"Tony is a stranger to me now; we're not an item, if that's what you're suggesting. We don't know each other any more. He called around when I got out of jail to see how I was, that's all. Maybe he wanted to carry on where we'd left off."

"And he's still calling around?"

She nodded.

"I get the feeling you don't even like him."

"We've both changed," she whispered, staring into the mug again. Benson was putting the story together in his own mind, and allowing Jess to affirm it for him.

Easy does it. "He scares me a little. He was very upset when I didn't seek him out once I'd been released." She swallowed, watching their reactions.

"And why didn't you?"

"My only concern was getting back on my feet and trying to form a relationship with my teenage son again. I'm not interested in a relationship with him, or with anyone. And Christ, he's let himself go."

"How has he taken the news that you're not interested in rekindling your old romance?"

"He's not happy about it. I think that's why he keeps calling round, hoping I've changed my mind." She studied Benson.

Eddie said, "He's not exactly pushed the boat out, though, has he?"

"He's a junkie. He thinks he looks wonderful."

Benson nodded, eyes focused somewhere beyond the confines of the small bedsit, mind obviously elsewhere too.

Jess coughed. "If there's nothing else, I'd like to enjoy my cold chicken."

The chair creaked as Benson stood. "I'll be sending someone around to take a statement from you about the burglary."

"What? Why?"

"It won't take long. It's only about the burglary here. And you might not know it yet, but I'm doing it for your own protection. Okay?"

"Sounds like a waste of time to me."

"Get your locks changed," Eddie said.

Chapter Fifty-Eight

Benson started the car but didn't drive away from outside Jess's house. "What do you think?"

"She's a smart cookie. And she was very convincing about Marchant. If I wanted someone to think I had nothing to do with someone's death, I'd play happy Karma about it too. And she played it well."

"You think she had something to do with it?"

"I think she knows about it. And I wouldn't be surprised to hear that she knows Tony's involved with it."

Benson cleared his throat. "Shoes?"

"Nike Cortez."

Benson swallowed. "I have enough to pull her in."

"Any lawyer would have her back out in twenty minutes. Leave her. You know she didn't do Marchant, and you'll never prove conspiracy, even if you *can* find this Tony geezer. And right now, she's just flattened any theory of her being at Doc Bolton's murder by saying someone nicked her jacket. She's not daft, Tom."

"What about her knife drawer?"

"Mish-mash of crap in it. Nothing to say the knife in that jacket pocket belonged there."

"Do you think she killed Bolton?"

Eddie stared forward. "Fifty-fifty."

"Fat lot of fucking use you are."

"She's scared stiff of him – this Tony geezer."

"I know. She's worried every time he comes round."

"She had a knife."

Benson snapped his head around. "She what?"

"I saw her bring it out from under the mattress. I was watching in the wardrobe mirror."

"Why the hell didn't you say something?"

"What? Charge her with not keeping a sharp object in a drawer? She keeps it there for self-defence, you can tell."

"Oh, you can tell, can you? Have you forgotten that she stabbed and killed her ex? She's an expert, you idiot."

"Ah, yes, I'd forgotten that. If you believe the verdict, of course." Eddie stared at Benson from the corner of his eye.

"You don't?"

Eddie shrugged. "You've read all the crap on that case, not me. But if she was telling the truth back there, then surely it's a possibility that he did it."

"And left her to carry the can?"

"I think the murder was more important than the consequences. If Tony killed Sebastian, he didn't give any thought to what happened next."

Benson blew exasperation through his lips. "You think having the coat stolen was a bit convenient?"

"Let me put it another way: If Tony killed Doc, then he planted her coat not only to deflect guilt away from himself, but to directly implicate her."

"And?"

"And what?"

Benson tutted. "You started your sentence with 'if'. I don't like ifs."

"Look, either she killed Doc and inadvertently left her own coat there – very clumsy. Or Tony did it, and deliberately left her coat there for us to find."

"Did he steal her shoes too? Nike Cortez; you said so yourself."

Eddie was silent. Eventually, he turned to Benson, shrugged. "I can't explain—"

"I can. She killed Doc Bolton for his part in sending her to prison. A two-year-old—"

"She didn't!"

Benson stared at him. He looked forward again, tapping the steering wheel. "Why would Tony kill him?"

Eddie shook his head.

"Come on. You've obviously got a fucking theory."

"You shouldn't be asking why Tony would kill Doc Bolton; you should be asking why he framed Jessica Ripley."

"This is beginning to sound like a Disney movie."

Eddie said, "I don't know what's going on inside that relationship, but I can tell you she's only a couple of degrees away from a breakdown. Hence the constant fear and hence the knife."

"You could do psychology as a sideline," Benson smirked. "Make a fortune."

"Yeah? And you could be a private investigator."

"You think so?"

Eddie grinned. "You'd never make a penny, but think of the status: Tom Benson, PI."

"Bastard."

"I could mistake you for Tom Selleck, easy. Grow a moustache and you could be his twin."

Benson filled the car with profanities and took off back towards the station; Eddie said, "Where are you going? I don't work in that shithole any more!"

Benson closed his eyes and cut across the traffic to get onto the M621. "I keep forgetting that you walked out."

"Pushed, mate. I was pushed."

"How are you going to get back in?"

"They'll invite me back before long. Watch this space."

"How do you work that one out?"

"Just a hunch."

"Like I said. So full of shit."

* * *

Eddie got out, grateful to note that Wendy's car wasn't parked outside his cottage. He bent and peered back into the car at Benson. "Did the Wicked Witch of the West submit that coat and knife from Doc's scene?"

Benson shrugged. "I've never had to look over CSI's shoulder before."

"Yeah, well, you'd better make a start. They're top priority – pay the premium, get it turned around quick. Twenty-four hours, Tom, don't fuck about."

"If it's hers, it means nothing anyway – she's just said it was stolen. And we can't prove who put it there."

"You think? The answer was right there staring at everyone in that scene."

Benson looked confused. "How do you mean?"

"Ask the lady in charge of your CSI department. She should know." Eddie slammed the door and began walking.

The car pulled up alongside, and the window opened.

Benson called out, "Come on, Eddie, tell me."

Eddie carried on walking, pulled his collar up.

"Eddie! It's my fucking case. Tell me."

Eddie turned and blew Benson a kiss as he put the key in the door.

"Bastard!"

Eddie slammed the door.

The first thing that struck him was the silence. It struck him so hard that it stopped him in his tracks on the way to the kettle. This was bliss. It was like the old days when all he had to worry about was himself and a spider called Winston. But all that had stopped about the time MCU had knocked on his door. And it stopped for Winston about five minutes later when someone from Major Crime stepped on him. Good ol' days.

And now he had Charles living here; and Wendy the Aunt Sally lookalike was here more often than not, too. The house was starting to smell like a prostitute's handbag. And that got him thinking in a whole new direction, and the thinking stopped at Troy.

Troy had Eddie's number. Why hadn't he called to say he'd left Charles's house, *thanks for letting me use the sofa*? Or something like that, anything really, just to say he was okay, and he'd locked the door on his way out, and I promise not to attack you any more, that kind of thing.

Eddie took out his phone, checked it for missed calls or text messages, and there were none. He hit dial and waited for the voice to tell him to leave a message. "Ring me, Troy. Let me know you're okay."

He put the phone away and reached for the kettle. He was tempted; just a quick coffee before making the most of being alone – relaxing to Floyd with no need for headphones. But he couldn't, could he?

He sighed, locked the door on his way out and climbed aboard the Discovery.

Chapter Fifty-Nine

As soon as the cops left, Jessica had burst into tears. There had been an inexplicable feeling of dashing towards a death that it was impossible to escape. Like being on a collision course, and finding out someone had removed the steering wheel. It was an hour before she'd surfaced again. And when she had, she felt different, somehow. Although the steering wheel was still missing, she had control of the accelerator pedal. And taking her foot off it allowed her time enough to see if there was still anything left in the world worth fighting for.

It was raining again as she stared. Only this time there was a chill wind as well, and every now and then it would flick rain at her through the open sides of the bus shelter. It made her blink, and then it made her squint. If it wasn't for her nerves, she would be getting angry by now.

The cause of the nerves strolled into view.

Michael walked along Heath Road alone this time, and Jess's eyes widened a fraction, her heart stepped up a gear and she jerked as though ready to stand, the annoying rain forgotten. But she turned the heat down, breathed more deeply, and tried to relax.

He was her son, she reasoned. They'd not seen each other for a few years, and hadn't had a chance to bond yet, that was all. It wasn't as though they'd grown apart; it was that they'd never had the chance to grow together in the first place. And he would understand that when she pointed it out to him.

How could he not understand?

Who would choose a foster parent over true blood? No one, that's who.

* * *

Eddie tried the front door, hoping it might be open. It was not, and the longer he stood here the more conspicuous he felt, the wetter he grew, and the angrier he became. He knocked, and despite the noise of traffic behind him, he could hear footsteps coming to the door. If it was Jess who answered, he'd have to come clean, and he'd have to make her understand why he needed access to her bedsit.

He turned around, and watched his blue van on the kerbside, hoping no one would recognise it. He'd taken notice of Benson and the need to find out who Tony was, and decided the best way of doing that would be to find something he'd had hold of. And the only place Eddie knew he'd been was here.

Eddie had called ahead, asked Sid to leave the CID office, sneak back into the CSI office, grab his van keys and bring them to him in the car park. Of course Sid had done it, and of course he'd been full of questions. None of which Eddie had answered.

The door opened and a blond-haired kid of twenty swayed on the top step. "Hey."

"Is Jess in, do you know?"

The kid stepped aside. "No idea, man. Don't fucking keep tabs, know what I mean?" He shuffled into his own bedsit halfway along the dusty hallway. Eddie peeked in on his way past, and he could see a black-haired male in there too. He saw his eyes, the way they couldn't stay still, and a shiver ran up Eddie's back.

Eddie knocked on Jessica's door. No reply. He listened, and knocked again. Nothing.

The noise of the traffic died and Eddie snapped on a pair of gloves. He shoved the door. He could see the frame giving way in the middle where the Yale lock bolt sank into it. He pushed his foot in at the bottom of the door, causing some tension, and then he shouldered the top and the damned thing sprang open and Eddie nearly fell inside.

It was quiet. Eerie. Clean.

* * *

Now Jess stood, and her hand clutched the side post of the bus shelter. Cold water ran inside her sleeve. She let traffic pass by and crossed the street through a mist of white spray, watching him. As she drew closer, he looked up from his feet, pulled away from his thoughts, squinting into the rain. He noticed her.

His eyes opened, and his pace slowed. His face was pale.

"Michael." Jess smiled, reaching out to him. "I was just, I was..."

"You're not supposed to be here." He stood still as she approached, pulled away from her shaking hand.

She stopped a couple of feet away from her son. He was the same height as her now. How he'd grown big and true. A fine young man indeed. She smiled at him; a genuine smile, full of the pride she felt for him. He might have been brought up by someone else, but she had given him his foundation, and it was that foundation that saw him tall and muscular right now, handsome. She looked him up and down. He wore his school uniform, a dark blue blazer with an embroidered badge stitched onto the left breast. The Latin motto arcing across the top of it said, 'Scientia et Veritas', and its English equivalent mirrored it at the bottom: 'Knowledge and Truth'.

He opened his mouth to speak.

Was it possible to embrace the sound of words? She got ready to snuggle into them, clicking the switch inside that would record his voice in full Dolby surround. The anticipation was crushing her; Jessica held her breath, put living on hold.

"Why don't you fuck off?" His eyes were cold, his face calm with a strange fury under the skin, ready to break out and throttle her. "If you don't fuck off right now, I'll call the police. Okay? Stay the hell away from me."

Her smile cracked and then shattered like a broken window. There was no light inside her. She was a husk.

"I told you that I don't want nothing to do with you. Why can't you get that, eh?"

"I only want you to know that I love you, Michael. I want you to know that we can be a happy family again. Just you and me." She smiled at him again, and was about to reach out and touch his arm when he slapped her hard across the face.

The queue of people at the bus shelter gasped. When she turned to look at them, one or two of the women had their hands at their mouths; one old man was getting to his feet. She smiled at them, palmed away their concerns, and looked back at Michael as a thin trail of blood ran across the crease in her chin and then dissolved in the rain.

"Why won't you give us a chance? I'm a decent woman, Michael, a nice woman." She laughed. "Really, I am."

Michael unlatched the gate.

"They hurt us both when they locked me up, but there's no need to stay apart now. Don't you get it?"

* * *

He dropped his fingerprint kit on the floor and turned a full three-sixty. It was a small room; enough space for a single bed, a wardrobe that was slowly collapsing sideways, and a chest of drawers that looked like a stutter of misaligned carpentry. To the side of the bed was a tall, slim window. The dirty net curtains over it swayed in a breeze that whistled through the ill-fitting sash window frame. Eddie took a peek outside to the back yard: an empty washing line and a gate hanging off its hinges. Sad.

Then there was the kitchenette. A single countertop with a stainless sink and a cupboard beneath it.

He sighed. There were few places in here with surfaces good enough for a fingerprint examination, and even fewer that would still hold Tony's marks. Either Jess would have touched them since and obliterated them, or she would have cleaned.

There was only one place that Eddie could think of that might still have Tony's fingerprints.

* * *

Michael closed the gate and turned to walk up the path, without even a backward glance.

"No one has given me a chance," she said. "Everyone has been awful to me, Michael. Everyone," she called. "It's about time someone… you… It's about time *you* gave me a chance!" She clutched the gate. "Michael, you will hear me. I just want to talk. Come back."

He closed the house door behind him, and Jess's voice cracked.

"Michael. Please!"

She gripped the gate, hands white, nails digging into the wet wood. She shook it and felt a scream brewing in the blackest part of her guts. Someone touched her on the shoulder and she spun around. It was the old man from the bus shelter. "Are you alright, love?"

She snarled at him. "Fuck off and mind your own business, granddad. Interfering bastard!" Jessica let the rain wash her tears down her face, and she walked away, her hands curled into claws, muttering to herself as she sobbed.

On the journey home, she clawed at her face – physically and emotionally. She wanted to pull her eyes out – she didn't want to see her son walking away any more. She wanted them to be together, forever. And that he'd chosen Valentine over her… it was killing her to think of it. Killing her.

She stood on the doorstep, trying to get the key in the lock, but her hands were shaking and her heart was collapsing so violently that she thought she wouldn't even make it inside before she fell over dead of a broken heart. How she hated what they'd done to her; the whole world was taking it in turns to kick a fallen woman.

Eventually, she got the door open, then kicked it shut behind her. Still sobbing, she walked up the hallway.

* * *

The bathroom was tiny, barely enough room for a man to stand without tipping into the bath or scraping along the wall to reach the toilet. He pulled the light cord and saw what he was up against.

The toilet was very old, a monstrosity made of green porcelain. The perfect place to throw up in, Eddie thought. But the toilet seat was in good order. A stack of cleaning fluids and bleach lined up next to the toilet rolls on the edge of the bath said she'd tried to do the best with what she had, and that added to the picture of Jess in Eddie's mind; how she soldiered on regardless of the shit that life threw her way.

Eddie unlatched his kit and took a moment to listen to the noises of the house before he became absorbed in the examination. Satisfied that he was alone and wouldn't be disturbed by the junkies next door, he lifted the toilet seat and charged the brush with a little aluminium powder. And then he held his breath and powdered the underside of the seat.

Amid the yellow stains that dotted the surface, a set of four fingerprints came up almost instantly. There were many more too, overlapping, some smearing others, some obliterating others. But Eddie was happy; there were four very good marks. He wasted no time. He prepared an acetate, then tore off a length of rubber lifting tape and gently rolled it onto the marks.

They peeled off almost perfectly, as though it were rigged as a practical examination. Getting results this good was a rarity.

They'd soon know who Tony was.

He rolled the lifted tape onto a small rectangle of clear acetate and filed it away inside his jacket pocket, put away the brush, the tape and the powder, and latched his kit box. The front door slammed shut.

He froze. Jaw hanging open.

Eddie put the seat down, yanked the light switch, and returned to the bedsit in a panic, listening to Jess's footsteps along the hall outside.

* * *

Jess closed the bedsit door behind her. Even though her nose was blocked with tears, she could still smell them, those men who'd visited her this morning. Eddie, his name was; she could smell his aftershave as though he were still in the room.

A gust of wind whistled through the window and the net curtain billowed. Through it she saw a tall man walking away with a briefcase in his hand.

Chapter Sixty

Eddie parked outside the fingerprint bureau at Bishopgarth in Wakefield. He left the engine running and tapped on the fourth window from the right. It opened and a hand reached out. "You know I could get disciplined for doing this, Eddie?"

"Where's your sense of adventure?"

"The mortgage company took it."

"Look, I just need a name. Afterwards you can throw this away, no one's the wiser."

"You owe me big time."

"I will be forever in your debt." Eddie laughed.

"Does that mean you've no intention of paying me?" Leo laughed and poked his head out.

"Seriously," Eddie said, "thanks—"

"Whoa, boy. Let's not get too serious, okay? It's just a name. Gimme a day or two, eh?"

"You're a hero, Leo." Eddie climbed back into the van. "Let DI Benson know if you get a hit."

"Bottle of Glenfiddich wouldn't go amiss."

"I won't forget." Eddie waved and drove away, leaving Leo shaking his head.

* * *

Eddie swapped his van for the Discovery and pulled up outside his dad's old house. His heart sank to see Wendy's Audi already there. He wondered how long she could get away with parking it here in this insalubrious Leeds neighbourhood before the wheels and satnav were stolen. He shrugged; maybe the local youths would think it belonged to a drugs baron and leave it well alone.

He didn't cut the engine at first, just sat there wondering how to play it. How far had she got her talons into him, exactly?

Eddie's mind shot forward at a thousand miles an hour. He saw a train of events that began from this very spot, from this impending meeting. He saw Charles becoming indignant; he saw Wendy holding Charles's arm, supporting her man and encouraging him to cut ties with his wayward son, and not listen to anything more from him. He saw Charles moving out, back into his own home, but with her giving the orders. She'd make sure Eddie stayed away.

And he could see Charles and Wendy married inside six months, a rewritten will, and a fatal coronary within a year. That would be as much nagging as one man like Charles could stand.

That would be goodbye. Eddie's eyes flickered as he suddenly realised he was thinking about Miss Moneypenny. He also realised his mouth was open in shock.

He shut off the motor, climbed out, and approached the front door. He knocked, thinking it the right thing to do, despite having his own key. He had hoped that Troy would answer the door. Of course Wendy would be angry that he'd been using Charles's house as lodgings for some junkie, but better that, Eddie thought, than having the junkie running riot somewhere.

That Eddie had spent considerable time and money repairing the house ought to count for something, anyway. Shouldn't it?

The hinges creaked and Eddie looked at Charles's eyes, hooded by folds of skin that had been taut only last week. "You've aged by about ten years," he said quietly. He peered over Charles's shoulders but didn't see her anywhere. "Dad, don't let her—"

"Well! If it isn't the silent property developer! Come in, come in."

Eddie looked at Charles as he stepped aside.

"I see how it is now," Wendy snapped. "Getting this place ready to sell from under your own father's feet! You are a callous, greedy boy."

Eddie looked across at her. "Wendy, shut up. I was doing this for you, Dad, should you ever…"

"Should I ever decide to move out?"

"Well—"

"You only had to say, Eddie," said Charles. "I would have gone. I didn't want to outstay my welcome."

"No, no. You misunderstand, Dad. I never—"

Wendy interrupted. "Really? It's quite plain, Eddie. It's lucky I was here to pick up the pieces. When a son abandons his father—"

"Last chance to shut your mouth before I shut it for you, okay?"

Wendy gasped.

"Eddie," said Charles. "No need for all this. We'll call it quits, son. Thanks for doing the house up – I appreciate it – and thanks for letting me stay with you. I enjoyed our time together. But now," he said, "I think we'd better go our separate ways. What do you think?"

"What do I think? Dad, she's poison. Walk away while you still can."

Charles shook his head. "Out you go. Go on, please. Let's not have a scene."

"Dad? You're not serious?" His earlier vision was working out just right.

"And don't think we haven't noticed you're back on the booze!" Wendy shouted as the door started to close.

Eddie was confused for a moment, but then he realised what had happened. He stopped the door closing, said, "Dad, let me in. Two minutes." Eddie didn't give negotiation a chance. He pushed the front door open and walked past them both and into the back room, into the parlour.

On the dining table was the bottle of Courvoisier. And even from here, with the daylight coming through the window beyond, he could see it was now only half full. "It's my challenge. You need to get your own."

Next to the bottle was a plain white mug with dregs of brandy in the bottom, and next to it a dinner plate. On the dinner plate were a dozen cigarette ends, some foil gum wraps, and two tiny plastic bags. Eddie picked them up and saw the residue of white powder inside them.

He dropped them, closed his eyes. "Oh you fucking idiot, Troy."

Chapter Sixty-One

Benson looked around the CSI office, at the empty desks, all the monitors showing the West Yorkshire Police screensavers. No one was there to get angry at them. The whole place seemed like a waste of electricity. He knocked on Eddie's door, and then corrected himself; Nicki's door. He would have to get used to that. There was nothing he could do to change things so he might as well stop thrashing against the system and learn to live with it.

Nicki was sitting at her desk, a pen and a sheet of paper with what looked like lists of names before her. She looked up, smiled, and went back to her list.

Benson coughed. "The coat," he said. "The one at Bolton's scene."

Nicki put down her pen and looked up at him. "What about it?"

"Did you submit it for DNA analysis?"

She nodded. "Yes, and the knife we found in the pocket, actually." She sighed. "If you'd checked the computer you'd find out when I did it."

"Never was very good with technology," Benson said.

She smiled politely at him, picked up her pen. But Benson didn't leave. "Anything else I can help you with?"

"I was chatting with Collins. He said you'd know who hung that coat up on the stand at the far end of the kitchen."

"He did?"

"Said it was on show to everyone in that scene."

"So what does it matter who put it there?"

Benson leaned against the door frame. "The owner of the coat says it was stolen from her. And there's now a chance that Bolton's killer was a male."

Nicki swivelled her chair, confusion on her face. "If we've traced the owner of the coat, why have I spent eight-hundred pounds having it examined—"

"On priority, I hope."

"On priority, yes. Again, the computer—"

"Again, I don't do computers if there's a person around. Okay?"

She offered a patronising smile.

"Who put that coat there, Nicki?"

"I don't know. I don't know what he's talking about." Nicki's eyes roamed as though looking around the office for the answer. "I have no idea. And I don't think he knows, actually. It's of no relevance."

"Really?"

"So Bolton will have put it there, I suppose." The shrug said she didn't know, but was settling for any answer just to get rid of Benson. "He's trying to make me look bad, Inspector Benson. Don't pay him any attention."

Benson nodded. She was full of shit. He left the office just as Weismann entered.

* * *

"He's a very stubborn man."

"Who? My dad?"

"No, not… Well, yes, him too. He gets an idea in his head and listens to no one who might have a different opinion." Weismann looked across the van at her. "It's no way to run a department, Nicki. No one says he has to make it a democracy, but it shouldn't be an autocracy either – that's when errors creep in, working practices suffer—"

"So tell him, not me."

"He won't listen to me. You try it." Weismann took a deep breath and stared forward, trying to weave a way through this minefield without becoming another victim. "The last thing he needs," he continued, "is 'yes' people. If Collins was right about one thing, it's that. It's a very unhealthy thing, surrounding yourself with people who agree with you."

Nicki snatched a glance at him, her eyebrows raised.

He sighed. "I've tried!"

"So who's stubborn?"

"What?"

"You were saying. He's stubborn."

"Oh. Collins."

"Stubborn? I thought he bowed out quite elegantly under the circumstances, actually. He could have kicked up more of a stink. But I suppose he would have faced disciplinary proceedings for the things that went on in that office."

"So you said."

"I feel a 'but' coming on."

And yes, there was a 'but'. Yet he felt disinclined to share it with her. Nicki was in the middle of pulling CSIs from division to float the office until a more permanent solution could be found, but it would be a week before anyone took up residence in the office. If the whole thing had been handled with a little more finesse then none of this nastiness need have happened, and people wouldn't have walked out. Forensic operations wouldn't be suffering. The office would still be viable.

And they *were* suffering. Substantially. And that's where Weismann was feeling the pressure – he was head of CSI and he was feeling the pressure from above and from below.

For a moment, he reflected on his own words – was he a 'yes' man? Surely, if he'd had more strength, he could have prevented this idiocy in the first place? But, when you accept a favour from your boss, such as being made Head of CSI, it becomes much more difficult to protest about doing something similar for his daughter.

Weismann sighed; it was a horrible situation, and he didn't feel at all proud of himself right now. He looked across at Nicki, but knew she didn't feel anything other than victorious, which was a shame.

She'd even tried to talk her way out of coming to this scene, but she couldn't. *She* was it; there was no one else they could send.

It was as though Collins had known all along that the series of deaths wasn't at an end yet, and now he was standing by watching the entire department fall flat on its face. But if that happened, it wouldn't just be something funny for him to laugh at, it wouldn't just be a lesson well learned for Crawford or even for him; it would be an internal affairs matter that would drag on for months; it would be interviews in front of the senior leadership team. And it would mean justifying their actions; how they ousted Jeffery, how they reacted to Eddie Collins's handling of his office, and how they reacted after he – possibly with just cause – relinquished control as requested, and then walked out of the office, followed by all of his staff.

No one had seen that one coming.

There was something about Collins that Weismann hated – he thought it was his arrogance, his lack of humility. And yet, regrettably, there was something about Collins that he respected.

Nicki pulled up in the middle of the road. Across it were two strips of blue and white scene tape. There were vans and police cars parked all over the place.

"So what's the 'but'?" she said.

"Ah, yes. The 'but' is that you might have bitten off more than the pair of you can chew."

She pulled the handbrake on, cut the engine and stared at him, as though he'd just become her new best enemy. She pouted, eyes half shut, arms folded, like a teenager waiting for words of wisdom from a parent who really should have known better than to challenge her.

Weismann turned slightly in his seat, rubbed a hand down his chin, and took a breath. He nodded towards the house with the PCSO standing outside. "This is where your decision and your father's decision will either bear fruit or will knock you off your pedestal."

"Pedestal?"

"Listen! This is the sharp end, Nicki. This is the only thing of importance in your life right now; not the office, not Eddie Collins, not impressing your father."

"I don't—"

"Shut up. Please."

The pout grew an inch and she stared forward, chastened.

"This is a murder scene, Nicki. Forget your pride and your vanity. This absolutely has to be a perfect examination without anyone hand-holding you. People are relying on you to get it right."

"I will get it right."

"And people are waiting for you to get it wrong."

"I said—"

Weismann palmed her comment. "Okay. But if you feel uncomfortable at all, or out of your depth—"

"I've been doing this job—"

"For three years. Yes, your father said."

So why do you always try to talk your way out of it?

* * *

Weismann held a clipboard and walked behind Nicki up the short path leading to the front door. He offered his name to the scene guard, who entered it onto a log below Nicki's. Nicki had the camera and her small box of forensic kit. He pulled up his face mask, stretched the gloves on his hands into a fist, and stepped forward. He had a bad feeling about this.

Once in the hallway, Weismann pushed the front door closed with a knuckle and said, "What are you going to do about body recovery? We'll need a tent to shield—"

"I have one in the van."

Weismann nodded as she turned away. "What about someone to give you a hand—"

"I'm quite capable of handling this alone, actually, thanks. And before you ask, I've arranged for a biologist to attend. And I've let the coroner's officer know; she'll contact the pathologist and request he visit the scene."

All well and good, thought Weismann, but she hadn't even viewed the body yet. Who was to say they'd even be needed?

"Now, I'm going to put stepping plates up the stairs." She thrust her chin forward in an assertion of power. "So you might want to make a note of that" —she indicated his notebook— "and then we'll go on up and see what all the fuss is about, yes?"

"Okay, I'll help you—"

"No, you won't. You'll do nothing. In fact, I don't understand why you're here, unless you're hoping I'll mess up so you can report it to my father?"

"Nicki, I don't want you to mess up; why would you say that?"

"Because you don't agree with how we did things."

"No. No, I don't agree. But it's done now. And my only concern at the moment is this scene."

"You need have no concerns on that score. This scene is in very safe hands."

Weismann nodded slowly. He stood back, clutching the notebook to his chest. "I'll wait while you get the plates," he said. "I want to see what's up there."

Chapter Sixty-Two

Nicki put the last plate on the top step and lurched onto the landing. She didn't watch Weismann ascending shakily behind her; she was awestruck by what she'd seen in the bedroom and the massacre that was waiting for her. She swallowed, regretting her earlier bravado.

Standing here, she realised there were a lot of things she regretted. And most of them began with her dad.

"Well?"

Nicki looked around, surprised to find Weismann was already by her side. "I, er… I think we need more stepping plates. It's a good floor in there. Don't want to er… You know. Footwear marks." Her mouth was watering. "Back in a minute." She set off back down the stairs.

A full fifteen minutes later she was back with another armful of stepping plates.

Weismann had run out of tunes to hum, had run out of conversations to have with himself, and was instead standing by the bedroom doorframe, peering in at the body and at the attempt someone had made at becoming a butcher.

"Here I am. Sorry I kept you waiting." She dropped the plates on the landing and cringed at the noise they made, like a thousand church bells chiming at the same time. She nodded a brief apology at Weismann and then laid a short trail out across the laminate bedroom floor, arriving a couple of feet short of the dead man and his cleaved face.

She swallowed, and then she noticed Weismann sniffing the air.

"Can you smell mint?" he asked.

"Oh. I used a little Vicks, actually. Would you like some?" Her eyes watered.

"Shall we get on?"

Nicki nodded, and turned back to the man. He was on his back, halfway between sitting and lying – the position he would have assumed if reclining in a deckchair. He was leaning against his upturned bed frame. He had a hand missing, chopped off at the wrist at an angle; she couldn't see it, but she could make out the ends of the radius and ulna glistening white among the red meat. The other hand was draped strangely across his right knee, only connected with his forearm by a string of white – a clump of nerves, or a tendon.

Nicki blinked rapidly.

Her eyes drifted down to his open crotch area. The clothing there was in shreds, and his… She peered closer, torchlight picking out details she wished it hadn't. There were two hefty cuts, one of them down to the inside of his thigh bone. She could see bone clearly; his leg looked like a freshly butchered steak.

She looked away.

Among the collection of dust and empty crisp packets on the floor were a pair of socks, three used condoms, clumps of dust-encrusted hair, and dozens of chewed fingernail ends, ragged. Nicki closed her eyes and took a long slow breath.

But the scene didn't get much better when she eventually opened them again and saw his penis lying on the floor, partly covered by his scrotum. Blood everywhere. She suddenly felt warm as her eyes drifted north to his face. When they got there, she felt hot. Her mouth watered even more. She could hear her rushed breathing inside the mask, could feel sweat trickling into her eyes. Her whole body was prickling. She dropped the torch, turned and ran straight into Weismann as she headed for the doorway.

"Nicki?" Weismann was up on his feet quickly, following her to make sure she was okay. He was right behind her as she ran across the hall into the bathroom.

She pulled her mask down and slid to a halt, panting. It smelled of faeces in here.

On the toilet was another body that no one had told them about. It was a woman, head tilted to one side as though she'd nodded off. It was cleaved almost from her shoulders. A sheet of blood had cascaded down her side, down her arm. On the floor was a spread of blood a couple of feet wide that had crusted at the edges.

A single delicate droplet of blood hung from one of her long brown fingernails, ready to fall, but frozen in place by coagulation, pursed by haemostasis.

Across the wall to the right was more blood. Part of Nicki's mind suggested it was cast off, and another part insisted it was arterial spray. The last part of Nicki's mind made her turn away from the woman and throw up all over Weismann.

Now it smelled of vomit in here, too.

Chapter Sixty-Three

Eddie was sitting in his car, looking at the house where he used to live as a kid. Back then there were maybe two or three cars parked in this street; now it was like driving through a slalom. What rankled most was knowing that his dad was stuck in there with a woman he couldn't stand because he was just too proud to admit it.

Someone had shown him a bit of attention, and he'd fallen down on one knee like a love-sick prick. If only he could see what he looked like from the outside; if only he could see what *she* looked like from the outside. If only he could, he'd run a mile.

Eddie's thoughts turned back to Troy just as Sid answered the phone.

"Eddie, is that you?"

"How you doing, Sid?"

"I'm helping Melanie out with research and whatnot. I'm not working in there, in CSI; I told them I wouldn't work under that" — Sid's voice lowered— "under that cow. I told them, Eddie, she's ruined that office, ruined it! But I couldn't walk out of the building, you see. I know it was the great show of strength or maybe the show of dignity on your part, whatever you want to call it, but I just couldn't join in. You do see that, don't you, Eddie? I really need to keep my job. I'm sorry."

"You know what I've missed about you, Sid?"

"No, what?"

"Fuck all."

"Ah, you haven't changed."

There was a smile in Sid's voice, and it somehow popped out onto Eddie's face too. It was good to talk to him again.

"There's been a murder."

"Sid, this is Leeds – there's always a murder."

"I know, I know, but *she's* gone to it – Nicki. And Weismann has gone with her."

"Should be interesting."

"She won't last two minutes, Eddie. You know how she always wriggled out of dealing with bodies… Well, I mean, I know I couldn't deal with them either, but that's not the point, is it? It's her job, and she should be able to do—"

"Sid. Do me a favour."

"What? I am quite busy, Eddie."

"You shock me. Listen, just find out for me if Nicki sent the coat and knife from Doc Bolton's scene away for DNA analysis."

"Give me a minute."

Eddie could hear Sid attacking a keyboard.

"So what are you doing with yourself while you're not at work?"

"I am still at work, Sid, just not in the office. You know what I mean; I'm keeping my finger in the pie."

"What you do in your own time is your own business." Sid laughed. "Right, here we are, the exhibit list for Doc's case. Yes, she sent them off, twenty-four-hour turnaround. So, a day for transport and admin… should get the results later today. But I'd say tomorrow morning at the earliest – you know what they're like."

Eddie nodded. He did indeed; getting a genuine twenty-four-hour turnaround was like getting an insurance company to pay out. "One more thing. Any idea where Troy lives?"

"Troy? Oh, Eddie. I think you should leave him alone. He's trouble."

"I think he's *in* trouble, Sid."

"Ah; going to his rescue? What a lovely gesture."

"It's not a gesture. I'm trying to help him."

"And everyone says you're a twat, can you believe that?"

"Who? Who says I'm a twat?"

Sid was laughing down the phone, and Eddie found himself smiling again. It felt good, but he wouldn't tell anyone he'd done it. No point having a reputation as a twat and then ruining it all by smiling. It would be a bit like having a reputation as a twat and then going out on a date. The smile limped off Eddie's face and dragged a sneer into position.

He looked to his right, saw the curtains twitching in his old front room. Doubtless Wendy was in there slagging him off to his dad again. "Sid?"

"I'm looking, hold on."

"Do you know anything about Facebook?"

"You're joining Facebook?"

"No, not me, you dick. Can you find someone on there for me?"

"Who?"

Eddie frowned. What the hell was her surname? "I only know her as Wendy."

There was a long pause before Sid said, "That could take a little while, Eddie."

"Was that your best attempt at sarcasm?"

"I thought it was quite good! Anyway, how come you're after someone called Wendy? Melanie says you're dating—"

"Yes, I am. It's not for me." He sighed.

"Congratu—"

"Sid, listen. I'm running background checks on some cow who's… Never mind, just get me some details about her."

"Like what?"

"Actually, you'll be able to find her through my old man: Charles Edward Collins."

"Aw, were you named after your dad?"

"No. His name's Charles, Sid. Get a grip."

"Okay, leave it with me. I'll see what I can do. Anyway – Troy: his address. He lives in Harehills."

* * *

On his way to Harehills, Eddie thought about Troy, and about what he'd said in the parlour last night when Eddie had asked why he'd gone back on the drugs again. *I'd lost my chance, Mr Collins. Nothing to keep me off them any more.*

"Chance?" Strange choice of word when all he meant was that he'd lost his job. "I'd lost my chance."

Eddie drove along York Road, past the old fire station and past the old police station, headed up the dual carriageway under the walkway, and took his next right along Harehills Lane.

Back-to-back terraced houses – hundreds of them. Identical. Kids vandalised them so they knew which was their street. He drove along slowly, staring. Dereliction and deprivation were the only things in abundance around here. He felt sorry for the mucky kids running around in the streets, the old men sitting on stone steps smoking joints and watching the high-heeled tarts strutting to the shiny black four-by-fours belonging to their pushers, pimps, and punters.

Number 49 came up on his left, and Eddie's jaw nearly bounced off the steering wheel. He stared at the house. It was like a glistening jewel in a field of cow shit, like a single smile in a sea of tears. Eddie came to a halt outside. It wasn't one of the red-brick terraces; it was a large detached house, painted white. In the front garden were palm trees, a water feature, a well-landscaped lawn amid a plethora of late-blooming plants and shrubs. On the roof was a row of solar panels, and the red eyes of a pair of high-end CCTV cameras glowed under the eaves.

Eddie climbed out, locked and double-checked the car doors, and then walked to one of the stone pillars either side of the driveway. He pushed a button as he looked across the driveway for Troy's black Astra.

"Hello?"

Eddie looked into the small camera set into the wall. "My name's Eddie Collins. I work with Troy. I wondered—"

The black and gold wrought-iron gates folded inwards and Eddie crossed the threshold. He was surprised to find this house on this estate, but he tried to cast aside all the preconceived images of the occupants that came to the fore. He couldn't help one image, though; it came and refused to be ushered aside. It was of a drugs baron. Look at the security here, he thought; look at the easy distribution, the opulence paid for and no doubt maintained by a choke-hold on the local community and their addictions. It stank of cliché.

The front door opened before Eddie got anywhere near it. A man stood in the shade; as Eddie approached, he could tell he wasn't looking at a typical drug baron.

Not many drug barons wore knitted green tank tops and tweed golfing trousers. He had garters on his shirt sleeves. His face, pleasant enough for a man pushing fifty, was as pristine as his front garden was immaculate. And when he smiled, Eddie wished he'd been wearing his sunglasses.

The man thrust out his hand. "Marlow." Eddie felt compelled to shake. The hand was cold, smooth, like he was a mannequin with full AI robotics. His eyes were green with perfect whites and there was not a single whisker on his face. The resemblance to Troy was uncanny.

"I work with him."

The man's eyes squinted up a little. "He mentioned an Eddie Collins once."

Eddie shrugged and smiled. "Guess I'm just popular."

The man did not smile. "How may I help you, Mr Collins?"

"I'm looking for Troy. I wondered if you'd—"

"Is he missing?"

"Well, no; not missing, as such."

"If you work with him, how is it that you cannot find him? He is either missing. Or he is not missing. Which is it?"

Eddie blinked, something he had yet to see those green eyes do. "I was expecting to meet with him today, but he didn't show up."

Marlow gave it some consideration.

"Are you his father?"

"I am."

"Has he been in touch?"

"Obviously not. Is he using drugs again?"

"I beg your pardon?"

"I assume you are not hard of hearing, so you are shocked at my question. But not because I mentioned the drugs. Shocked because you know he's using again, but felt it inappropriate to let me know. Are you trying to cover up for him, Mr Collins?"

"Either you know where he is. Or you do not know where he is. Which is it?"

"This was his last chance." Marlow was completely expressionless, despite Eddie's impersonation. Not a twitch in the eyebrows, not a smirk or a frown to be found on that wonderful, wrinkle-free face.

Eddie found himself staring at the face and had to pull back from tapping it to see if it was made of plastic. "I'm sorry, I don't quite follow."

"You don't have to. Goodbye, Mr Collins."

"Wait, wait. What's up with the lad? He just needs some help."

"He received help three years ago, Mr Collins. Now is the time for discipline and action."

Eddie got back in the Discovery and watched as the gates clanged shut. A shiver scooted up his back, and he thought his first assessment of this house had been woefully inaccurate. It was actually a cowpat in a field of jewels. Eddie started the engine, and thought about it from Troy's perspective. A scream in a sea of smiles. No wonder he did drugs.

"Where the hell are you, Troy?"

Chapter Sixty-Four

Four miles away from his family home and from Eddie Collins, Troy snuggled beneath a fire hydrant on the sixth floor of a block of respectable flats. He was still drunk, and he was still high. He tended to keep his eyes closed most of the time because opening them caused his vision to spin like he had vertigo.

The external walkways and the exposed concrete landings funnelled the cold wind. Troy found it almost comforting, but it was cold enough to make him wrap his arms even tighter around himself and pull his knees up closer to his chin.

Though his mind was offline for most of the time, occasionally it entered a kind of analytical – no, visionary – state. Images came to him, circled his mind and fell onto the little projector screen that someone had set up so he could watch his own private movie show as he waited.

There were pictures of Eddie; how bolshie he was, how 'always right' he was, how aloof and condescending he was. Eddie Collins was a first-class bastard – he'd proved that when he upped and left the office when Crawford and his bitch of a daughter had asked him to. Just like that!

But Collins wasn't all bad – despite setting him up with a fake drugs test.

He'd hated Collins first thing this morning; would have killed him, given the chance. But he'd turned things around a bit since then. One of the images on the projector now was Collins in the kitchen, mug of coffee in hand, confessing his own addiction. He wasn't daft; if they shared a common flaw, they would become allies. Well, in that respect it had worked – they had become allies of sorts, and Troy no longer hated him enough to stove his head in with a fire extinguisher, or stab him with one of his own kitchen knives. Now, he thought, they shared a common dignity, a brotherhood.

"The Brotherhood of Falsehoods!" he shouted, and began to laugh.

The laughter stopped abruptly as the projector showed him Collins's 'challenge' on the mantelpiece: the brandy bottle. He'd got a kind of satisfaction from drinking half of it, and had thought about pouring the rest away, but decided it would be more of an insult if he left some. *There's always time for a relapse, Collins.* Brothers they might be, but he still warranted a poke in the ribs every now and then.

Collins was off the list. Troy believed him when he said he'd try to get him his job back, and that, when clean, Troy was an asset at any scene.

He chewed gum and smiled. For once he felt trusted. And he trusted Collins to stick to his word.

In this concrete echo chamber, he could hear everything. He could hear the front door of the block slamming in the wind down on the ground floor. He could hear people chatting in the two creaking lifts. He could hear people in the surrounding flats arguing, babies crying, music playing. He pulled the hood tighter over his ears – the noise was playing hell with his images, but also the wind was giving him earache.

The image that came to mind was—

The lift door opened.

Troy pressed pause on the image inside his head; opened his eyes – clear and focused, no vertigo – and waited silently, holding his breath. He heard heels on the false floor inside the lift, and then heard them clattering on the concrete out here on the windy landing.

Troy got to his feet, wobbled slightly, and steadied himself against the piss-stained wall. She walked towards the external walkway and Troy took off after her.

"Oi!" he shouted.

She turned. And when she recognised him, Nicki screamed and tried to run.

Troy barged into her, grabbed her, lifted her.

She was over the railing before she knew what was happening. Clinging onto his hood, she was spinning, legs spiralling, kicking to stop her motion. And when she did stop, she swung a hand up and grasped the rail.

Troy glared at her as she screamed, as she held onto the railing by four fingertips, the other hand clamped onto his hood. He was halfway over the rail himself, but it didn't register – all he saw was the utter terror in her eyes and her legs kicking in mid-air. Frenzy. A nail-snapping shin-scraping frenzy.

She smelled of puke.

"Please, Troy!"

He looked from her eyes to her fingers. She had three fingertips now on the rail. The rail had been painted white a couple of years ago by the look of it. You could see the rust coming back through. He could see how white her fingernails were. And he could see how wide her eyes were, and her mouth as she screamed.

Now she only had two fingers on the rail. Then one.

Troy twitched. His hoodie was taut over his right shoulder, digging in because she was pulling like crazy, and his head and upper body were getting closer and closer to her face; how she screamed! It was deafening. His t-shirt had ridden up, and the rail was cold against his exposed stomach. He tried to look up again, but the spinning came, and he felt sick, and everything spun faster and faster, and he tried to cling on...

His sweater pulled over his head and that was when his eyes opened.

She twisted as she fell through the air, screaming, fingers clawing at nothing.

He found himself on his back, staring up at the dirty concrete of the seventh-floor balcony above, and panting like crazy.

Troy got up, steadied himself against the rail, and ran for the stairs.

Chapter Sixty-Five

Weismann stepped out of the shower, rubbing his hair dry.

He looked at the phone sitting on the cistern lid and heard people outside in the locker room. There was nothing like police banter: either you joined in with it or you were chased out by it. It wasn't bullying in the truest sense of the word, but it was certainly a close relative.

Even though most of his clothes had been protected from Nicki's vomit by the scene suit, he'd binned his shirt when he got back to the nick, unpacked a spare and hung it in the shower room to let the creases drop out. But his other clothes were out there in the locker room.

He tied the towel around his waist and reached for the door. He hadn't even unlocked it before he heard his name mentioned. He paused, drew closer to the frosted glass panel and listened.

"Place is fucked," said someone.

"Job's fucked!" agreed someone else.

"What's the point of working your bollocks off, climbing the ladder when they promote from outside anyway?"

"I got no respect for him."

"Me neither. Nor his sidekick, Weismann. It's just another stepping stone for them. They got no interest in this place. They couldn't give a shit about the job."

"Empire-building."

"Exactly!"

"They'll be gone this time next year."

"Yeah, and some other wanker will do exactly the same again."

"But in the meantime, we have to live with it."

"I know."

"Look at CSI. They fucking gave it away! It's ruined. Now what do we do?"

"Exactly."

"We ought to get Weismann to do our forensic stuff for us, cos that Nicki lass is as much use as a woodpecker with a rubber beak. See how he likes it then."

"Place is fucked."

The door squeaked open and they disappeared; Weismann heard, "Job's fucked," just as they left.

He unlocked the door and stepped out, headed towards his locker, phone in hand. He sat down on the bench; his shoulders slumped as he scrolled to Collins's number.

* * *

The door squeaked and Benson heard one of them say, "Job's fucked!" He looked at them as the locker room door closed, and unfolded his arms as they approached.

Benson pointed at the locker room. "He in there?"

One of them nodded. "He's in there alright."

"Couldn't fail to hear us. We were loud enough," said the other.

Benson nodded again, "Thanks, lads. Appreciate it."

* * *

"Eddie?"

"Hello?"

"It's Victor Weismann here."

Eddie tensed slightly, his eyes grew hard, and his mind threw a red alert, ready for more shit coming his way. "What now?" he said. "Want my locker key? Or do you need the pen back that I stole last week?"

"Keep the pen," Weismann said.

Pushover.

"So what's up?"

"I need you at a scene."

Eddie looked confused. "I thought Wonder Woman was on the ball? She's thought of everything, don't forget, how to—"

"Shut up. Nicki's not doing the scene."

Eddie smiled. That was a deliberate omission on Weismann's part and Eddie could smell it like he could smell the car on fire somewhere nearby. He wound up the window. "Don't ever tell me to shut up." He took a moment, mellowed and said, "I'm listening."

"Meet me in your office in half an hour."

"*My* office?" He grinned at the phone. "My office?"

No response. He looked at the handset, frowning. "Hello? Bastard."

Chapter Sixty-Six

"Eddie?"

He stopped in the foyer, staring at the double doors. It was so quiet in here that he could hear his forehead sweating. He swivelled left, and there she was. Miss Moneypenny.

"You're not allowed to smoke in here."

He looked down at the cigarette lodged between his fingers. "Sorry," he said. "Didn't realise."

Once back outside, he finished smoking it, wondering how much more awkward his conversations with Moneypenny could get. Eddie replayed this morning's confrontation with his dad and Wendy. He'd seen the pain in his father's eyes battling with the pride on his face. One of them was a lie, and he knew it was the pride.

It was nice being wanted. But it was horrible being used.

He peered through the door at Moneypenny as she spoke on the phone. And he wondered who wanted whom, and who was using whom.

He dropped the cigarette down a drain and entered the foyer again just as she put down the phone. She looked up, smiled at him. It wasn't the wholesome smile she'd had before, and it wasn't the coy smile he'd so admired in her. It was a polite smile, the kind of smile she'd give to anyone who walked through here. "I think we need to talk," she said.

And he didn't know why, but Eddie's heart boomed – just once, a huge thud like he'd been kicked in the chest by a pissed-off donkey. "Sounds ominous."

"Tonight? Seven?"

"I think I'm going to be working late. I got a call from Weismann."

She nodded her understanding and looked away. "How's Troy?"

"No idea. Look…" He twitched.

"Yes, go on, off you go. We'll chat another time."

"Yeah, definitely." Eddie couldn't bring himself to look down at her cleavage as he swept by her and through the double doors. But an overwhelming flood of coldness came over him as he ascended the stairs. It made him sad, which made him angry.

He focused the anger, squinted, and blasted through the CSI doors.

Weismann was waiting, arms folded, perched on the edge of Sid's desk. As Eddie walked up the office towards him, Sid peered around Weismann and his face lit up. "Eddie!"

Eddie was happy to see him again, but now wasn't the right time to show it. Now was the right time to keep the anger bubbling. He thought of Moneypenny again, he thought of Troy being a prick last night, and he thought of Troy's father being a wonderful role-model for a drug user, and the anger soon returned. "Kettle on, Sid."

"What? No 'hello, Sid, how are you, Sid'?"

Eddie stared at him. "Please."

Sid tutted, and stood. "I want you to know that the tea fund is seriously depleted. We have no biscuits… well, we do, but they're cheap horrible things that have gone limp. And no one likes a limp biscuit…" He looked at Eddie, and Eddie looked at Weismann.

Sid put his nose in the air and walked towards the kitchenette. "I know when I'm not wanted. It's like a sixth sense. You've either got it or you haven't. Well, I'm not buying any more biscuits," he called back, "unless I'm working in this office!"

Eddie stood before Weismann. "Is he? Working in this office?"

Weismann unfolded his arms and continued to stare at Eddie as though they were a pair of stags ready to lock antlers.

Eddie shrugged, turned around and walked away.

"Eddie."

He stopped. Waited. Turned back. "Don't you think this is all a bit melodramatic? You asked me—"

"Nicki can't do scene work."

"Why not?"

Weismann paused for a moment or two, long enough for Eddie to become impatient and turn away again. "She's not good with blood."

"Don't you think she's in the wrong fucking job, then?"

"I'm so annoyed—"

"Oh no you're not. You haven't seen me annoyed yet!" Eddie stormed up the office, and Weismann's stance altered in those seconds, ready to cower. "She burned this place and she burned everyone in it. She was in the wrong job from day one and you must've known about it, just like her fucking useless father must have known."

"I didn't! I had more important things to do than monitor her tolerance for blood, Christ's sake. You see a CSI and you assume they're good with blood and gore. Christ. Taking over a department full of people who don't trust you is bloody hard, Eddie."

"You don't say."

"Taking over an office whose boss has been blown out to obscurity is near impossible."

Eddie stared at him. "I forgot my violin. Sorry."

"She's still in charge."

"What?"

"She's office-based; no need for her to visit scenes. It's a compromise. Best I can do."

Eddie searched Weismann's eyes, waiting for the punch line. He saw none. "I don't know how things were done in Nottingham, but that role here in MCU is certainly not office-based."

"You'll be senior examiner. She's the manager."

Eddie blinked. He smiled, about to slap Weismann on the arm and congratulate him on a prank well executed, but... "You're serious, aren't you?"

Weismann nodded.

"That's not a great incentive for me to stay. And if that's the best you can do, *arrivederci, amigo*."

"You still work for me, Eddie," Weismann said. "You're *my* resource, and I deploy you as I see fit. And right now, I want you at a double murder in Morley."

"No."

"Eddie. I'm warning you."

"Like I give a shit." It took a while, but eventually a smile punched its way onto Eddie's face. "You saw that old bag at my house this morning, didn't you?"

"What about her?"

"She gave me some good advice. She said that I am totally dispensable, and that the world will not collapse without me in it. I've been giving that some thought, and much as I hate the old cow, she's absolutely right on that score."

"Walking out again?"

"Yep." He rocked his head from side to side, mocking. "I'm walking out. For the last time. No fanfare required. Have a garibaldi and celebrate the good times without me. Don't forget the party-poppers."

"Eddie."

"Listen, I know you're stuck in an awkward spot here. On the one hand you've got Crawford breathing down your neck, and tin-tits in her new tiara, ready to scream 'Daddy' if you don't do as she says. And on the other hand, you've got bolshie Collins who's going to spit out his dummy and walk away if you don't give him his old job back. I can see you're in a dilemma. Well, let me make this a bit clearer for you, boss: I love my job."

"What?" Weismann feigned a laugh.

"I care about the victims and I care about justice – I know how clichéd that sounds, by the way, but it's true. She loves the status and the salary. But I love the job. I love the blood, and I love sniffing out clues among the dead and twisted. I can do that shit all day and all night. And put that together with the people I have working for me, and you've just about got Utopia – but don't tell them I said that.

"Don't get me wrong, I hated every single one of the useless bastards when we first met, but now we trust each other; we get along well, like second nature. How many people can you steal coffee from and they don't mind? How many people can you ridicule for wearing black nail varnish and they don't mind? We take the piss out of each other.

"She will never have that. Don't you understand, Weismann? She'll never work in an office full of people who will tolerate her, let alone pull out all the stops for her. Why? Because she didn't earn their trust. She stabbed people in the back to get where she's got, and worse than that, she spied on people, used private information to get where she got.

"I was helping Troy because he has a good foundation, and it was the best way of getting him back on course without butchering his career. But she climbed all over him, and me, to get a promotion she didn't deserve or earn. People will never respect that. Even if she filled this place with new people, word gets around. And how long before her true persona comes out? What happens when one of them needs her advice at a scene?

"And when she needs that one last job doing, she'll have no goodwill and no trust to call on in getting that job done. She will lose out, and ultimately *you* will lose out too."

Weismann looked away, thinking.

"So. If you think that I can work in the same office as her, taking orders from her, you're mistaken. I really couldn't live with myself. It's nothing to do with the way she stabbed me in the back; it's because I wouldn't be able to look Kenny and Sid in the eye ever again." Eddie reached inside his jacket, and he handed Weismann a pen. "Here," he said. "Now I owe this place nothing."

Weismann took the pen. "You can't leave."

"Why," asked Eddie, "you saying my head won't fit through the door?"

"Okay." A sigh fell out of Weismann's mouth that rounded his shoulders and seemed to shrink him by several inches. "She's out."

"What?"

"Leave it with me. She's gone."

Eddie looked at him through the corner of his eyes. "You're saying this just so I'll work your double murder, aren't you?"

"You're right, okay? She's no good to me."

"How has she got through the last three years, or however long she was at Division?"

Weismann shrugged. "Never worked serious crime. Always volume."

Eddie thought about that and nodded. "What about her dad?"

Weismann took the breath back in again, but his shoulders remained rounded. "I'll deal with him later." He looked Eddie in the eye, held out his hand. "I give you my word."

"Seriously?"

Weismann nodded, and Eddie shook hands.

"You can come out now, Sid."

"Oh, thank God for that. I was getting cramp back there, right in my calf; you know when you can feel it starting to bite? Another minute or two and I would have screamed, I know I would." He paused, looked at Eddie. "Do you have any Fiery Jack?"

Eddie laughed, and gave Sid a hand with the tray of drinks. "Get Kenny back here, Sid. And give Troy a ring, too." He looked at Weismann, eyebrows raised.

Weismann considered this for a moment. "Yes. Seeing as the drugs test was a fake, we can't exactly call him a junkie, can we?"

Oops, thought Eddie.

Chapter Sixty-Seven

Eddie climbed into the van and crushed his knees into the dashboard. He screamed and pulled the seat release lever. "Short-arsed bastard woman!"

Then he climbed out again, knowing that it was better to check the van for stock now than to wish he'd done it when he got to the scene.

Twenty minutes later, as he shoved an armful of stock into the drawers and checked the camera flash batteries, Benson surprised him.

"You got your job back, then?"

"Until someone else has their eye on it."

Benson was smiling at him, arms folded.

Eddie stopped loading the van. "What?"

"Bet you had to promise to be a good boy, eh? No more back-chatting, no more smart-arsing."

"I'm back on my terms. Her arse is out the door."

"On your own terms?"

"Yep."

"Someone put in a good word for you?"

"Like I know anyone who'd do that."

Benson chuckled to himself. "Yeah, well, luckily for you I'm with you on this one."

Eddie closed his eyes and looked skyward. "Why? What have I done to piss off the gods today?"

"Charming!"

"All I want is some peace and quiet, not some bastard bemoaning the state of his marriage and eating Mars bars at me."

"I ain't saying a word, mate," Benson said. "My lips are sealed. You won't know I'm here. And for the record, I'm not keen on working with you on this one, either. I'd rather have had that Nicki woman, better looking—"

"She tried it once already."

"Tried what?"

"The scene I'm about to go and work."

"Really?"

"She hurled all over it. So I imagine it'll be very pleasant." He found a small tub of Vicks in a dashboard nook. "Here," he said, "treat yourself."

* * *

During the journey, Benson turned to look at Eddie. He opened his mouth to speak; as though expecting it, Eddie snapped his head around and glared.

Slowly, Eddie put a finger to his lips and blew a shush.

"What? I was only going to say—"

"I don't care what you were only going to say. Stop. Now. I'm thinking."

Benson turned forward again, and had there been an audience present, would have rolled his eyes for their benefit. As it was, he felt a little embarrassed at being told off for nothing; felt his cheeks flush. "His name is Sidmouth. John Sidmouth."

Eddie stared at him.

"He lives with his mother."

"Can't you tell me all this shit when we get there? I like a surprise, okay?"

"I'm only saying."

"Don't. Just… just don't."

Benson shrugged. "You're going to need to—"

"We're half a mile away. It'll keep, okay? I like to think while I'm driving."

Benson laughed. "Yeah—"

"Do you feel that?"

Benson's eyes widened, hands flat on the seat. "What?"

"That." Eddie wobbled the steering wheel. "Feels like the front wheel's coming off. I bet that stupid bitch kerbed it."

Benson looked on, worried, as Eddie pulled over.

"Have a look."

"What?"

"Take a look at the wheel. I'll do this" —he shuffled the steering wheel again— "and you check the wheel."

"Yeah, yeah, okay." Benson nodded. "Good idea." He climbed out.

Before his feet had hit the pavement, Eddie drove away.

He watched him in the rear-view mirror, waving a fist. And had Eddie's mind not been occupied by thoughts of a more serious nature, he would have found it hilarious; Benson was shaking his fist like a cartoon villain. Eddie resisted the temptation to laugh and contented himself with a quick shake of the head and a crafty grin.

What pulled at his mind now, as he wound through the estate toward the street in Morley, was Troy and his whereabouts. He could understand him not wanting to go back to his parents' house – Christ, who needed parents like them? – but where *had* he gone? Where would he go? His dealer? He wondered just what kind of mental state the lad was in today.

As he stopped at the scene tape stretched across the road, he stared through the windscreen, focused on nothing at all, his mind miles away. Actually, not miles away; it was here, but it was hours away – hours in the past. "Nicki," he whispered.

She can't do scene work.

He sat there, eyes growing wider. Officers walked past the windscreen and peered inside as Eddie sat motionless, growing colder and colder. "No. Troy." He reached for his phone, and called Weismann. "It's me."

"What's up?"

"Where's Nicki?"

"Look, if she messed up the scene—"

"Where the fuck is Nicki?"

"She's upset, gone home—"

Eddie closed his eyes. "Listen to me very carefully. Find out where she lives and get a unit round there now. Now. Do not stop to pick your fucking nose. Just do it."

"What's—"

"Troy's missing. I think—" The line clicked off, and Eddie knew Weismann was on it already. He sat there for a minute or two longer, hoping he was wrong, but the shiver skittering through his scalp told him he wasn't. Who knew what Troy might do if he was pissed off at her – or even if she was just her usual arrogant self, provoking him, poking him, laughing at him. It was people laughing at him that Troy found the most disturbing, Eddie knew. That, and being without a job any more.

The scene through the windscreen began to coalesce before him, and eventually Eddie was back in some street in Morley that had grown temporarily famous. He spotted the press sixty yards away, behind a length of cordon tape, waiting for something to happen. Among them, no doubt, was Wilson – a man Eddie knew from a previous case.

In fact, it occurred to him that he'd had more than his fair share of press as friends. Oops, there was that word again – friend. Okay; he'd *known* his fair share.

The scene was in full swing: eight or ten officers from the Operational Support Unit in a straight line along the road, backs bent, each one scanning a shoulders-width strip of tarmac as they shuffled slowly across. The press had taken their shots and were busy chatting about who was shagging whom. Officers leaned against beat cars chatting, or doing work on their mobile devices – or playing games on their phones. Waiting. Everyone was waiting. And, he supposed, it was him they were waiting for.

He climbed from the van. Up and down the road, at the kerb edge, were rows of wheelie bins.

The OSU sergeant looked up and said, "Ooh, hello – CSI are here again to vomit all over the fucking place." The rest of the line laughed.

Eddie looked at him.

The sergeant, enjoying his new status as 'funny-as-hell, much-loved-sarge', stuck his chest out and grinned. "Stinks round here."

Eddie closed the van door and gazed skywards, as though in thought. "And yet, even over the top of the vomit, we can still smell your breath."

The officers in line stopped scanning the road, straightened and laughed even louder. The sergeant stared daggers at Eddie, then shouted, "Alright, alright. Let's get on with the job."

Eddie watched them, still chuckling, as they inched their way across the road, shifting up a few yards before returning in the other direction. He looked from them, and the bins caught his attention again. Eddie peered into one; it was still full. Of course – the refuse wagons couldn't get through because of all the coppers.

One of the officers who'd been engrossed with his mobile device lifted the cordon tape up and Benson stepped through, jacket hooked over his shoulder, scowl on his face. "You bastard, Collins," he said. "I fucking hate you. No, I mean it. I really fucking hate you."

Eddie refrained from smiling. "When you've composed yourself, you might want to ask the OSU sergeant to search the bins."

Benson's eyebrows rose. "Can't help yourself, can you? Always got to be poking your nose in someone else's business."

Eddie thought about that for a moment, conscious that it was the same thing Troy had told him last night – how he couldn't help being a good Samaritan. "Just thought—"

"Yeah, well, don't. It was on my list. I've been doing this for a few years, Collins, and I'm not completely—"

"Stupid?" asked Eddie.

"Fuck off. Pull a stunt like that again and—"

"You'll lose another two pounds?"

Benson closed his eyes and took a deep breath. "Shall we make a start on the scene?"

"What? You're coming in there with me?"

Chapter Sixty-Eight

"It stinks in here," Benson said, screwing his face up.

"I'm sure the dead will forgive you." Eddie tore a scene suit down the leg. But Benson was right; there was a peculiar odour in this house, and not all of it was vomit. It seemed that Nicki had not only thrown up on the footpath a few yards from the OSU line, she'd hurled in here too, in the hallway, and Eddie already knew she'd puked upstairs on the landing.

"What the hell had she eaten?"

Eddie stopped himself from answering. He'd begun to think about Nicki again – and about Troy. He peered up the stairs at the precarious rows of stepping plates. "She trying to kill herself?" He pulled the plates up, handed them to Benson. "Stack them by the door."

Before long, he reached the damaged step, the one with a gash through the carpet and splashes of blood that stretched up the walls. There was more blood in the torn wood; something had chopped right through flesh and into the step. An axe? Eddie pointed it out to Benson. "Don't step here, okay?"

Benson nodded, and they reached the landing with its splashes of vomit across the carpet. Benson peered past Eddie into the bedroom, and Eddie saw his mouth fall open behind his mask.

"What did you say his name was?"

Benson didn't take his eyes from the scene. "John Sidmouth. He's a Probation Officer."

"Is that supposed to mean anything to me?"

"What? No, no. It won't mean anything to you because you ejected me from the bloody van before I could get to that part."

"Alright, alright, keep your wig on."

"Hello?"

Benson and Eddie looked back down the stairs as someone else wearing a white suit and mask similar to their own – except without the gash down the leg – entered the hallway.

"Kenny. Good to have you back," said Eddie.

"Christ. What a stink."

Benson glared a warning at Eddie.

"Yeah, Benson's here; sorry 'bout that." Eddie winked at Benson.

"Not even funny the first dozen times you said it." Benson shook his head. "I still hate you."

Kenny climbed the stairs, automatically avoided the damaged step, and was standing at their side moments later. "Wow," he said, "another angry one." He looked at the dead man. "Christ, look at his heel. Bet that stung a bit." He leant towards Eddie and whispered, "Where's the mad cow?"

"You mean Kay Scarpetta? She threw up and left."

Kenny laughed. "Is that like *Eats, Shoots and Leaves*?"

Eddie took a breath, hands on hips, and said, "Have you been drinking?"

"No, why?"

"What the fuck are you talking about then?"

He mumbled, "Doesn't matter."

"Correct. It doesn't."

"She *left* left, or she left, soon to return?"

Kenny had a knack for asking far-reaching questions without even intending to. "I don't really know how to answer that," Eddie said, the cold feeling crawling up his back again. "She's not around any more – I have Weismann's word on it."

"Wouldn't trust him as far as I could throw him."

Eddie shrugged. "It's as good as we'll get for the time being."

"So what do you want me to do?"

Eddie nodded over his shoulder. "Since you've been sitting with your thumb up your arse for the last few days, you can have the half-naked female in the bathroom."

The creases in Kenny's forehead smoothed out as his eyebrows tried to kiss the back of his neck.

Eddie smiled. "You can do her if you want, and I'll do him."

"On it." Kenny almost skipped to the bathroom doorway. He took in the sight, and the eyebrows sprang back like furry roller blinds. He let out a disappointed 'sheesh'. "You bastard. I thought she was gonna be a stunner with her tits out. This is like something from *Saw*."

Eddie joined him and stared at the mass of blood across her bare flesh. "I did give that impression, didn't I? Sorry. But on the bright side, she's been letting off some cracking farts. You could have a competition with her."

Kenny ignored him, folding his arms. "Not going to be a lot of scope for Low Copy."

"I don't think he touched them, Kenny."

"Nah, maybe not. What we looking at, then? Footwear marks on the bathroom and bedroom floors?"

"Pretty much. Tape her if you can, bag her head, hands and feet, and then we'll bag her out here on the landing. Okay?"

"Gotcha. Let me get the floor out of the way first though."

"Yep," said Eddie, "I'll do the same in the bedroom."

Benson nodded towards the woman on the toilet. Her head hung limply to the right, a slice of neck exposed down to the spine like the executioner had fucked up and missed. "What do you mean, no scope for Low Copy?"

"Locard's Law, mate. If he touched her, throttled her for example – we can try to get his DNA from her throat, or from her arms if he grabbed her. But I don't think there was any contact. I think he walked in here and took a swing or two."

"Machete?"

"Gesundheit."

"I mean, was it a machete?"

Eddie slid past him, ready to collect his kit from the front yard and begin his part of the scene. "Axe."

Chapter Sixty-Nine

Eddie beckoned Benson into the room and closed the door. "I want to keep as much ambient light out as I can."

Benson nodded, as though that would have been his suggestion too.

On his knees, Eddie laid the torch on the floor and arced it left and right a dozen or so times.

Benson watched him, fascinated. "Whenever I think about forensicating a scene like this, you know, looking for footwear, I always imagine fancy gear like they have on CSI Miami. Not a torch."

"CSI Miami is television, Tom. And if you need a more accurate assessment: it's shit television. This is real life. Okay?"

"Smart arse. I was only saying."

"There's equipment we could use to attract all the dust from the laminate onto a length of black foil. ESLA: Electrostatic Lifting Apparatus. Sounds impressive, doesn't it?"

"So why don't you use it?"

"Like CSI Miami, it too is shit. It's fine on really dusty floors, but on a well-used floor like this, all it does is ruin the footwear marks you're looking for."

"Okay."

"And check your dictionary next time you're trying to impress someone: forensicating doesn't exist. Prick."

"Instead of picking on me, how about you tell me what you know about Mr Sidmouth and his scene so far?"

"Christ, I've only just started."

"See. Not as smart—"

"How about you finish telling me about him, and we'll take it from there, huh?" Eddie turned off the torch. Blackness.

When the light goes, the sound amplifies to compensate. And sometimes, when there's no sound *and* no light, your imagination fills in the gaps with something home-made, something created especially for you.

Eddie saw Sidmouth running upstairs, fear pulling his eyes wide, driving his heart into the red zone. He saw the axe pinning him to the stair, heard him screaming his lungs into hot ragged strips, until the pursuer yanked it free from his heel and continued the chase. He saw Sidmouth limping in here, dragging his damaged foot into his room, where he felt safe – safe, that is, until this happened. Despite the shredded lungs, he'd still be screaming – who wouldn't?

And then the axeman got to work.

Except there was more, wasn't there?

"Sidmouth is an Offender Manager."

"A what?"

"Probation Officer. Prisoners out on licence, you know…"

"Ah, yeah, you already said." Eddie turned on the torch again, lighting the room, and swapping all of those grotesque home-made images for grotesque real ones. He paused. "You're fucking kidding, right?"

"What? No, I'm not. Why?" Benson was squinting.

"You think Jessica Ripley did it?"

Benson tugged his mask off. "I have an open mind."

"Is she on his workload?"

Benson huffed. "Even if she is, I'm not saying she'd do this."

"She is, isn't she? On his workload?"

"Yes, she's on his workload."

"So the first thing your open mind did was to check and see if Ripley—"

"But so are dozens of others. She went there yesterday, wanted him to sign off on another visit to see her son."

"And?"

"He didn't do it."

Eddie sighed out of his mask. "He didn't sign off on her request to see her son. Why not?"

"I don't know, do I?" Benson went quiet, and then said, "He was supposed to. The man who's taken over part of his workload said there was no reason not to agree to Jessica's request without a second glance."

"But he didn't?"

"I just said that, didn't I?" Benson looked across to Eddie. "Is that enough of a motive for her to do this?"

"No, probably not, but look at all that shit." Eddie pointed his torch at the porn mountain. "That's not something a rational man has. He's a fucking weirdo, and he's a fucking weirdo who still lives with his mum."

"Abusing his power, maybe?" Benson's eyebrows rose up his forehead.

"Even if it was an abuse of power, she didn't do this, Tom. You've got to be looking at that Tony fella for this. He likes axes, remember? And because of… this." He waved an arm in case Benson hadn't seen the carnage. "There's so much energy. So much strength needed. Look at the overturned bed. Look at the damage on Sidmouth's body."

Benson did a mini-shake of his head, the kind of thing you'd do if you were organising your thoughts, lining them up until they made more sense. "Why would *he* do it?"

"Framing her, just like the other murders. And if he was Jessica's Offender Manager, it's the perfect murder to frame her for."

"He didn't frame her for Marchant's murder."

"No. He didn't." Eddie slid in to a short period of thought, and then said, "I wonder if it all started with Marchant; this thing between Tony and Jessica. Tony killed Marchant for messing up

Jessica's life, and she doesn't like it because it brings suspicion on her – obviously."

"And you think Tony's worried she'll grass him up if we put too much pressure on her?"

"Makes sense. And so he's killing her enemies, making it look like she did it."

"So she gets sent down again," Benson said.

Eddie nodded. "It's a decent theory."

Benson folded his arms. "But why wait all these years to kill Marchant?"

Eddie blew out a sigh, and shrugged. "No idea."

Benson slid the mask back on and focused on the scene. "Why the hell kill the mother?"

Eddie stood, rubbed his face with the back of his gloved hand, saw the shine of fresh grease there and went to change his gloves. "The mother couldn't keep quiet; that's a given, mate. When she hears her boy screaming his tits off, she's shitting herself – probably quite literally. All she can do is whimper. Offender goes to see what the noise is, finds her on the bog."

"Being on the bog is offensive is it?"

"No, but no self-respecting murderer leaves witnesses alive. You never watched The Sopranos?"

"I preferred Morse." Benson crouched down. "What footwear marks have you found?"

Eddie shouted, "Kenny?"

"What?"

"Kind of footwear marks on the bathroom floor?"

There was a pause, then, "Zig-zags."

"Nike Cortez?"

"We have a footwear bureau for identifying them."

"Could it be Cortez, Kenny?"

"You're the saddo who knows his footwear patterns, mate. To me they're just zig-zags."

Eddie turned back to Benson. "They're Cortez. And in here, too."

"You saw them?"

Eddie pointed the torch beam directly at a good right shoe impression in the dust where the bed had been. "There." He stood, widened the beam out, and, keeping away from the path trodden by the offender, made his way towards the victim. He shone the torch on Sidmouth's face, at the shoe-shaped bruise across his cheek, and then looked back at Benson.

Benson groaned and stood up. "You'rc shitting me?"

Eddie said nothing.

Benson shook his head. "It's her. Look at the size of it!"

"Even for a copper, that's a fucking big conclusion to jump to. It doesn't suit you. You're usually more cautious than this."

Benson pulled his hood down, and his cheeks were flushed red. "Same size as the shoe at Doc Bolton's scene, wouldn't you say?"

"It is. And I happen to think that Tony was at Bolton's murder."

"Bollocks, Eddie. You said yourself that everyone at Bolton's scene would spot who had killed him, remember?"

Eddie nodded. "Well, the jury is still out on that one."

"Tell me. You think she killed Bolton, but Tony killed everyone else, right?"

Eddie breathed deeply. "No. I originally thought she killed Bolton because there were no footwear marks leading to the coat stand where her coat was found hanging."

"So?"

"So it meant that Bolton took it from *her* and hung it up to dry. He's not going to take a woman's coat off a burly tramp, is he?"

"And now?"

"And now I think Tony took off his shoes and hung the stolen coat up there himself once Bolton was dead."

"That still doesn't explain the small, female-sized Nike Cortez, does it?"

Eddie shrugged.

"Does it?"

"No. It doesn't. Okay?"

"But you still think it's Tony?"

Eddie nodded. "A hunch."

"You're a man of science, but you're relying on a hunch? You cretin. And don't forget she had a knife under her mattress while we were there. She's not as innocent as she makes out."

"Look, we're just going around in circles here." Eddie followed him out, dropped the gloves into a black bin bag, and flapped his hands, trying to dry the sweat off. "She was afraid. It was there in case Tony got rough."

"You're supposed to be impartial."

"And you're supposed to be open-minded."

Benson sighed. "Isn't that the same thing? Anyway, never mind, just hurry up in there, I've organised officers to recover his computer and whatever other shit he's got."

Eddie's phone rang. He split the tear in his suit leg higher and pulled the phone from his pocket. 'Weismann' flashed on the screen; he pressed the green button.

"Hello? Hello, can you hear me? Fucking phones." He shouted to Kenny. "Back in a minute, mate, I have to take this."

Eddie and Benson parted company in the hallway. Benson went out to order OSU to search all the bins up and down the street, and Eddie called Weismann back.

There were clicks and crackles, but eventually he heard Weismann just clearly enough to catch something like an address before his voice became unreadable. There was an anticipation that hurried Eddie out of the house, already searching his pockets for the van keys, but someone in a white suit was blocking his way.

The suit smiled at him, and Eddie's attention was divided, but it landed firmly on Weismann's side when heard the word 'dead'. "What? Who's dead? Weismann, I can't hear you."

Eddie shut the phone off, and growled, thoughts spinning – an address, a death. And then the suit was there again, holding a hand out. She was smiling.

"Sally?" Sally Pemberton, the biologist who always seemed to gravitate towards Eddie's jobs these days. Good-looking lass, he thought, but a pain in the arse. Eddie looked at her smile, looked down at her petite hand, and tried to work out if he should shake or not. He decided not – it wasn't fucking LinkedIn. "Who requested you? I didn't request you."

"Erm…" Sally put her hand away as though it was an absurdity.

"Hurry up, love. I have another death to get to." Eddie stared off over her shoulder, wondering which one was dead: Troy or Nicki. He could feel anger at the whole messy situation forcing its way down his trachea.

"Nicki," she said. "Nicki Murphy. She requested me."

He looked down at her, noted the dismay on her face, felt bad about it, but felt disinclined to lift her mood when his own had just turned so fucking sour. "Follow me." He, trudged back up the stone steps and into the hallway. He pointed up the stairs. "Don't tread on that one, the one with the blood on it. Right?"

She nodded.

"Kenny, put a marker on this damaged step."

"Righto."

"And the biologist is here." He heard Kenny mumble; 'wasting my time' was definitely in there somewhere.

"Seems no one's very keen on seeing me today."

"Try being me, love. Even people in my office have an injunction out against me." Eddie looked at her, and almost felt guilty. "Don't take it personally; you lot just tend to fuck up people's days, that's all. Comes with the territory." And then up the stairs to Kenny, he shouted. "I got to go, mate. I'll be back as soon as I can."

"Can't tell you how many times I've heard that piece of shit before."

Chapter Seventy

Eddie sat in his van as dusk painted the street a darker hue and stole a layer of colour. He was lost in thought as he waited for the copper to find the keys to a beat car that was blocking the road.

Usually he would have been bouncing off the ceiling for them to get the car moved, and would even have considered pushing it away with the van. But right now he felt disinclined to rush to the address that Weismann had given him. In fact, he felt like driving straight past the address and terminating his journey somewhere on the coast; Whitby, perhaps, or Filey. Somewhere quiet, somewhere he could just disappear.

He didn't want to know who had died, and he didn't want to know how. It was someone else's turn for all that shit, thank you very much – his shoulders weren't wide enough to accommodate anyone else's shit these days. Irrespective of who it was, he wasn't sure he could cope with the inevitable fall-out of another in-house death, especially if it was an in-house murder. He'd never rest again if that had happened.

He peered out of the side window, thumbs running circles around each other as he waited. The death house was to his right. He could see bursts of light through a frosted window as Kenny fired the flash in the bathroom. Eddie peered to his left. There was a dirt track that led nowhere at the end of a terrace of houses. Although the light was dimming, he could see that at the back of the dead-end lane was a chain-link fence with a growth of straw-coloured grass and weeds at its feet. Beyond it was a field.

But the thing Eddie found interesting was the streetlight. There wasn't one. The nearest streetlight behind him was fifty yards uphill on the left; the nearest one in front was forty yards downhill and on the right pavement.

That little hole was unlit. That little hole was black.

This job came in this morning, but it would have happened last night, overnight, probably. It would have been pitch black in there. And there was no excess parking on this street – you had to breathe in just to walk on the fucking pavement. But if you were parking a car, or prepping for a bit of a murder or two, it'd be good to have a jumping-off point, wouldn't it? A place to come back to afterwards if it had all gone according to plan.

Eddie climbed out of the van, clicked on his torch as the copper waved a set of keys at him from across the road. "Five minutes," Eddie said.

"I've just—"

"Shut up." The copper sulked and was about to walk away, when Eddie said, "Don't you dare disappear. Just wait for me." Eddie walked through the moths flitting back and forth in the light from the van's headlamps and stood on the footpath pointing his light into the dark track.

Around him, the noises of the scene disappeared. The incessant police radio chatter, the sounds of distant sirens, traffic on the nearby roads, all faded away. Eddie was in the zone.

He cast the beam low across the silty, damp mud; there were footwear marks. Zig-zags, as Kenny would have said. A concentration of them near the gable end of the terraced house, and more coming and going towards the chain-link fence. Had he stashed something there, the murderer? There were no tyre tracks, so he'd come and gone on foot. But the 'foot' was odd. It was small – female-sized, like those at Doc's scene, like those across the road there inside Sidmouth's house.

No way could they be Tony's footwear impressions. Too small.

And Eddie found that a bit sad. When he looked at Jess, he saw someone afraid, someone scared to open their door, someone whose sleep was as thin and broken as his own. She wasn't a killer; she was a victim. So these footwear marks came as a shock, and Eddie considered them: Either Jessica Ripley was a better actress than he'd given her credit for – had completely beaten Eddie's bullshit detector, or another female was involved.

There was another alternative: Tony had tiny feet.

Eddie sighed; felt pulled in two directions at once, and was unable to determine the correct path to take.

The torchlight picked out something else. A faint red stain on a clump of grass, and next to it an impression in the soil. The impression was wedge-shaped, and the red stain was concentrated at the thinnest end of the wedge. So it *was* an axe. And then, as though the murderer had just let it fall while attending to other matters, there was the impression of a shaft, a handle. It was a hatchet.

Eddie scurried towards the chain-link fence and the shit-coloured grass, avoiding a dog turd by sheer luck and less than an inch. Beyond it was a flattening of the grass where something had been sitting for a while – a bag, perhaps?

The dead-looking grass and the dog turd were of no value, but Eddie closed in on the flattened spot, searching inch by inch. He came up empty.

Back out on the footpath, he took out his phone, and as he waited for an answer he summoned the sulking copper with the keys. "Throw some cordon tape across this gap. CSI will be here soon. Okay?"

There was no response from the copper.

Eddie got in his face. "I said okay?"

"Okay."

"Good. Move your fucking car first."

There was no reply from Weismann's phone, so Eddie, now back in his van, rang straight through to divisional CSI control and booked the next available officer. "And make sure they take a soil sample."

Seatbelt on, cigarette between his lips, Eddie engaged gear and set off for the address Weismann had given him. His nerves prickled the closer he got.

And when he arrived – a smart block of flats with its own semi-enclosed car park – the place was alive with police vehicles, blue lights flashing on some, making Eddie squint. Fire crews were in attendance, several ambulances too, and the noise was enormous. Among the vehicles were two or three from news networks, and a Peugeot he recognised as belonging to Weismann. He parked the van as close as he could, about fifty yards away, then lit another cigarette, locked the van and walked towards the thing he'd been dreading all day.

Here, at the roadside, crowds of people gathered; in the flats, windows were open, curtains tied back as people watched the arse-end of this circus. The juicy bit, of course, was around the back. Eddie dodged around people, avoiding eye contact, and made his way to the outer cordon.

There were the obligatory kids on bikes poking fun at the emergency services and there were the dealers keeping an eye on things from a safe distance. Eddie approached the cordon and spoke with a PCSO who was on scene guard, and on edge.

For a change, the lift smelled not of piss but of lavender or jasmine. He didn't know which, but it was a pleasant surprise. The pleasure didn't last long; the red digit changed to a 6 and the door slid open. Eddie stepped out and the cold wind slapped his face. More cordon tape flapped, more police radio traffic echoed around the concrete landing.

Divisional CID, already in scene suits, were at the railings peering over, determined to ruin the scene in order to feel a frisson that only a one-hundred-foot drop seemed able to give.

Pretty soon they would be officially handing the scene over to MCU, the process probably already underway, and CSI from another force would fingerprint the railing being leaned on by these fine detectives right now.

Eddie shook his head at their tourist mentality.

"You want to go in?" The PCSO's hand was poised on the tape, ready to lift it for Eddie.

"No. Thanks," he said. He turned to leave, eyes fixed on the lift's call button when something shiny caught his eye. Beneath the hydrant, tucked away into its own concrete alcove, was something flashing at him. The flashing was a Wrigley's chewing gum wrapper; a foil one that acted like a tiny mirror as it flicked around in the alcove's breeze. "Troy. You stupid fucker."

Chapter Seventy-One

Back on the ground, Eddie wove through the melee and found himself staring at a sheet of grey plastic held to the ground by a brick on each corner. There was a body-sized bulge in its centre, and next to it was a hoodie; it was blue with a white stripe down the centre.

Feeling despondent, Eddie made his way around the front of the building. Someone nearby said, "Oi."

Eddie turned around and the blow to his face took him clean off his feet. He landed on his back, shoulders first; his face was on fire, and the wind was knocked out of him. He was disorientated, but felt the thud in his side as the boot went in. He snatched consciousness but things were grey and hazy, the sounds around him coming clear and focused one second and then buzzy, distant the next.

He tried to draw a breath and got nothing other than a hitching in his chest.

There was screaming. He could hear raised voices and the crowd jeering, some women screaming, and when his eyes opened, he could see the PCSO shouting urgently into his radio, and he could see him struggling with a man. And before long, another man in a suit, wearing braces, joined the tussle. Eddie shook his head; it seemed to clear the sound, though his vision was still blurred.

Crawford slapped him around the face. He was on him; he was all teeth like a rabid dog. Eddie could see the tendons in his neck standing out, and his eyes were wide, fierce, and his fists were pummelling the air right in front of Eddie's face, his claws trying to grab Eddie by the throat. Lips pulled back, hatred gushing. Crawford was screaming like an animal on the kill. No; like an animal wounded.

Eddie realised the scene tape was there for Nicki.

But the thing Eddie noticed – the only thing that he *really* noticed – were the tears flicking from Crawford's overflowing eyes, dripping from his chin and from the end of his nose as he swung his head around, and how they shimmered with blue lights.

Tears everywhere. Pain everywhere.

Chapter Seventy-Two

There were people banging on the walls when he opened his eyes. Someone was standing over him. For an awful moment, Eddie thought they were going to beat him to death, but as his vision cleared he managed to work out that the fuzzy person blocking the light from the ceiling was dressed in a green paramedic's uniform, and the banging was kids throwing stones at the ambulance.

"You okay?"

Eddie squinted, tried to take a deep breath and had to open his mouth.

"It might be broken. Your nose."

Eddie wiped a sleeve under his nose and was rewarded with a blistering white-hot pain. He winced, saw the blood on his arm, and winced again. "Have you got any paracetamol?"

"You're concussed. We'll need to take you to the LGI, they'll want to keep you in overnight for obs."

"What?" Eddie tried to sit up, but the fuzzy guy rested a hand on his shoulder. "I love the NHS," Eddie said, "and I love the doctors and the nurses and the paramedics. Really I do. But get your hand off me. I ain't going anywhere for obs overnight."

The paramedic took away his hand. "And we appreciate it that you love us all so much. But you're giving us twice as much work to do if you fall over again and split your head open. Twenty-four hours, that's all."

Eddie was nodding. "Okay," he said. "Just give me some paracetamol. And if you could let my boss know?"

"Sure. Was he the short one? Tie and braces?"

Eddie tried to nod, but his head just wobbled as though it had dislocated itself. He groaned again. "Yep. Looks like a penis. Can't miss him."

"Back in a minute."

The fuzzy shape disappeared and the bright ceiling lights made Eddie close his eyes again. Still the banging on the side of the ambulance continued. The back end of the vehicle lifted slightly as the paramedic climbed down. Eddie immediately climbed off the gurney, steadying himself with a strap dangling from the ceiling. A moment later he was back outside, patting his pockets for his van keys. As he unlocked the van door and opened it, a familiar hand landed on his shoulder, and Eddie sighed into the night.

"Come on, Mr Collins, let's get you checked out."

Eddie turned and saw the paramedic, and beside him a man wearing a crumpled tie and braces. Eddie found it interesting to note the blood smeared across Weismann's chin. "I appreciate your concern. But I'm fine."

"Eddie—"

"Thank you." Eddie stared at the paramedic. "Goodbye."

The paramedic looked between Eddie and Weismann, and simply turned and left them.

Eddie sighed. "Get it out of your system, and then *you* can fuck off as well."

Weismann walked around the other side of the van, climbed in just as Eddie had, and closed his door. He tutted, "What? I have things to do."

"We got here too late."

"I figured that out all by myself. Now we have to find out where the hell Troy is."

Weismann looked forwards. "And where the hell do you start looking for a shadow among shadows?"

"Isn't it our job to find people?" Eddie went a white cold, and felt the last dregs of strength running out of the soles of his feet. He could practically see them – his strength and energy sloshing around together in the footwell. He swallowed, looking out of the side window as a couple of hot tears threaded their way through the whiskers on his face. "Fucking prick. I always said…"

"You should rest."

"Who's doing their scene?"

"I'll get North Yorks down to help."

"Make sure you don't use Michael Penny. Fucking useless."

Weismann nodded as though making a mental note, but Eddie knew he'd forget about it as soon as he got out of the van. Weismann would want to shove that scene as hard as he could into someone else's hands.

"It's in the hands of the IPCC, anyway," said Weismann, opening the van door and stepping out into the night right next to a black Astra. "We'll run it with them. But it won't be a long job."

Eddie looked at him.

"There were at least two people who filmed it all."

"Filmed it? Instead of helping?"

"Someone tried to, apparently. Didn't get there in time."

Eddie was speechless.

"Look," Weismann's voice was low and calm. "The attack on you. That was being filmed too."

Eddie swallowed the pain, and shook his head anyway.

"I have to ask you if you want to pursue it. The assault on you, I mean."

"Pursue it?"

Weismann nodded.

"Put yourself in his shoes," Eddie said. "Would you have done anything different? I wouldn't."

"But he—"

"Listen… Victor, isn't it?"

Weismann nodded.

"His daughter is dead. I hope my nose *is* broken. I wouldn't want it straightening; I'd like to keep it bent so I could remember this every time I looked in a mirror. I'd think of Crawford, a man who will spend every minute of his life from tonight without his daughter. It would be worth it never to forget."

"But it's not your fault."

"I kinda think it is. If I hadn't rigged up that false drugs test, Troy wouldn't have been so paranoid, and Nicki wouldn't have used it as ammunition against me, catching him in the cross-fire. She'd still be alive." He tried to smile, and he thought he'd done a fairly good job of it. "You got any paracetamol?"

Weismann stared forward, tormented by blue strobes. The light shone on his dampened face, and Eddie turned away so as not to see it. "I thought the way they muscled their way into West Yorkshire was wrong," said Weismann. "But I didn't complain because Crawford got me this job too." He cleared his throat. "Don't get me wrong, I'm good at my job, and I'm glad to be here rather than in Nottingham. But I'd rather have been invited than being part of a package that your top brass couldn't turn down."

"Can't believe they acceded to blackmail."

Weismann shrugged. "It's not unheard of to get one top man who brings others along too. But as I say, I'll be a good asset, I think." He bit his lower lip for a moment. "And I'm sorry. About Jeffery."

"And Nicki?"

Weismann smiled ruefully. "Not exactly an asset, and that's why all this isn't your fault. She was poor at her job; if she'd been any good at it, would she have needed to bring attention to your alternative style of management? They both saw you as an easy gateway to her getting a quick and painless promotion up the ladder."

"Painless?"

"Indeed. What I'm trying to say is don't blame yourself for tonight, Eddie. It's a culmination of a series of bad events, that's all. People who couldn't moderate their own behaviour. It's a series of events that could only have happened to them."

"Circumstances built for the dead?"

"Something like that," he said. "Listen, why don't you take a few days off? You'll need to rest before your body seizes up."

"Nice idea. But we're back to one CSI."

"I think there's help on the way."

When Eddie didn't reply, Weismann nodded. "Take it easy. I'll catch up with you tomorrow."

"We'll never see him again, will we?"

"Crawford?" Weismann shrugged. "He's angry. He's already arranged a meeting with the Senior Leadership Team tomorrow to put his case forward."

"His case?"

"For your permanent removal." Weismann palmed away Eddie's imminent protest. "Don't worry about it; I'll be there, and I've made it perfectly plain that I want you to stay." He swallowed. "He's overstepped the mark, and I think he'll be out, not you. Early retirement or resignation."

"No one's concerned that he's rigged up a meeting the day after his daughter is pushed to her death?" Eddie stared forward. "What's wrong with the man?"

"He's very driven."

"He's fucking mad, is what he is."

"Just… just don't worry about tomorrow, Eddie."

Eddie started the engine. He gave Crawford twelve months. At the end of it he'd be a shell of a man, just waiting to never wake up again.

He drove to a garage where he bought a packet of paracetamol, a bottle of water, and some wet wipes to clean the blood off his face. Then he called at Mac's for food and coffee.

Twenty minutes later he was back in Morley. During those twenty minutes he thought of Troy, and he thought of Troy's parents. Those thoughts slipped across to Nicki's parents, and finally landed on Nicki herself. When that happened, Eddie turned them off like they were a torch. Some things should be saved until their rightful time and place, until they could be dealt with properly.

He lit a cigarette, cracked the window open, and stared at Sidmouth's house. Kenny's flash popped through the landing window even more prominently now that it was fully dark outside. "No rest for the wicked." He opened the door.

Chapter Seventy-Three

There's an unwritten rule that says you shall never, under any circumstances, visit a crime scene for any other purpose than to examine it.

Eddie nudged the front door open, slid inside, closed it with a heel, and shouted, "Grub up!" He nodded at Kenny's shouts of hurrah, and dropped the covered box of food and drink onto the coffee table in the lounge, and made sure the curtains were closed.

He was fairly sure that nothing relating to the crime upstairs had happened here in this room, and so rather than eat in the van in full view of the public and any dregs of the press still hanging about, he thought the sofa might be more welcome. Eddie was suddenly starving.

When Kenny entered the lounge, peeling off however many pairs of gloves he now wore, there was a grumble in his stomach and great relief on his smiling face. "Thanks, mate, you've no idea—what the fuck happened to you?"

"I told McDonald's their fries tasted like maggots." Eddie smiled, but it turned to a frown moments later as he heard footsteps on the stairs. Kenny had already dived into the box for a burger and a coffee.

"Sally." Eddie screwed his eyes up. "Shit. I forgot."

And then she appeared. "Hi, Eddie. Jesus, what happened to your face?"

"I just came from a fucking fancy dress party, alright?"

She peered closer. "Excellent makeup."

"Tuck in," he nodded towards the box, "before *he* eats it all."

Sally licked her lips and peered inside the box. "There's only one meal left."

"I already ate. I got it for you."

"Ooh, thank you – I'm ravenous!" She pulled out a burger and a box of fries, sat down and reached back inside for the coffee. "Very kind."

Eddie licked his lips longingly, looking at the coffee. "What's left to do?"

Kenny spat food as he talked. "We already shifted the woman out of the bathroom. Body snatchers came for her about half an hour ago. So that room is finished."

"Footwear?"

Kenny sighed. "Yes, Eddie. I got footwear. You need to see someone about this fetish of yours."

"Very good." He turned to Sally. "You finished in there too?"

She nodded. "It wasn't a long job. Two blows to the neck. Nothing else, just cast-off; three nice neat arcs."

"Three?"

"The first one is an arc of the male victim's blood as the weapon travelled to the female victim, I should imagine. I've swabbed it anyway, and we can check later, but it all helps in forming a picture, a sequence of events."

"I don't think there's much doubt about what happened, do you? How far have you got with Dickless Dan?"

"Go have a look," said Kenny. "We got a shitload of footwear, including one from his face. It might be good to try UV, actually, at the mortuary. But it's clearly the same shoe as on the bedroom floor."

"He stamped on his face," Eddie said.

"Looks that way. It's not a kick, anyway."

Eddie nodded slowly.

"And his dick is in a knife tube. A small one." He laughed through a mouthful of burger.

Eddie looked away.

"Seriously," Kenny said, "what happened to your face?"

"Seriously?"

Kenny nodded.

"Nothing to worry about. Hurry up, we've got work to do." Eddie walked out of the room, took a suit from a stack on a CSI foldout table in the hallway, and struggled into it. He pulled on a couple of pairs of gloves as he mounted the stairs. "I presume all general photography's done?"

"Yep."

Even the lingering smell of puke couldn't dispel Eddie's hunger as he peered from the landing into Sidmouth's bedroom. He stepped inside, noted all Kenny's camera gear dumped in one corner and all Sally's shiny cantilever boxes in another, next to Kenny's forensic kit and a stack of packaging materials.

On the laminate floor were several clean rectangles where Kenny had peeled away adhesive footwear lifters. Outside on the landing were Nicki's stepping plates, no longer needed. There were other clean areas on the floor, much smaller than the footwear lifters, and next to them were white labels with exhibit reference numbers on them. These were blood spots that Sally had marked and then swabbed – no doubt asking Kenny to photograph them first.

All that was left to do was to process Sidmouth.

Eddie's face throbbed, his jaw ached, and even his neck felt sore – like he'd suffered whiplash. He just wanted to lie down and go to sleep. But he couldn't leave all this to Kenny. He looked at his watch. It was already after ten, and there was a shitload of work still left to do.

Of course, he could elect to leave the body here and attack it fresh tomorrow. But Benson wouldn't be too pleased about waiting longer for the post mortem; they needed results, confirmation that he died of the obvious wounds and there wasn't anything being concealed by them – no drugs in his system, things like that. Often the 'straightforward' murders were anything but; things that looked like ducks and quacked like ducks sometimes turned out to be peacocks.

Better safe than wrong.

"What we doing about the hand?"

Eddie jumped. "Jesus, Kenny! There were nearly three deaths in this house then. Twat!"

Kenny laughed, "That would have been funny as fuck."

"You're such an arse. Tape the hand, if you can find any clean bare skin to tape. Then bag it; it goes into the body bag with him."

"Do we need to exhibit it separately?"

"No. This isn't disaster victim identification. I'm fairly happy it belongs to him."

"'Kay."

"When you pull him forwards, spin him over and get some close shots of his heel. Scaled, obviously. I'm going to swab blood from the stair, and then I'm going to cast the split in the wood."

"Why?"

"Striation marks. If we can match them to a tool, we might match the tool to an offender."

Kenny nodded, "Ah, so that's what we do. Thanks."

"Can you think of anything else?"

"Yes. What happened to your face?" He was looking at Eddie, arms folded, but his voice was soft, serious.

Eddie looked away, undecided whether it would be right to tell Kenny about Troy and Nicki. If he didn't tell him, if he found out from someone else tomorrow… well, he didn't think Kenny would thank him. But if he told him now, then it would take Kenny's mind off what he was doing. Hell, he might even have to leave the scene. And Eddie couldn't finish things all by himself. "Tell you later. Let's get this shit finished first, eh?"

"Ah. It's bad then?"

Eddie tried to smile. "Don't suppose you saved me any fries, did you?"

* * *

It was after three in the morning when they finally finished with the body and waved him goodbye as the body snatchers, followed by an officer in a beat car, took him away in a plain black Mercedes van. Sally peeled herself out of her wet scene suit; Kenny looked away, Eddie did not. She promised to get the swabs off to the lab by lunchtime, and to submit a report the same afternoon. Eddie and Kenny watched her taillights disappear.

"What are we going to do about fingerprinting?"

Eddie looked at his hands, damp, white and wrinkled after being gloved for so many hours. They trembled. He was beyond hungry, and felt himself sinking into the blackest pit of exhaustion. His face hurt. But there were still several hours of fingerprinting to get through. All the doors and door frames from the front door, the bathroom and bedrooms, the bannister rail, all needed examining.

It was probably safe to assume that the attacker had been wearing gloves and had touched nothing anyway. But to assume would be foolish. The only assumption they allowed themselves was that this place needed a fingerprint exam.

"I'm not sure I can last another four hours."

Eddie nodded. It was something that they would have to leave until the morning – until later in the morning, rather. But who would do it? Eddie and Kenny would be asleep until lunchtime. And Eddie didn't want to lean on divisional CSI too much; they'd already be doing him a favour by taking both post mortems and processing the dead-end alleyway.

It didn't look good, and Eddie didn't know what the hell he was going to do about getting some staff.

"We'll have to come back in the afternoon."

Kenny nodded.

Eddie lit a cigarette. "That suit you?"

"Yep. Right now, I just want to get out of here. We've got hours of fucking computer work in front of us."

"Okay," Eddie said, "let's gather our shit and our evidence and lock it down till later."

Chapter Seventy-Four

A small sliver of orange light from the landing guided her to his side. She watched him; marvelling at how still he was, and how recognisable – even after all these years. There were still features of that adorable two-year-old in him; if asked what they were, she wouldn't be able to give a definitive answer, but it was the same face. It was her little man. It was Michael.

As quietly as she could, she sat on his bed and pointed the gun at him.

He stirred and, as though aware of someone's presence, his eyes flickered open.

She smiled, and he was about to scream when she shushed him by putting a finger to her own lips.

He scooted up the bed, cramming himself into the corner of the wall as though it might protect him. It wouldn't.

"Stay quiet, Michael." She nudged the gun at him.

"You!" he shouted.

"I said stay quiet." She cocked the gun, and his eyes snapped away from hers to focus on it.

"You're not going to kill me," he said, still pushing himself away from her, speaking through small scared breaths.

"You think? You don't want to be with me. You said so. And if I can't have you…"

"Wait." He thrust his palms out. "Wait. There's no need for this, we can sort something out."

She smiled, shuffled up the bed a little, and whispered, "I'd hoped you'd eventually see it my way. We were made to be together, Michael. You're all I've thought—"

"Mum!" he shouted.

"You fucking stupid boy," she snarled, jumping up. She hid behind the door as it opened.

Valentine stood in the doorway. "What? What's up?" she said, hand still on the door handle.

Jessica pointed the gun at the door at roughly head height, and swivelled her head to look at Michael. Even in the comparative darkness, she knew he'd be able to see her when she mouthed, "Try me," and raised her eyebrows.

Michael looked back at Valentine, rubbed a hand down his face. "Nothing," he said. "Nightmare, that's all."

"You been watching horror films again? I told you—"

"No. I haven't. I'm sorry I woke you."

Jessica heard Valentine's breathing slow down, heard her swallow.

"Okay. Go back to sleep, yeah? See you in the morning."

The door closed. Even after it had latched and the handle rattled slightly as Valentine took her hand away, even when she heard footsteps down the hall, Jess stood still, watching Michael.

"Wow," she whispered, "you were nearly down by a mother then."

"How did you get in here? What do you want?"

"Shh, quieten down." She came towards the bed again. "Do you know what hydrochloric acid is?"

"What?"

She sighed. "I'm going to be here a long time if—"

"Yes, yes, I know."

"Good. It's nasty shit, Michael. Imagine the damage it could do to Valentine's face." She watched his eyes screw up and saw him recoil slightly. "Nasty stuff."

"You're sick."

"I'll swap sick for desperate. Do you know York Road?"

"Which bit—"

"Near the cop shop; near Burger King."

"I know it, yes."

"Be at Burger King tomorrow night at seven. Make sure you're in a car," she said. "And whatever you do, do not be late. Do not tell anyone, and do not bring anyone. Got it?"

"I'm fourteen. I can't drive."

"Really? I hear that you're the wrong crowd, Michael. And stealing a car again will be the least of your worries if you're not there on time. Got it?"

An hour later, Jessica hurled the plastic handgun into a field.

DAY 7

Chapter Seventy-Five

On the way back to the ranch, Eddie veered off track and collected more food and coffee from Mac's; he ate as he drove. He felt much better, less shaky, as he entered the foyer, arms full of exhibits, balancing a coffee in his one free hand, choking on the cigarette between his lips, stinging eyes watering. And then he remembered Moneypenny gently reminding him he shouldn't be smoking in here.

Grudgingly, he rested his coffee on the reception desk and went back outside to finish smoking.

Once back in CSI, he realised Benson must have left hours ago, and was probably fast asleep at Mrs Benson's side. Lucky bastard, he thought. But given all he'd heard about Mrs Benson, maybe not.

Eddie and Kenny launched headlong into the computer work, with Eddie disappearing inside his office for a smoke only twice, until they'd all but done. Kenny looked up, hands behind his neck, stretched, and said, "It's half past seven!"

"Bollocks."

"I'm done," Kenny said. "I'll take the exhibits to the store on my way out." He looked across at Eddie. "You okay to book me off?"

"Absolutely, mate. Thanks for… you know, cheers."

"Well?"

Eddie looked up, puzzlement on his face.

"What happened to your clock?"

Eddie chewed his bottom lip. "They called me away, remember?"

"I remember. I had to work it by myself, don't forget."

"Come on." Eddie helped with the exhibits. He grabbed his car keys and kicked his way out through the office doors. He whispered,

"Troy went after Nicki." Eddie carried on walking, and then realised he was alone. Kenny had stopped yards back, jaw slack.

"What?"

Eddie walked back to him. "She lived alone – block of flats up in north Leeds. She's divorced, apparently, and this was the first step—"

"Get a move on, Eddie. I'm nodding off."

Eddie licked his lips. And then just blurted out, "Troy pushed her off a sixth-floor walkway."

"You're kidding?"

He stared at Kenny. "Hilarious, isn't it."

"She dead?"

Eddie nodded. "When I got there, Crawford's fist seemed to think it was my fault."

Kenny stared into the distance. "Fucking hell."

"Weismann's being good about it. He doesn't think we'll see Crawford again. We've got a reprieve."

"This is just so messed up." Kenny laughed, a violent expulsion of spent air. "What the hell am I supposed to feel?"

"Before we knew about Troy and Nicki, Weismann said we were back in here. We're back on our own merit, not just because they're out of the frame."

Kenny was just staring at him, mouth open still.

"You okay?"

"Okay?" Kenny unglued his feet from the floor and continued towards the stores. "I'm just fucking giddy." There was no smile on his face, just coldness, blankness. "Just… fucking giddy."

Eddie followed him down the stairs and along the corridor.

"You never know who you're dealing with, do you?"

"Nope. He was back on the drugs. Blamed her for losing his job—"

"Well, she *was* responsible."

With the exhibits signed in, Kenny turned to Eddie. "How do you feel about it?"

"I've been putting off feeling anything. I wanted to get Sidmouth's scene out of the way. I'll probably start thinking about it on my way home."

Kenny nodded. "This is so fucked up. Troy in custody?"

Eddie shook his head. "He's on his toes." He patted Kenny on the back. "You want to take the rest of the day off? Come back tomorrow?"

They walked back along the corridor and turned left through the double doors into reception. Kenny sniffled. "Nah. I'm better off working, I think. I'll be back as soon as I've had some kip, okay?"

Eddie nodded, saw Moneypenny carrying her first cup of tea across to her desk. "I'll catch you later," he called after Kenny. "Ring me if you need anything."

"You wouldn't pick up even if I did."

Eddie paused. "Yeah, that's true. But it's the thought that counts."

Kenny waved and walked away.

Eddie stared at her. Intermittently he'd been thinking about her – and about relationships in general. He wasn't doing very well in this one. But he consoled himself with the knowledge that at least he was trying. That knowledge almost made him feel good about himself. He gritted his teeth, took a breath that made his ribs hurt, and began walking across the open floor, towards the door and away from awkward questions.

"Eddie?"

He closed his eyes, stood on the spot, and then turned to face her, something like a smile on his face – one picked off the shelf for use in case of emergency. "Hi. How are you doing?" He walked towards her.

"You look awful." She put down her tea, and her hand rested against her mouth, eyes crawling over his face. "What on earth happened?"

Eddie looked down. Here it comes, he thought.

"Have you been working all night?"

He could feel his eyes prickling with dryness, could feel his headache coming back, and could feel his nose and lip throbbing again. And his neck pain had returned to chime in unison with his ribs.

He gritted his teeth again, and decided relationships were wonderful things – for other people. Eddie was designed to be alone, and to stay that way. He sighed; all he wanted was a shower and his bed. Oh, and some more paracetamol. And a cigarette.

"What's happened to your eye?" She came closer. "Oh God, and your nose? And your lip!"

"Calm down," he whispered, "it's not as bad as it looks." There was that smile again – second-hand but just as good as new; reassuring, but obviously false. "I have some bad news." Eddie reached across the counter and rested his fingertips on her shoulder, wondering if he should touch her hand. He licked his lips again, discomfort making itself evident.

What the hell do other people do in this situation?

I wonder if I could get away with just sending her a text.

This is why I should just be alone; there's nothing I can give another person but heartache.

"What?" She touched his hand, and Eddie almost pulled it back, but bravely kept it there, absorbing the heat of her skin.

"Troy is missing, and Nicki is dead." He heard the sharp intake, he watched her eyes widen further, and he felt her hand grasp his. "There was no easy way," he said, "you know, to tell you."

"Why?"

Eddie stared, then shrugged. "I'm just not very good—"

"Why is she dead, Eddie?"

"Ah. Speculation at the moment." He looked around; the foyer was still empty, thankfully. He closed in another few inches, whispered, "Troy pushed her off a balcony."

With a thump, Moneypenny sat down, her eyes staring into nothing, her hand still at her mouth. It fell away, and left behind a perfect 'O'. "That's… that's awful."

Eddie swallowed. He was no good at this shit. He saw the pain in her eyes – pain that she wasn't really entitled to feel. She didn't know either of them well enough to look this hurt. Or was that him being selfish again? Did he have the monopoly on feeling third-party pain? Pain by proxy? Maybe she was a different animal than he was. He dealt with strangers' deaths every day and it left almost no trace.

Sure, he felt sorry for them – who wouldn't? – but he was able to move through life without their ghosts pulling at his trouser leg. But look at Moneypenny, almost immobile with torment. It endeared her to him, and had the time been right, he would have tried to reassess his own stance on How One Should Feel Upon the Deaths of Others. But for now, he'd shelve it.

He couldn't understand the depth of her empathy. And it made him question his own – so shallow that you could see right to the bottom where the paint was flaking.

Two different animals.

He looked away, feeling emotionally stagnant, but his eyes drifted back to her. She was beautiful even in grief. She was so beautiful that he was tempted to comfort her again, a hand on the shoulder perhaps, a comforting murmur in her ear.

Maybe I should get a book. Understanding People for Dummies, or something.

"Hey," he said, making a start. "You okay?"

She had tears in her eyes. Actual tears.

He stared; no comforting hand would sort those out. "I have to go," he said. "I've been on a double murder all night. I'm wiped."

She nodded absently, and then she seemed to latch on to what he'd said. "Listen. About the other night..."

Oh crap, he thought. Here it comes, three out of ten if I'm lucky. Next time I'll think of somewhere better, classier. She deserves something swish. Next time I'll pick her up, chauffeur her – treat her well. He brought out the smile again, dusted it off, dented but serviceable.

"I don't think we should, you know… I don't think we should go out again."

"You want to stay in? I can get a takeaway—"

"No. Eddie. I mean I think we should… I think maybe we should call it a day. You know…"

Eddie was gobsmacked. It was his turn for his mouth to form a perfect 'O'. "Oh. Yes, yes, of course. I was just about to say the same thing! Incompatible…"

"Are you okay?"

"Absolutely," he beamed. "It's the right move. Definitely." He was laughing and shaking his head, the jester desperately trying to laugh his way off stage. He pointed a finger at her, winked, and said, "Here's to you, kid," and he walked away. Eddie felt pain and revelled in it. Secretly he smiled. He had some emotions after all!

"Eddie? I'm sorry," she called after him.

He spun around and gave her another wink. "Don't be. It was good while it lasted." The smile dropped off his face as soon as his back was turned. It was a cheap smile, after all; no returns, no guarantee.

She called, "Oh – Eddie?"

He stood still again, feeling jagged and spiky now that he had become a human being with real feelings – fragile feelings.

"My name. It's—"

"Moneypenny." He closed his eyes, and the smile this time was genuine. He nodded. "Your name is Moneypenny." He walked to the door, and left the building. Although Melanie had told him Moneypenny's name, he'd made an effort to forget it. Successfully.

His mind was so full of other people and their shit, and all on top of being awake for twenty-five hours with a creeping exhaustion so ready to overwhelm him that he almost screamed when he saw Sid in the car park.

Eddie sighed and lit a cigarette.

"Eddie! Eddie!" Sid was waving, running towards him with his flared trousers flapping behind him, handbag swinging in his hand, red nail polish glinting in the day's new light.

"Have you joined a Mott the Hoople tribute band?" Eddie squinted against the light, and then squinted at Sid's hair as he drew closer, the sun shining through the ringlets. "What the fuck happened to your hair?"

"Huh? Don't you like it?"

"It looks like you've glued two plates of noodles to your head. Did someone do that to you while you were asleep?"

"Cheeky. This cost seventy-five—" He gasped. "What the hell happened—"

"Seventy-five? Want me to beat them up for you?"

"It's a wig, silly. And what happened—"

"Thank God for that. You look like Shirley Temple."

"Who?" Sid tutted, lips pursed. "Anyway— Wait, are you crying?"

"What? Don't talk shit; I've been yawning so hard that my jaw almost fell off, that's all."

Sid looked at him. "Right," he said. "Anyway, never mind all that now; we have two new starters coming in today."

"Good. Set them off with fingerprinting Sidmouth's house – first floor only."

"Sidmouth?"
"Just… Check in with CID, they'll give you the details."
Sid clicked his fingers. "Oh! Also, I found out about Wendy."
Eddie took a step back. "Who the fuck is W— Oh. Wendy!"

Chapter Seventy-Six

Despite his tiredness – a tiredness that should have been too extreme to permit driving – Eddie's fury had kept him awake and focused all the way to Charles's house, and it had kept his knuckles white on the steering wheel.

But when he pulled up outside, her car wasn't there. He gave a quick knock on the front door to make sure Charles wasn't in there by himself. But there was no response.

He lit another cigarette, climbed back into the Discovery, aimed it towards his own home, and made a phone call on the hands-free. He was there twenty minutes later, the sun full up now, gracing the thin clouds that skipped across a cold sky. Her car was parked out front.

He slammed the car door. No matter how hard he tried to calm down, he could feel the pressure building inside his chest, could feel his fingertips tingling, but he was unaware of the snarl that curled his top lip.

He barged into the cottage. There they were in the lounge, like a pair of love-sick puppies, lusting over each other across a table with tea and biscuits still on it. Eddie stared at their stunned faces. If he'd been a cartoon character, Eddie would have been a bull; head down, hooves kicking up dirt, ready to charge.

"Eddie?"

His attention turned solely to Wendy. "Get out of my fucking house."

"Eddie!"

"Shut up, Dad."

"How dare you?" Wendy said, and stood. "I demand you show some respect—"

"If you don't get out of my house – now – you're going through that fucking window, woman."

Charles stood, circled around Wendy, and came towards Eddie. "What's going on? What the hell happened to your face?"

His eyes never left Wendy's. "Ever heard of romance scamming?"

"What?"

"Romance scamming. Have you heard of it?"

Charles stopped, ran fingers through what little hair he had left. He turned towards Wendy, then back to Eddie. A weak and withered laugh tripped out of thin pale lips. "No."

"Tell me you haven't signed anything, Dad."

Charles stuttered, "Signed anything? No, I haven't, but signed what, I mean what—"

"She's a con artist. Her real name is Clarissa Hardisty, and she lived in London until last year."

"I don't have to put up with this!" Wendy walked over to Charles. "Come on, let's get out of here. We don't need to stay here and listen to these delusional accusations. I know of a perfectly fine—"

"Is he right? Is Clarissa your real name?"

"Charles. Do you even hear yourself? Don't tell me you believe his nonsense. My name is Wendy." She held his hand, then came in close and kissed him on the cheek. She whispered, "And I love you. Don't forget that." She set off walking then, pulling Charles like a leashed pet, but he stood his ground, causing her to turn around again and face him.

There were tears in his eyes.

There was anger in Wendy's. "Charles." She closed in again. "I'm leaving now. You can come with me and we can start living the rest of our lives together, just as we planned. We can do all those things we set our hearts on. But you have to do it now. I'm not waiting."

Charles's eyes drifted across to Eddie. Eddie shook his head.

Charles looked back at her. "Why? I thought we had something special." He glanced away, as though reminiscing. "Holidays in Paris. Trips to Italy..."

"It was all fake, Dad. Sucking you in, getting you to sign over your house. She wanted this one, remember? Until she found out I owned it. But when she found out you had your own house, and it was refurbished... She saw pound signs."

"Shut up," said Charles. He looked at Wendy. "I just have to know," he said, his voice cracking. "I just have to know if you ever really loved me."

She let go of his hand. There was a whisper of a smile on her painted face, like a trace of poison on a kiss, an easy-come, easy-go shrug of the shoulders. "Pathetic." She turned and headed for the front door, where Eddie stood, waiting.

He pulled his arm back, ready to punch her in the face – an eye for an eye, for the blow she'd dealt his father. But as she neared and Eddie took his aim, someone grabbed his arm.

"It's okay, Eddie, thanks. We've got it from here."

She stopped dead, the smile gone. Her jaw was limp, her eyes wide as she stared at the two suited gentleman standing in Eddie's doorway.

"Clarissa Hardisty, you are under arrest on suspicion of fraud. You do not have to say anything, but it may harm your defence if you do not mention when questioned something which you later rely on in court. Anything you do say may be given in evidence."

"Are you having a laugh?"

One officer looked at the other, took his cuffs out and reached for her.

"Charles! Tell them, Charles, do something! We're together, we're in love. Charles. Charles, tell them!"

Eddie and his father watched her being helped into the back seat of a plain car. One officer came back to them. "Do you have her car keys? Where's her handbag?"

Charles, in something of a daze, got them from the side of her chair and offered them over. "Fraud? What has she done?"

The officer took the bag and the keys. "Someone will come by later to collect her car, alright?"

Eddie nodded.

"Well?" asked Charles.

The officer sighed, leaned against the door. "She's operated for years down south: London, and Sussex. She's also wanted for fraud in the Midlands. Over the last year she's been in Yorkshire, and she's already put two men through what you were going through."

"Which is what? I still don't know."

"She befriends lonely men. Earns their trust. She finds out whether they have a house, whether the mortgage is paid off. And then she manipulates the system and gets a mortgage on the property, or she forges documents to transfer it into her name, and then sells it. When she gets the money, you never see her again."

Charles stared, wide-eyed, at the officer.

"Cheers, Eddie." The officer patted Eddie on the arm, nodded at Charles and left.

Eddie watched Charles. His own anger had dissipated, but he still felt as though he needed justice for his father. He still felt cheated, and he saw the same feelings in Charles, but he also saw a void opening up, an empty space that Wendy – or whatever her damned name was – had filled.

Charles might have been perpetually under the thumb, always at her beck and call, but he had company. He had a woman, he had romance of a sort, and he had… he had *someone.*

"You okay?"

Charles looked incredulous. "What?"

"You want a brew?"

"Do I want a brew? No, I don't want a bloody brew!" Charles stepped closer. "Couldn't handle it, could you? Couldn't handle me having a woman and you not. You were always jealous. You little bastard."

"What?" Eddie took a step back. "Jealous that she was screwing you over for your house? Oh yes, obviously. I can see how you'd think I was jealous of that."

Charles slapped Eddie across the face, and left.

Eddie stood there stunned, new blood trickling from his nose and a renewed pain in his whole face. He followed Charles outside. "Dad—"

"Leave me alone, Eddie."

"Dad."

Charles faced him as the car disappeared from view. "I was happy. It might not have looked that way from where you were standing; I know she could be a bit domineering. But I was the happiest I've been since… well, since your mum passed away. And you couldn't stand it, could you? You had to destroy it, my happiness. You had to destroy what we had."

"I was trying to save you from—"

Charles nodded. "You were helping me? Well, you succeeded. You won. You really helped me, Eddie. Thank you."

Eddie watched him walk away. "Where are you going?"

Chapter Seventy-Seven

Jessica let out a sigh, silently thanking God that the knock on her door wasn't the coppers again. "I was wondering when you'd show up."

Tony tried to peer over her shoulder into her flat. "I didn't know if I'd still be welcome."

She opened the door further and let him in; watching, arms folded, as he slumped into his usual chair. She kicked the door closed. Not only was she relieved that he wasn't the coppers, she was relieved that her plan could now proceed unhindered.

"Any chance of a tea? I'm gagging."

Jess put the kettle on, picturing the Stanley knife under her mattress. She closed her eyes, looking for an excuse – other than the mess it would cause – not to use it here and now. She tried to remember the good times they had shared twelve years ago, before all the life-changing surgery that the justice system had given them. And the harder she thought about it, the more those supposed good times slithered away from view.

"You're always gagging for a brew." She looked at him out of the corner of her eye, and bit the inside of her lip before saying, "I only have green tea."

"Green tea? What the hell's green tea?"

"It's good for you. Tastes a bit like cough syrup, but it's full of vitamins."

And why did those good times slither away? she wondered. Was it because they actually weren't good times? Was this just a veil of nostalgia fabricated by wishful thinking? They were 'times', but if she remembered correctly – and fair enough, it was a dozen years ago – there was no 'good' in there at all.

"Is that the only tea you've got? I ain't keen on all that foreign muck."

The search for a balance between the old days they'd shared, and the future she had planned for them, just wasn't there. There was no degree of quality in their past that could prevent this new future from happening. Not now; she'd put in too much effort to let this slip by. "Do you want a drink or not? I'm not a bloody café, Tony!"

He raised his hands. "Alright, alright. Keep your hair on." He slid backwards in the seat, and then tried to change the subject. "Did it all go okay? With whatsisname?"

"Sidmouth? You can say it, you know. He isn't coming back to haunt you."

"It went okay, then?"

She nodded, poured water. "He suffered. Not enough, but a little."

"Feel better?"

Jess slammed the kettle down. "Feel better? What? I haven't just taken a Lemsip for a cold, Tony! I haven't put some Savlon on a fucking scratch." She took a pace towards him, and her eyes were black with anger. "Do you know what that man did to me? And do you know what I've had to do to get his face out of my head? Do you?"

"Sorry," was all he said.

She watched his small dark eyes until he looked away. She could smell him. He turned her stomach. Grotesque. "Here," she said, and with sweating fingers, handed him a mug of very green tea.

He held the cup to his nose. "It smells vile."

"Don't even think about wasting it! That was expensive."

He sipped and grimaced.

"Police have been round. About Marchant."

Tony shuddered. "Figures. Did they say anything about the other one, the pathologist?"

"No." She failed to mention their interest in Tony, or how naughty he had been to steal her jacket and her knife.

"There you go, then. They haven't linked them. You're safe."

"They'll be back. And I think they'll be taking me away this time."

Tony rolled a smoke, watching her all the time. He lit it, spat out a stray bit of tobacco. "What are you saying?"

"Take me back to your place. It's too dangerous for me here."

He was already shaking his head before her sentence ended. "I keep myself to myself, Jessy. You can understand that, can't you? I need to keep private."

"I see. Like that, is it? You've been sniffing around me like a dog ever since I got out. And now I give you a chance to…" She searched for the phrase. "Now I give you the chance to turn back the clock, you turn up your nose instead? How's that work, then?"

Tony paused. Smoke curled up his face as he studied her, sipping from the cup again.

She could tell by his expression that he was trying to work out what she meant, and what to say next.

He said it. "Thinking of grassing on me, Jessy?"

She smiled, just broadly enough to worry him.

"I trust you," he said.

"Yeah? Well, we all need something to believe in, don't we?"

"Ain't about turning the clock back, girl. I like my invisibility. I'll do anything to protect it."

"How fucking lovely for you."

He puffed on his cigarette, supped his tea. Thinking. "Don't you think you're going underground a bit too early? There's still one man on that list."

"The forensic guy, yeah, I know. I don't need your list, Tony." She tapped her head. "It's up here."

She saw him take a breath, watching her, looking up and down her body, and that's when she knew he'd relent and invite her over. He stood, put his empty mug on the draining board. "Thanks for the lousy tea," he said. "The answer's still no."

She went cold.

"Can't, Jessy. Sorry, love."

"You bastard. You're just going to hang me out to dry? I'll be in cuffs by tomorrow unless I find somewhere!"

"Scout around. There's loads of places up Burley way."

Jess pointed a threatening finger. "I will not go down alone again. I will not wear those cuffs by myself." Her voice shook, and her eyes stung.

He closed the door behind him, and Jessica's mouth fell open. He obviously knew the end was coming. But the future she had planned, for Tony at least, depended on being back at his place, and it had to be tonight. She couldn't let him leave the building without her. She opened her bedsit door and saw him reaching for the door handle at the end of the hallway. "Tony."

He turned and eyed her.

"Okay," she said.

He smiled at her. The wrinkles around his eyes turned into furrows and his teeth glinted a sick brown through grey lips. "Okay what?"

"Enough of the games. You want me. And you can have me, we can be together again. But not here. You take me somewhere safe, and you keep me safe till it's blown over."

Tony pulled away from the door handle, and then shuffled along the hallway towards her, grinning like a kid getting everything he wanted for Christmas. Eyes sparkling. And when he reached her bedsit doorway, he took her by the throat. The smile fell away. The eyes went dim. "Have you mentioned me to the cops?"

She grabbed his wrist, tried to pull his hand away, and couldn't. She couldn't breathe, and she could feel the pressure rising inside her head, her eyes ready to pop. "No," she whispered. "No."

He relaxed, and she took a long breath, dry-coughing it all back out. "Better not be playing me, Jessy. I'll kill you if you're messing with me."

"I wouldn't—"

"Understand?"

She stared at him, rubbing her throat. "I understand."

"Good, cos it ain't never going to blow over."

She stared into his eyes, noticing their constricted pupils. "Let me grab my bag. We'll get a taxi to yours." She thundered back inside the flat, leaving Tony swaying slightly in the hallway.

In the back of the taxi, Tony just about had the presence of mind to relay his address to the driver before his head fell backwards, and he fell into a deep sleep. It was an address that Jessica didn't expect to hear.

* * *

By the time they had arrived at Tony's house in Headingley, he was blitzed.

Jess looked through the dirt-smeared glass, and asked the driver, "You sure this is the address he gave you?"

"Listen love, I don't know what your game is, but I'm losing money while we sit here discussing the retentive capabilities of my memory."

She opened the door, and then leaned forward and paid him, slid an extra tenner into his hand and asked if he'd mind helping her boyfriend out of the car. "Silly sod's had too much again." She smiled. "And I can't manage him by myself."

"What's your game?"

"I beg your pardon?"

"With him." He nodded towards Tony. "No way is he your boyfriend. You gonna do him over?" He winked at her.

"How fucking dare you! Are you suggesting I'm on the game?"

The driver see-sawed his hand as he smiled at her. "It crossed my mind."

Jessica held out her hand. "Give me the tenner back, you cheeky bastard."

"Okay, love, no need to get twisted about it; I was only joking."

"Are you going to help me or what?"

The driver didn't look happy.

She slammed the door again, sat back in the seat, and folded her arms. "He'll probably throw up in a minute. We'll just wait and see, shall we?"

It took them only a few minutes to get Tony to his front door. The taxi driver took Tony's limp arm from around his shoulder and let him sink to the floor. "G'night, love." Halfway back to his car, he turned and said, "You should think about getting him to a hospital."

"I will. Thanks." She stared at him as he climbed back into the car.

Jessica opened the rucksack and pulled out a small torch; she took a look around, but knew it would be clear. Tony was very careful where he lived; like he said, he liked his seclusion. It was dark, cloud stole the moonlight, and the sound of the taxi driving away faded into the background rumble of the traffic on the main road several hundred yards away.

This wasn't where she'd expected to end up. She'd expected to be in the basement of some derelict old mill, or a lousy hostel. But this wasn't a slum at all. This was a regular house, standing out by itself, close to the bustle of life – but not too close. And up there under the eaves was an alarm box, and she wouldn't be at all surprised to learn the place was hooked up with CCTV.

She shone the torch at Tony's face, and noticed how sweaty he was, and how his eyelids flickered – a good sign at least. And when she put her fingertips to the side of his neck, she felt how slowly his heart was beating. Perhaps there wasn't as much time left as she'd hoped. It was time to search him for the keys.

"Tony, Tony…" She slapped his face. Eventually, his eyes slid halfway open, but he seemed unable to focus. "What's your alarm code?"

His eyes slid closed again.

This time she hit him hard enough to make her hand tingle. "Tony! Alarm code. Now!"

He slurred, "One, two, three, four."

"You're kidding, right? Who the hell uses one, two, three, four?"

"Zactly," he mumbled.

"Can you stand?"

He shook his head, and then cringed, digging his nails into the floor.

"Feel sick?"

"The fuck d'you give me?"

"Shut up and give me the keys or we're spending the night on your doorstep."

He slowly opened his eyes; they were already glaring at her. "Inside pocket. Left." His eyelids drifted down again.

Jessica yanked the jacket open, searched the pockets in both his coats, brushed aside his feeble attempt to grab her wrist, and eventually found the keys.

Despite her heart banging inside her hollow chest, she put aside her fears and her hopes, silenced the beeping alarm, dragged Tony into his hallway, and slammed and locked the door. She turned on the lights.

She ran up the stairs, searched all the rooms up there, then ran back downstairs and searched the open-plan ground floor. He was still in the same position when she returned to him ten minutes later.

His breathing had slowed considerably, and she hoped he wouldn't expire before she'd set things in motion. It was very important to her that he should be alive until she chose otherwise.

Chapter Seventy-Eight

During one of Tony's slender bouts of consciousness, she managed to get his overcoats off and a fresh surge of body odour hit her like a brick. She gagged, but just managed to keep her guts under control. Eventually, she got him into a chair at the kitchen table. While he was drifting in and out of awareness, she took the chance to hide some of the contents of the rucksack she'd brought with her. And now she sat in an armchair in the lounge, with her knees up under her chin and her arms tight around her legs, rocking back and forth, watching him.

His eyes opened slightly, then slid closed again. Ten minutes later they opened fully, and his head swivelled towards her like it was motorised. His eyes looked at her, but she had the feeling he was seeing nothing. He looked dead.

"Is this your house?"

The sound of her voice caused him to jump. He looked terrified. Was this what junkies did for fun? "Is it your house, Tony?"

"Yeah."

"If you're a tramp, how come—"

"Jessy. You don't know… what you're fucking with. Bail while you still can."

"I'll be leaving soon. After I've done you."

He tried to laugh, but failed. "What you give me?"

"Methadone."

"Jesus. Killing me. Hospital." He looked like a puppy that had just been kicked. Pleading.

"Don't worry about that. I'll make sure I kill you before the methadone can." She reached down and slapped his face, and was surprised to note that he barely responded. She could feel anger pulsing in her temple. She looked around. "So how come you only play at being homeless?"

He slurred, "Green tea? Bitch."

"I'll be giving you something else soon: the ultimate freedom." She grinned, pleased that she'd managed to keep him alive so long, but aware that he might not last much longer. Time to get a move on.

"Why, Jessy? We're s'posed to be lovers."

"I'll ignore that – I'll put it down to delirium. And I won't even answer the first question." She stood, ready to make a start.

"You know… about Sebastian." Clear. A statement, not a question.

Her fingertips prickled. Just the mention of his name caused her to tense up. "Couple of days ago, you were very good at offering me sympathy," she said. "But you nudged it just a little too far."

He struggled to swivel his head around and look up at her, confusion in his faraway eyes. "How d'you mean?"

"The coppers didn't believe me when I told them the smoke alarm was blaring at me; there was no such sound on the three-nines recording. And they said the grill was cold, which it would have been by the time they'd thought to check." She bit her lower lip to stop the tears, and eventually said, "Only me, Michael, and Sebastian knew the smoke alarm was going off. Just us – and the person who came into the kitchen and killed him. That person was you."

He stopped struggling to keep looking up at her, and his chin fell to his chest.

"It wasn't even brought up in court. And I never mentioned it to you." She crouched beside him, grabbed his chin through his filthy beard, and pulled his face around so he could see her. And she asked, "Why did you do it? I can't believe you'd let me suffer for twelve years when you knew the truth."

His eyes began to close so she slapped him with her free hand.

"Answer me, or I'll cram a full twelve years' worth of pain into whatever life you've got left."

"Horrible fucker. Got paid to kill him."

Jess let go of his face, and she dropped backwards onto the chair, her mouth open and her mind reeling. "Who paid you?" When he didn't answer, she scrambled to her feet and grabbed his face again. "Tony! Tony, who paid you? What do you mean?"

"Was just a scam." He paused. "Never had no feelings for you. Just business."

"Who fucking paid you?"

His rolling eyes finally found her. "Stanley."

"Stanley? Sebastian's brother?"

Tony squinted at her, and he managed a smile of sorts. "Was you shagging him?"

Her eyes widened at the insinuation.

"While you was with Sebastian?"

"Don't be ridiculous," she spat. But she said it too fiercely, looked away too quickly, and she knew that he knew.

Tony continued. "He got back in touch. Few weeks ago. Your brief was making noises. Wanting more money."

"Marchant? He knew?"

"If you went down, they'd stop looking."

Jess almost screamed. "He fucking knew!"

"He was in on it. Coming up for retirement. Got greedy. Shut him up with a pickaxe."

Jessica's fury almost twisted her mind away to somewhere black again, but she pulled it back, aware that she had things to do. Important things. "But why would Stanley—"

"Jessy. What's everything always about?"

"Money?"

"Their dad was dying. Big inheritance." He tried to move his arm, tried to grab her wrist – just to hold it, or to pull her close, she didn't know. But she kept it out of his reach.

"Nothing personal, Jessy. Liked you."

She sighed. "Business is business, right?" She sat on the cold floor, her back against the kitchen unit, in much the same position she'd found herself after taking her revenge against Bolton. And she found that she was shaking, much as she had done then, but this was not the fear she'd felt in the pathologist's house. It was anger.

Jess had been angry her entire life, had lived in close confines with it for over a decade, and had seen it eat away at other inmates' minds until they'd harmed themselves, or someone else. It was vile. And now she was experiencing it again, undiluted by time – full fat, high-octane anger – and she glared at Tony as his piece-of-shit eyes rolled around inside his empty skull, drifting in and out of consciousness.

It took a long while for the penny to drop, but eventually it did. Her mouth opened again, and her spine shuddered like someone had electrocuted her. "You set me up to kill the others too, to mask Marchant's death. You even told me you'd killed him as a favour to me!"

His lolling head steadied, and eventually became still, eyes fixed on her. "You were entitled to your revenge. Still are."

"You bastard!"

"Never thought you'd go down for Sebastian's murder. Thought… thought they'd say suicide. But when they charged you… well, like you said. Business.

"I reckon," he slurred, "when they knew I did him in your house, they got Marchant to point the finger at you."

"You mean Stanley got my own lawyer to pin it on me? Why would he do that?"

Tony raised his eyebrows, challenging her. "This time, ain't nothing to do with money."

Jess sat there in the cold kitchen, marvelling at how shit her life actually was. Not only did someone kill her ex-husband and fail to make it look like suicide, but the police then fucked up and charged her with his murder. And Marchant locked her in the cell himself.

And now, no doubt, the police would have her lined up for another three deaths.

She stared at Tony. *Make that four.* "And is that why you dressed as a tramp? To make me think you'd been pining for me all those years?"

"Stanley… Married now. They want your boy."

The creases on Jessica's forehead pulled tightly together. She shrugged, "Married? Do I know her?"

"Valentine."

When it all goes awfully wrong for you, Jessica, remember today. This was the beginning of it all.

Jessica's mouth fell open and her eyes glided away as she remembered meeting Michael's foster mother, and the private meeting they'd had. *Stanley's wife?* "I won't agree! I didn't agree back then, and I won't agree now. I'll never agree!"

"They knew that." He almost looked at her, but couldn't manage to move his head upwards. He did, however, manage to grow a smile on his pale lips. "It's why they want you… jail… again. Should've taken… fifty grand… Jessy."

His head rolled around and settled against his chest again. He grunted.

"Tony?" She nudged him with her foot. There was no response. She scooted across to him and felt his neck with her fingertips.

"Shit!"

She stood, nudged him again, harder. "Don't you dare fucking die on me! How fucking dare you, you bastard!" She kicked him, and his head lolled again, but there was no other movement.

Jessica hurried out to the cupboard underneath the stairs, where she'd left the stuff from the rucksack. She snapped on a pair of latex gloves and got to work. "This is what happens when you rush things," she told herself. "This is what happens when the fucking cops call round before you've got your ducks in a row." Tony's death was a killing too soon, she knew that: there was one more increment to click through, one more killing to make her whole again. And if she'd done that one before Tony, the police would have suspected him of them all.

Not now, though. Thanks to Tony infuriating her, they'd probably soon figure it out. But she had a contingency plan.

Chapter Seventy-Nine

Eddie woke after four and half hours' sleep and fell out of bed. On his way to the bathroom, he stubbed his little toe on the bedside table and screamed, hopping along the corridor, huffing at the pain. Twenty minutes later he dripped shower water all over the hallway carpet as he found himself staring into the full-length mirror.

He was mesmerised by the creases. The last time he looked this closely there had been none. And the grey hair at the sides, all stuck up in clumps like he had a blind barber – where the hell had that come from? And were they hairs poking out of his ears? And more out of his nostrils?

"Fuck."

He was about to go and put the kettle on when some ignorant bastard knocked at his front door. Eddie groaned and shuffled through the lounge, praying it was just the window cleaner, someone he could get rid of in ten seconds flat.

The door, like his joints, groaned. Benson stood in the rain looking pissed off and cold.

"What?"

"Are you going to let me in? It's fucking raining, Eddie. It's only polite to let someone in when it's raining."

Eddie grunted and stepped aside.

"And now go and put some clothes on. No man wants to see another man's Walnut Whip while they're talking."

Eddie turned and shuffled away. "Make me a coffee, Benson."

* * *

"I put Khan on tracking down that Tony fella."

"Did he get anywhere?"

"Nope. But Leo Brightman called, got me a name from the fingerprints you lifted."

Eddie raised an eyebrow. "So my undercover work came up trumps, eh? I always knew I should have been a covert operative. I could be the new Jason Bourne."

"You don't have the figure for it."

Eddie stared at Benson's gut.

Benson ignored him. "I don't want to know where you got that fingerprint from—"

"No, of course you don't. You'd rather remain ignorant and just have the fucking answers to life's little problems land in your lap. It's people like me who make people like you look good, and don't you forget it." Eddie was pointing a finger, and he'd become much more serious than he'd intended.

"Down, boy."

"Well, come on. Don't back away from me, Benson, join me. I'm pushing your investigation forward and you've got your nose in the fucking air over where I got a fingerprint from and whether it's legal and all that bollocks. If you're going to get high and mighty with me, you might as well forget the name Leo got for you and wait for your meathead Khan to track him down."

"Okay, okay. I'm sorry, alright?"

Eddie nodded. "Yeah, I should bloody well think so. My dad said something to me last week that hurt. He said I was selfish. And I'm standing here proving that I'm not."

Benson took a little step back. "Okaaay," he said. "Back to business?"

Eddie shrugged. "Just saying."

"Tony Longbottom's real name is Anthony Hardwick. He's a monster. He's known to us for three counts of Section 18 wounding, and he got away with an attempted murder charge up in Newcastle in '99. Rumour has it he fancies himself as a bit of a hitman, and I think he's playing a bigger role in these murders than meets the eye. I know he did Marchant, and I wouldn't be surprised if he did Bolton too." And then he stopped, and thought. "No idea why he'd do Sidmouth, though."

Eddie sipped the brown liquid that Benson had claimed was coffee. To him it tasted how he imagined sieved vomit would. "You want another?" he said, waving the mug at Benson and walking towards the kitchen.

"No. Now listen—"

"I thought we'd agreed that he did Sidmouth and tried to frame Jessica for it so she'd get sent down again."

Benson was halfway through constructing a word, complete with pointing finger, when he paused, dropped his arm, and said, "Good point."

Eddie fixed a fresh coffee, one that actually tasted like coffee. "So you were saying you got Khan on the job?"

"I did, yes. There was no Tony Longbottom driving for any Leeds bus company between 2004 and 2006."

"So he was using another alias, or his real name."

Benson shrugged as Eddie lit a cigarette and breathed it like it was a honeysuckle bouquet. "Nope, certainly not his real name. But why would he use an alias?"

"So people like you couldn't find him? So people like Jessica…"

Benson turned to him. "Go on."

"So she wouldn't know who he was."

"You're saying he topped Sebastian?"

"We've been through all this."

"Yes, we have. But now we find out he doesn't exist as Tony Longbottom."

"Seriously" —Eddie grinned— "who would *choose* to call themselves Longbottom?"

"But Jessica Ripley—"

"You're fucking obsessed."

"Of course I am. She's the centre of this series of deaths, Eddie, even if she's not the killer. Marchant's dead; she was his client. Bolton is dead; he worked her case. Sidmouth is dead; he was her Probation Officer."

"They're called Offender Managers now."

"Whatever. Shut up." Benson slid a pause into the conversation that was like white noise in a nightclub. Then, thinking aloud, he said, "Having said that, she's been bothering his office, looking for him."

"Sidmouth's office?"

"Yes, Sidmouth's office. Keep up. She's been there asking to see her son. Sidmouth was the one who signed her off, let her go and see him provided she kept to the conditions of her parole." He rubbed his chin, "They've given her another Offender Manager to sort out those appointments."

"You told me. But if she's been seeking him out even after he was dead, doesn't it tell you that she didn't kill him?"

"No. It tells me she's a wonderful actress."

"Whoa. Come on, she's no actress. You saw how scared she was."

"Bollocks," Benson said.

"Listen. She didn't kill Sebastian. If she had, why would she go around killing everyone who was involved with her case? She can't hold a grudge against them if they were right, can she? Do you see what I mean?"

"Suppose so."

"And in all my years of doing this shit, I've never yet seen anyone commit suicide by stabbing themselves in the heart. Never."

"I have."

"Well you would have, wouldn't you? You're as bad as my dad: if I've got an elephant, he's got a bag to put it in." He sighed, stared at Benson and drew on his cigarette. "Just acknowledge me for once, and say, 'Hey, Eddie, you're right'."

Benson's eyebrows knotted in confusion. "You really are so full of shit, Collins, it's a wonder you don't explode through your arsehole."

Eddie downed the coffee and wiped a sleeve across the drop hanging off his chin. "Which all adds weight," he said, "to the killer being Tony. Anthony. Whoever."

"Well" —Benson turned to face him— "we'll soon see."

"I already don't like where this is going."

"You'll need to get your van from MCU."

Eddie looked to the ceiling, closed his eyes. "I just want one fucking day off. Is that too much to ask? I'm knackered, Tom."

"If you're right that Tony is the killer, you can have all the rest you can manage, beginning tomorrow," Benson said. "He won't be killing anyone ever again."

Chapter Eighty

Jess snapped on the gloves, felt nauseous, but swallowed it down and got to work. She picked up the hatchet in her right hand and worked from behind him to keep the angles true.

There wasn't much room for a swing – the thick end of the hatchet banged into his chest – but she found that she didn't need much of one. The blade was sharp like a razor; all she needed to do was drag it along the skin and it left behind a red trail of weeping blood that gathered and teemed across the hairs on his arm and dripped onto the table. Fascinating. Horrific. Same measure.

She stood, arched her back, and knew it wasn't enough. At this rate he'd heal before he bled to death. She leaned in close again, her chest against his right shoulder, her left ear near his mouth. He breathed hot rancid breath against her, and even when the axe cut deeper, that breathing didn't change.

She cut along his arm towards his wrist, and saw it jump as though it'd caught an electric shock somehow. She saw the muscle, and she saw the miniature fountain as the blade severed an artery. The blood flowed fast, washing across the side of his arm, and flowing across the table to pour over the edge and onto his lap.

From there it dripped onto the floor, splashing like water. Blood *is* thicker than water, but not by much, and it travels a long way before it dries. And the blood splashes hit the chair leg, and they hit Tony's legs, hit his shoes, and left a shadow beyond them, clear of blood.

More blood hit the floor and splashed onto Jess's shoes, leaving a shadow of clean floor beneath them too.

As the blood slowed, and then stopped, she took a step back and breathed hard, fighting tears that had appeared from nowhere.

She was confused by them, by this sudden surge of an emotion that had been so lacking with Bolton and the others. She extended a gloved hand to rest it on his shoulder. "Goodbye, Tony," she whispered. "It was good to know you."

But the anger came then, blew apart the sadness, obliterated any feeling she ever had for this bastard, and she swung the blade at his head.

* * *

But she stopped the hatchet in mid-arc, less than six inches from his stupid fat fucking dead head.

Jessica screamed and sank to her knees, stinging tears blinding her. This was the culmination of all the hatred her mind had nurtured, and to let it run free right now would mean the destruction of the entire house, the annihilation of his body, and quite possibly even of herself. She breathed hard, long, deep breaths that scalded like heartburn. She stood, closed her eyes, made herself breathe through her nose, slower, shallower. Eventually the pressure inside her head subsided.

No. I mustn't. Stick to the plan. No point in ruining everything now.

She curled Tony's flaccid hand around the hatchet shaft, got plenty of his blood on there, and got his fingerprint in there too. And then she carefully put the weapon on the table. She took a step back and peeled off her second pair of gloves, shoving them inside a resealable plastic bag that she kept in her left back pocket. From another plastic bag in her right back pocket, she took a clean pair of gloves and pulled them with difficulty onto her sweating hands.

She took out the key from the front door, cleaned it, and replaced it, making sure the door was locked. She picked up Tony's CAT hat that had fallen on the hall floor inside the front door, and she retrieved the one that she'd worn at Sidmouth's murder and put it on the table facing Tony – it seemed only right. She smiled, and then carried on with the plan.

Jess watched him sink a little further towards the table, but essentially nothing changed; he was just settling into his new position. And now it was time to leave. She stepped onto his heavy, filthy overcoat and shuffled towards the back door on it. Once there, she put the bottle of methadone into the inside pocket, having torn off the label long ago. And then she snagged the heavy coat with the hook end of a wire coat hanger, opened the back door, and slid the wire beneath it.

As she pulled the door closed, she yanked on the wire hard enough for the hanger to release the coat and to pull out from under the door before it closed fully. The effect was a closed and locked door with an overcoat bunched up behind it, and the ultimate effect would be suicide – no way out for a would-be murderer.

Chapter Eighty-One

If you die when there's no one looking, do you still die? Of course you do. Lots of people die alone. Scary thought, having no one there at the end.

Eddie contemplated this as he parked the van on the public side of the blue and white tape. No matter how often he parked a van next to a strip of scene tape, he'd never get bored, but he would always get nervous.

Of course, he'd never be stupid enough to tell anyone that.

It was the nerves that kept him on his toes; it was the nerves that kept him awake, and kept him looking when all the others had gone home for the night. And he suffered from nerves because he knew he wasn't perfect; he had to work hard not to miss things, and he took it hard when he did.

When he missed things, he punished himself, and looked harder the next time, edged closer to other people's expectations of him. But he was still afraid of missing things – not because of those expectations but because of the people he'd be letting down: the victims. If he never missed anything at a scene, he wouldn't be nervous.

But how do you know if you've missed something at a scene?

He wondered what it would be like to die alone.

Even when Eddie had been in relationships, and even now that his dad was living with him – however temporary that situation might turn out to be – Eddie had always been fundamentally alone. Perhaps it was a sad thing to admit to, but like the nerves, he'd never tell anyone out loud.

Dying would be one of two things: the most enjoyable experience of his life, finally getting the peace he'd longed for; or the most terrifying thing ever. It would have him screaming that he'd got it all wrong and he needed a second go at life.

Either way, best or worst, it would be the last experience of his life.

He wondered if all his longing for peace and quiet and solitude had taken him down the wrong fork along the lanes of life. He wondered if everyone had been put on this earth to mingle and make friends, to enjoy the company of other humans and to sink into the shallows of polite laughter and polite nods while passing someone on the corridor, leaving behind all sense of deep thought, giving it up for mediocrity, for insincerity.

Giving it up just to fucking fit in. Surrendering contemplation for the acceptance of others.

You arrive with your mother surrounding you, but you always leave through the darkest door with no one holding your hand. Cold. Silent. Alone.

And no matter how brave you were when dying, you never qualified for a medal. It was so easy that everyone could do it. Everyone *would* do it sooner or later.

He shivered, pulled out a cigarette, set it on fire and inhaled deeply, still contemplating death in general while those outside his van contemplated death in the particular, in between wondering what to have for dinner or where to sneak off for a piss.

Eddie cracked the window, sighed smoke towards it and focused on the turmoil inside his head. These were the moments he longed for; these rare moments when he and his mind could sever the contact with his surroundings and fall into deep thought, the abstract and the playful: turmoil within smooth, infinite blackness. Death.

He threw the cigarette out of the window, slid out from the driver's seat into the rain, pushed the door closed, and looked at his new place of work.

It was shit.

Or, at least, it was very mediocre. It was a small, detached, brick house with white-framed UPVC windows and hanging baskets with dead flowers draped over the sides. It had its own narrow driveway and a concrete path with moss encroaching from the dampness of a low brick wall on one side and a claggy lawn full of weeds at the other.

He and Benson stood out of the rain, protected by the hatch door of the van as they pulled scene suits and black overshoes on.

"Khan put the door in. Found him in the kitchen."

"Fuck's sake. What's wrong with you? You know he doesn't have a clue when it comes to forensic work. Did he dick about with my scene?"

"I sent him to see if we were on the right track; I didn't know he'd find him dead, did I? Anyway, the alarm went off, so he wouldn't have been in there too long." Benson shrugged. "Come on, he knows how to play it, Eddie. He won't have messed with things he shouldn't."

"So he didn't use the fucking floor while he was in there doing his search?"

"What search?"

"Come off it. You mean to tell me he found a body and immediately tiptoed back out the front door with his hands in his pockets? He'll have had a good poke around before he called it in."

Benson's head bowed and he resumed his slow amble towards the scene guard who stood before the rusting grey gate at the foot of the concrete path. "Okay, no, I can't guarantee it. Anyway, he's a copper, his first duty is to protect life."

"Pretty hard to do that with someone who's already dead."

They both signed in with the scene guard, uttering nothing other than their names and numbers. Eddie looked at her as she tapped their details into a mobile device. Her collar number was 249, and when she looked up he saw she had the most wonderful deep hazel eyes, a kind face, a Marilyn Monroe smile. He found himself staring at her, captivated.

Benson nudged him, and they walked up to the house until they stood outside the front door, admiring those dead hanging baskets as water dripped from them.

What the hell was going on? Was he entering his second puberty or something?

"I fucking hate this weather."

"Be boring if it was sunny all the time," said Benson.

"What? That's what I like about you: always got a differing opinion, even if it *is* bollocks. You can never just agree, can you? Always picking a fight."

"Shut up, Eddie. Let's go and have a look, eh?"

Chapter Eighty-Two

Eddie swung the door open and stepped onto the 'welcome' mat.

How appropriate.

Benson rustled in behind him and they peered through into the kitchen at the body.

"Did Khan find any ID?"

"Utility bills in the name of Anthony Hardwick."

Eddie stared at Benson from the corner of his eye.

"Okay, yes, so he might have had a quick look around."

They stood on stepping plates in the kitchen.

Benson took a pace back from Eddie and watched him.

Eddie folded his arms and melted into the scene.

He saw Tony – Anthony – his heavy overcoat on the floor inside the back door as though he'd been in a rush, or he'd been too intent on carrying out the deed bouncing around inside his head to worry about anything else.

Though Eddie wasn't religious in the slightest, each time he saw a suicide he always did the spectacles-testicles-wallet-and-watch thing, and whispered, 'There but for the grace of God go I'. And today was no different.

He pictured Tony, eyes almost glazed over in some drug-induced or booze-induced stupor, tripping into the closest of the chairs that sat around a small, glass-topped dining table crushed up against the kitchen wall. He saw him take off the CAT hat and throw it on the table. He saw him take the razor-sharp hatchet and use it like a scalpel, coursing a red line down his exposed left forearm. Just enough to part the skin.

The fingers tingled. Hot blood trickled down his wrist and dripped onto the glass. It hurt, but not too much. Perhaps Tony's vacant, apathetic mind had found it fascinating, and perhaps any pain that might have lingered soon fled, leaving behind nothing more than another task under way, like making lunch. Not the beginning of the end, nothing so monumental, nothing so catastrophic. Nothing so fatal. Routine. Back in a minute.

This time, perhaps, he gripped the hatchet a little tighter in his right hand, made a fist with his left, and held his breath. He didn't swing the hatchet, he just cut. The sharp blade entered his forearm and parted meat on its way down to the cluster of wrist bones; he could feel his arm being tugged at, and it felt like a stranger was doing it.

There was pain this time, and an electric shock that caused his fingers to twitch, and he winced. The blood came faster, and the nerves in his fingers stopped working. There was no pain there, and he smiled, amazed. His arm was on fire, but it was bearable, and the hot blood flowing over it seemed to cool it. There was a little steam, and the blood ran fast enough now that he could hear it dripping onto the table even as everything else turned to white noise. It ran across the glass and it poured off the edge, spattered on his leg and onto the floor.

Lots of it.

He could see a little fountain of it pumping in his wrist.

Tony put the hatchet down. It had done its job. He dipped the index finger of his right hand into the blood on the table, and on a clean part of the glass, wrote: SORRY.

He laid his right hand on the table, but it slid sideways, landed in his lap, and then slipped off that too, to finish its life dangling by his right side.

Tony blinked for the last time, and then his chest became still. His eyes closed and his head fell forward onto his chest. And the house seemed to grow cold and die too.

Eddie saw the last drop of blood drip from the tip of Tony's finger, and was reminded of Sidmouth's mother.

He shuddered just as Benson's voice brought him back. "Okay, Eddie?"

He nodded.

* * *

"Nasty way to go," Eddie whispered.

"You need a drink?"

He shook his head. "We should get to work." He turned to Benson and saw his face was white. "Front door. Locked from the inside?"

Benson nodded, shuffled on his stepping plate, suit crinkling. "Key's still in the lock. Door's smashed to fuckery thanks to Khan, but the key's in the lock, yes."

"Key on the inside rear door mortice lock?"

Benson nodded. "But it's not locked with that lock."

"Locked on the Yale?"

Another nod.

"We need to check the windows."

"I did that. All secure."

Eddie nodded. "I'm happy it's a suicide, then."

"Of course, the killer could have just gone out of the back door, latched the Yale."

Eddie thought about it. "Yep, could have, but his overcoat is right up against it, not pushed up against the wall like it would be if the door had been opened against it."

Benson took a look; sure enough, it was bunched up against the door like a draft excluder. And then he took another look at Eddie, worried that he was affected by this much more than usual.

He often wondered what happened inside Eddie's head when he disappeared at scenes like this. He'd worked with dozens of CSIs and never seen anything like it; it was like Collins was watching it happening, like he was a bystander.

Whatever it was, it was creepy, and he didn't much like it. But, on the plus side, it always seemed to be eerily accurate.

* * *

Eddie was thinking about the PCSO outside, and what a wonderful pair of… eyes she had. He could hear Benson breathing hard behind him. It almost made him laugh as he stood there with his arms folded. Benson treated Eddie like his own personal psychic, reading a scene and coming up with something prophetic, giving him the answer like some kind of *deus forensis*.

Well it didn't work like that. Sure, he liked to look hard at a scene, to actually see it, and to read it if he could. There was nothing magical about it; it was a case of seeing something, like that bloodless shadow on the floor by the chair, and asking questions. When the answer that best fit the situation came to mind, then that was almost always what had happened. It wasn't science, it wasn't magic. It was just common sense. It was logic.

There were several factors that had to be borne in mind when looking and seeing things like this. First, staging – had someone set this thing up to look like something it was not? And then, lack of preservation – had someone inadvertently, or otherwise, messed up the scene and destroyed or altered clues?

For now, it was the shadow that had Eddie's attention. Blood isn't the thick, glutinous fluid most people imagine; it's marginally more viscous than water, and it flows and splashes and travels just as easily and just as far as water does. The thing Eddie liked best about it right now, though, was that it was bright fucking red, and stood out on a white kitchen floor like a murder in a suicide scene.

Potentially.

"I think that was a nice touch." He pointed to the word SORRY written in blood on the table. "I wonder what he's sorry for? Causing a mess? Leaking blood everywhere? Killing people? Blaming people? Giving me four hours' sleep?"

"Killing himself?" Benson asked. "He must have family."

Eddie wasn't listening. That shadow was a doubt that hissed at him like a slow leak in a tyre; it was the only thing that turned him from 'it was suicide' to 'was it suicide?' Nagging.

The CAT Diesel Power cap was on the table right in front of him. It was as soiled as you'd expect a well-worn cap to be. Much of the bright yellow was now mucky and subdued, blackened over the years where grubby fingers had handled it. The peak at the front was almost entirely black; the seam where the peak joined the main cap was sweat-stained, and that in turn had attracted even more dirt.

In short, it was filthy; well-loved and well-worn.

And yet… Eddie stared at it as he'd stared at the rest of the scene; was drawn to it. He didn't know why.

Chapter Eighty-Three

"Okay," Eddie said. "I can't do all this by myself. I'm going to get Kenny over here." It was a little after 2pm; enough time for him to be rested. Eddie took out his phone and dialled.

Kenny was there within the hour, and by the time he'd walked across the stepping plates to the back door, Eddie had pulled everything out of the overcoat, and laid out the contents of a rucksack he'd found, and photographed it *in situ* in the cluttered cupboard under the stairs.

"What we got?"

Eddie stood, arched his back, and the camera that hung on a strap around his neck bounced off his stomach. "Hope you brought me a coffee."

"It's outside."

Eddie closed his eyes in gratitude.

"This," Eddie swept his arm towards Tony's body, still slumped in the chair, "is our little serial killer."

"Is that right?"

"The guilt got too much for him." Eddie looked Kenny in the eye. "The weight of death too heavy a burden to bear."

Kenny sighed. "You're not in one of your Shakespeare moods again, are you? I thought you'd grown out of that shit, I really did. And, I'll be honest with you, I wasn't disappointed."

"Okay, no need to get so personal. I thought it was pretty good, actually."

"It wasn't. Sorry."

"Be like that. Anyway, he *was* sorry, look, he even wrote it on the table in his own blood. Therefore, we can all gather round and forgive him in a wonderful ceremony of life over death."

"Any more of that and I'm leaving. Okay?"

Eddie sniffled and pulled out a small notebook he'd found inside the overcoat. "It's a list of names."

"Names?"

"Christ, do I have to explain everything to you, Kenny? A name is—"

"Whose names, Eddie? And snap out of it, I'm still tired, and it wouldn't take me much to walk straight back out of here and get my head down again."

"Okay, keep your wig on." Eddie looked at the book. "Thomas Marchant."

"The pickaxe guy?"

"One and the same, Kenny." He read the next name. "Stanford Bolton."

"Doctor Faeces himself."

"A certain Frank Cooper."

"You're fucking kidding!"

Eddie showed him. "See? Even when he's dead, people want to kill the bastard." He read the last name on the list, and his eyebrows met in the middle, and he looked up at Kenny.

"Who?"

"Jeffery Walker."

"*Our* Jeffery Walker?"

"No, Kenny. Just *a* Jeffery Walker. Of course our Jeffery Walker, you—"

"Kidding."

Eddie shook his head.

"How sure are you that this piece of shit is the killer?"

"I love how you hit the fucking nail on the head dead centre every time, Kenny. That's the very question I've been asking ever since I got here."

"Well?"

"Ninety percent?"

Kenny took a big breath. "So there's ten percent says you should warn Jeffery that he's on a hit list."

"I suppose so, but…"

"Don't take the chance, Eddie."

Benson's voice boomed from the doorway. "Where's the ten percent, Eddie? I thought we'd scored the full ton with this one."

Eddie beckoned him in. "If you were going to slash his wrist like that, where would you stand?"

They all looked at the clean shadow.

"Precisely," Eddie said.

"That it?"

Eddie and Kenny looked at Benson. "It's enough to make me nervous," Eddie said.

"Anything else?"

"Not yet."

Benson nodded. He looked from Eddie to Kenny, and back again. "Tell him."

"What's all this stuff?" Kenny indicated the contents of the rucksack laid out on brown paper.

On it were a pair of Nike Cortez trainers. But they weren't like normal trainers. These had slits cut into the sides of the shoes, just above the dense rubber tread of the sole. Through these slits was threaded a belt, one on each shoe: black leather, brass buckle. The belts were shortened so they'd buckle up around someone's feet rather than their waist.

"Odds-on those are the trainers that left those marks at Bolton's scene," said Eddie.

"And Sidmouth's scene. They're blood-spattered."

Eddie looked at the trainers as though trying to see inside them. He got on his knees, took out his torch. "Interesting."

"What's interesting?"

Eddie pointed the torch inside the right shoe, moving the belt aside so Benson and Kenny could see a little more clearly.

"What am I looking at?" asked Benson.

"There, see the blood on the edge of the slit on the inside surface?"

"What about it?"

"We need to swab it," said Kenny. "Whoever made these slits cut themselves."

"Or," Eddie said, "we could check Tony's hands now; see if there are any cuts." He looked at Benson.

Benson shrugged. "When have you ever needed my agreement to do something? Just take a look."

Eddie looked at Kenny. "Shall we?"

"Won't be easy, Eddie. His hands are covered in blood."

"Let's take a look, eh?"

They spent a full ten minutes inspecting Tony's hands, the drying blood flaking from his skin as they flexed it. They discovered no cuts at all. Of course, the pathologist would have a better look once all the blood had been washed away. "Might want to ask Prof Steele to pay special attention."

"I will," Benson said. "What was the deal with Ripley's coat at Bolton's scene? You never did get around to telling me, and Nicki couldn't tell me."

"It's a psychological stamp I put on that scene, really. If this man mountain here" —he nodded towards Tony— "asked you to hang up his wet coat – a coat three yards too small for him – would you? No, because you wouldn't allow this man mountain inside your fucking house, never mind letting him make himself at home in your kitchen."

"But how do you know that Bolton hung up the coat?"

"No Nike Cortez approaching the coat hooks. No Cortez after the breakfast bar."

"Ah," said Kenny, "but he might have taken those contraptions off, and taken off his own shoes, and walked over there in his socks."

"He might have. But he didn't. He's not thinking about the footwear database. And if he was, then he's beaten us, because we don't have a sock database."

"Still at ninety percent?" Benson asked.

Kenny looked dubious. "But he *was* thinking about the footwear database – he made these, didn't he?"

Eddie conceded the point. "Yep. If, on the other hand, a good-looking woman asked to use your phone or whatever, and you're a randy old goat like Bolton, you'd have her in there and partly undressed quicker than anyone could say sex scandal. That's what made me think the Bolton murder was initially done by Jessica, not him. But Kenny's right: Tony could've killed him, and hung up the coat to make it look like she'd been in there. Add that to the Cortez footprints, and any investigator would think she was responsible. And she did say he'd stolen her coat."

"And the knife?"

Eddie crouched, picked up the slender knife. It had *Messermeister Park Plaza* etched into the blade. "How much are these?"

Kenny shrugged.

Benson said, "I bet you wouldn't see any change from a hundred and fifty quid."

"For one fucking knife?"

"The point is," Eddie said, "you don't see many of them around – but Bolton had some in his kitchen. Chances are this belongs in his knife block."

"Looking more and more like he's your man, Eddie," said Kenny.

Eddie thought about it. Everything pointed to Tony. The only thing that didn't was the leaking tyre, the clean shadow next to the chair. He stared at it.

Kenny followed his gaze. "Could the shadow have been caused by him, and then he moved his foot to where it is now before he died?"

Eddie winked. "*Before* he died? Not after?"

"Smartarse."

"Can't tell," Eddie said. "He has blood spatter on the uppers of both shoes anyway."

Benson sighed.

"Okay," Eddie said. "I'm happy he's our man."

"Really?"

Eddie nodded, hands on his hips, and bit his lower lip. "Yep. He's good for Marchant, Bolton, and Sidmouth."

"And you're happy he tried to frame Jessy Ripley for all of them?"

Eddie turned to face him.

"Well?"

Eddie nodded.

"If that's the case, you don't need to tell Jeff he was on some stupid fucking list. Thing like that can send a man insane." Benson turned to leave.

"Why didn't he kill Jeffery?" Kenny asked.

"Kenny. Stop it with the questions. Especially the ones I can't answer."

"Where are you going now?"

"I'm going to go and tell Jessy," said Benson, pulling a Mars bar from his pocket.

Eddie made a 'stop' gesture. "You can't do that; we haven't finished our investigation yet."

"You said it yourself: how soul-destroying it is, not knowing."

"I said that?"

"I don't give a shit whether you did or not. I'm going to tell her."

"Let me come," Eddie said.

Benson paused, then nodded. "Okay. Why?"

"I want to see her face."

That made Benson squint. And it made Kenny ask, "So you're not finishing this scene then, Eddie?"

Eddie grinned. "I'd rather shit on my hands and clap. He's all yours."

Chapter Eighty-Four

Benson switched the hands-free phone off. Weismann had given his blessing for him to speak with Jessica, relieved that they'd found the serial killer that had made Leeds jumpy for the better part of two weeks.

He had enquired after Eddie, and Eddie had spoken for himself that he was still alive. Just.

Benson rolled the car to a gentle stop outside Jess's flat and turned the engine off. "Please leave the talking to me, okay?"

"Never crossed my mind to do anything else."

Benson stared at him. "Lying bastard. What's bothering you?"

Eddie sighed, looked front. He licked his lips and lied, "I think you're rushing this. I think you should take your time – wrap up Tony's scene, and wrap up Sidmouth's too."

"Is that still going?"

"Course it is. They're not ten-minute jobs, Tom. I have people there fingerprinting right now."

Benson rubbed his chin. "Tony went in there and killed Sidmouth and his mother, and I'll bet you twenty quid he never touched a thing in that house. Not one thing."

Eddie nodded. "Agreed. Got to do it, though—"

"I know you've got to do it; I'm just saying, that's all."

"But what's your rush? Why don't you wait till we've wrapped the scenes up before you go and tell her that her boyfriend's topped himself?"

"I thought you said you were a hundred percent with Tony's scene?"

"I am."

"So what's the problem? I'd rather put her mind at rest. I remember you saying how scared of life she was. And if I can put those fears aside for her, then maybe she won't be so scared any more. And that's a good thing. Isn't it? Well? If she's not scared any more, she might open up about Tony's involvement with the Marchant killing. We could use some help, you know."

Eddie reached for the door handle.

* * *

Benson knocked and moments later the door opened.

Her eyes were red and she looked withered, aged by worry.

Eddie's mouth opened, and he found himself staring at her.

"Hi, Jess. Can we come in, love?"

She nodded and disappeared into the darkness. Eddie saw the shock in Benson's eyes.

"See?" said Benson. "That's why I had to let her know now."

Eddie followed Benson inside, closing the door behind him.

The door to her bedsit was open, and they entered quietly. "You okay, love?" Benson said.

She sat motionless on the bed, next to the bedside cabinet. Eddie stood, thumbs hooked into his jeans; he tried to be relaxed but couldn't help staring at her, amazed at how much more fragile she looked than the last time he'd seen her.

"What can I do for you?" Her voice was a whisper; something delicate, vulnerable.

Benson cleared his throat. "I just wanted to let you know that we've found Tony Longbottom."

Her eyes widened slightly, and she seemed to curl inwards as though subconsciously protecting herself from him. She took a breath and said, "You got him? Has he been arrested?"

Eddie felt satisfied with her reaction.

"He won't be bothering you any more. I'm afraid I have some bad news, Jessy."

She bit her top lip, brought her hands up to her face.

"Tony is dead, love."

A whimper.

Benson stood, reached out to her, but seemed afraid to go too close. "We found him a few hours ago in his house. It looks like he took his own life."

She looked at him, her hands fell away, and her face twisted into confusion before she asked, "He had a house? I thought he was homeless."

"No… He had a house." Benson moved closer to her, put his hand on her shoulder. Eddie stepped sideways so he could still watch her.

"He killed himself?"

"I can't say anything further on that just now, but it seems he did, yes."

"Why? Did he leave a note or anything?"

Eddie stood by the sink and watched her, and he could see her chin beginning to wobble, see her eyes filling up. No one was that good an actress. She was genuinely relieved, and the realisation that Tony wouldn't interfere with her any further signalled the collapse of a self-preservation wall; it was like watching the outside world crashing back into a life she'd sealed herself away from.

Eddie sniffed the air, and found himself looking into the sink. A white cup with the dregs of a green fluid drying in the bottom. Green?

He looked back at Jessica. He noticed her eyes too, how – through the new tears – they flitted to a Morrisons carrier bag next to the wardrobe, time and again. Eddie wanted to look in there. It was like an itch, it was like the leaking tyre, a slow hiss constantly in his range of hearing. His imagination told him there was a pair of bloodstained jeans inside that she hadn't had the time to dispose of yet.

The blood on those jeans belonged to Tony.

This was half of that last ten percent.

Eddie's heart clattered. There wouldn't be another chance.

"Mind if I look in the bag?"

Jessica looked at Eddie over Benson's shoulder. Benson turned, then he too saw the bag.

"Why?" she said.

Eddie shrugged. "It's just my job. I'm a nosey bastard."

"I'd rather you didn't."

That made Eddie prickle with wonder. "Take me a minute, that's all."

"Eddie," Benson warned.

"It won't take me—"

"No, please."

Eddie snatched the bag and Benson stood before him, gritting his teeth. He stared into Eddie's eyes. He whispered, "We don't have a warrant for any of this shit. We're not here to do any of this shit. Apologise to the lady and put the bag down."

Last chance.

Eddie looked at Benson, looked at Jessica, and then the bag. He nodded. "Okay. Sorry." As he went to put the bag back, he opened it and tipped the contents across the bed.

"Eddie!"

She screamed at the sight of the blood.

Eddie's eyes lit up and he grinned.

But it was short-lived. The blood was on a pair of pants, and more on some jeans.

Jess barged him aside and scooped them back into the bag, sobbing.

Eddie put his hands out, "Sorry," he said, "I'm sorry, sorry—"

"Get out, Eddie!"

Eddie looked at Benson.

Benson snarled. "I said get out."

He went to touch Jess, to apologise again, when she turned on him. "Leave me alone, you fucking creep!"

"I said I'm sorry."

"Get out!"

Eddie grew hostile. "I just need to know—"

"Collins! Out! Now!"

Eddie grabbed her arm. "Show me your trainers."

Jessica turned and slapped him across the face; and then she pushed him, and he instinctively grabbed her and she fell with him, both of them falling into Benson as they hit the floor. Eddie thought of the knife under her mattress – where was it? But all he saw as he went down was the fingers of her left hand. Just the fingers. And the sticking plaster wrapped around the little finger.

She hurriedly prised herself off him, straightening her clothes hastily as she stood, sweeping her hair behind her ears. "Get the fuck out of my house," she panted.

Eddie pulled himself up using the chair by the door, hands out, palming away her anger. "I'm going," he said. "I'm sorry—"

"And if you ever come in here to do any fingerprinting while I'm out again, I will have you prosecuted for burglary."

"What?"

"I found your powder under the toilet seat."

Eddie gritted his teeth.

"Now get out."

He looked at Benson, who looked away – no support there – and then back at Jessica. As he left, he saw it. Just the briefest flicker of a smile.

Smug.

* * *

Eddie smoked his second cigarette leaning against Benson's car, tapping his foot, waiting for him, as a light rain fell. And when Benson did emerge and walked down the steps towards him, all he said was, "Think yourself lucky she isn't pressing charges."

"Look, I have my—"

"No. *You* look, Collins. Is Tony guilty of these murders or not?"

"I… Well, of course."

"Eddie?"

"Yes. He is."

"Then what the fuck are you playing at? I'm basing my decisions on the shit coming out of your mouth. I'm trusting you. You can't go pointing the finger at Tony, and then change your fucking mind. Forensics rule this case. You can't—"

"I know." He stared at Benson over the top of the car. And he flicked away his cigarette, and set off walking. "I know," he said.

"Eddie?"

Eddie waved and carried on walking.

He walked the four miles from Jess's bedsit to MCU in just over an hour, and by the time the gates rumbled open to let a car out, and Eddie walked in, he was wet through, and more confused than ever by what circled his mind. It hadn't stopped raining for the whole journey. And he'd loved it.

Tony was a definite for Marchant's murder – they had the CCTV of him acquiring the axe.

He was ninety percent for Bolton's murder. He'd gone to Jessica's bedsit and stolen her jacket and a knife, and he'd planted them at Bolton's scene in the kitchen, on the coat hook right at the back of the kitchen where they found no footwear marks. Tony had killed Bolton, then taken off his belted Cortez trainers and his own shoes, and gone and hung the coat up, pinning the murder on Jess.

But then there was Sidmouth.

He was the odd one out. He was nothing to do with Jessica's past. He was to do with Jessica's present. And judging by what they found in his bedroom, it wasn't a long stretch of the imagination to work out that he'd been taking advantage of Jess, and she'd got a little bit pissed off at him.

Tony had known the police would suspect him of abuse, and would automatically think a client – Jessica – had killed him. Tony was a very clever man.

Eddie might have been happy with that conclusion if it wasn't for that smug smile. She should have been in tears still, but she'd smiled instead. Had the tears prior to that little tussle been just good acting as well?

That and the clean shadow made up the whole ten percent.

And he hated indecision. He liked black and white; mistrusted grey.

Eddie stopped outside the glass doors of the reception foyer. They'd become dirty again. He knew Moneypenny would be in there, and he felt awkward enough without adding to it. He wanted to see Sid, though; he wanted to know how Tom and Jerry were doing with the fingerprinting at Sidmouth's scene.

He took a deep breath and turned around. It would all wait. For now, he was overflowing with work, and everything to do with it. And as he walked to his car, fishing the keys out of his pocket, he began to think about Nicki again, and about Troy, and about how trying to do the right thing always caused so much pain. And really, it wasn't even trying to do the right thing, it was just trying to look out for people – in this case, Troy.

Why did trying to help people – genuinely help people – have to end in such tragedy? Where was the motivation to continue helping people? Well, he'd learned a lesson: fuck 'em. Fuck 'em all.

And then there was his dad and that Wendy woman.

He sighed again. Things had gone by so fast over the last few days that he hadn't had the chance to touch base with any of his feelings recently, let alone spend any time with his dad.

Without knowing it, he'd climbed into the Discovery, and lit another cigarette, and was pointing the car through the slowly opening gates. He was looking forward to getting home and taking a shower to wash away the aches from the walk from Holbeck. He knew that he couldn't rest or concentrate properly on anything else until he'd resolved that conflict inside his head – the slow air leak from that fucking tyre.

Chapter Eighty-Five

Eddie unlocked the cottage door and slid inside, heeling it closed behind him. For a moment he stood and listened to the rainwater dripping from him and landing on the floor, splashing like Tony's blood had.

He felt cold, and that was good because whenever he felt hot, his mind worked itself into a rage easily. Cool was… cool.

Charles cleared his throat and Eddie looked around, happy that his dad was back, but a little disappointed that his peace and quiet was now a thing of the past. He tried to hide the regret but its corner pierced through. "If you want an argument you can fuck off and find someone else. I ain't interested."

"Would you like a coffee?"

Eddie looked at him with suspicion.

Charles held out his hands. "No strings."

Eddie nodded, lit a cigarette and took a long drag. He stood still, trying to hear the raindrops hitting the floor, but was no longer able to. Instead he could hear the tobacco burning and his dad shuffling around on the kitchen floor. Outside the rain still fell, and Eddie thought he could just hear it grazing the windows.

Moments later, Charles handed him a mug of coffee. "I'm sorry," he said, "for having a pop at you earlier."

Eddie looked at him, but he was thinking about Jess. He nodded and walked off towards the shower.

"That it? Just a nod?"

Eddie slammed the door.

* * *

He dried himself and walked into his room to dress. As he entered the bedroom, he thought he might put on some Pink Floyd – maybe *Wish You Were Here*, something mellow to keep him cool. But as he closed the bedroom door behind him, his mobile phone danced on the bedside table.

Eddie tutted, slid a pair of boxers on and then accepted the call.

"Eddie?"

"No, it's Alice fucking Cooper!"

"It's me, Jeffery."

Eddie closed his eyes. "Hi, Jeffery, sorry about—"

"I've had some time to donate to that case you mentioned."

"Jessy Ripley?"

"Jessica Ripley, yes."

"And?"

Jeffery took a deep breath. "Your research checks out; she's the common denominator in the case. Don't you remember saying the common denominator was Jessica Ripley? You were right."

"Doesn't mean she killed Sebastian, though, does it?"

"No, no. It doesn't mean that. But what I found curious were the victims since she was released from prison. There's the lawyer, Marchant; there's the pathologist, Bolton; and I don't know if you're aware, but—"

"Probation Officer and his mother, yes. We're aware of them."

"I was going to ask if you were also aware that I was the scene examiner on Sebastian's case?"

Eddie went cold. "Yes. We'd worked that one out too."

"I was the one who said there was a possibility of a third-party involvement. The door to the flat – she said she often left it open because the kitchen window was painted shut and it was the only way to get any air into the place."

"You said that?"

"And it was buried. Marchant buried it."

"What? Didn't you tell Cooper?"

"Cooper was as much use as a chocolate fireguard."

"We, well I, think that a man called Tony Longbottom – who's actually called Anthony Hardwick – might have been responsible for Sebastian's death. He had the opportunity."

"I found him just now while searching, yes. But did he have a motive?"

"If he did, I don't know what it was."

"And you think he's been killing everyone responsible for convicting Jessica Ripley?"

That ninety percent question again. "Yes."

"You don't sound too sure."

"I'm sure."

"Am I in danger?"

Eddie swallowed. "No, you're fine, Jeffery. Anthony committed suicide."

"Yes, I saw that, too. You're happy it's suicide?"

Eddie was nodding, "Yep, it's suicide. Sealed room suicide."

"Sealed room?"

Eddie sat on the bed, dragged a hand down his face. "Front and back doors locked, windows secure, and the body inside. No way in or out."

"And you're happy?"

"Yes. Yes, I'm happy."

"Okay, thank you. But you're not happy, and you're not sure. You haven't sworn at me once. I know when doubt is eating you, Eddie."

"There's no doubt, Jeffery," he lied. "Are you… are you okay?"

Jeffery sniffed. "Yes. I have more to do on a search I'm running, then I'm heading home. Bit of luck, I should be in time to miss Coronation Street."

"Okay. Catch you later." Eddie hung up and felt awful. Even if he were safe, which he *was*, perhaps they ought to have had the courtesy to let him know he'd been on some kind of list before he found out for himself.

Never mind; too late now.

Eddie dressed, grabbed his lanyard, wallet, and cigarettes, and walked into the lounge, ready for round two. Charles stood there like a twig with clothes on. "We need to buy you an appetite," said Eddie.

"Women, eh? Who needs them?"

Eddie stole a glance at the clock on the oven door and smiled at Charles. "I have a confession to make."

"You do?"

"I *was* jealous of you. You know," he shrugged, "you'd found someone to be with. You'd finally got someone you could hold tight. I wanted that; I was jealous of you."

Charles nodded. "It's nice. Well, it *was* nice. Till she ended up in a cell."

"Shit happens," Eddie shrugged again. "I never made it past first base."

"But you were brave enough to give it a go. That's worthy of a pat on the back, Eddie."

"I *was* brave, wasn't I?" He looked at the ceiling, a smile broke across his face, and then it clouded over again. "I was silly though. I don't think I'll be doing it again. I like things the way they are."

"Me too. And I want you to know that I forgive you."

Eddie nearly swallowed his tongue. "Beg your fucking pardon?"

"Hey, no need for an argument. I just want you to know that I've been thinking about it, and I don't hold it against you."

Eddie blinked. "You don't hold it against me? I really ought to punch you in the nose for that. I saved your house from being owned by a con artist who made politicians look honest. I saved your arse from getting too involved with a woman so evil she makes Cruella de Vil look like a candidate for a Dogs Trust Award. So what you really mean is 'thank you, Eddie'."

"What? No, I mean—"

"You don't get to forgive me, and you're not entitled to not hold it against me. All you get to do is thank me. For once, I got involved in your stupid antics and luckily this time I managed to pull you out of the fire before you got too badly burned."

"But—"

"Listen! You would have got burned, you stupid old fucker. Your dick, or your need to be dominated by a drag queen, was leading you down the road to oblivion, and I fucking pulled you back! So don't you fucking dare be in a mood with me when I saved your sorry fucking arse! You stupid old man!" Veins stood out in Eddie's neck, and his face was the colour of an overripe plum.

Tears glistened in Charles's eyes. "How could you?"

Eddie felt like shit, like he'd kicked a puppy. "How could I what? How could I smash up your laptop so you can't use Facebook ever again?"

Charles took a sharp breath. "You didn't?"

"No. I didn't. But I should have done." He stepped closer, licked his dry lips and tried to calm down. "I hope you learned your lesson over this, Dad. There are bad people out there."

Charles stared at the floor. "There are bad people in here too."

"Yeah, blame me if you like, I don't care; I stopped you—"

"No, you don't care. That's perfectly obvious. It's like a bloody dictatorship."

"You think I'm oppressive? Am I as oppressive as your psycho girlfriend was?"

Charles snarled at him, folded his arms, and whispered, "If the cap fits, Eddie."

"You cheeky—" Eddie stared at his father, accusatory finger at the ready, when he stopped. He stared at Charles, saw the snarl smooth out, saw the creases disappearing.

"Eddie? You okay?"

Eddie stared into the distance. "If the cap fits."

Chapter Eighty-Six

Eddie ran to the Discovery and slipped on the gravel. He picked himself up, cursing, slapping mud and leaves from his wet jeans as his phone rang. He crawled inside the car and answered.

"Eddie?"

Eddie looked at the phone. "Benson. Did you dial my number?"

"Yes, of course I—"

"Then it's me, isn't it? Why do you keep asking if it's me! Of course it's—"

"Shut up, you prick, and listen to me. We found a motive for Tony Longbottom's involvement in Sebastian's murder."

"Go on."

"His house. Bought for cash, twelve years ago."

"And?"

"Khan traced the origin of that money: Stanley Archibald. Sebastian's brother."

Eddie started the engine and got the AC fighting the misted-up windows.

"He was a hitman?"

"Of sorts. Stanley stood to gain a small fortune if Sebastian wasn't alive to lay claim to his dying dad's money."

Eddie glanced at the cottage. "Families, eh?"

"There's more. Stanley and his wife, Valentine, are fostering Jessica's son."

"You're shitting me. How could anyone let that happen?"

"Valentine was having fertility treatment for years. She can't have kids of her own."

"They're stealing Jessy's kid?"

"They'll be turning him against her, yes."

"You sure Tony has a motive for all the other murders too?"

Benson paused, coughed. "Wait a minute – *you* said he was responsible."

"I know what I said!"

"He doesn't have a motive for Sidmouth or even Bolton – unless we're working along the lines of their deaths being gifts for Jessy – or orders from Stanley, to shut them up."

"No. She killed them." Eddie screwed his eyes shut. A moment later he heard a noise that sounded like Benson punching something.

"What?"

Eddie sighed. "She played us. She made an idiot out of me, Tom. The CAT hat on the table."

"You're making no sense. The hat? What about it?"

Eddie put the car in gear and wheelspun away from his house. "The more I looked at it, the more I could see something was wrong with it."

Benson was now yelling down the phone. "What, Eddie? What was fucking wrong with it?"

"It was too small for him. No way would it fit on his head. It's a plant."

"Ripley?"

"She wore it at Sidmouth's murder, left it on Tony's table, but forgot to make the strap bigger."

"We got the results through for the coat found at Bolton's scene, too," said Benson.

"Academic now."

"It was hers; wearer DNA on the collar," Benson said anyway. "She planted it there after she killed him. No one broke into her flat and stole it. Another nail in her coffin."

"Like I said, it's academic."

"Where are you going now?"

"Gonna search Ripley's flat," Eddie said. "You get over to Stanley's. Take care of the boy – she'll be coming for him."

"What if she's there, at her flat?"

"She won't be."

Eddie hoped she was; there were a couple of things he'd like to straighten out with her.

* * *

Eddie pulled on the handbrake outside Jessica's flat and raced up the concrete steps. He banged on the door and eventually the blond-haired junkie answered it. His face was a wreck.

"You again."

"Fuck off," Eddie said, and barged past.

"If you're looking for Jess, she's gone."

Eddie stopped, and turned just as the junkie slammed the front door closed. "Where?"

"Like she'd tell me. She just bust us up and took our gear." The junkie opened his bedsit door, and the dark-haired kid showed his face above the quilt on the sofa. His eyes were swollen shut.

"She did that?"

He shivered. "She took our methadone."

Eddie looked at them. "The fuck for?"

The kid shrugged, teeth chattering.

Eddie took a step forward, his forehead creased by a lack of understanding. "If you're not on drugs and you take a load of methadone, what happens?"

"Who? You mean me?"

Eddie growled. "This is why drugs are bad for you! One more IQ point and you'd be a glass of fucking water."

"I don't get you, man."

"Not you. I'm speaking hypothe— I'm not talking about you specifically. If a person isn't on drugs and they take—"

"Depends how much."

The dark-haired junkie shouted, "It'll unravel your brain and fry it."

"It's like you're in an echo chamber."

"It's like a tranquiliser."

"Too much," said the blond one, "and it'll kill you."

"'Specially if you drink too."

"Drink?" Eddie said.

"Now who's a glass of water? Booze, man. It don't mix with booze."

"Slows your heart down."

"Happened to a mate of mine. Killed him."

Eddie kicked Jessica's door open and marched inside. There was nothing in there. Empty. Except for the Morrisons bag. He tipped it out, nudged aside the bloody pants and saw clearly that they were sitting on top of a pair of bloodied jeans. He straightened the jeans out; there was a little blood in the crotch area, matching the leakage in the knickers, but most of it was halfway down the thigh and there was a healthy spatter along the bottom cuff of the right leg.

That clean shadow on Tony's floor.

Eddie took them to the window, and the tepid daylight emphasised the spatter. These were the jeans she'd worn when she killed Tony. "Can't fucking believe we fell for it. One name left."

* * *

Eddie tore along the inner ring road. It was a dual carriageway that barrelled right through the city centre, right underneath the buildings, as though it didn't give a shit what was in its way; it was a rude road, it was doing its own thing and sticking up a finger to anything that got in its way. Eddie loved that road, but wasn't so keen on the forty limit; where he could, he hit sixty and on the long stretch past the speed cameras, he managed almost eighty. The cameras flashed and Eddie didn't even notice, let alone care.

He kept his eyes on the road, unblinking, weaving through the dregs of the rush-hour traffic that stretched up to the horizon a mile away. In the distance was Killingbeck police station. And sitting inside Killingbeck police station, carrying out some research in an attic room that most people didn't even know existed, was Jeffery.

Jeffery would be completely unaware of the danger he was in, and despite Eddie trying his phone several times along the journey, no one picked up. Eddie tapped the steering wheel, cheeks throbbing as he ground his teeth. Then he leaned on the horn and punched the steering wheel.

Five minutes out.

Chapter Eighty-Seven

Jessica pulled the red coat a little tighter around her shoulders, made sure her hair was tidy in a tight bun up on the top of her head, and watched as the automatic floodlights came on in the car park. The illuminated sign over the front door of Killingbeck police station grew brighter as the daylight faded.

She took a long breath, planted a smile on her face, and walked through the rain towards that front door with confidence, as though she owned the place. The heat inside the foyer pulled at her coat and it wasn't long before she unzipped it. She walked past the front desk, manned by two bored-looking women trying to deal with the problems of a crowd of youths who didn't know how to say please or thank you. To the side was a door with a card reader lock mounted on the wall.

She touched the ID card against the reader. It bleeped and the red light on top turned green. She heard a magnetic latch click, and the door opened into a brightly lit corridor with the buzz of overhead tubes and the smell of a busy, twenty-four-hour station. To her left was the back end of the front counter; this part wasn't seen by the public. She leaned against it. Police officer after police officer came there to collect batteries for their radios and to dump exhausted batteries in a blue plastic box.

The walls were filled with 'Wanted' posters – something she'd always thought was a myth produced for television – and handwritten posters reminding officers not to forget to file their reports before going off duty. Then there were the monitors. She counted eight, all showing the car parks and the rear courtyard of the station, where all the liveried vehicles were parked.

"Excuse me," she said to a female member of staff who was busy tapping a keyboard. "I don't mean to interrupt, but I'm looking for Jeffery Walker."

The woman looked up and said, "Who?"

"Jeffery Walker. He's not long been transferred over here."

"Hold on." The woman typed again, squinting at the screen.

Jessica swallowed, and she could feel the sweat patches growing under her arms. Here she was, inside a major police station, officers all around her, and she had to check her resolve, because if this woman didn't give her a location soon, she was likely to turn right around and walk out again. She drummed her fingers on the counter.

"Ah," the woman said, "found him. His name is spelt wrong. Anyway, he's up in the Gods." She saw Jessica's confusion. "Not from round here, eh?"

"Bradford," Jess said with an apology in her voice. She nudged the plain glasses a bit further up her nose, and smiled.

"No worries. Go through those double doors, take your second left and use the stairs or the lift to get to the third floor. When you reach the third-floor landing, it's the room in the far right corner. Operational Research Facility. Room GD13."

"That's brilliant, thank you."

The woman smiled and went back to her computer.

Relief flooded her. Jess blundered through the double doors and promptly forgot the directions.

* * *

Eddie screeched into the car park, and tried Jeff's phone one more time. Still no reply. "Bastard." He rammed the phone back into his pocket just as it rang.

"What's up, Tom?"

"Michael is missing. And so is his foster mother's car."

"You're joking! What is it?"

"What?"

"What make of car is it?" Eddie stepped out into the rain, scanning the car park.

"Just a minute. I'll ask."

"What?" The line cracked and the call died. "Piece of shit!" Eddie screamed at the phone. He ran through the rain towards the foyer lights. Inside, a group of youths were heading for the exit, and Eddie circled them, grabbed his lanyard and hit the entry box with it. He shouldered the door, but nothing happened. The door remained closed.

He pulled back and tried the card again. Nothing. Then he looked at the card holder fastened to the lanyard. It was empty. No card.

What the fuck?

And then he remembered how Jessica had fallen into him at her flat. She must have taken the card when they all hit the floor.

"Hey," he looked through the hatch into the front counter, and shouted, "get the door for me, love."

One of the counter staff approached, arms folded.

"I lost my card." He showed her the empty card holder on his lanyard.

"Do you work here?"

"MCU, over in Morley."

"Sorry, *love*: no card, no entry."

"Come on! Someone's in danger. Please – I need to get to him."

"What's your name?"

"Eddie Collins."

She returned to her computer, tapped on the keyboard.

Eddie closed his eyes, trying to stifle his anger, trying to resist kicking the shit out of the locked door, and wondering how far he'd get if he just followed someone through the next time it opened.

"What's your management number, Eddie?"

"287656."

The woman leaned close to her colleague and they engaged in a bout of whispering.

The fire was growing. "Look," he said, "what if I can get someone to come and vouch for me? Would that be okay?"

"Who?"

"Jeffery Walker. He's my old boss."

The woman raised her eyebrows. "Wow, *he's* popular today!"

Eddie almost leapt over the counter. "What do you mean?"

"Someone was just here asking for him a minute ago."

"Fuck. Please, you've got to let me in; he's in danger."

"My colleague's ringing him now."

"He won't be able to answer if he's fucking dead, will he? Let me in!"

"Problem?"

Eddie turned and there stood a bedraggled-looking Crawford. Eddie knew he was going no further. "Jeffery Walker is in danger."

"Someone's just gone up to see him," said the woman.

"She's the one he needs protecting against! Please!" Eddie screamed, then continued more calmly. "Send someone up to his office. Please. Get him some fucking help even if you won't let me in."

Crawford dropped his briefcase and stared right into Eddie's eyes.

"You're wasting time. You're wasting *his* time." Eddie knew that Crawford wasn't listening, he knew Crawford was picturing what it would be like to pulverise Eddie's face. Again. "Crawford," Eddie shouted, "this isn't about us, it's not about you and me! Christ's sake, it's about Jeff! Come on!"

Crawford looked like shit. Not only did it look like he hadn't slept in a year; it looked as though he'd attacked his eyes with sandpaper and spray-painted his skin grey. He wasn't sharp any more; no more catalogue advert for funky men's fashion. Today he barely qualified as blunt, appeared to have recently stepped out of a tumble dryer. For the life of him, Eddie couldn't understand why he was here – one day after Nicki's death. "Calm down, sir," Crawford said, his red eyes blazing. "The lady is doing all she can. No need for that kind of language in here."

"What? Look," Eddie said, stepping closer. "Let's make sure Jeff is okay first, eh? And then you got me, right? You take me somewhere quiet and you get to punch me till you break your knuckles, okay?"

Crawford leaned in close. "Amazing. You can read my daydreams. Don't worry, I *will* break my knuckles on you one day. But it won't bring back Nicki, will it?"

"I'm sorry." Eddie padded him away. "I'm desperately sorry about Nicki; I didn't mean for anything like that to happen. But right now, this isn't about me or you, or Nicki. It's about stopping someone else dying…" He looked around; people stared, but remained inactive. "Fuck's sake! What do I have to do? He's in danger! Go and fucking check on him! If he dies, this is on you, Crawford!"

"Know all about killing people, don't you, Eddie?"

"Sir," one of the staff said to Crawford. "So you *do* know him?"

Crawford raised a finger to silence her and took a step closer to Eddie – just as the door opened and an officer came out. Eddie pushed him aside and thundered into the corridor.

"Oi! Stop him!"

Eddie took to the stairs.

* * *

Out in the car park, a black Astra missing a spoiler slowly came to a halt.

Chapter Eighty-Eight

The door sign said GD13; it looked like someone had tried to change it to GOD, but failed. Jessica touched the door with her fingertips, listened, and heard someone typing. She stepped inside, and was surprised to find only one person in there. He stopped typing and turned around to see who the visitor was.

Jeffery's mouth dropped open.

"Hello, Jeffery."

His eyes were wide and he raised his hands. "I'm not Jeffery," he said. "He's gone home."

"Why do you have your hands up?"

Jeffery licked his lips.

She walked to him, took hold of the ID card that hung around his neck. She looked at the picture, read the name, and let go. "Again. Hello, Jeffery."

"Jessica, I tried to help you. Honestly. They wouldn't allow my testimony. Marchant blocked it."

She was nodding. "I believe you," she said, "and I thank you for trying to help." She shrugged and took out her last steak knife. "But I need a clean slate. You understand."

* * *

Eddie's lungs screamed. Alarms sounded throughout the building, Crawford was chasing him up the stairs, and it sounded as though there might be more officers following. To Eddie's dismay, and despite appearances, Crawford was a lot fitter than he was. But he could see the third-floor landing coming up, and summoned the energy to get to GD13 first.

He pushed through the door just as Crawford grabbed the collar of his jacket and drove a punch into his kidney – the one he'd damaged years ago. Eddie went down with his face screwed up, unable even to scream, and looked up towards Jeffery's desk.

"Fuck me," Crawford whispered through panting breath as two officers crammed into the doorway behind him.

"Now do you fucking believe me?" Eddie clawed his way to his feet and edged towards Jeffery. "Jeffery?"

Jeffery stared at him. His eyes flicked to Crawford, and then back to Eddie.

"I'll get you an ambulance. Just… Just hold on, mate." Tears bubbled in Eddie's eyes as Crawford backed towards the door with his hand over his mouth. "You're going to be just fine, Jeffery, just stay with me, mate. Stay with me." Eddie looked around, searching for Crawford. He saw him cowering by the door, and was going to shout that *he* did this, that this was *his* fault. But Crawford was in tears. An officer reached across to him. Crawford batted his hand away.

The knife sticking out of Jeffery's neck throbbed slowly, and from the exposed length of its handle a stream of hot blood spewed in pulses that mirrored the knife's movement.

Eddie saw Jeffery swallow, saw him open his mouth. And then Jeffery blinked again before his eyes went wide. His blood pressure had dropped; he was entering cardiac arrest. And all Eddie could do was offer an open hand and some words that meant nothing. He stepped even closer, leaned down and brought his hand up to Jeffery's whitening face and drooping eyes. "I'm so sorry," Eddie whispered, embracing him. "Please forgive me."

Jeffery's eyes slid closed. The pulsing stopped. Blood still flowed, matched now by Eddie's tears.

"Eddie…"

Eddie watched as Crawford took to his feet.

"I'm going to crucify you for all this. I won't rest until—"

"Shut up, you arrogant knob." Eddie stood. "If you want to make yourself useful, find the woman who did this!" Eddie barged past him, and through the door. One of the two officers who'd followed them up here accompanied him back down the stairs.

"Sir." The remaining officer put his hand on Crawford's shoulder, and Crawford yelled at him to get the hell away. As the officer's boots went down the stairs, their echoing sound thinning into the distant alarm, Crawford looked up again at Jeffery, and he blinked away the tears.

Chapter Eighty-Nine

She took the lift. On the ride down, she took off the spectacles, shook out her hair so it flowed down her back just as Jeffery's blood had flowed down his chest. She took off the coat, turned it inside out, and put it back on again, now bright yellow.

She could hear an alarm coming from somewhere.

The shiny stainless-steel panel containing the button assembly showed her how she looked – completely different. Confident. She smiled. Job done. And already, though she was still inside a police station, with dozens of officers probably looking for her, she felt relaxed. No matter how it ended now, she'd done what she set out to do, and it felt good.

She had rebuilt herself increment by increment. And although she'd never be whole again, this was as close as it was possible to come. Even though each of those increments was theft, and so damaged in some way, there was no better way of getting back into one piece. Except, perhaps, by forgiving those who had wronged her. But Jessica Ripley wasn't the forgiving kind.

There was a buzz running through her as the lift hit ground and the doors opened.

She stepped out into the corridor and stopped. She was in the middle of a corridor that she didn't recognise – this wasn't the ground floor. Her heart thwacked in her chest and she forced herself to turn left in order to be doing something rather than attract attention by doing nothing.

She turned left and left again, and found herself in the courtyard she'd seen on the monitors earlier. Now she knew where she was. Down two flights of concrete steps, past a building that blew hot air at her through a vent, and there was the car park she'd waited in.

All she had to do now was walk over the road and sit in Burger King until Michael arrived. He might even be there already. He would be a punctual kid, she just knew it. She'd told him seven o'clock.

Her heart swelled with pride, with bliss. It was hard to describe such an unfamiliar emotion. She'd dreamed of feeling it before, often – a hundred times, a thousand – but now that it was here, it was of a magnitude even her dreams couldn't accommodate.

She felt like crying, but she insisted upon maintaining a certain control until this was all over and she and Michael were a long way away from here. And despite his earlier reluctance to join her in this new life, she knew that he'd accept it soon.

Threats were wonderful things.

Of course coercion wasn't the ideal way to begin life over again – she knew that. But eventually he would grow to know her, and he would grow to love her. How could he not? They were mother and son.

Jessica reached the kerb, heart hammering in her chest. Over the road was Burger King. Fifty yards away. She looked right and stepped out into the path of a silver car. It was on the wrong side of the road, and hit her dead centre. Glass smashed, the car bucked, and Jess pinwheeled into the centre of the road. In a swirl of tyre smoke and steam, the car slid to a halt.

She lay on her back, struggling to breathe; sipping smoke-laden air as ribs crunched. Her head buzzed, and confusion ran rampant in her swelling brain, but she brought the driver into focus as he bent to her. "Michael." She tried to hold out a hand to him, but her arm wouldn't work. The tears shimmered his image.

Traffic swerved around them, horns sounded as cars stopped; and on each kerb, a small crowd popped into being. Windows at Burger King darkened with onlookers.

He knelt at her side. "I'm fourteen years old. I'm old enough to steal cars, remember? And I'm old enough to hate you." He cleared his throat. "And just so we're clear, I know that Stanley is my real dad. He told me all that. We're a family: him, Valentine, and me. You're not wanted. Fuck off and die."

He stood to leave, a smirk on his face, when someone grabbed him around the throat and pushed him back down to the wet pavement, only yards from his mother's face as she sobbed.

Eddie made sure the lad couldn't move despite his bucking and despite his screaming. He looked at Jessica and panted, "Jeffery was a good guy. Not like the others. He tried to help you." He cleared his vision with a jacket still slick with Jeff's blood and left a red trail across his face that slowly washed away in the rain. "I hope you survive your injuries and spend the rest of your days inside."

Only a minute or so passed before a single voice cut through the screams and the sirens. "Eddie?"

Eddie turned and saw Weismann. He closed his eyes and just nodded. "I know," he said.

"We need to talk."

Chapter Ninety

In the back car park at Killingbeck police station was what appeared to be a big metal box – just a bit smaller than a shipping container – with ventilation slits up one side and a smoke stack sticking out of the top. Inside this big metal box was a massive diesel engine that acted as an emergency electrical generator. It was kept at a steady temperature with a fan either blowing out through the vents or sucking in through them, depending whether it was getting too hot or too cold.

The metal box rested on a concrete pad and was surrounded by a low brick wall. And the whole ensemble was roughly below the corridor running from room GD13.

He was found almost an hour after the alarms had been shut off and the RTC on the road outside had been dealt with. He was found, half on and half off the big metal box, by a police officer. The fans had been running inside, blowing warm air out; Crawford's blood had trickled down the side of the metal box and into the ventilation slits where, according to his statement, the fan 'blew something wet' into the officer's face as he walked past.

North Yorkshire CSI would conduct a forensic examination of the body, the container, and the wide-open window on the corridor outside GD13, and would conclude that it was suicide.

No one had taken any notice of a black Astra leaving the car park, and no one had seen Troy and Crawford's verbal and violent exchange along the corridor from where Jeffery's body was cooling.

Chapter Ninety-One

Two days later, just as Jessica Ripley was heading back to ICU after her third operation in the Leeds General Infirmary, Eddie smiled across at Troy. "I'm glad you came over. If you want your job back… we could use an extra set of hands. Busy as hell these days."

"No one's looking for me?"

Eddie was confused. "Looking for you? Why would anyone be looking for you?"

"Nicki."

Eddie shook his head. "You weren't there, Troy. Fuck's sake – she jumped."

"Is that what they think?"

Eddie's confusion deepened. "Do you know differently?"

He was quiet a moment; chewed his gum.

"Do you want to come back or not? I have things to do—"

"I'm listening."

"Hey, don't do me any fucking favours. If you don't want the job, you know where the door is."

"Like I said. I'm listening."

"Tell me about it. The drugs thing."

Troy was shaking his head, chewing.

"So get out then. I haven't got time to dick about with you. I need to know you're off them. This is your second chance, you idiot, the one I promised you."

"Who says I want it?"

"Course you do. You reckon you're the best. And the best always want more."

Troy looked at the veneer on the lounge door, the one that was a foot too short and had an extra bit tacked on. "You getting along with your dad again now?"

Eddie smirked. "Kind of. He's a stubborn bastard. But then, so am I. We'll work it out, I suppose."

"I hate my dad. He drove mum to suicide. She was never good enough for him. Could never hope to keep him happy. He's an elitist bastard and he took great pleasure in bringing me up to be just like him.

"Only I was nothing like him. I could *never* be like him. I like freedom, I like things that aren't perfectly symmetrical, you know? There's something almost magical about flaking paint. Just like there's something almost magical about clouds messing up a perfectly blue sky, or a cow turd in a lush green field." He chuckled. "Does that make any sense at all? Everything in his life has to be perfect; he couldn't tolerate imperfection, even in his own body – his own face! He was obsessive about it. He's had loads of plastic surgery – all kinds, not just face lifts. He had plastic surgery to stop him sweating! Did you hear that? He had plastic surgery under his arms and on his top lip and on his forehead to stop him fucking sweating!"

Eddie thumbed the leather and chrome armrest. "I get it, Troy."

Troy huffed. "Good. Now imagine living under that kind of pressure. Imagine coming home with anything less than an 'A' in your exams. Imagine shitting yourself on the walk home. Imagine the pain when he found out."

Eddie watched the torment twisting Troy's face. He said nothing; just listened.

"When I turned sixteen, I told him to fuck off. He told the doctors that a car had knocked me off my bike. I remember him looking at me as he told them that. I remember him saying, 'Didn't it, Troy?'

"At eighteen I was gone; he didn't see me for dust – that was the year my mum ended it all. But I didn't really have any place to go so I slept rough, took whatever jobs I could get. He found me, dragged me back home, and enrolled me at Leeds University. He wanted me to be a doctor; had some grand idea about me studying plastic surgery and making a fortune. Can you fucking believe it? I rebelled in the purest way I could think of: I went out and I bought some cannabis. When he came home I lit a spliff right in front of him, right in his own lounge.

"He went straight back out, and didn't come back for almost an hour. By which time I was wasted. I woke up as he smashed my big toes with the brand new hammer he'd gone out to buy."

Troy dragged a sleeve under his nose. "I gave in. But I told him I'd had enough of medicine and wanted to study forensic science instead. That was the only time he compromised in my entire life. He figured if it kept me off the drugs and kept me straight, he'd allow it. He also made the decision to continue having plastic surgery rather than wait for his incompetent son to do it on the cheap. Prick. Can you imagine what I'd have done if I took a scalpel near his face?" He laughed. "I'd have taken his eyes out. He'd never see perfection again. I often wonder if *he* thought that too – maybe that's why he allowed me to change my degree.

"Anyway, I got a job with West Yorkshire Police and I was the best CSI they'd ever had – got the highest grades they'd ever seen. My father acknowledged my success with a nod. No champagne. Just a nod.

"The hours were long – well, you know – there was always lots of overtime to be had. The pressure at work was almost unbearable too, the procedures and the policies ground me down and I needed something to help me keep afloat."

"Amphet."

He nodded. "It was great at first, like being given an additional twenty-four hours in every day, like being given an extra set of hands, two brains… you get the idea. Life was easy. And then it wasn't; it began to feel like everyone else was dragging me down, holding me back with how slowly they did things, you know? I got annoyed easily, and I started picking fights. I felt like I was unravelling.

"But instead of taking less of the drugs or coming off them altogether, I took more. Stupid. I went on and did coke and pretty soon I couldn't get out of bed without doing a line."

Eddie uncrossed his legs and leaned forward. "So how did you manage to come off them when you knew there was a random drugs test coming along?"

"I didn't. I got a sample of piss from a blocked urinal the day you told me about it, and I just carried it around in my jacket the whole time until it was needed. And I took downers for a while."

"And you stole my challenge. I told you to get your own challenge!"

"Sorry." Troy shrugged. "I found out that Benzo doesn't really mix with Courvoisier. Sorry again. I wanted some booze, and I'd never tried it before."

"Nicki found out, too, huh?"

"Yep. But that was only partly the drugs' doing. I mean I was fucking angry with her. I was furious, and I thought throwing her off the balcony was just fine. I kept saying how the mighty fall, how the mighty fall. And she did. Bitch nearly took me with her!"

"And her dad?"

"Third floor window at Killingbeck." He clapped his hands once, hard. "Splat onto a metal box," he grinned. "But do you know why he had to go?

Eddie leaned back in his chair and folded his arms. "I can read you like a Ladybird book. You killed him so that no one else in authority could stand in the way of you getting your job back?"

Troy's grin flourished. "Wow, you've really thought this through, old man. That's right. I know the others in the office sort of know about it, and I know you do too – but you're alright, Eddie. You were all for giving me another shot. And now *they're* gone… So, if you're offering the job back…

"It really was my last chance. If I failed at something again, I think he'd slice me up. Dad, I mean. So do we have a deal? I can start back tomorrow. What do you think?"

"What do I think?" Eddie stood up. "I think you had a bad childhood. But then so did a lot of other people. You grew up being very good at shifting blame onto others and creeping through life feeling like you deserved special treatment. I wouldn't give you a job cleaning my fucking shoes."

Troy's mouth fell open. "I thought—"

"I don't give a shit what you thought, you moron." Eddie closed in on Troy, and he whispered, "If Benson wasn't in the next room, I'd rip your fucking head off."

In a panic, Troy almost made it to his feet before Eddie landed a punch in his guts.

Benson barged into the room, followed by Khan and two other plain-clothed officers. "Whoa! Eddie, leave him alone, leave him. He's not worth it."

Eddie stood over Troy, fists ready to turn his face red and runny.

Khan hoisted Troy to his feet and said, "Troy Ainsley, I am arresting you on suspicion of the murders of Nicki Murphy and Lloyd Crawford…"

Benson pulled Eddie into the kitchen.

Eddie asked, "Did you get it?"

"Course we did. All on tape."

He expected Benson to be all smiles, but he was sullen.

"What did Weismann say to you?"

Eddie's gaze dropped to the floor, and a sigh shuddered free. "I wasn't listening. Just blah, blah, blah. He didn't have to say anything anyway. I fucked up; I *know* I fucked up. She pulled a blinder, and I fell for it."

"You shouldn't blame yourself, Eddie."

"For Jeffery's murder? Who else is to blame? I steered you wrong."

"She steered us both wrong."

"Bitch worked it out so well."

"Yep." There was a long pause. "The hospital has been in touch. She stopped breathing and died two hours ago."

Author's Note

I write crime thrillers, and have done since 1996, the same time I became a CSI here in Yorkshire. All of my books are set in or around our biggest city of Leeds. I don't write formulaic crime thrillers; each one is hand-crafted to give you a flavour of what CSIs encounter in real life. Every book is rich with forensic insight to enhance your enjoyment.

Get in touch.

For more information, or to sign up for my Reader's Club, visit AndrewBarrett.co.uk. I'd be delighted to hear your comments on Facebook (and so would Eddie Collins) and Twitter. Email me and say hello at andrew@andrewbarrett.co.uk

You can make a big difference.

Did you enjoy this book? I hope you did. Honest reviews of my books help bring them to the attention of other readers. So if you've enjoyed this book I would be very grateful if you could spend just five minutes leaving a short review.

Reader's Club Download Offer

GET A **FREE** BEST-SELLER AND A **FREE** SHORT STORY.

Building a relationship with my readers is one of the best things about writing. I occasionally send newsletters with details of new releases, special offers, and other news.

Sign up to the Reader's Club at www.andrewbarrett.co.uk, and I'll send you these **free** goodies as a thank you:

The Third Rule, the first book in the Eddie Collins series – a 500-page best-seller.

The Lift – a first person short story. Climb inside Eddie's head and see life as he does.

Subject to change without notice

Did you enjoy ***The Death of Jessica Ripley***? What's next?

Buy This Side of Death to find out what makes Eddie tick, and who tried to stop him.

Try a CSI Eddie Collins short story or a novella. Read them from behind the couch!

Have you tried the SOCO Roger Conniston trilogy?

How about a stand-alone psychological thriller that will leave you shocked?

Thanks!

The idea for this book came originally from one of my best friends; also a CSI, Graeme Bottomley. Thanks, Botts.

Together we wrote some fantastic scripts for television. The scripts got to the top at the BBC and at YTV, they also made waves at Sky and other places the names of which have become blurred by time. Those short-sighted people back then, ten or twelve years ago, wouldn't take a punt on something new, and something I believe is still fresh and innovative today, killed the desire to write in one of the most talented and passionate screenwriters I've ever read. Botts is the absolute master of dialogue and humour. He's one of the few writers I envy, and I wish that he'd pick up his pen and write some more.

To Kath Middleton, and Alison Birch, the editor from re:Written, a huge thank you for making sure the first draft wasn't the final draft – you will always be the first people to read my books, and consequently always the first to point and laugh at my errors. It's because of you that this book has turned out as well as it has, and it's because of me that you had so much work to do to get it there.

A special thanks to Noelle Holten for the advice she kindly gave concerning the probation service. Any errors are wholly my own – sometimes I just don't listen. And to the tireless Sarah Hardy of Book on the Bright Side Publicity and Promo who probably had a hand in bringing this book to you – thanks to you, and to the wonderful world of bloggers who are the lifeblood of the book universe.

Thanks to Patti for reading this thing and putting my mind at rest. And to Nicki Murphy – the *real* Nicki Murphy – for offering herself to this crazy writer come what may. I think you performed with elegance!

Thanks also to Helen Boyce in THE Book Club on Facebook, to my friends in the UK Crime Book Club, my Andrew Barrett page, and Rudi, Patti, and the gang in my Exclusive Readers Group for their constant encouragement – who knew readers could be so assertive, demanding… and kind. To those who suffer my newsletter (sign in at andrewbarrett.co.uk), a big thank you for helping me shape this book, and for all your encouragement – you haven't a clue how valuable that is.

The Death of Jessica Ripley

Is dedicated to Sarah Barrett. Thank you, dear, for being there.

Published in the United Kingdom by The Ink Foundry.

Printed in Great Britain
by Amazon

50950330R00265